fleshed out the people who make up that world."—*National Catholic Reporter*

"One of those rare works of fiction that both wound and heal." —*O Magazine*

"Epic. . . . If Jones . . . keeps up this level of work, he'll equal the best fiction Toni Morrison has written about being black in America." —*Speakeasy*

"You will be rewarded many times over by Jones's masterful ability to convey even the most despicable aspects of the nation's history with humanity and poetic language. This . . . magical novel will touch you in a profound way."—*People*, "Critic's Choice"

"Extraordinary. . . . There's a music, a mobility, a seductive elasticity in the way Jones lays out his fictional terrain. . . . Nothing . . . quite prepares readers for the imaginative leaps and technical prowess of *The Known World*."—*Seattle Times*

"Fascinating. . . . There is grief and fear, genuine affection and envy in this complex and fine novel."—*Philadelphia Inquirer*

"A major achievement."—*Time Out New York*

"Superior storytelling. . . . Jones's characters are vividly and fully drawn, and by writing in omniscient point of view he offers readers a layered, complex portrait of America on the cusp of the Civil War." —*Rocky Mountain News*

"A brilliant debut."—*St. Louis Post-Dispatch*

"Stunning. . . . Too much cannot be said about Mr. Jones gifts as a storyteller and a stylist. . . . Words flow quietly and build toward frequent crescendos that are breathtaking. Dialogue is pitch perfect, landscapes seem authentic, and personal squabbles are always adjudicated with wisdom."—*Washington Times*

"Once you start the book you are hooked. When you finally lay it down, you are not only informed about slave life in the antebellum South but also deeply moved. Consider this novel necessary reading." —*Fort Worth Star-Telegram*

"Complex, beautifully written, and breathtaking. . . . The last chapters present us with scenes of redemption, and the very last sentence of the book will knock the wind out of you with the depth of its compassion."—*QBR: The Black Book Review*

"Fascinating . . . poignant. . . . A complex and fine novel."—*Baltimore Sun*

"Heartbreaking . . . fascinating."—*Newsweek*

"Its biblical rhythms . . . lend depth to a story about profound moral confusion."—*Denver Post*

"Astonishingly rich."—*Kirkus Reviews* (starred)

"Ambitious . . . fascinating . . . this book is an ideal choice for book clubs."—*Library Journal* (starred)

"Vivid. . . . An epic novel."—*Booklist*

"The most powerful, deeply realized novel I've read in a long time. Edward P. Jones has crafted a modern masterpiece, which not only tells an unforgettable story, but does so with such elegance, grace, and mystery that it, finally, staggers the imagination. This novel is what literature should, and can, be."—Jeffrey Lent, author of *In the Fall* and *Lost Nation*

"An immensely moving novel which manifests quite marvelously the irony and sorrow, the joy, pain, mystery, and poignant humor of our transient human existence in the known world—a strong, intricate, daring book by a writer of deep compassion and uncommon gifts." —Peter Matthiessen

© 1992 Jerry Bauer

EDWARD P. JONES won the PEN/Hemingway Award and was a finalist for the National Book Award for his debut collection of short
stories, *Lost in the City*. A recipient of the Lannan Foundation Grant
and a Lannan Literary Award, Mr. Jones resides in Washington, D.C.
The Known World—winner of the 2004 Pulitzer Prize and the
National Book Critics Circle Award, and a finalist for the National
Book Award—is his first novel.

THE KNOWN WORLD

EDWARD P. JONES

AMISTAD
An Imprint of **HarperCollins***Publishers*

FIRST AMISTAD PAPERBACK EDITION 2004

Designed by Claire Vaccaro

Printed on acid-free paper

The Library of Congress has catalogued the hardcover edition as follows:
Jones, Edward P.
The known world / Edward P. Jones.—1st ed.
p.   cm.
ISBN 0-06-055754-0
1. African American plantation owners—Fiction. 2. African American
slaveholders—Fiction 3. Plantation life—Fiction. 4. Virginia—Fiction.
5. Slavery—Fiction. 6. Slaves—Fiction. I. Title.
PS3560.O4813 K58 2003
813'.54—dc21   2003040389

ISBN 0-06-055755-9 (pbk.)

06 07 08 ❖/RRD 30 29 28 27 26 25 24 23 22

TO MY BROTHER,
JOSEPH V. JONES

and, again,

TO THE MEMORY OF OUR MOTHER,
JEANETTE S. M. JONES
who could have done much more in a better world

ACKNOWLEDGMENTS

I am very grateful to: Dawn L. Davis, my editor, who may well have believed from the first word; Lil Coyne (grandmother to Steven Mears), a woman of small stature who stood on the night shore and held the lantern up as high as she could; Shirley Grossman (wife to the late Milton), who took up the lantern some nights so Lil could lie down where she stood and rest; Maria Guarnaschelli, the editor of *Lost in the City*; the Lannan Foundation and Jeanie J. Kim; Eve Shelnutt, who, though the water rose every hour on her shore, never failed to answer the telephone; Eric Simonoff, my agent, who may well have believed before the first word; and John Edgar Wideman, a kind and generous man.

My soul's often wondered how I got over. . . .

Liaison. The Warmth of Family. Stormy Weather.

The evening his master died he worked again well after he ended the day for the other adults, his own wife among them, and sent them back with hunger and tiredness to their cabins. The young ones, his son among them, had been sent out of the fields an hour or so before the adults, to prepare the late supper and, if there was time enough, to play in the few minutes of sun that were left. When he, Moses, finally freed himself of the ancient and brittle harness that connected him to the oldest mule his master owned, all that was left of the sun was a five-inch-long memory of red orange laid out in still waves across the horizon between two mountains on the left and one on the right. He had been in the fields for all of fifteen hours. He paused before leaving the fields as the evening quiet wrapped itself about him. The mule quivered, wanting home and rest. Moses closed his eyes and bent down and took a pinch of the soil and ate it with no more thought than if it were a spot of cornbread. He worked the dirt around in his mouth and swallowed, leaning his head back and opening his eyes in time to see the strip of sun fade to dark blue and then to nothing. He was the only man in the realm, slave or free, who ate dirt, but while the bondage women, particularly the pregnant ones, ate it for some incomprehensible need, for that something that ash cakes and apples and fatback did not give their bodies, he ate it not only to discover the strengths and weaknesses of the field, but because the eating of it tied him to the only thing in his small world that meant almost as much as his own life.

This was July, and July dirt tasted even more like sweetened metal than the dirt of June or May. Something in the growing crops unleashed a metallic life that only began to dissipate in mid-August, and by harvest time that life would be gone altogether, replaced by a sour moldiness he associated with the coming of fall and winter, the end of a relationship he had begun with the first taste of dirt back in March, before the first hard spring rain. Now, with the sun gone and no moon and the darkness having taken a nice hold of him, he walked to the end of the row, holding the mule by the tail. In the clearing he dropped the tail and moved around the mule toward the barn.

The mule followed him, and after he had prepared the animal for the night and came out, Moses smelled the coming of rain. He breathed deeply, feeling it surge through him. Believing he was alone, he smiled. He knelt down to be closer to the earth and breathed deeply some more. Finally, when the effect began to dwindle, he stood and turned away, for the third time that week, from the path that led to the narrow lane of the quarters with its people and his own cabin, his woman and his boy. His wife knew enough now not to wait for him to come and eat with them. On a night with the moon he could see some of the smoke rising from the world that was the lane—home and food and rest and what passed in many cabins for the life of family. He turned his head slightly to the right and made out what he thought was the sound of playing children, but when he turned his head back, he could hear far more clearly the last bird of the day as it evening-chirped in the small forest far off to the left.

He went straight ahead, to the farthest edge of the cornfields to a patch of woods that had yielded nothing of value since the day his master bought it from a white man who had gone broke and returned to Ireland. "I did well over there," that man lied to his people back in

Ireland, his dying wife standing hunched over beside him, "but I longed for all of you and for the wealth of my homeland." The patch of woods of no more than three acres did yield some soft, blue grass that no animal would touch and many trees that no one could identify. Just before Moses stepped into the woods, the rain began, and as he walked on the rain became heavier. Well into the forest the rain came in torrents through the trees and their mighty summer leaves, and after a bit Moses stopped and held out his hands and collected water that he washed over his face. Then he undressed down to his nakedness and lay down. To keep the rain out of his nose, he rolled up his shirt and placed it under his head so that it tilted just enough for the rain to flow down about his face. When he was an old man and rheumatism chained up his body, he would look back and blame the chains on evenings such as these, and on nights when he lost himself completely and fell asleep and didn't come to until morning, covered with dew.

The ground was almost soaked. The leaves seemed to soften the hard rain as it fell and it hit his body and face with no more power than the gentle tapping of fingers. He opened his mouth; it was rare for him and the rain to meet up like this. His eyes had remained open, and after taking in all that he could without turning his head, he took up his thing and did it. When he was done, after a few strokes, he closed his eyes, turned on his side and dozed. After a half hour or so the rain stopped abruptly and plunged everything into silence, and that silence woke him. He came to his feet with the usual reluctance. All about his body were mud and leaves and debris for the rain had sent a wind through the woods. He wiped himself with his pants and remembered that the last time he had been there in the rain, the rain had lasted long enough to wash him clean. He had been seized then by an even greater happiness and had laughed and twirled himself around and around in what someone watching him might have called a dance. He did not know it, but Alice, a woman people said had lost her mind, was watching him now, only the first time in her six months of wandering about in the night that she had come upon him. Had he known she was there, he would not have thought she had sense enough to know what was going on, given how hard, the story went, the mule had kicked her on the plantation in a faraway county whose name only she remembered. In her saner moments, which were very rare since the day Moses's master bought her, Alice could describe everything about the Sunday the mule kicked her in the head and sent all common sense flying out of her. No one questioned her because her story was so vivid, so sad—another slave without freedom and now she had a mind so addled she wandered in the night like a cow without a bell. No one knew enough about the place she had come from to know that her former master was terrified of mules and would not have them on his place, had even banished pictures and books about mules from his little world.

Moses walked out of the forest and into still more darkness toward the quarters, needing no moon to light his way. He was thirty-five years old and for every moment of those years he had been someone's slave, a white man's slave and then another white man's slave and now, for nearly ten years, the overseer slave for a black master.

Caldonia Townsend, his master's wife, had for the last six days and nights only been catnapping, as her husband made his hard way toward death. The white people's doctor had come the morning of the first day, as a favor to Caldonia's mother, who believed in the magic of white people, but that doctor had only pronounced that Moses's master, Henry Townsend, was going through a bad spell and would recover soon. The ailments of white people and black people were different, and a man who specialized in one was not expected to know much about the other, and that was something he believed Caldonia should know without him telling her. If her husband was dying, the doctor didn't know anything about it. And he left in the heat of the day, having pocketed 75 cents from Caldonia, 60 cents for looking at

Henry and 15 cents for the wear and tear on himself and his buggy and his one-eyed horse.

Henry Townsend—a black man of thirty-one years with thirty-three slaves and more than fifty acres of land that sat him high above many others, white and black and Indian, in Manchester County, Virginia—sat up in bed for most of his dying days, eating a watery porridge and looking out his window at land his wife, Caldonia, kept telling him he would walk and ride over again. But she was young and naively vigorous and had known but one death in her life, that of her father, who had been secretly poisoned by his own wife. On the fourth day on his way to death, Henry found sitting up difficult and lay down. He spent that night trying to reassure his wife. "Nothin hurts," he said more than once that day, a day in July 1855. "Nothin hurts."

"Would you tell me if it did?" Caldonia said. It was near about three in the morning, two hours or so after she had dismissed for the evening Loretta, her personal maid, the one who had come with her marriage to Henry.

"I ain't took on the habit of not tellin you the truth," Henry said that fourth evening. "I can't start now." He had received some education when he was twenty and twenty-one, educated just enough to appreciate a wife like Caldonia, a colored woman born free and who had been educated all her days. Finding a wife had been near the end of a list of things he planned to do with his life. "Why don't you go on to bed, darlin?" Henry said. "I can feel sleep comin on and you shouldn't wait for it to get here." He was in what the slaves who worked in the house called "the sick and gettin well room," where he had taken himself that first sick day to give Caldonia some peace at night.

"I'm fine right here," she said. The night had gotten cooler and he was in fresh nightclothes, having sweated through the ones they had put him in at about nine o'clock. "Should I read to you?" Caldonia asked, covered in a lace shawl Henry had seen in Richmond. He had paid a white boy to go into the white man's shop to purchase it for him, because the shop would have no black customers. "A bit of

Milton? Or the Bible?" She was curled up in a large horsehair chair that had been pulled up to his bed. On each side of the bed were small tables, just large enough for a book and a candelabrum that held three candles as thick as a woman's wrist. The candelabrum on the right side was dark, and the one on the left had only one burning candle. There was no fire in the hearth.

"I been so weary of Milton," Henry said. "And the Bible suits me better in the day, when there's sun and I can see what all God gave me." Two days before he had told his parents to go home, that he was doing better, and he had indeed felt some improvement, but on the next day, after his folks were back at their place, Henry took a turn back to bad. He and his father had not been close for more than ten years, but his father was a man strong enough to put aside disappointment in his son when he knew his flesh and blood was sick. In fact, the only time his father had come to see Henry on the plantation was when the son had been doing poorly. Some seven times in the course of ten years or so. When Henry's mother visited alone, whether he was ill or well, she stayed in the house, two rooms down from her son and Caldonia. The day Henry sent them home, his parents had come upstairs and kissed his smiling face good-bye, his mother on the lips and his father on the forehead, the way it had been done since Henry was a boy. His parents as a couple had never slept in the home he and Moses the slave had built, choosing to stay in whatever cabin was available down in the quarters. And they would do it that way when they came to bury their only child.

"Shall I sing?" Caldonia said, and reached over and touched his hand resting at the side of the bed. "Shall I sing till the birds wake up?" She had been educated by a black woman born free who herself had been educated in Washington, D.C., and Richmond. That woman, Fern Elston, had returned to her own plantation after visiting the Townsends three days ago to continue making part of her living in Manchester County teaching the freed black children whose parents could afford her. Caldonia said, "You think you've heard all my songs, Henry Townsend, but you haven't. You really haven't." Fern Elston had married a man who was supposed to be a farmer, but he lived to gamble, and as Fern told herself in those moments when she was able to put love aside and see her husband for what he was, he seemed to be driving them the long way around to the poorhouse. Fern and her husband had twelve slaves to their names. In 1855 in Manchester County, Virginia, there were thirty-four free black families, with a mother and father and one child or more, and eight of those free families owned slaves, and all eight knew one another's business. When the War between the States came, the number of slave-owning blacks in Manchester would be down to five, and one of those included an extremely morose man who, according to the U.S. census of 1860, legally owned his own wife and five children and three grandchildren. The census of 1860 said there were 2,670 slaves in Manchester County, but the census taker, a U.S. marshal who feared God, had argued with his wife the day he sent his report to Washington, D.C., and all his arithmetic was wrong because he had failed to carry a one.

Henry said, "No. Best save the singin for some other time, darlin." What he wanted was to love her, to get up from the sickbed and walk under his own power and take his wife to the bed they had been happy in all their married days. When he died, late the evening of the seventh day, Fern Elston the teacher would be with Caldonia in his death room. "I always thought you did right in marrying him," Fern would say, in the first stages of grief for Henry, a former student. After the War between the States, Fern would tell a pamphlet writer, a white immigrant from Canada, that Henry had been the brightest of her students, someone she would have taught for free. Loretta, Caldonia's maid, would be there as well when Henry died, but she would be silent. She merely closed her master's eyes after a time and covered his face with a quilt, a Christmas present from three slave women who had made it in fourteen days.

Moses the overseer walked the lane of the quarters down to his cabin, the one nearest the house where his master and mistress lived. Next to Moses's cabin, Elias sat on a damp tree stump before his own cabin, whittling a piece of pinewood that would be the body of a doll he was making for his daughter. It was the first thing he had ever given her. He had a lamp hanging from a nail beside his door but the light had been failing and he was as close to working blind as a body could get. But his daughter and his two sons, one only thirteen months old, were heaven and earth to him and somehow the knife cut into the pinewood in just the right way and began what would be the doll's right eye.

Moses, a few feet before passing Elias, said, "You gotta meet that mule in the mornin."

"I know," Elias said. Moses had not stopped walking. "I ain't hurtin a soul here," Elias said. "Just fixin on some wood." Now Moses stopped and said, "I ain't carin if you fixin God's throne. I said you gotta meet that mule in the mornin. That mule sleepin right now, so maybe you should follow after him." Elias said nothing and he did not move. Moses said, "I ain't but two minutes off you, fella, and you seem to wanna keep forgettin that." Moses had found Elias a great bother in the mind from the day Henry Townsend drove up with Elias from the slave market, a one-day affair held out in the open twice a year at the eastern edge of the town of Manchester, in the spring and in the fall after harvest. The very day Elias was bought by Henry some white people had talked about building a permanent structure for the slave market—that was the year it rained every spring day the market was held, and many white people caught colds as a result. One woman died of pneumonia. But God was generous with his blessings the following fall and each day was perfect for buying and selling slaves, and not a soul said anything about constructing a permanent place, so fine was the roof God himself had provided for the market.

Now Moses said to Elias, "If you ain't waitin for me here when the sun come up, not even Massa Henry will save you." Moses continued on to his cabin. Moses was the first slave Henry Townsend had bought: $325 and a handshake from William Robbins, a white man. It took Moses more than two weeks to come to understand that some-

one wasn't fiddling with him and that indeed a black man, two shades
darker than himself, owned him and any shadow he made. Sleeping
in a cabin beside Henry in the first weeks after the sale, Moses had
thought that it was already a strange world that made him a slave to
a white man, but God had indeed set it twirling and twisting every
which way when he put black people to owning their own kind. Was
God even up there attending to business anymore?

With one foot Elias swept the shavings from his other foot and
started whittling again. The right leg of the doll was giving him trouble: He wanted the figure to be running but he had not been able to
get the knee to bend just right. Someone seeing it might think it was
just a doll standing still, and he didn't want that. He was afraid that
if the knee did not bend soon he would have to start again with a new
piece of wood. Finding a good piece would be hard. But then the right
leg of his own wife, Celeste, did not bend the way it should either, so
maybe in the long run it might not matter with the doll. Celeste had
been limping from her first step she took into the world.

Moses went into his cabin and met the darkness and a dead hearth.
Outside, the light of Elias's lamp leaned this way and that and then it
dimmed even more. Elias had never believed in a sane God and so had
never questioned a world where colored people could be the owners of
slaves, and if at that moment, in the near dark, he had sprouted wings,
he would not have questioned that either. He would simply have gone
on making the doll. Inside Elias's cabin his crippled wife and three
children slept and the hearth had enough embers to last the night,
which promised to be cold again. Elias left the doll's right leg alone
and returned to the head, which he already thought was as perfect as
anything he had seen made by a man. He had gotten better since
carving the first comb for Celeste. He wanted to attach corn silk to the
doll's head but the kind of dark silk he wanted would not be ready until early fall. Immature silk would have to do.

Moses was not hungry and so did not complain to his wife or the
boy about the darkness. He lay down on the straw pallet beside his

wife, Priscilla. Their son was on the other side of her, snoring. Priscilla watched her husband as he slowly drifted into sleep, and once he was asleep, she took hold of his hand and put it to her face and smelled all of the outside world that he had brought in with him and then she tried to find sleep herself.

That last day, the day Henry Townsend died, Fern Elston returned early in a buggy driven by a sixty-five-year-old slave her husband had inherited from his father.

Fern and Caldonia spent a few hours in the parlor, drinking a milk-and-honey brew Caldonia's mother was fond of making. Upstairs during that time, Zeddie, the cook, and then Loretta, Caldonia's maid, sat with Henry. About seven in the evening, Caldonia told Fern she had best go on to bed, but Fern had not been sleeping well and she told Caldonia they might as well sit together with Henry. Fern had been a teacher not only to Caldonia but to her twin brother as well. There were not that many free educated women in Manchester County to pass her time with and so Fern had made a friend of a woman who, as a girl, had found too much to giggle about in the words of William Shakespeare.

The two women went up about eight and Caldonia told Loretta she would call her if she needed her and Loretta nodded and went out and down to her small room at the end of the hall. The three, Fern and Henry and Caldonia, started in talking about the Virginia heat and the way it wore away a body. Henry had seen North Carolina once and thought Virginia's heat could not compare. That last evening was relatively cool again. Henry had not had to change the nightclothes he had put on at six. About nine he fell asleep and woke not long after. His wife and Fern were discussing a Thomas Gray poem. He thought he knew the one they were talking about but as he formed some words to join the conversation, death stepped into the room and came to him: Henry walked up the steps and into the tiniest of houses, knowing with each step that he did not own it, that he was only renting. He was ever so disappointed; he heard footsteps behind him and death told him it was Caldonia, coming to register her own disappointment. Whoever was renting the house to him had promised a thousand rooms, but as he traveled through the house he found less than four rooms, and all the rooms were identical and his head touched their ceilings. "This will not do," Henry kept saying to himself, and he turned to share that thought with his wife, to say, "Wife, wife, look what they done done," and God told him right then, "Not a wife, Henry, but a widow."

It was several minutes before Caldonia and Fern knew Henry was no more and they went on talking about a widowed white woman with two slaves to her name on a farm in some distant part of Virginia, in a place near Montross where her nearest white neighbors were miles and miles away. The news of the young woman, Elizabeth Marson, was more than one year old but it was only now reaching the people of Manchester County, so the women in the room with dead Henry spoke as if it had all happened to Elizabeth just that morning. After the white woman's husband died, her slaves, Mirtha and Destiny, had taken over and kept the woman prisoner for months, working her ragged with only a few hours rest each day until her hair turned white and her pores sweated blood. Caldonia said she understood that Mirtha and Destiny had been sold to try to compensate Elizabeth, to settle her away from that farm with its memories, but Fern said she understood that the slave women had been killed by the law. When Elizabeth was finally rescued, she did not remember that she was supposed to be the owner, and it was a long time before she could be taught that again. Caldonia, noticing her husband's stillness, went to him. She gave a cry as she shook him. Loretta came in silently and took a hand mirror from atop the dresser. It seemed to Caldonia as she watched Loretta place the mirror under Henry's nose that he had only stepped away and that if she called loudly enough to him, put her mouth quite close to his ear, and called loud enough for any slave in the quarters to hear, he might turn back and be her husband again. She took Henry's hand in both of hers and put it to her cheek. It was warm, she noticed, thinking there might yet be enough life in it for him to reconsider. Caldonia was twenty-eight years old and she was childless.

A lice, the woman without a mind who had watched Moses be with himself in the woods, had been Henry and Caldonia's property for some six months the night he died. From the first week, Alice had started going about the land in the night, singing and talking to herself and doing things that sometimes made the hair on the backs of the slave patrollers' necks stand up. She spit at and slapped their horses for saying untrue things about her to her neighbors, especially to Elias's youngest, "a little bitty boy" she told the patrollers she planned to marry after the harvest. She grabbed the patrollers' crotches and begged them to dance away with her because her intended was forever pretending he didn't know who she was. She called the white men by made-up names and gave them the day and time God would take them to heaven, would drag each and every member of their families across the sky and toss them into hell with no more thought than a woman dropping strawberries into a cup of cream.

In those first days after Henry bought Alice, the patrollers would haul her back to Henry's plantation, waking him and Caldonia as one of them rode up on the porch and pounded on the black man's front door with the butt of a pistol. "Your property out here loose and you just sleepin like everything's fine and dandy," they shouted to him, a giggling Alice sprawled before them in the dirt after they had run her back. "Come down here and find out about your property." Henry would come down and explain again that no one, not even his overseer, had been able to keep her from roaming. Moses had suggested tying her down at night, but Caldonia would not have it. Alice was nothing to worry about, Henry said to the patrollers, coming down the steps in his nightclothes and helping Alice up from the ground. She just had half a mind, he said, but other than that she was a good worker, never saying to the two or three white patrollers who owned no slaves that a woman of half a mind had been so much cheaper to buy than one with a whole mind: $228 and two bushels of apples not good enough to eat and only so-so enough for a cider that was bound to set someone's teeth on edge. The patrollers would soon ride away. "This is what happens," they said among themselves back on the road, "when you give niggers the same rights as a white man."

Toward the middle of her third week as Henry and Caldonia's property, the patrollers got used to seeing Alice wander about and she became just another fixture in the patrollers' night, worthy of no more attention than a hooting owl or a rabbit hopping across the road. Sometimes, when the patrollers had tired of their own banter or when they anticipated getting their pay from Sheriff John Skiffington, they would sit their horses and make fun of her as she sang darky songs in the road. This show was best when the moon was at its brightest, shining down on them and easing their fear of the night and of a mad slave woman and lighting up Alice as she danced to the songs. The moon gave more life to her shadow, and the shadow would bounce about with her from one side of the road to other, calming the horses and quieting the crickets. But when they suffered ill humor, or the rain poured down and wetted them and their threadbare clothes, and their horses were skittish and the skin down to their feet itched, then they heaped curse words upon her. Over time, over those six months after Henry bought Alice, the patrollers heard from other white people that a crazy Negro slave in the night was akin to a two-headed chicken, or a crowing hen. Bad luck. Very bad luck, so it was best to try to keep the cussing to themselves.

The rainy evening her master Henry died Alice again stepped out of the cabin she shared with Delphie and Delphie's daughter, Cassandra. Delphie was nearing forty-four years old and believed that God had greater dangers in store for everybody than a colored woman gone insane, which was what she told her daughter, who was at first afraid of Alice. Alice came out that evening and saw Elias standing at his door with the whittling knife and the pinewood in his hands, waiting for the rain to end. "Come on with me," she sang to Elias. "You just come on with me now. Come on, boy." Elias ignored her.

After she came back from watching Moses in the patch of woods, Alice went back down the lane and out to the road. The muddy road gave her a hard way but she kept on. Once on the road, she veered away from Henry's place and began to chant, even more loudly than when she was on her master's land.

Lifting the front of her frock for the moon and all to see, she shimmied in the road and chanted with all her might:

> *I met a dead man layin in Massa lane*
> *Ask that dead man what his name*
> *He raised he bony head and took off his hat*
> *He told me this, he told me that.*

Augustus Townsend, Henry's father, finally bought himself out of slavery when he was twenty-two. He was a carpenter, a woodcarver whose work people said could bring sinners to tears. His master, William Robbins, a white man with 113 slaves to his name, had long permitted Augustus to hire himself out, and Robbins kept part of what he earned. The rest Augustus used to pay for himself. Once free, he continued to hire himself out. He could make a four-poster bed of oak in three weeks, chairs he could do in two days, chiffoniers in seventeen days, give or take the time it took to get the mirrors. He built a shack—and later a proper house—on land he rented and then bought from a poor white man who needed money more than he needed land. The land was at the western end of Manchester County, a fairly large slip of land where the county, as if tired of pushing west, dipped abruptly to the south, toward Amherst County. Moses, "world stupid" as Elias was to call him, would get lost there in about two months, thinking that he was headed north. Augustus Townsend liked it because it was at the farthest end of the county and the nearest white man with slaves was a half a mile away.

Augustus made the last payment for his wife, Mildred, when she was twenty-six and he was twenty-five, some three years after he bought his own freedom. An 1806 act of the Virginia House of Delegates required that former slaves leave the Commonwealth within twelve months of getting their freedom; freed Negroes might give slaves too many "unnatural notions," a delegate from Northampton County had noted before the act was passed, and, added another delegate from Gloucester, freed Negroes lacked "the natural controls" put on a slave. The delegates decreed that any freed person who had not left Virginia after one year could be brought back into slavery. That happened to thirteen people the year of Augustus's petition— five men, seven women, and one child, a girl named Lucinda, whose parents died before the family could get out of Virginia. Based primarily on his skills, Augustus had managed to get William Robbins and a number of other white citizens to petition the state assembly to permit him to stay. "Our County—Indeed, our beloved Commonwealth—would be all the poorer without the talents of Augustus Townsend," the petition read in part. His and two other petitions for former slaves were the only ones out of twenty-three granted that year; a Norfolk City woman who made elaborate cakes and pies for parties and a Richmond barber, both with more white customers than black, were also permitted to stay in Virginia after freedom. Augustus did not seek a petition for Mildred his wife when he bought her freedom because the law allowed freed slaves to stay on in the state in cases where they lived as someone's property, and relatives and friends often took advantage of the law to keep loved ones close by. Augustus would also not seek a petition for Henry, his son, and over time, because of how well William Robbins, their former owner, treated Henry, people in Manchester County just failed to remember that Henry, in fact, was listed forever in the records of Manchester as his father's property.

Henry was nine when his mother, Mildred, came to freedom. That day she left, a mild day two weeks after harvest, she walked holding her son's hand down to the road where Augustus and his wagon and two mules were waiting. Rita, Mildred's cabin mate, was holding the boy's other hand.

At the wagon, Mildred sank to her knees and held on to Henry, who, at last realizing that he was to be separated from her, began crying. Augustus knelt beside his wife and promised Henry that they would be back for him. "Before you can turn around good," he said, "you be comin home with us." Augustus repeated himself, and the boy tried to make sense of the word *home*. He knew the word, knew the cabin with him and his mother and Rita that the word represented. He could no longer remember when his father was a part of that home. Augustus kept talking and Henry pulled at Mildred, wanting her to go back onto William Robbins's land, back to the cabin where the fireplace smoked when it was first lit. "Please," the boy said, "please, les go back."

Along about then William Robbins came slowly out to the road, heading into the town of Manchester on his prized bay, Sir Guilderham. Patting the horse's black mane, he asked Henry why was he crying and the boy said, "For nothin, Massa." Augustus stood up and took off his hat. Mildred continued holding on to her son. The boy knew his master only from a distance; this was the closest they had been in a very long time. Robbins sat high on his horse, a mountain separating the boy from the fullness of the sun. "Well don't do it anymore," Robbins said. He nodded at Augustus. "Counting off the days, are you, Augustus?" He looked to Rita. "You see things go right," Robbins said. He meant for her not to let the boy go too many steps beyond his property. He would have called Rita by name but she had not distinguished herself enough in his life for him to remember the name he had given her at birth. It was enough that the name was written somewhere in his large book of births and deaths, the comings and goings of slaves. "Noticeable mole on left cheek," he had written five days after Rita's birth. "Eyes gray." Years later, after Rita disappeared, Robbins would put those facts on the poster offering a reward for her return, along with her age.

Robbins gave a last look at Henry, whose name he also did not know, and set off at a gallop, his horse's black tail flipping first one pretty way and then another, as if the tail were separate and so had a life all its own. Henry stopped crying. In the end, Augustus had to pull his wife from the child. He turned Henry over to Rita, who had been friends with Mildred all her life. He lifted his wife up onto the wagon that sagged and creaked with her weight. The wagon and the mules were not as high as Robbins's horse. Before he got up, Augustus told his son that he would see him on Sunday, the day Robbins was now allowing for visits. Then Augustus said, "I'll be back for you," meaning the day he would ultimately free the boy. But it took far longer to buy Henry's freedom than his father had thought; Robbins would come to know what a smart boy Henry was. The cost of intelligence was not fixed and because it was fluid, it was whatever the market would bear and all of that burden would fall upon Mildred and Augustus.

Mildred fixed Henry as many of the things she knew he would enjoy to take with them on Sundays. Before freedom she had known only slave food, plenty of fatback and ash cakes and the occasional mouthful of rape or kale. But freedom and the money from their labors spread a better table before them. Still, she could not enjoy even one good morsel in her new place when she thought of what Henry had to eat. So she prepared him a little feast before each visit. Little meat pies, cakes that he could share with his friends through the days, the odd rabbit caught by Augustus, which she salted to last the week. The mother and the father would ride over in the wagon pulled by the mules and call onto Robbins's land for their boy, enticing him with what they had brought. They would wait in the road until Henry on his stick legs came up from the quarters and out to the lane, Robbins's mansion giant and eternal behind him.

He was growing quickly, eager to show them the little things he had carved. The horses in full stride, the mules loaded down, the bull with his head turned just so to look behind him. The three would settle on a quilt on a piece of no-man's-land across from Robbins's plantation. Behind them and way off to the left, there was a creek that had never seen a fish, but slaves fished in it nevertheless, practicing for the day when there would be better water. When the three had eaten, Mildred would sit between them as Augustus and Henry fished. She always wanted to know how he was treated and his answer was almost always the same—that Massa Robbins and his overseer were treating him well, that Rita was always good to him.

The fall that year, 1834, just dropped away one day and suddenly it was winter. Mildred and Augustus came every Sunday even when it turned cold and then even colder than that. They built a fire on no-man's-land and ate with few words. Robbins had told them not to take the boy beyond where his overseer could see them from the entrance to his property. The winter visits were short ones because the boy often complained of the cold. Sometimes Henry did not show up, even if the cold was bearable for a visit of a few minutes. Mildred and Augustus would wait hour after hour, huddled in the wagon under quilts and blankets, or walking hopefully up and down the road, for Robbins had forbidden them to come onto his land except when Augustus was making a payment on the second and fourth Tuesdays of the month. They would hope some slave would venture out, going to or from the mansion, so they could holler to him or her to go get their boy Henry. But even when they managed to see someone and tell them about Henry, they would wait in vain for the boy to show up.

"I just forgot," Henry would say the next time they saw him. Augustus had often been chastised as a boy but though Henry was his son, he was not yet his property and so beyond his reach.

"Try harder to remember, son. To know the right way," Augustus said, only to have Henry do right the next Sunday or two and then not show up the one after that.

Then, in mid-February, after they had waited two hours beyond when he was supposed to appear on the road, Augustus grabbed the boy when he shuffled up and shook him, then he pushed him to the ground. Henry covered his face and began to cry. "Augustus!" Mildred shouted and helped her son up. "Everything's good," she said to him as she cradled him in her arms. "Everything's good."

Augustus turned and walked across the road to the wagon. The wagon had a thick burlap covering, something he had come up with not long after the first cold visit. The mother and her child soon followed him across the road and the three settled into the wagon under the covering and around the stones Augustus and Mildred had boiled. They were quite large stones, which they would boil for many hours at home on Sunday mornings before setting out to see Henry. Then, just before they left home, the stones were wrapped in blankets and placed in the center of the wagon. When the stones stopped giving warmth and the boy began complaining of the cold, they knew it was time to go.

That Sunday Augustus pushed Henry, the three of them ate, once again, in silence.

The next Sunday Robbins was waiting. "I heard you did something to my boy, to my property," he said before Augustus and Mildred were down from the wagon.

"No, Mr. Robbins. I did nothin," Augustus said, having forgotten the push.

"We wouldn't," Mildred said. "We wouldn't hurt him for the world. He our son."

Robbins looked at her as if she had told him the day was Wednesday. "I won't have you touching my boy, my property." His horse, Sir Guilderham, was idling two or so paces behind his master. And just as the horse began to wander away, Robbins turned and picked up the reins, mounted. "No more visits for a month," he said, picking one piece of lint from the horse's ear.

"Please, Mr. Robbins," Mildred said. Freedom had allowed her not to call him "Master" anymore. "We come all this way."

"I don't care," Robbins said. "It'll take all of a month for him to heal from what you did, Augustus."

Robbins set off. Henry had not told his parents that he had become Robbins's groom. An older boy, Toby, had been the groom but Henry had bribed the boy with Mildred's food and the boy had commenced telling the overseer that he was not up to the task of grooming. "Henry be better," Toby said to the overseer so many times that it became a truth in the white man's head. Now all the food Mildred brought for her son each Sunday had already been promised to Toby.

"We wouldn't hurt him to save the world," Mildred said to Robbins's back. She began crying because she saw a month of days spread out before her and they added up to more than a thousand. Augustus held her and kissed her bonneted head and then helped her up on to the wagon. The journey home to southwest Manchester County always took about an hour or so, depending upon the bitterness or kindness of the weather.

Henry was indeed better as a groom, far more eager than Toby had been, not at all afraid to rise long before the sun to do his duties. He was always waiting for Robbins when he returned from town, from Philomena, a black woman, and the two children he had with her. Henry would, in those early days when he was trying to prove himself to Robbins, stand in front of the mansion and watch as Robbins and Sir Guilderham emerged from the winter fog of the road, the boy's heart beating faster and faster as the man and the horse became larger and larger. "Mornin, Massa," he would say, and raise both hands to take the reins. "Good morning, Henry. Are you well?" "Yes, Massa." "Then stay that way." "Yes, Massa, I plan to."

Robbins would go into his mansion, to face a white wife who had not yet resigned herself to having lost her place in his heart to

Philomena. The wife knew about the first child her husband had with Philomena, about Dora, but she would not know about the second, Louis, until the boy was three years old. This was in the days before Robbins's wife turned beastly sour and began to spend most of her time in a part of the mansion her daughter had named the East when the daughter was very young and didn't know what she was doing. When the wife did turn beastly sour, she took it out on the people nearest her that she could not love. It got to be, the slaves said, as if she hated the very ground they had to walk on.

Henry would take Sir Guilderham to the stable, the one reserved for the animals Robbins thought the most of, and rub him down until the animal was at peace and the sweat was gone, until he began to close his eyes and wanted to be left alone. Then Henry made sure the horse had enough hay and water. Sometimes, if he thought he could escape the other tasks of the day, he would stand on a stool and comb the mane until his hands tired. If the horse recognized the boy from all the work he did, it never showed.

Henry waited eagerly at one end of the road Robbins took at least three times a week, and at the other end of the road, at the very edge of the town of Manchester, the county seat, was another boy, Louis, who was eight in 1840 when Henry was sixteen and an accomplished groom. Louis, the son, was also Robbins's slave, which was how the U.S. census that year listed him. The census noted that the house on Shenandoah Road where the boy lived in Manchester was headed by Philomena, his mother, and that the boy had a sister, Dora, three years his senior. The census did not say that the children were Robbins's flesh and blood and that he traveled into Manchester because he loved their mother far more than anything he could name and that, in his quieter moments, after the storms in his head, he feared that he was losing his mind because of that love. Robbins's grandfather, who had stowed away as a boy on the HMS *Claxton*'s maiden voyage to America, would not have not approved—not of Robbins's having lost himself to a black but of having lost himself at all. Having given away so much to love, the grandfather would have told his grandson, where would Robbins get the fortitude to make his way back to Bristol, England, back to their home?

The 1840 U.S. census contained an enormous amount of facts, far more than the one done by the alcoholic state delegate in 1830, and all of the 1840 facts pointed to the one big fact that Manchester was then the largest county in Virginia, a place of 2,191 slaves, 142 free Negroes, 939 whites, and 136 Indians, most of them Cherokee but with a sprinkling of Choctaw. A well-liked and fastidious tanner, who doubled as the U.S. marshal and who had lost three fingers to frostbite, carried out the 1840 census in seven and a half summer weeks. It should have taken him less time but he had plenty of trouble, starting with people like Harvey Travis who wanted to make sure his own children were counted as white, though all the world knew his wife was a full-blooded Cherokee. Travis even called his children niggers and filthy half-breeds when they and that world got to be too much for him. The census taker/tanner/U.S. marshal told Travis he would count the children as white but he actually wrote in his report to the federal government in Washington, D.C., that they were slaves, the property of their father, which, in the eyes of the law, they truly were; the census taker had never seen the children before the day he rode out to Travis's place on one of two mules the American government had bought for him so he could do his census job. He thought the children were too dark for him and the federal government to consider them as anything else but black. He told his government the children were slaves and he let it go at that, not saying anything about their white blood or their Indian blood. The census taker had a great belief that his government could read between the lines. And though he came away with suspicions about Travis's wife being a full Indian, he gave Travis the benefit of the doubt and listed her as "American Indian/Full Cherokee." The census taker also had trouble trying to calculate how many square miles the county was, and in the end he sent in figures that were far short of the mark. The mountains, he told a confidant, threw him off because he was unable to take the measure of the land with the damn mountains in the way. Even with the mountains taken out of all the arithmetic, Manchester was still half as large as the next biggest county in the Commonwealth.

The boy Louis, by 1840, could not be contained on the days when he thought Robbins was coming to see them. He bounced around the house Robbins had had built when Philomena was pregnant with Dora and he did not want her to be on the plantation near a wife who early on had suspected she was losing her husband of ten years. The boy would run up the stairs and look out the second-floor windows that faced the road, but when he saw no sign of the dust from Sir Guilderham, he would run back down and look out the parlor window. "I must be not lookin in the right place for him," he would say to whoever was in the room before flying back up the stairs. The teacher Fern Elston had already reprimanded Louis about leaving out the *g*'s on all his *ing* words.

There was no one else in the county who could have gotten away with putting a Negro and her two children in a house on the same block with white people. On one page of the census report to the federal government in Washington, D.C., the census taker put a check by William Robbins's name and footnoted on page 113 that he was the county's wealthiest man. He was a distant cousin of Robbins's and was quite proud that his kin had done so well in America.

Dora and Louis never called Robbins "Father." They addressed him as "Mr. William," and when he was not around he was referred to as "him." Louis liked for Robbins to set him on his knee and raise his knee up and down rapidly. "My horsey Mr. William" was what he sometimes called him. Robbins called him "my little prince. My little princely prince."

The boy had what people in that part of Virginia termed a travel-ing eye. As he looked directly at someone, his left eye would often fol-low some extraneous moving object that might be just to the side—a spot of dust in the near distance or a bird on the wing in the far dis-tance. Follow it as the object or body moved a few feet. Then the eye would return to the person in front of the boy. The right eye, and his mind, never left the person Louis was talking to. Robbins was aware that a traveling eye in a boy he would have had with his white wife would have meant some kind of failing in the white boy, that he had a questionable future and could receive only so much fatherly love. But in the child whose mother was black and who had Robbins's heart, the traveling eye served only to endear him even more to his fa-ther. It was a cruel thing God had done to his son, he told himself many a time on the road back home.

Louis, over time, would learn how not to let the eye become his destiny, for people in that part of Virginia thought a traveling eye a sign of an inattentive and dishonest man. By the time he became friends with Caldonia and Calvin, her brother, at Fern Elston's tiny academy for free Negro children just behind her parlor, Louis would be able to tell the moment when the eye was wandering off just by the look on a person's face. He would blink and the eye would come back. This meant looking full and long into someone's eyes, and peo-ple came to see that as a sign of a man who cared about what was be-ing said. He became an honest man in many people's eyes, honest enough for Caldonia Townsend to say yes when he asked her to marry him. "I never thought I was worthy of you," he said, thinking of the dead Henry, when he asked her to marry him. She said, "We are all worthy of one another."

Robbins was forty-one when Henry became his groom. The trips into town were not easy. It would have been best if he had trav-eled by buggy, but he was not a man for that. Sir Guilderham was expensive and grand horseflesh, meant to be paraded before the world. In 1840, when there were still many more payments to be made for Henry's freedom, Robbins had been thinking for a long time that he was losing his mind. On the way to town or on the way back, he would suffer what he called small storms, thunder and lightning, in the brain. The lightning would streak from the front of his head and explode with thunder at the base of his skull. Then there was a kind of calming rain throughout his head that he associated with the return of normalcy. He lost whole bits of time with some storms. Sir Guilderham sometimes sensed the coming of the storms, and when it did, the horse would slow and then stop altogether until the storm had passed. If the horse sensed nothing, a storm would hit Robbins, and he would emerge from the storm miles closer to his destination, with no memory of how he got there.

He saw the storms as the price to be paid for Philomena and their children. In 1841, awaking from a storm, he found a white man on the road back to the plantation asking if he was ill. Robbins's nose was bleeding and the man was pointing to the nose and the blood. Robbins rubbed his nose with the sleeve of his coat. The blood stopped. "Lemme see you home," the man said. Robbins pointed up the road to where he lived and they rode side by side, the man telling him who he was and what he did and Robbins not caring but just grateful for the company.

Robbins felt compelled to repay the kindness when two slaves caught the man's eye the second day he stayed with Robbins. The Bible said guests should be treated like royalty lest a host entertain angels unaware. The man had stepped out onto the verandah to smoke one of Robbins's cigars and saw Toby, the former groom, and his sister. Mildred's food had done things for the boy and his sister, marvelous things to their bones that Robbins's poor food could never have done. The man came inside and offered $233 for the pair, claiming that was all he had.

The three, the two children and the man who could have been an

angel, had been gone four days when Robbins realized what a bad sale
he had made, even if he took something off the price to express
his gratitude to an angel. He soon got it into his head that the man
had actually been a kind of abolitionist, no more than a thief, the
devil in disguise. The idea of the slave patrols began with that bitter
sale, with the idea that the storms made him vulnerable and that abolitionists could insinuate themselves and cheat him out of all that he
and his father and his father's father had worked for. But the idea
would take root and grow with the disappearance of Rita, the woman
who became a kind of mother to Henry after Augustus Townsend
bought his wife Mildred to freedom. Before the angel/man on the
road and Rita's disappearance, Manchester County, Virginia, had not
had much problem with the disappearance of slaves since 1837. In
that year, a man named Jesse and four other slaves took off one night
and were found two days later by a posse headed by Sheriff Gilly
Patterson. The escape and the chase had put such bile in Jesse's master that he shot Jesse in the swamp where the posse found him. He
had the four other escapees hobbled that night—sharp and swift
knives back and forth through their Achilles' tendons—right after he
cut off Jesse's head as a warning to his other fourteen slaves and stuck
it on a post made from an apple-tree branch in front of the cabin Jesse
had shared with three other men. The law ruled that Jesse's murder
was justifiable homicide—though the escaped slaves were headed in
a different direction from a white widow and her two teenage daughters, the five men were less than a mile from those women when they
were caught. No white person wanted to imagine what would have
happened if those five slaves had doubled back, heading south and
away from freedom, and got to the place with the widow and the girls.
Jesse got what was coming to him, Sheriff Patterson theorized as he
thought of the widow and her daughters. He did not put it in those
words in a report he made to the circuit judge, a man known for op-
posing the abuse of slaves. But Sheriff Patterson did write that Jesse's
master was punished enough having to live with the knowledge that

he had done away with property that was easily worth $500 in a seller's market.

In truth, the man William Robbins met on the road was not an abolitionist or an angel, and Toby and his sister never saw the north. The man on the road sold the children for $527 to a man who chewed his food with his mouth open. He met the openmouthed man in a very fancy Petersburg bar that closed down at night to become a brothel, and that openmouthed man sold the children to a rice planter from South Carolina for $619. The children's mother wasn't good for doing her job very much after that, after her children were sold, even with the overseer flaying the skin on her back with whippings meant to make her do what was right and proper. The mother wasted away to skin and bones. Robbins sold her to a man in Tennessee for $257 and a three-year-old mule, a profitless sale, considering all the potential the mother had if she had pulled herself together and considering what Robbins had already spent for her upkeep, food and clothes, and a leakproof roof over her head and whatnot. In his big book about the comings and goings of slaves, Robbins put a line through the name of the children's mother, something he always did with people who died before old age or who were sold for no profit.

Robbins usually spent the night at Philomena's, braving all her talk about wanting to go and live in Richmond. He would set out for his plantation just after dawn, weather permitting. There was almost always a storm in his head on the way back. He would have preferred to suffer one going into town, so as to enjoy Philomena and their children knowing the worst was behind him. No matter what weather God gave Manchester County, Henry would be waiting. That first winter after seeing the boy shivering in the rags he tied around his feet, Robbins had his slave shoemaker make the boy something good for his feet. He told the servants who ran his mansion that Henry was to eat in the kitchen with them and forever be clothed the right way just the same as they were clothed. Robbins came to depend on seeing the boy waving from his place in front of the mansion, came to know that the sight of Henry meant the storm was over and that he was safe from bad men disguised as angels, came to develop a kind of love for the boy, and that love, built up morning after morning, was another reason to up the selling price Mildred and Augustus Townsend would have to pay for their boy.

2

The Wedding Present. Dinner First, Then Breakfast. Prayers Before an Offering.

In the Bible God commanded men to take wives, and John Skiffington obeyed.

He tried always to live humbly and obediently in the shadow of God, but he was afraid that at twenty-six years old he was falling short. He yearned for earthly things, to begin with, and he rendered far more unto Caesar than he knew God would have liked. I am imperfect, he said to God each morning he rose from his bed. I am imperfect, but I am still clay in your hands, ever walking the way you want me to. Mold me and help me to be perfect in your eyes, O Lord.

God had not put it in his mind to take a wife until that autumn afternoon in 1840 in the parlor of Sheriff Gilly Patterson. Skiffington, who had been Patterson's deputy for two years, had come up at twenty years old with his father to Manchester, to a town and county in the middle of Virginia his father had seen only once as a child and had dreamed about twice as an adult. His father had long been the overseer on the North Carolina plantation owned by his cousin, and it was there that John Skiffington grew uneasily into manhood, grew into it among 10 or so white people and 158 or so slaves, the numbers changing only slightly year by year, owing to birth, owing to sales and purchases, owing to death. The night before John Skiffington's mother died, his father dreamed that God told him he did not want him and his son having dominion over slaves, and two days later the man and his son left North Carolina, carrying the dead woman in a pine box in a wagon the cousin bestowed on them. Don't leave your wife in North Carolina, God had said to the father at the end of the dream.

Sheriff Patterson's two nieces came down from Philadelphia in 1840 for a three-month stay, and the sheriff and his wife held one o'clock dinners most Sundays while the young women were there. The hosts would invite folks near and about for small gatherings, and it was on that autumn afternoon that it was John Skiffington and his father's turn. Patterson's wife was distant kin to William Robbins's wife, and Robbins and his wife came as well, though Robbins viewed the Pattersons, to say nothing of the Skiffingtons, as being two or three rungs beneath him and his.

John Skiffington and his father arrived first and John stepped out of a gray day into Mrs. Patterson's dull-blue parlor and saw first thing Winifred Patterson, a product of the Philadelphia School for Girls, an institution with one foot in Quakerism. He was not a shy man and he was bear-large. Winifred was not shy either, an unintended result of being at the Philadelphia School for Girls, and it wasn't long before he and Winifred—after the arrival of the Robbinses—had retired to a corner of the parlor and begun a conversation that lasted through dinner and into early evening. What surprised him most was why the female sex had not interested him before that Sunday. Where had God been keeping that part of his head and heart?

He saw her often after that, in Mrs. Patterson's parlor, or in church or on buggy rides accompanied by Mrs. Patterson and Winifred's younger sister. John became the only regular visitor at the Pattersons' Sunday dinners, and had to be told a few times by Mrs. Patterson, suppressing a titter, that it was rude and selfish to take Winifred aside before the other dinner guests had a chance to relish the worldliness that the Philadelphia School for Girls had instilled in her. By early January Mrs. Patterson told her husband that things were moving in

such a way that it might be best if Mr. Patterson summoned his
brother from Philadelphia, that the brother and John Skiffington
might want to talk. The brother arrived, the men talked, but Winifred
returned to Philadelphia in March, after the second frost that did
wonders for gardens that year. Skiffington visited Philadelphia twice,
and came away that last time in May with Winifred's promise that she
would marry him.

They married in June, a wedding attended by even the better
white people in the county, so liked had John become in his time in
Manchester as Patterson's deputy. His father's cousin was ill in North
Carolina but the cousin sent his son, Counsel Skiffington, and Counsel's wife, Belle, a product of a very good family in Raleigh. Though
John and Counsel had grown up together, as close as brothers, they
had no overwhelming love for each other. Indeed, had Counsel not
been a wealthy man he would have found his mild dislike of John
veering toward something most unkind whenever they met. But
wealth helped to raise him above what would have made other men
common riffraff and so he was more than happy to come to his
cousin's wedding in a Virginia town whose name his wife had to keep
reminding him of. And, too, Counsel hadn't been out of North
Carolina in five months and he had been feeling an ache to walk
about under a different sky.

Counsel and his wife, with some discussion from his dying father,
brought a wedding present for Winifred from North Carolina. They
waited to present it until the reception for family members in the
house John had bought near the edge of town for his bride. About
three o'clock, after matters had quieted down some, Belle went out to
where her maid was in the backyard and returned with a slave girl of
nine years and had the girl, festooned with a blue ribbon, stand and
then twirl about for Winifred. "She's yours," Belle told Winifred. "A
woman, especially a married one, is nothing without her personal servant." All the people from Philadelphia were quiet, along with John
Skiffington and his father, and the people from Virginia, especially

those who knew the cost of good slave flesh, smiled. Belle picked up the hem of the girl's dress and held it out for Winifred to examine, as if the dress itself were a bonus.

Winifred looked at her new husband and he nodded and Winifred said, "Thank you." Winifred's father left the room, followed by Skiffington's father. Counsel went on smiling; he was thinking of all those early days in North Carolina when his dislike for his cousin was taking root. The trip up to that nowhere Virginia town had been worth it just for the look on his cousin's face. "It's a good way of introducing you to the life you should become accustomed to, Mrs. Skiffington," Counsel said to Winifred. He looked at Belle, his wife. "Isn't that right, Mrs. Skiffington?"

"Of course, darling." She said to the wedding present, "Say hello. Say hello to your mistress."

The girl did, curtsying the way she had been shown before leaving North Carolina and many times during the trip to Manchester. "Hello. Hello, mistress."

"Her name is Minerva," Belle said. "She will answer to the name Minnie, but her proper name is Minerva. She will, however, answer to either, to whatever you choose to call her. Call her Minnie and she will answer. But her proper name is Minerva." Her first maid, received when Belle was twelve, had had a disagreeable night cough and had to be replaced after a few weeks with a quieter soul.

"Minerva," the child said.

"See," Belle said. "See." The night that Belle Skiffington would die, that first maid, Annette, grown out of a cough that had plagued her for years, would open a Bible in the study of her Massachusetts home, looking for some verses to calm her mind before sleep. Out of the Bible would fall a leaf from a North Carolina apple tree that she had, the night she escaped with five other slaves, secreted in her bosom for good luck. She would not have seen the leaf for many years and at first she would not remember where the browned and brittle thing came from. But as she remembered, as the leaf fell apart in her fingers, she would fall into a cry that would wake everyone in her house and she could not be calmed, not even when morning came. Belle's second maid, the one who had never been sick a day in her life, would die the night after Belle did. Her name was Patty and she had had three children, one dead, two yet alive, Allie and Newby, a boy who liked to drink directly from a cow's teat. Those two children would die the third night, the same night the last of Belle's children died, the beautiful girl with freckles who played the piano so well.

"See," Belle said again to Winifred. "Now I don't want you spoiling her, Mrs. Skiffington. Spoiling has been the ruination of many. And, sweet Winifred, I just will not have it." Belle laughed and picked up the hem of Minerva's dress again.

"Yes," Counsel said, winking at John his cousin, "my wife is the best evidence of the ruination that spoiling brings."

The morning after their wedding night Winifred turned to her husband in their bed and told him slavery was not something she wanted in her life. It was not something he wanted either, he said; he and his father had sworn off slavery before they left North Carolina, he reminded his bride. That was how his father had interpreted the final dream, as well as the ones he had been having for weeks. Wash your hands of all that slavery business, God had said in his dreams. The death of John Skiffington's mother was just God's way of emphasizing what he wanted. *Don't leave your wife in North Carolina.*

Skiffington sat up on the side of his marriage bed. He and Winifred were whispering, though Minerva, the wedding present, and his father were way at the end of the hall. Counsel and Belle would be leaving that day, but even with them gone Skiffington saw no way to rid themselves of the girl. Selling her would be out of the question because they could not know what would become of her. Even selling her to a kind master, a God-fearing master, did not ensure that such a master would never sell her to someone who did not fear God. And giving her away was no better than selling her. Winifred sat up in bed. They had both gotten up after their lovemaking the night before and put on their nightclothes, so unaccustomed were they to each other. She pulled the gown's collar tight around her neck and placed her hand over the garment at her throat.

"I had almost forgotten where I was," Winifred said, meaning the South, meaning the world of human property. She looked over at the window where even the heavy curtains could not hold back what was promising to be an extraordinarily beautiful day. Right then, she recalled the woman and her handsome husband in Philadelphia who had been thrown into jail for keeping two free black people as slaves. They had been slaves for years, confined to the house, and all the white neighbors knew the slaves by name, but people just thought they were part of the family. They even had the white people's last name.

"That was just Counsel," Skiffington said, a bit defensively. The South was home, and not at all the hell some in the North wanted to make it. "Not everyone can afford to give away a slave like that. They're expensive, Winifred. That was just Counsel, pokin at me. He can afford to take pokes at me. And they really wanted to please you. Make you happy."

"It hurts me to think about it," she said, and began to cry. He turned round in the bed and pulled her to him, placing his hand on the back of her head. "Please, John . . ."

"Shhh," he said. Then, after a while, he kissed the top of her head and put his mouth to her ear. "She might be better off with us than anywhere else." He was thinking not only about what would happen if they sold her into God only knew what but what their neighbors might say if they gave her to Winifred's people for a life in the North: Deputy John Skiffington, once a good man, but now siding with the outsiders, and northern ones at that. Skiffington asked his wife, "Are you and me not good people?"

"I would hope so," Winifred said. She lay back in the bed and

Skiffington got up to dress, for he was still the deputy, newlywed or not. There were more tears in her but she held them and busied herself watching her husband. Then he was gone. She started back crying.

Three rooms away, the wedding present, Minerva, heard her master leave and she came silently out of her room and studied the bare window nearest her and the hall and all the doors along the hall. The sun came full through the window and made most of the glass knobs on the doors glow. Then before her very eyes, bit by bit, the sun rose and the glow was gone. Minerva was barefoot, though Belle had more than once warned the child never to traipse around without her night slippers. Minerva had, though, remembered to put one of Winifred's shawls around her shoulders. "You will be in a proper house," Belle had instructed her, "and you must not go about with your shoulders bare. Now repeat what I have just told you."

Minerva went to the window nearest her and looked out to where the sun was still rising. She had an older sister back in North Carolina and every morning back home she could look down where the sun was coming up to the neighboring farm where her sister was a slave. They had been able to visit with each other about once every three weeks. Minerva, though she had traveled for days and days to get from North Carolina to Virginia, looked down to where the sun was rising, believing with a heart that had a long reach that she could see the farm where her sister was. She was disappointed that she could not. Though just a shout and a holler away from Belle Skiffington, the sister back in North Carolina would escape the devastation that was to come to Belle and almost all that God had given her. Minerva wanted to raise the window, thinking that the farm with her sister was just a little look-see beyond the windowpane, but she dared not touch it. Minerva and her sister would not see each other again for more than twenty years. It would be in Philadelphia, nine blocks from the Philadelphia School for Girls. "You done growed," her sister would say, both hands to Minerva's cheeks. "I would have held back on growing up," Minerva would say. "I would have waited for you to see me grow but I had no choice in the matter."

Minerva stepped away from the window and took one step down the hall and stopped. The child listened. She took two more steps and was near the staircase going down. She was not brave enough to go down the steps where she thought the rest of the household might be. In less than a week she would be brave enough, brave enough to even go to the front door and open it up and take a step onto the morning porch. The child now took more steps, passing her own room, and came to a partly opened door. She could see John Skiffington's father on his knees praying in a corner of his room. Fully dressed with his hat on, the old man, who would find another wife in Philadelphia, had been on his knees for nearly two hours: God gave so much and yet asked for so little in return. Minerva stepped on and finally came to the end of the hall where Winifred was still crying in her bed and did not hear the little girl knock once and then once again on the door that was ajar. Finally, Winifred heard. "Yes. Yes," she said. "Who is it?" Minerva touched the door with her baby finger and it opened some more. The child peeked into the room and looked about until she found Winifred. She took an innocent measure of the whole room and then stepped slowly up to the side of the bed. Minerva was more afraid than she had been out in the hall. She was even now missing Belle because Belle was a certainty she knew about and Winifred could see all that in her face. She touched the girl's shoulder, recognizing the shawl she had brought from Philadelphia in what she had joked to Skiffington was her "dowry trunk." Winifred lightly touched Minerva's cheek, the first and last black human being she would ever touch.

"I heard you cryin," Minerva said.

"A bad dream," Winifred said.

Minerva looked about the room some more, half expecting to see Skiffington. She was trying to remember all she had been taught about the proper decorum with a mistress. Concern about her well-being was certainly one thing Belle had told her about. "It a really bad dream?" the girl asked.

Winifred thought. "Bad enough, I suppose."

"Oh," Minerva said. "Oh." She looked around again.

"Are you hungry?" Winifred said.

"Yes, mistress," Minerva said, both hands now resting on the bed.

"Then we must eat. And we must find a new and better name for me. But first, you and I must eat."

Three weeks later William Robbins and four other major landowners summoned Sheriff Gilly Patterson and John Skiffington to Robbins's home. Robbins had not been able to let go of the sale of Toby and his sister to the man he had met on the road and he was able to convince the four others that something threatening was loose in the land. He was never definite about any of it, but if William Robbins said a storm was coming, then it did not matter how blue and pleasant the sky was and how much the chickens strutted happily about the yard.

Robbins expressed dissatisfaction with Patterson's vigilance, hinted that while Patterson and Skiffington slept, abolitionists were spiriting away their livelihood to some fool's idea of nigger heaven in the North. He had become convinced that the man on the road had come into their county and waited on the road and befriended him with the one aim of stealing Toby and his sister. Robbins, for the first time, broached the idea of a militia.

"This is a peaceful land, William," Sheriff Patterson said. "We have no need for anything more than what we got. Me and John are doing a good job." Patterson liked what little authority he had and was concerned that anything else would be a usurper. And he had never liked the idea of Robbins riding into town in broad open daylight any day of the week to be with a nigger and her nigger children.

"Gilly, how many slaves you got?"

"None, William. You know that." Four of the men were on Robbins's verandah, including the sheriff and three of the landowners. One of the landowners was standing beside Deputy Skiffington on the ground. Skiffington had had to hear Patterson's complaining about coming to Robbins's place all the way out there. "I ain't no fetch and carry, John," Patterson had said to Skiffington. "But thas what they're making me into. I didn't come across that Atlantic Ocean to be a fetch and carry man." All trace of the accent he had brought across the ocean as a little boy had disappeared a long time ago. He spoke like any average white Virginia man walking down the road.

Robbins said, "Well, Gilly, you don't know then. You don't know what the difficulty is in keeping this world going right. You ride around, keeping the peace, but that ain't got nothin to do with running a plantation fulla slaves."

"I never said it did, William. This is a peaceful place here in Manchester, thas about all I'm sayin," Patterson said. He liked the sound of the word *peaceful* right then and was looking for a way to use it again before he left.

"That was yesterday," Robbins said. "Yesterday's peace. Way yesterday. Even now, I can remember that mess with that Turner nigger and them others. Even now, even today. My wife talks about it. My wife cries about it. That wasn't something he could have thought of on his own. That abolitionist just about walked in here and walked out the door with my property."

"That ain't what I heard," Patterson said. "I heard it was a straight open deal. Straight sale, William."

"You can hear the wind but it ain't me whispering in your ear." Robbins stood up and walked to the edge of the verandah and crossed his arms. He had seen Philomena the day before and had come away with a sour memory of her talking about Richmond and how happy they could be there. The other men on the verandah stayed seated and Patterson leaned forward in his chair, studied the grain of the wooden floor.

Patterson said, "John and me'll do a little extra duty, if thas what got everyone tied up in a fritter. My job is to protect everybody, to make sure everybody can sleep right every night in a peaceful way, and if that ain't happenin, then I'll make it happen."

One of the landowners on the porch, Robert Colfax, said, "Bill, how that stick with you?" Neither Robbins nor Colfax would know it for a very long time but that day was the high point of their friendship. They were now heading down the other side of the mountain with it.

Robbins said nothing.

"Bill? How that set with you, Bill?" Colfax said.

Robbins turned round, uncrossed his arms and ran his hand through his hair. "I'll take that," he said. "For now, I'll take that. But if anything more were to happen . . ." He sat down again and raised the hand without his wedding ring and a servant appeared at his side. "Bring us something." "Yessir." The black man disappeared and reappeared soon after with drinks. Patterson said he wanted nothing to drink, that he and Skiffington had to get back. He stood and in a moment Henry appeared with his horse and Skiffington's horse.

"I promise peace and thas what I'll deliver," Patterson said. "Good day to one and all, gentlemen." He stepped out to the horse and Henry handed him the reins. Skiffington was already on his horse.

The men on the verandah and the landowner now alone in the yard said, "Good day."

Patterson hung on as sheriff for two more years, until 1843, when Robbins said Patterson was doing nothing as property just up and walked away. Tom Anderson, a forty-six-year-old slave, disappeared in 1842, but it was never clear if he had indeed run away. His master, a sometime preacher with the same name, owed $350 to a man in Albemarle County and had promised Tom the slave in payment. Rather than pay the debt, some said, Tom the preacher probably sold

Tom the slave and pocketed the $450 the world knew Tom the slave was worth. Tom the preacher always claimed "my Tom" had run away, even blamed the abolitionists, and he forever pleaded poor to the Albemarle man he owed the debt to. Since Tom the preacher had nothing more the Albemarle man cared about, the debt was all but forgotten, although in his will—revised for the last time in 1871 when slavery wasn't that kind of issue anymore—the Albemarle man listed "Tom Anderson, 46 Year Old SLAVE, red Hair," as one of his assets. In early 1843, after four other slaves had ostensibly run away, a very self-confident fourteen-year-old slave girl, Ophelia, disappeared, also without an explanation that satisfied everyone. Some white people attributed that disappearance to her jealous and possibly murderous mistress, who had been educated in Paris, Venice, and Poughkeepsie, New York, and who returned home to Virginia with a tomcat of an Italian husband who had never seen black people before coming to America. But slaves in Manchester County said Ophelia had met Jesus' mother one late afternoon on the main road people took to get to Louisa County and that Mary, hearing Ophelia sing, had decided right then that she didn't want heaven if it came without Ophelia. Mary asked Ophelia about coming with her and eating peaches and cream in the sunlight until Judgment Day and Ophelia shrugged her shoulders and said, "That sounds fine. I ain't got nothin better to do right at the moment. Ain't got nothin to do till evenin time anyway."

In the history of Manchester County, the end of Sheriff Patterson's long tenure when he was only thirty-eight would be a small thing— way down on the list of historical events, after the death in 1820 of the virgin Mistress Taylor in her hundred-and-second year and the snowstorm that brought ten inches in late May 1829 and the slave boy Baker and the two white Otis boys who burst spontaneously into flames in front of the dry goods store in 1849. Patterson stayed on but he was crippled and he never got over having been summoned by Robbins like a child out to his plantation, and a nigger child at that.

The last straw for all of them, from Robbins to Colfax to white men who could not even afford slaves, was that Rita thing, which grew into something larger than it actually was, thanks to Robbins. Rita, the woman who became a second mother to the boy Henry Townsend. After the Rita thing, everyone agreed that a change would do the whole county good and would put a stop to what Robbins had begun to call "a hemorrhaging of slaves." So Patterson resigned, took himself back to that English town near the Scottish border where his people had lived for centuries. He spent all the rest of his years as a sheep farmer and became known as a good shepherd, "a man born to it." His health improved tremendously from what it had been in America, but the health of his wife, a Scot from Gretna Green who was hard of hearing, never returned to what it had been in her early, happy years in the United States. Whenever people in that part of the world asked Patterson about the wonders of America, the possibilities and the hope of America, Patterson would say that it was a good and fine place but all the Americans were running it into the ground and that it would be a far better place if it had no Americans.

John Skiffington had come to love and respect Patterson, but it took him less than a day to consider the suggestion from Robbins and Colfax that he become the new sheriff, that he, as Robbins put it, "take up the mantle." Indeed, Skiffington believed he could be a better peacekeeper, given Patterson's growing irascibility. Though his marriage was two years old, he and Winifred still considered themselves newlyweds; two years wasn't even a full blink of God's eye. Skiffington wanted a good life for his bride and he thought a sheriff's life, and not that of someone's deputy, would bring that. He felt he might make a reputation that he could carry to a greater job elsewhere, even to something in Philadelphia, where Winifred often said she wanted to return. A man he knew in Halifax County had gone from deputy to state delegate in less than a generation, less time than it took for a boy to grow into a man. Skiffington loved the South, but as a man with a woman from the North, he gradually became comfortable thinking he could live happy in Philadelphia or in any other part of the country and consider himself just another American who had become what he was because of what the South had given and taught him. Whenever he and Winifred visited his in-laws in Philadelphia, Skiffington never returned to the South without paying his respects to the place where Benjamin Franklin had died. He considered Franklin the second-greatest American, after George Washington, and before Thomas Jefferson.

Though Manchester County had money for it, Skiffington did not at that time take on a deputy, having always thought that Patterson had taken him on as a favor to his father. He could do alone what needed to be done. But Skiffington, mindful of the Caesars who controlled all that did not belong to God, took a hint from Colfax and Robbins and assembled a team of twelve patrollers to serve as "nocturnal aides"—slave patrollers. He split Manchester County into three parts and appointed a nightly team of three men for each section. Except for one man who was Cherokee, they were all poor whites, the patrollers, and among them there were only two who had slaves to their names. One was Barnum Kinsey, then considered by everyone to be the poorest white man in the county, "saved," as one neighbor said, "from bein a nigger only by the color of his skin." Barnum's only slave, Jeff, was fifty-seven when his master became a patroller; the slave had been part of his second wife's dowry, along with five square yards of green silk that had wonderful golden lines running through it, silk so fabulous people said a person could get on it and ride away into the sun. Jeff died at sixty-two, after being unable to work for almost a year and after being cared for all that time by Barnum and his wife. Wherever he went after death, Jeff may have been grateful that in his last months, Barnum would read to him from Franklin's *Poor Richard's Almanac*. "You have to stop all this funnin me with that book, Mr. Barnum," Jeff would say, laughing. "You and that funny book will be the death of me." After Jeff died, Barnum had to put his first child from that second marriage to work in his fields. The child was four at the time and by then all the magical green silk with golden lines had been sold off or used up. Sheriff John Skiffington was to say one day of Barnum Kinsey that he was a good man unable to practice in a place that could be hard on people with his kind of religion.

Despite vowing never to own a slave, Skiffington had no trouble doing his job to keep the institution of slavery going, an institution even God himself had sanctioned throughout the Bible. Skiffington had learned from his father how much solace there was in separating God's law from Caesar's law. "Render your body unto them," his father had taught, "but know your soul belongs to God." As long as Skiffington and Winifred lived within the light that came from God's law, from the Bible, nothing on earth, not even his duty as a sheriff to the Caesars, could deny them the kingdom of God. "We will not own slaves," Skiffington promised God, and he promised each morning he went to his knees to pray. Though everyone in the county saw Minerva the wedding present as their property, the Skiffingtons did not feel that they owned her, not in the way whites and a few blacks owned slaves. Minerva was not free, but only in the way a child in a family is not free. In fact, in Philadelphia years later, as she paid for all those posters with Minerva's picture on them, Winifred Skiffington was to think only one thing—"I must get my daughter back. I must get my daughter back."

In Skiffington's day, the sheriff's office sat next to the general store on Manchester's main street; it was moved to a larger facility across the street and next to the hardware store after the War between the States. Skiffington kept a Bible in the jail, on the northwest corner of his desk, and he kept one in his saddlebags. He found it a comfort knowing that wherever he might be, God's word could be picked up and read. He turned twenty-nine the month he became sheriff. The town and the county went into a period of years and years of what University of Virginia historian Roberta Murphy in a 1979 book would call "peace and prosperity." For the people who depended upon slaves, this meant, among other things, that not one slave escaped, not until after Henry Townsend died. The historian—whose book was rejected by the University of Virginia Press and finally published by the University of North Carolina Press—would also call Skiffington "a godsend" for the county. This historian was especially drawn to the quirks of the county. In 1851, she noted, for example, a man of two slaves at the eastern end of Manchester had five chickens born on the same day with two heads. Two of the chickens were even said to do a kind of dance when the harmonica was played. People came from as far away as Tennessee and South Carolina to see the five chickens for a charge of one penny. In the history of the county, the chickens, all of which managed to live until 1856, were a momentous event ten places below the tenure of John Skiffington as sheriff, according to this one historian, who became a full professor at Washington and Lee University three years after her book was published.

The Rita thing, which would ultimately bring Skiffington to the job of sheriff in 1843, began with Mildred and Augustus Townsend buying their own son Henry from William Robbins. Augustus and Mildred came to pick up their boy a few days after they made the last payment. They waited on the road that Sunday and about noon Rita, the second mother to Henry, came out with the boy. His groom clothes belonged to Robbins so he came out to his parents barefoot and in some secondhand clothes that Robbins had thrown in for free because the Townsends had never been late with a payment. There was nothing to do but for the boy to get into the back of the wagon after he and Rita had hugged good-bye. "I see you later, Rita," Mildred said. "I see you later," Rita said. "I see you later, Rita," Henry said. What would amaze all involved was that Robbins never suspected the Townsends, and Henry, who became as close to Robbins as Robbins's own son Louis, would never say a word. Rita came out into the road, which she knew she was not supposed to do, and stood with her arms folded when she was not waving bye-bye to the boy. The moment the wagon took off, she began to vomit, and all she could think, between the tears, was how much she had enjoyed that dinner, now lost to the road. And she vomited again—thinking that this time it was that little breakfast of one stolen egg and a slice of an old pig's ear that would have been green in another hour or two if she hadn't cooked it. She took the bottom of her frock and wiped her mouth. Being that it was noon, the sun was high. The sun for a moment went behind a cloud and when it emerged, she took a step toward the departing wagon. She wiped her tears and then she began to run, and in the moments it took for the sun to go behind another cloud, she had caught up with the wagon and had hold of the back of it. Augustus wasn't driving the wagon very fast because he had his family together again and all time was now spread out before him over the valley and the mountains forever and ever. Henry soon took hold of Rita's other hand. Augustus and Mildred were facing ahead, toward home. "Daddy," Henry said quietly as he watched Rita. His legs dangling off the edge of the wagon, he alone was facing back, toward the Robbins plantation. "Daddy." Augustus turned in his seat and saw Rita. "What you doin, woman?"

"Don't leave me here. Please don't leave me here," Rita managed to say. The wagon was dragging her when she wasn't able to run along and it was all Henry could do to hold on to her. Augustus stopped. She climbed aboard and pulled Henry into her arms. "Please please. Lord Jesus, please."

"Go back now," Mildred said and Augustus repeated her words. The sun was coming full again and the clouds drifted away and so there was even more light on what wasn't yet a crime, just a minor offense—two lashes of the whip on Rita's back and a scolding to the free and clear Townsends, even the boy, who should have known better even if his parents were to claim they didn't. "You go back," Mildred and Augustus said together. Henry, beginning to understand the weight of the problem, began to cry, but he clung to Rita as much as she was clinging to him. Augustus got down and pulled at Rita. "Go way. Go way, woman," he said, looking about, waiting for Robbins or the overseer or some slave to come out and bear witness to it all. Augustus trembled and he saw the sun move in that doomed way a dying man sees a clock's hour and minute hands move; worse was the promise from the much faster second hand on the clock that all their backs would be whipped raw before sundown. "Please go way, Rita. Please."

"Don't leave me here, Augustus. I never been bad not one day to Henry. Tell him, Henry, bout what a good mother I been to you."

"Yes, Daddy, she been a good mother." He turned and looked at Mildred. "Mama, she been a good mama."

"It don't matter. Don't kill us like this, Rita." Augustus raised his hands and shook them at the universe. "Bad mother, good mother, it don't matter." He knelt to halt the tears. Mildred got down and came to him. "Augustus," she said and she was followed by Henry saying, "Daddy, daddy." In less than an hour, he had said "Daddy" more times than he had in three years. Augustus stood up. "Augustus," Mildred said. She touched his chest and he knew. "We all be dead by mornin," he said. He got back up on the wagon, and after he had taken the reins, he was silent as he saw time rolling back toward him from the valley and from the mountains. Mildred told Rita to lay down and she and Henry covered her with a blanket. When Mildred got back up, her husband said, "You got your free papers?" "Yes," she said. "You got yours?" They were the same questions they had asked before setting out every Sunday from home, but now he added, "You got Henry's bill a sale?" "Yes," Mildred said. Augustus nodded and commanded the mules to go. "Up," he said. "Go up." He looked back once and when he saw the gray lump that was Rita and saw even farther back the opening to Robbins's plantation where he had been and his wife had been and his child had been, he commanded the mules to go faster.

He sat all night waiting and thinking of what he could do. Rita, as if trying to disappear, went to a corner of the kitchen in the house Augustus had not long completed. She told the Townsends she was afraid to accept a bed upstairs, lest she have the comfort of it to get out of her mind for the rest of her life. No one came Monday and no one came Tuesday. Very early that Tuesday morning Augustus began collecting the walking sticks he had carved and which he was sending to an Irish merchant in New York. He wrapped each stick in burlap. After he had placed the third one in the wooden box, he stopped and looked over at Rita, sitting up and asleep in the corner. "Rita," he said in a whisper. She woke and immediately stood up, sensing the end. She could not see all the white men and all the white men's horses who had come for her, but she nevertheless raised her hands high to surrender. "Come here," Augustus whispered. He took out the three wrapped sticks and told her to get in the box. Her first thought was a coffin but only white people got coffins that nice.

When she was in it, with her head just an inch or so from the top and her feet with a little less than that from the bottom, he put wrapped walking sticks to either side of her. He had planned to send at least forty sticks to the merchant in New York, but he judged now that the box would take no more than seventeen. Rita's people had always been people of more bones than meat and muscle, and at long last that was a blessing. Augustus had always wondered what type of New York people bought his walking sticks, what kinds of places they wandered to with them, and that was one thing on his mind as he wrapped sticks and smiled at Rita. There was one stick upon which Augustus had carved Adam at the base. Adam was holding up Eve who was holding up Cain who was holding up Abel and so on and so on. After fourteen or more other figures, including his idea of the king and queen of England, there was George Washington. Rita, not knowing, not caring what was on the stick, but knowing only that she might get another day of sun, took that wrapped stick of Adam and his people and held it. "You get out now and lemme make some holes for the air." Once he finished, he put her back in and fitted the top on

the box. "How that?" he asked her through one of the holes once the
top was on. "It be good. It be real good, Augustus," she said. Before he
woke her in the corner, she had been dreaming of work—she had
planted seeds in her rows and finished long before everyone else and
she was waiting for the overseer to direct her to more work. Just before Augustus whispered her name, she had raised both her hands so
that the overseer might see that she was waiting and was not just
slacking.

Near the end of Augustus's work on the box, after he had padded
it with burlap, Mildred and Henry came down from upstairs and
watched Augustus. It was a little after six in the morning. One rooster
crowed, then another, and then another. The four people took the box
and the sticks out to the wagon. "Fill these here with water,"
Augustus said, handing two flasks to Henry before stepping back to
consider the box. Augustus put a clean rag with a few biscuits next to
the right of where Rita's head would go. Augustus moved a stick just
a bit and put the filled flasks in the space on the other side of where
her head would be. He was surprised at the ease of how he worked, no
trembling of the hands, as if he had been born just to put a woman
in a box and send her to New York. He believed whistling inside or
outside the house was bad luck, but right then as he worked, he was
tempted to whistle. Finally, he turned to Rita, held out his hand and
helped her up onto the wagon and into the box. Before he nailed her
in, Mildred said, "Rita, honey, I see you in the bye and bye. Lord
willin." Rita said, "Mildred, baby, I see you one day in the bye and
bye. The Lord wouldn't hurt us so we couldn't see each other in the
bye and bye." Rita held on to the stick with Adam and Eve holding
up their descendants, and that was the last the three of them ever saw
of her. Mildred would dream about her often. She would be walking
in a cemetery and would come upon a body, Rita's, that had not yet
been buried. "I see you later," the dead Rita would say. "Yes, you
promised you would," was all Mildred could manage as she picked up
a shovel to begin digging.

Henry accompanied his father into town to the shipping agent, talking to Rita the whole trip, and by two o'clock the box was gone. The father and the son watched the train go away, waiting for it to stop on the tracks and back up and have all the world come up to pay witness to the crime of stealing a white man's property. But the train did not stop. "How she gon do her business?" Henry asked when the train and the people and the engine smoke were all gone. "A little bit at a time," Augustus said.

About halfway the trip home, the man realized that these had been his son's first days of freedom. He and Mildred had planned a week of celebration, culminating with neighbors coming by the next Sunday. Augustus said, "You feelin any different?"

"Bout what?" Henry said. He was holding the reins to the mules.

"Bout bein free? Bout not bein nobody's slave?"

"No, sir, I don't reckon I do." He wanted to know if he was supposed to, but he did not know how to ask that. He wondered who was waiting now for Robbins to come riding up on Sir Guilderham.

"Not that you need to feel any different. You can just feel whatever you want to feel." Augustus remembered now that Henry had told on him to Robbins about pushing him some years ago, and it occurred to him that if Robbins were ever to learn about Rita, Henry would be the one to tell him. He wondered if all would have been different if he had bought the boy's freedom first, before Mildred's. "You don't have to ask anybody how to feel. You can just go on and do whatever it is you want to feel. Feel sad, go on and feel sad. Feel happy, you go on and feel happy."

"I reckon," Henry said.

"Oh, yes," Augustus said. "I know so. I've had a little experience with this freedom situation. It's big and little, yes and no, up and down, all at the same time."

"I reckon," Henry said again. The strange thing was that it would be the second black person Henry Townsend bought—not the first, not Moses who became his overseer—who would trouble him after the purchase. He knew by then what Augustus and Mildred felt about what he was doing. That second person was Zeddie, the cook, and he purchased her from a man down from Fredericksburg who had a lot of five slaves to sell and had the most informative leaflet full of the history of those slaves. Much of what he had written was just fiction, because that was the kind of slave sellers Fredericksburg, Virginia, produced. Being black, Henry could not in those days purchase a slave outright in Manchester County. He got his second slave through Robbins. It might well be that—in addition to thinking about his parents—Henry didn't feel Zeddie was worth the money Robbins paid for her; Robbins had been trying to teach him after he sold Moses to Henry that every man felt he had been snookered after buying or selling a slave. She a good cook, the Fredericksburg man—patting his watermelon-sized stomach—said to Robbins about Zeddie, her handkerchief-covered head down, her hands clasped before her, her feet in mere wisps of shoes that would have blown away had she not been standing in them. Henry stood at the very back of the market, and a stranger seeing him might have thought he was someone's servant waiting for the market to close and have his master take him back home. Using Henry's money, Robbins did all Henry's purchases of slaves before 1850 when a delegate from Manchester had the law changed. Most white men knew that when they sold a slave to Robbins, they were really selling to Henry Townsend. Some refused to do it. Henry was, after all, only a nigger who got big by making boots and shoes. Who knew what kind of ideas he had in his head? Who knew what a nigger *really* planned to do with other niggers?

"You just think any way you want," Augustus said to Henry as the wagon neared home, "and it'll be fine."

It was forty-one hours before Rita in the box got to New York. The box was opened with a crowbar by the merchant's wife, a broad-shouldered Irish woman he had met on the HMS *Thames*'s twentieth trip to America. The Irish woman's first husband had died only one day out of Cork Harbor, leaving her alone with five children. The captain had the husband's body—coffined only in the clothes the man had died in and his head wrapped in a piece of family lace—tossed overboard after ten Lord's Prayers and ten Hail Marys were spoken by the man's oldest child, a boy of eight. The boy, Timothy, had struggled through ten of each when the captain, a German Protestant, thought one of each would have done. An Irish prayer was obviously worth only a tenth of what a German prayer was worth. The boy could not bear to see his father go and everyone assembled could tell that in all the words of the prayers. A month into the voyage the Irish woman's youngest child died, a girl of some five months—twenty Lord's Prayers and twenty Hail Marys from Timothy. A coffin of lace for baby Agnes, that lace being the last of the family fortune.

Mary O'Donnell had been nursing that baby, and the day after Agnes was committed to the sea, her milk stopped flowing. She thought it only a natural result of grieving for Agnes. She would go on to have three more children with her second husband, the seller of Augustus Townsend's walking sticks, but with each child the milk did not return. "Where is my milk?" Mary asked God with each of the three children. "Where is my milk?" God did not give her an answer and he gave her not one drop of milk. With the second and third children, she asked Mary the mother of Jesus to intercede with God on her behalf. "Didn't he give you milk for your child?" she asked Mary. "Wasn't there milk aplenty for Jesus?"

Mary O'Donnell Conlon would never live comfortably in America, would never come to feel it was her own dear country. Long before the HMS *Thames* had even seen the American shore, America, the land of promise and hope, had reached out across the sea and taken her husband, a man who had taken her heart and kept it, and America had taken her baby—two innocent beings in the vastness of a world with all kinds of things that could have been taken first. She held nothing against God. God was simply being God. But she could not forgive America and saw it as the cause of all her misery. Had America not called out to her first husband, not sung to him, they could have stayed home and managed somehow in that county in Ireland where children, even old children, had the pinkest cheeks.

Mary Conlon's hair stayed all black until her dying day. She would wake one morning as an old woman with a gray hair or two or three and the next morning those gray hairs would be black again. "Such strong black hair," she would say to God when she was seventy-five, "such hair and all I wanted was a little milk." Her children stayed devoted to her, but none was closer and more devoted than Timothy, who was affectionately known as his mother's pet. He had worried himself sick on the ship to America, thinking his mother would be the next to die. Not even a million Lord's Prayers and a million Hail Marys would have let him consign his mother to the sea.

It was Timothy, then twelve years old, who was at his mother's side when she opened the box from Augustus Townsend. "Don't send me back," Rita said in the darkness as each nail was pried loose and the top of the box was gradually separated from the body of the box and the feeble light little by little began to seep in on her. Each nail Mary pried loose made such an awful noise to Rita, awful and as loud as the coming of an army. As the light came in, Rita began to feel ashamed because of her waste. A seven-hour stretch out of Baltimore had had her lying on her stomach because the handlers ignored the Manchester shipping agent's words marked in black paint on the top—THIS SIDE UP WITH EXTREME CARE. Mary gave no expression when she first heard and then saw the black woman through the first good opening. Rita, once the box was open all the way, covered her eyes because even that weak light in the storeroom was too much for her to bear. "Don't send me back. Don't send me back." Rita did not know if she was in New York or merely in a house only a plantation away from William Robbins. She could barely move and her mouth was dry because she had allowed herself only five sips of water during the entire trip. A journey into possible death could take a long time and so water shouldn't be wasted. Her body was too dry to even produce tears, and her words came out as if her mouth were stuffed with rags. Slowly, she opened her eyes and saw Mary. "Don't send me back." And then, seeing the boy Timothy for the first time, Rita's stiffened arms managed to offer the stick of Adam and Eve and their descendants to him. The boy, who was as expressionless as his mother, took the walking stick as if that was what he had been waiting for all along.

3

A Death in the Family. Where God Stands. Ten Thousand Combs.

Loretta, Caldonia Townsend's maid, came down from the house about sunrise the next morning and opened Moses's cabin door after one knock and told him their master Henry was dead. He scratched at his whiskers. "How long?" he said. "Last night," she answered. Priscilla, Moses's wife, came up behind him, her hand to her mouth. "Oh, Lord," she said. "Massa dead." She turned to her son who was sitting before the hearth, eating cornbread and gravy. "There been death in the family," she said to the boy. He considered his mother for a second or so then went back to eating. Something told the boy that his mother, with the dead master on her mind, might not eat her portion, so he took her food as well.

"Loretta, whas gonna happen to all us now?" Moses said, thinking that her being up in the house gave her more to know. Priscilla came up closer behind her husband and Loretta could see the third of her body that wasn't obscured by the man.

"I don't know, Moses. We just have to wait and see." The three of them were thinking of the six slaves of the white family just down the road a piece, the six slaves who were so close by they were like family to the slaves at Henry's place. Those six were good workers and had made their owner quite wealthy in a small Manchester County kind of way. Loretta said, "We just gon have to wait and see which way the wind gon blow." The white man down the road had died four months ago, and at first the widow, his third wife and mother to his two children from his second marriage, told the slaves they would not be sold off. But before the white man could even get settled in his grave, his widow had sold them to finance a new life in Europe, which she knew about from two fanciful picture books she had treasured and hidden for years in the chimney from her husband. One of the books showed what an artist claimed were the Paris fashions of 1825. There were nearly thirty years separating the year of the fashion picture book and the year the widow finally got to France, so all the material of her dreams, the fashions of 1825, was no doubt out of style by the time she arrived. White people said she took the dead white man's two children with her to the new life in Paris, but colored people, slave and free, said that didn't happen, that the woman had sold the children once she was safely out of Virginia. Negroes said that somewhere in the world, known or unknown, someone might not think twice about buying two happy white children with plump cheeks and able to write and sing like angels and do basic ciphering.

Priscilla now stepped even closer to her husband, and most of the third of her that Loretta could see disappeared. Priscilla said, "I would hate to go from Massa Henry's place. I would hate all that not knowin again where in the world I was." The six slaves down the road—along with the animals and the land and its equipment—had brought the widow just a tad over $11,316, which supplemented the $1,567.39 her husband had in the bank and buried in the backyard. Only the land remained where it had always been after the widow sold everything; all else, including the slaves, was scattered to the farthest winds. No two slaves ended up together. Five of them were related by blood. One, Judy, was married to a young man owned by Henry Townsend. Another, Melanie, not seven months old, was just getting used to solid food, had begun to crawl and so had to be watched every waking second. Nicknamed "Miss Frisky" by her maternal uncle, the baby Melanie—her parents bragged to any soul who would listen—had the spirit of three babies and would crawl and crawl all over the world until someone picked her up to stop her or until her hands and knees wore out.

Moses scratched his whiskers again, and things were so quiet beyond the crackle of the fire in his hearth that someone passing in the lane could have heard his fingers going over his whiskers. Right then, Elias came out of his cabin next door, carrying an empty water bucket. He nodded "Morning" to the people in Moses's doorway, but no words were spoken by anyone. Loretta nodded "Morning" to Elias; she depended on Moses to tell him about the death of Henry.

"Moses," Loretta said after Elias had passed, "just about everything can wait till Henry is safe in his grave, till we put the master down. You hear what I'm sayin?"

"I hear you," Moses said. "I hear you good."

Loretta said, "Is there any trouble down here from anyone? Is there any trouble from somebody that might spoil that man's trip to the grave?"

"You best tell her bout Stamford," Priscilla said. Stamford was forty years old, desperate for any young woman he could get a hold of. A man had told Stamford when he was no more than twelve that the way for a man to survive slavery was to always have a young woman, "young stuff" was how the man put it. Without "young stuff," a man was destined to die a horrible death in slavery. "Don't you be like that, Stamford," the man had said more than once. "Keep your young stuff close by."

"Whas the problem with Stamford?" Loretta said, her eyes on the top of Priscilla's head, which was now just about all she could see of her. "Is it Gloria again?" Gloria was Stamford's latest young stuff.

Moses said, "That might be finished. I think she kicked him out day fore yestiddy. Stamford probably out there with nobody and he ain't a happy man when that happens."

"Please check him, Moses," Loretta said. "Don't let him start up somethin. We can deal with Stamford after the funeral. I don't want a lot of Who-Shot-John when we start puttin Henry in the ground."

"I'll check him," Moses said, "or I'll break him in two tryin."

"No breakin, Moses." Loretta looked down the lane to where a little girl was standing with her hands on her hips, staring at her. Loretta knew her name, had helped the girl into the world. *Say good mornin to me, honey chile. Say good mornin to Loretta.* "No breakin, just checkin. And I hope you ain't wrong about what trouble Stamford is, the way you was wrong bout Elias."

"Elias still trouble to my way a thinkin," Moses said.

Loretta looked from the girl and said to Moses, "Mistress Caldonia and Miss Fern want you get evbody to come out front maybe in another hour, after breakfast," and she looked to find that the little girl was gone. Where the girl had stood was where the sun would first come over the horizon. "Go tell em Henry dead." He nodded. He was barefoot. They both knew where he was on the pole of who was and was not important on the Townsend plantation, so he did not tarry when she told him to do something. Once, not long after Henry had purchased her for his bride, Loretta had spent weeks thinking Moses might make a good man for her, a tolerable match, but one morning she had awakened to hear him out somewhere screaming at someone or something. A scream so loud all the morning birds quieted down. He went on screaming until Henry came out and told him to hush. That morning he screamed was so cold she hurt her hand cracking the water in the face basin. And as she put on her clothes, wishing for warmth, she knew that he would not do. Loretta turned from Moses and Priscilla now and stepped away from their door.

Heading back to the house, she met Elias, carrying a bucket of water from the well.

"Tell Celeste that Henry be dead," she said.

"You stick a needle in him to make sure?" Elias said. "You poke him and poke him to make sure?"

At first, before remembering everything, she did not understand what he could mean by that and her mouth opened in a small *O* of surprise. Once upon a time he would have been a better man for her. Loretta looked down at the water, at the way it came right up to the lip of the bucket. There was none spilled behind him, which said something about the way he moved through the world, even with his head unbalanced with part of one ear gone. "He dead, thas all," Loretta said. "I know dead when I see it, Elias. It don't put on a face to make him look like nothin else but dead. Master dead." It was said by many a slave that a servant's feeling about a master could be discerned on any given day by whether the slave called him "Master," "Marse," or "Massa." "Marse" could sound like a curse if the right woman said it in just the right way. Alice, for one, said "Massa," but it came up out of her like a call from a tomb. "Master dead," Loretta said again, and it struck Elias that he had never heard her say "Master" before. He felt compelled to repeat her words, as if to make it so once and for all. "Master dead." She went around him and disappeared into the fog, which the sun was fast burning off. Back in the house, she stood at the kitchen window and watched the world come up out of the fog. There was no need to tell Zeddie, the cook, to fix breakfast or to tell Zeddie's man, Bennett, to fix the fire. For the moment, death was giving all the orders. All was quiet. Loretta was thirty-two years old. When the day came when all the slaves were slaves no more and decided that they should choose a last name for themselves, she would not pick Townsend or Blueberry or Freeman or Godspeed or Badmemory, as many would. She would choose nothing, and she stayed with nothing even when she decided to marry.

Moses made to go down the lane of cabins, eight on one side of the lane and eight on the other side, laid out just the way Henry Townsend had seen them in a dream when he was twenty-one years old and without a slave to his name. Moses thought at first he might send his son or another child to tell all to gather in the yard of the house, but as he stepped out of his cabin and saw the sun-filled fog fraying away to nothing, he realized that this was one of the last things he would ever do for his master. Not knowing that Loretta had already told him, he went to Elias's cabin first, the one next to his own, and Celeste, Elias's wife, came to the door. Whether she sensed something or was about to take in some morning air, Celeste opened the door before he could knock. "Master dead," Moses said. "So it is," she said, and stuck her head out the door just so and looked up toward the house, as if there might be a sign on the verandah announcing the news. "We gotta get up to the house," Moses said. "Elias," Celeste said to her husband, turning around to face him. "That Henry gone." She could tell in his eyes that he knew already and had just not bothered to tell her. The smallest smudge of dirt on one of his children's cheeks was important, but the death of his master was no more than the death of a fly in a foreign place he had never even heard of. Celeste had no love for Henry either, but death had taken all his power and now she could afford a little bit of charity. "That Henry be dead. Let God be kind," she said, and limped to Elias, to her three children playing on a pallet. The limp was a horrible one, and it pained most humans to see because they thought it must pain her to move. They shot animals for far less, Moses once thought after Henry brought her home. But she was a good worker, limp or no limp.

Moses went back and forth across the lane and told all. All of the cabins, save one, were occupied. A man, Peter, had died in that one and his widow, May, had abandoned it, to give Peter's spirit time and space to prepare to go home. Before Moses had reached the last cabin on his side of the lane, the one Alice, whom he called the "Night Walker," shared with Delphie and her daughter, Cassandra, the slaves were filling the lane. A few women had cried, remembering the way Henry smiled or how he would join them in singing or thinking that the death of anyone, good or bad, master or not, cut down one more tree in the life forest that shielded them from their own death; but most said or did nothing. Their world had changed but they could not yet understand how. A black man had owned them, a strange thing for many in that world, and now that he was dead, maybe a white man would buy them, which was not as strange. No matter what, though, the sun would come up on them tomorrow, followed by the moon, and dogs would chase their own tails and the sky would remain just out of reach. "I didn't sleep well," one man across the lane from Elias said to his next-door neighbor. "Well, I know I sure did," the neighbor said. "I slept like they was payin me to, slept anough for three white women without a care in the world." "Well," the first man said, "sounds like you gotta hold a some of my sleep. Better give it back. Better give it back fore you wear out my sleep usin it. Give it back." "Oh, I will," the neighbor said, laughing, inspecting loose threads on his overalls. "I sure will. Soon as I'm finished. Meantime, I'm gonna use it again tonight. Come for it in the mornin." They both laughed.

It was often the case that Alice, the Night Walker, would be standing just inside her door when Moses opened it each morning, dressed and ready to work, as if she had been standing at the door waiting for him all night. She was waiting now and she was smiling, the same smile she had for everything—from the death of a neighbor's baby to the four oranges Henry and Caldonia gave each slave on Christmas morning. *"Baby dead baby dead baby dead,"* she would chant. *"Christmas oranges Christmas oranges Christmas oranges in the mornin."*

"I don't want no foolishness from you, woman," Moses said now. He turned and saw Stamford, the seeker of young stuff, in the middle of the crowd, eyeing Gloria, who didn't want to be his young stuff anymore. "Master dead," Moses said to Alice. "No foolishness this mornin, woman." Alice went on smiling. "Master dead master dead master be dead." "Hush, girl," Moses said. "Respect the dead the way they need to be respected." The story went that the mule that kicked Alice in the head when she was years younger had been a one-eyed mule, but no more ornery for being one-eyed than any other mule. The story continued that when she regained her senses, moments after the kick, she slapped the mule and called it a dirty name. This was before Henry bought her for $228 and two bushels of apples from the estate of a white man who had no heirs and who was afraid of mules. It was the dirty name that made everyone know she had gone down the crazy road, because before the kick Alice had been known as a sweet girl of sweet words.

"Moses?" Delphie came up behind Alice, her cabin mate.

"Master dead," Moses said. "You and Cassie get Alice and come up with evbody to the house."

"Master dead, Moses?" Delphie said. "Whas gonna come of us?" She would be forty-four in a few months and had already lived longer than any ancestor she had ever had, every single one of them. She did not know this history of eons about herself; there was only the feeling in her bones that for some time she had been venturing into a place unknown, and that feeling made her hope for a road that would not cut too deeply into her feet and her soul. To live to see fifty was a wish she was beginning to dare to have. My name is Delphie and I'm fifty years old. Count em. Start at one and count em. One Delphie, two Delphie, three Delphie . . . Before she had reached forty her only wish was that the world would be kind to her daughter Cassandra, or "Cassie," as some people called her. Now a second wish was beginning to creep up on her, and she was afraid that wishing to see fifty might make God turn his back on the first wish about her daughter. God might say: *Make up your mind about them wishes, Delphie, I ain't got all day and you ain't got but one wish comin to you.* Delphie said to Moses, "We gon leave here? Be sold off?"

"I don't know no more than it's mornin time and that master dead," Moses said. "You and Cassie get Alice and come on up to the house like evbody else."

"Master dead master dead master be dead," Alice chanted.

"We comin," Delphie said. She looked at her daughter and Cassandra hunched her shoulders. The two had been purchased together, one of the few times God had answered Delphie's prayers. She wondered now if she should pray for Henry's soul. It came to her as she stepped off toward the house that a prayer for a man who was one of God's children would not be wasted. She prayed every day that her food would stay on her stomach, prayers that were dozens of words long. So ten words for the soul of Henry Townsend could be spared. Delphie saw Stamford two people behind Gloria, the woman who did not want him anymore. If he touches Gloria, Delphie thought, I will strike that fool man down right out here in the open.

There was a crowd in the lane now and Moses made his slow way through it, through the uncertainty of twenty-nine adults and children. At his cabin he found Priscilla and Jamie, his son, who was playing hand games with Tessie, the oldest child of Elias and Celeste. Moses stepped off toward the house and all the rest followed, the children skipping along the way they did on Sundays, their day off. All the children, except those in their parents' arms, were in front of all the adults. Everyone found Caldonia on the verandah, and with her were Augustus and Mildred, Henry's parents, on one side and on the other side was Fern Elston the teacher, who was holding Caldonia's hand. Augustus and Mildred had arrived less than an hour before. Behind Caldonia were her mother and twin brother. Loretta the maid was in the doorway and behind her stood Zeddie the cook and Bennett, her man. The fog was gone and the day was once more moving toward beautiful.

Caldonia stepped to the edge of the verandah and raised her head for the first time since she had walked out her front door. She was wearing the black mourning dress and the veil that her mother had brought with her. The sun was full in her face but she did not shade her eyes. She had been crying before she came through the door, and she knew that the tears would soon come back so she wanted to hurry to get at least a few words out. Fern put one arm around Caldonia and Caldonia raised her veil.

"You know now that our Henry has left us," she said to her slaves. "Left us for good, left us for heaven. Pray for him. Give him all your prayers. He cared about you all, and I have no less care than he did. I have no less love." She had not considered beforehand what she would say. Every word was not original, was part of something she had heard somewhere else, something her father may have told her as a bedtime story, something Fern Elston may have long ago put into Caldonia's head and the heads of dozens of other students. Caldonia said to the slaves, "Please do not worry yourselves. I am here and I will not be going anywhere. And you will be with me. We will be together in all of this. God stands with us. God will give us many days, good and bright days, good and joyful days. Your master had work to do, your master wanted better things for you and your children and this world, and I want them for you as well. Please do not worry. God stands with us." Something she had read in a book, written by a white man in a different time and place. Henry had always said that he wanted to be a better master than any white man he had ever known. He did not understand that the kind of world he wanted to create was doomed before he had even spoken the first syllable of the word *master*.

Caldonia faltered and began crying and Augustus, her father-in-law, took her into his arms, and then, not long after that, he put her in her brother's arms and her brother led her into the house, followed by her mother and Fern Elston and Loretta.

Augustus came down the steps and Mildred came after him. They knew all that was in the hearts of the slaves, they knew all that they were thinking. The slaves came to them, wordless. Augustus had come down not to accept their condolences but because he knew now, after hearing Caldonia speak, that the death of his son would not set them free. He knew that not one of them had ever believed that death would free them—that was not the benevolent way their world moved through the universe. But he himself had believed, had hoped from the moment of the knock at his door at two that morning. "Augustus, I'm sorry, but Mistress say to say to you that Master Henry dead," Bennett had said, holding his pass in one hand and the lantern in the other so his face might be seen in the darkness. Augustus had believed in Caldonia, had always believed in her, having seen from the beginning a light in her that had failed in his own son born into slavery. But the light was not in her words. So he and Mildred came down the steps to offer their own condolences. They went through the crowd, hugging men and women, kissing the faces of the children, for they had come to know them over the years.

It was before they reached the end of the crowd that William Robbins came up to the house in a surrey driven by his son, Louis. Louis and Caldonia and her twin brother, Calvin, had been schoolmates, all taught by Fern. Robbins sat in the backseat with Dora, Louis's sister, another of Caldonia's schoolmates. Robbins got out of the surrey and went around and helped Dora out. None of the slaves moved; with a black master and mistress, a white man was now a day-to-day rarity for many of them. Robbins took off his hat and went to the steps and up to the door and his children followed. Augustus watched the white man all the way. Robbins had not once looked around, but at the door, a storm went off in his head and it made him turn around. "Sir?" Louis said. "Sir?" Robbins came to the end of the verandah and looked down at everybody. "What have I told you?" he asked the assembly. "Have I not told yall?" Dora asked her father what was wrong. Except for the skin a shade and a half darker and the differences in their age, Dora was the very image of the daughter Robbins had with his white wife. "What have I told yall?"

A wind, gentle but insistent, drifted through Robbins's head and the storm quieted, and in a moment or so he raised a hand in greeting to the crowd. The people did not react. Robbins knew something had happened in the minute just gone by but he could not know what, could not know in what way he may have disgraced himself, even before a passel of slaves. He remembered now that he was there because a man he had cared about was dead. Henry, good Henry, was dead. Dora came behind her father and put her hand softly on his shoulder. "Let's go inside now," she said.

Robbins turned and opened Caldonia's door without knocking. His

two children followed. Calvin came out of the house and went down
to everyone to say that Caldonia wanted no one working that day or
the next day, when the funeral was planned. "Moses," he said, "if
anyone needs anything, just let me know." He meant whatever anyone needed to make a coffin and grave for Henry. Stamford, trying to
impress the woman who did not want him anymore, made a show of
shaking Calvin's hand and saying he was sorry to hear about poor
Master Henry. Calvin nodded. Calvin wanted to stay on down there
with them but he feared that he would not be welcome the way
Mildred and Augustus were. He and his mother had thirteen slaves to
their names, but he was not a happy young man. Whenever he talked
to her about freeing them, as he often did, Maude, his mother, would
call them his legacy and say that people with all their faculties did not
sell off their legacies.

No other slave came to Calvin and he made to go away. Augustus
said to his back, "Tell Caldonia we be back up directly." Calvin
nodded again and began walking to the house. His father had died
a slow death three years before, shriveling and drying up like a leaf
in a rainless December, and Calvin always suspected that his mother
had poisoned him because his father had been planning to free all
their slaves—their legacy. "Sweet Maude, I want to go home to God
with a clean mind," Calvin's father kept saying. After his father's
death, Calvin stayed on with his mother, in their house, surrounded
by the legacy he did not want, because Maude told him she, too, was
not long for this world. He stayed also because he wanted to be close
to Louis, William Robbins's son, whom Calvin loved but who could
never love Calvin back. Calvin now walked away from the gathering
of slaves and Augustus and Mildred and reached the top of the stairs
and stopped, stood there for a long time, only two feet or so from the
door.

The slaves and Mildred and Augustus went down to the lane to the
cabins. Even now with Henry gone, especially now, Mildred and
Augustus had no plans to stay in the house their son and his slave had

built. They would stay in the cabin they had just left only days before, after Henry had assured them that he was getting well.

The slaves Henry Townsend left his wife were thirteen women, eleven men, and nine children. The adults included the house servants Loretta, Zeddie, and Bennett, who lived and worked in the house. At any one time some adults and children might be working in the house, depending upon the tasks that needed to be done and whether they might be needed in the fields. As the crowd made its way back down to the lane, some of the children were at the front, and at the head of those children was Elias and Celeste's oldest, Tessie. She began skipping but an adult told her that a human being had died and skipping should be left off to another day. Tessie would soon be six years old and being the child of her parents who she was, she listened and stopped skipping. Tessie would live to be ninety-seven years old, and the doll her father was making for her would be with her until her last hour. She and the doll, long missing the corn-silk hair Elias her father had put on it, would outlive two of her children, and the doll would outlive her. Beside Tessie that day going back down to the lane was Jamie, the son of Priscilla and Moses the overseer. The boy leaned toward mischief and he was the fattest slave child in four counties, eight years old and the best friend of Tessie. Jamie always talked about him and Tessie marrying one day but that was never to be.

Five-year-old Grant, the oldest of Tessie's brothers, held her hand as they went down to the lane. Grant and another boy in the lane, Boyd, also five, had been plagued by identical nightmares for weeks. What Grant dreamed one night, Boyd would dream the next. And then, days later, the reverse would happen, and Boyd's dream would go across the lane and settle into Grant's dreaming head. "You just be tryin to do what I be doin," they teased each other under the safety of the sun. They were both terrified of going to sleep but they had found a strange enjoyment in comparing the dreams, remembering and sharing some detail that the other boy may have forgotten. "You see that big giant man in the blue hat comin at you?" "Whatn't blue atall. Was all yellow." "Well, I saw blue." "You saw wrong." In recent days the nightmares had eased off, and there was talk that with the coming of fall, the dreams would end altogether. Elias carried their third child, Ellwood, thirteen months. Celeste limped beside her husband. She was three months pregnant with their fourth child.

Two other children at the head of the crowd that day were three-year-old twins, Caldonia and Henry. The twins had had a bad spell the year before, seized for nearly two weeks by a paralyzing and fever-ish malady that the white doctor could not understand and so could not cure. He did recommend that the whole plantation be quaran-tined and John Skiffington, the sheriff, used his patrollers to make sure that was done. Each day and night of the children's illness Caldonia was with them, leaving only to go up to the house to change clothes. Finally, Delphie, who knew something about roots, told the mother of the twins to have them sleep with the tops of their heads touching, and in two days the children were up and about. Delphie surmised that a bond had been created while the twins were in the womb and that that bond had been cut to their detriment with their births. Only sleeping head-to-head could repair that bond, making them ready for the rest of their lives together. The twins would live to be eighty-eight years old. Caldonia would die first, and though her brother Henry had a good and happy life with a good wife and many offspring with their offspring, he decided to follow his sister. "She's never led me wrong in all this time," he said to his best friend over drinks the night before he decided to up and die. "I don't think she'll lead me wrong this one last time."

Also at the head of the crowd were Delores, seven years old, and her brother Patrick, three years younger. Delores would live to be ninety-five years old, but her brother would die when he was forty-seven, shot three times by a man as Patrick came out of the man's bedroom window after being with the man's wife. The night Patrick was killed he had had a choice—go down to the bottom and spend the night playing cards or go through that man's bedroom window where the wife was waiting, all wet and hungry and everything. "I need what you got, P Patrick," the wife had said to him earlier that day. "I need it bad." The cards had not been falling right for Patrick that week. He had already lost $53 and owed one evil man $11 more, so he thought he would have better luck with that man's wife. "Give me what you got, P Patrick."

Augustus and Mildred would again stay in the cabin they had been in when they visited during Henry's illness. Peter and his wife May had lived in that cabin until about five weeks before when two horses, frightened by something in the barn only they could see, ran Peter over in their effort to escape. May's child was now seven months old and as everyone walked back down to the lane, the child was carried by a neighbor next door to where Peter and May had lived. Peter, after being trampled by the horses, had been carried back to his cabin and that was where he died. May had abandoned the cabin for the requisite month to give Peter's spirit time to say good-bye and then find its way to heaven. But after that month she had not returned. May, known for her stubbornness, would decide the day after Henry Townsend's funeral that Mildred and Augustus's being in the cabin a second time was Peter's way of telling her that he was home and settled in. She returned to the cabin.

Though there was to be no work in the fields that day, there were things to be done if the world was to go on. Milking cows, a mule to be shod, eggs collected, a plow to be repaired, cabins to be swept if more dust and dirt were not to join what was already inside. And the bodies of slaves and animals required nourishment and fires needed tending to. They, all of them except the children under five, went to work, having decided that food could wait until the chores of the morning were done since they had the rest of the day to themselves.

Mildred and Augustus shared in all the work, as they were not strangers to labor.

About noon Calvin and Louis came down and told Moses the grave should be dug. There was a good-sized plot at the back and off to the left of the house where Henry had planned for himself, Caldonia and their generations to be buried. It was on the same piece of land where slaves were buried, but separate, the way white slaveowners did it. The slave cemetery was nearly empty of adults, unlike the generations of men and women who were in other slave cemeteries in Manchester County. Henry Townsend had not been a master long enough for his adult slaves to die of old age and populate the cemetery. In that slave cemetery there was Peter, the man trampled by horses. People believed one of two things: that the beasts had sensed something unholy in the barn and stampeded to escape it, or that the horses had sensed something holy just beyond the barn door and needed to be near that thing. Whatever the case, Peter, father to an unborn girl, was in the way. The cemetery also held Sadie, a fairly new purchase by Henry at the time of her death. A tall woman of forty who, five years before, fell asleep on an empty stomach after fourteen hours in the field and never woke up. Beside Peter in death, she had been mostly alone in life, owing perhaps to her newness to the plantation. No husband, though she had lain twice with a man from another plantation. That man's master, a white man of five slaves to his name, allowed the slave to come to Sadie's funeral, though he warned Andy that if the funeral went on too long, as nigger funerals sometimes did, Andy was to step away and come straight back home. He wrote Andy a pass that expired at two o'clock in the afternoon. There were ten infants in the slave cemetery, five girls, five boys, only two of them related; none had seen their second year of life. No two had died of the same thing. An inability to digest even mother's milk, an infection from a burn from a flying ember, a silent, unexplained death during the night as if not to disturb her mother's sleep. One had died strapped to his mother's back as the woman worked in the fields, two days before the end of harvest, the day Loretta the maid and Caldonia the mistress were away and Zeddie the cook took sick and was unable to look after the baby. The only child over two years in the cemetery was twelve-year-old Luke, a gangly boy of a sweet nature, dead of hard work on a farm to which he had been rented for $2 a week. A boy Elias and Celeste had loved. Henry had Luke's mother brought in for the funeral from two counties over, but no one could find his father. Both cemeteries were on a rise, both guarded by trees, some apple, some dogwoods, a stunning magnolia, and some trees no one could make head or tail of. The cemeteries were separated by a hop, skip and a jump.

Calvin, Caldonia's twin, dug into the ground first, dug down more than a foot and came up and gave the shovel to Louis. He, like Calvin, was not a man used to hard labor, but that was not obvious from the way he worked. Louis handed the shovel over to Augustus, who worked until Calvin told him he had done real good and that he might want to give the shovel to Moses. Once Moses was in the hole, William Robbins came out of the house followed by Dora, his daughter. Robbins stood without words at the site for nearly half an hour and watched the men work and then he turned and went back into the house with Dora. After the funeral the next day, he would not see the plantation again until the day Louis married Caldonia. Up in the house, as the men worked on the grave, Henry Townsend had been washed and dressed and laid out on his cooling board in the parlor.

Elias was next and he dug down and then he gave the shovel to Stamford, forty years old. Stamford, in addition to chasing young women, could be a most disagreeable man if he was idle too long. When he was honest with himself, Stamford knew his days with Gloria were at an end. He was now studying on Cassandra, Alice's cabin mate, but Cassandra had already told him once she wouldn't go with an old dog full of fleas. Gloria, twenty-six, loved biscuits, loved to open them hot and soak them in molasses when she could get it. Stamford knew how to cook biscuits the way she liked, but that had

not been enough. They had fought all the time; once it was an all-
night battle and they, bruised and sore, were unfit for the fields the
next day. After a week of the fighting, Henry had Moses separate
them. It was a good thing, people said, because in another week Gloria
would have killed him. Stamford had a plan to make Cassandra like
him, the third plan that summer. That day weeks later when
Stamford would see the crows fall dead from the tree, before he himself walked out toward death, he would say good-bye to Gloria and he
would say good-bye to Cassandra, to all that good young stuff that the
man had once advised him would allow him to survive slavery.
"Without all that young stuff, Stamford, you will die a slave. And it
will not be a pretty die."

When Stamford was done, Calvin took the shovel back and before
long six feet were finally ready for Henry. The men then collected the
lumber from the wagon Augustus and Mildred came in and took it to
the second barn, where they made Henry a coffin. The wood was
pine, which just about everybody in Manchester County, in Virginia,
was buried in. The slaves sometimes got pine, if they had always done
the right thing and their masters thought they deserved it.

Sometime after two o'clock William Robbins left with Dora and
Louis, he off to his plantation and they off to the house they shared
with their mother outside the town. The rest of the day wore itself
away and nothing good and nothing bad happened.

A lice, the woman who wandered in the night, had started being
restless way long before bedtime. "Just leave her be," Cassandra
kept telling her mother, Delphie, who wanted some way to calm
Alice. The three shared their cabin with an orphaned teenage girl. In
the end, leaving her alone was just what Delphie had to do and she
shook her head as Alice went out the door. Alice had a minor cut on
her foot from walking all about the night before, the night her master died. But the cut did not prevent her now from strolling up and

down the lane, chanting, "Master dead master dead master be dead."
Moses did not go out that evening to be alone with himself in the
woods, but before he went to bed he did go about the plantation to
make certain all was well. He told Alice to hush three times and that
last time she did, choosing then to only pace up and down the lane. If
Augustus and Mildred in May's cabin heard Alice chanting about
their dead son they made nothing of it. Finally, Alice sauntered off
toward the smokehouse.

Caldonia and Calvin and their mother came down to the lane once
that evening to ask Augustus and Mildred to please come and stay in
the house. They declined, as they had twice before that day. Mildred
might have gone up, had she not been with Augustus. Fern Elston
came down to the lane as well, the first time she had ever done so. She
felt she owed it to Henry. In her life after this day, she was always to
come down to the lane when she visited, whether Caldonia was with
her or not. Something had shifted with Henry's death, but the greatest shifts were to come very soon, after the gambler Jebediah Dickinson entered her life. Before this day, she had always stayed up in the
house during her visits, preferring not to mingle with "any slave that
was not house broken," as she put it. But the gambler who lost his leg
would change everything and she was never to see the world the same
again, despite all the defensiveness and reticence she displayed with
the white Canadian in August 1881. One evening in the November
that was only months away, Fern, walking in the lane beside Caldonia,
would think how Jebediah the gambler would now be in Baltimore, if
the horse and wagon she gave him held up. In a different world, she
would think before she and Caldonia and Loretta turned to go back
up to the house, she might have found something with him, one leg
or not, dark skin or not. She would not have even had to teach him
how to read and write, because he came to her knowing that already.
I have been a dutiful wife.

Moses and Priscilla came out of their cabin and joined the small
group as they went down the lane. The evening smoke of supper fires

hung thick all about them. Caldonia, still veiled, knocked at a few doors and poked her head inside one or two cabins to ask if there was anything anyone needed. All the children liked her, Mistress Caldonia. Her mother Maude had been saying all day that she had to take care of her "legacy," but as Caldonia went about what Henry, following William Robbins, had called "the business of mastering," she did not think she was doing anything more than escaping for a spell from a house that was twice as large as it had been the day before. Moses spoke to her all the while as she walked, letting her know what he and the slaves would be doing when they returned to work, what his tasting of the soil had told him about the crops. His droning on and on was a bit soothing, far more than Calvin's hand on her arm or the children's smiling up at her. His talking told her in some odd way that one day the pain would at least be cut in half.

At the end of the lane, they turned around. Fern stopped and stood alone and looked out beyond the lane, to the fields. When she turned back, Alice was in front of her, telling Fern that the master was dead. "I know," Fern said. "We know that." "Then why ain't you ready?" Alice said. Fern looked back toward the fields and when she turned around again, Alice had gone away. In four generations, Fern's family had managed to produce people who could easily pass for white. "Marry nothing beneath you," her mother always said, meaning no one darker than herself, and Fern had not. Her mother would not have approved of the gambler who lost a leg. "Human beings should never go back. They should always go forward." Some of Fern's people had gone white, disappearing across the color line and never looking back. She saw some of her kin now and again, a sister, cousins, in Richmond, in Petersburg, carriaging away with fine horses down the street, and she would nod to them and they would nod to her and go on about their business. Fern's husband was also a gambler and he was slowly gambling away their little fortune but there was nothing she could do about it. She was never to know anyone to go to Baltimore and return to tell her about it. *I have been a dutiful wife.*

The lane quieted after they returned to the house. Moses and Priscilla went into their cabin and shut the door for the night. Alice the wanderer came back to the lane, walking up and down. In their cabin, Augustus and Mildred lay down and held each other. One of them started talking—they would not remember which one it was—all about Henry, from his birth to his death, starting a weeks-long project of recalling all that they could about their son. If they had known how to read and write, they could have put it all in a book of two thousand pages. Up in the house, Calvin lit another set of candles, preparing to sit the night with Henry. Louis was soon to return to share the duty, and Zeddie's man Bennett would join them sometime during the night. As Calvin lit the candles, Loretta covered Henry's face with a black silk cloth—she felt he had best rest before the trip in the morning.

Alice set off and she was no sooner out in the road than she began chanting again. Loud, as if she were trying to reach the rafters of heaven. In a little more than a mile from the Townsend plantation Sheriff John Skiffington's patrollers came upon her. "Master dead master dead master be dead."

"What you doin out here?" asked Harvey Travis, the man with the Cherokee wife. He knew Alice was crazy but he thought his job required asking a question even if there was no logical answer. There were three of them, the patrollers, the same number as always for that section of the county.

Alice went on chanting and then she did a dance.

"Oh, let her alone," Barnum Kinsey said. "She just that crazy woman from Nigger Henry's place."

"I'll do what the hell I want!" Travis said. He liked Barnum better when Barnum had been drinking, when he was liable to be quiet.

"I'm just sayin, Harvey, that you know by now she ain't no more harm. Probably even more crazy than usual since Henry died."

"Master dead master dead master died."

"I'm gettin plenty tired of seein you out here like this," Travis said. "I never sleep good after I see this thing dancin in the road. My skin start crawlin." The third patroller started laughing, but Barnum was silent. There was a weak moon and the third patroller was holding a lantern. Skiffington had been rotating the patrollers again and the man with the lantern was new to this part of the county, and though the others had assured him there was nothing to worry about, his wife, pregnant with their second child, had sent him out with a lantern. "We should start chargin Nigger Henry every time we see one a his niggers in the road."

"Henry dead. I told you," Barnum said, and the patroller with the lantern laughed again. He was very young. "Ain't you listened to a word she been sayin." Barnum, that morning, had promised his wife that he would not drink anymore. They had cried together and ended up on their knees, praying. Their children came in and seeing their parents praying, the children had gone to their knees as well. This was Barnum's second set of children, the first set having grown up and went far out into the world to forget a father who loved them but who was, in the eyes of that world, little more than a nigger.

Alice danced past the man in front with the lantern. She pointed at Travis. "Hey, now!" he said, frightened that she was doing something evil. "Damn!" The other patrollers laughed at him.

"Master died master died master died." She kicked her legs out and pointed at Travis and his horse.

"Dear Lord!" Travis said. "Leave her, boys. Just leave her," and he rode around the woman, who was still kicking and still chanting. The other two patrollers started moving as well.

Barnum stopped. "You better go on home. I want you to go on home now." Alice told him again that the master was dead. She did not stop kicking. "I know," Barnum said, "but you best go home." The men rode away.

After a time, Alice went down the way the men had come. She shook the dirt of the road from her frock. She wouldn't get back to her cabin until about four-thirty that morning; several times in the past she had not gotten home until about noon. What moon there was was now gone. She began to chant after a few yards and was just as loud as she had been in the beginning. On a day before the mule kicked her in the head, an African woman who spoke very little English had told her that some angels were hard of hearing, that it was best to speak real loud when talking to them.

> *I met a dead man layin in Massa lane*
> *Ask that dead man what his name*
> *He raised he bony head and took off his hat*
> *He told me this, he told me that.*

Elias finished the doll for Tessie his daughter the night of the day they buried Henry Townsend. He put the whittling knife on the ground beside the tree stump he was sitting on and held the doll for some time in both his hands, feeling empty and restless now that the task was done. Since his marriage to Celeste, it had helped to always have something for his hands to do when he could not shut them down in sleep. His legs never shut down—they kicked and twitched in his sleep and Celeste always threatened to tie them down for the night. "I tell you, husband, you plannin on cripplin me some more with them runnin feet."

He ran his finger over the face of the doll and then he kissed its forehead. He had wanted it to look like Tessie but he knew he had fallen far short of that. He needed something else now for his hands, and soon. Maybe some carved figure for his oldest son, a horse. He had seen a boat once, that last day with his mother, but he did not think he could do a boat the way the first one lived on in his head, a silent brown giant sailing away under a blue sky. Any boat he would try to carve might turn out like that first comb for Celeste his wife. And besides, where could his boy sail it? Down, down in a well where he could not even see it? He would tell Tessie that the doll had the face of his own mother, for her idea of what her grandmother looked like

would probably be the same as his memory of her, and that memory
had shredded down to nothing over the thirty years.

Elias stood up and brushed the shavings from his shirt and pants.
He was alone in the lane. The indirect pledge he had made to Henry
once upon a time was now no more. But that did not matter, dead man
or no dead man. Elias looked up and found the winking stars in a clear
part of the sky that were supposed to have guided him away. How
ready he had been, at ease, legs powerful, heart desperate to beat
under another moon and sun. He sat down again and put the doll
inside his shirt and leaned over to pick up another piece of wood. It
was nearing nine-thirty. As he took up the knife, Alice came out of
her cabin and danced down the lane and stood before him with her
hands on her hips. They had rarely spoken because nothing she said
ever made sense. "Whatcha makin now?" she said, surprising him.
"Somethin for my boy." "Well, you just make it good, make it to last,"
Alice said. He waited for her to follow up with some nonsense, but she
just stood as she had been. Maybe the moon, or the lack of it, determined her ways. "Don't be late," Elias said to her. "Don't be late goin
out and about." "Don't you be late neither," she said and danced away.
He watched her, and for the first time he was afraid for her. He would
begin at the horse's head, which would be the hardest part. No boat.
Why put such a notion in a boy's head anyway? He put the wood in
his left hand and the knife in his right, and then he began to cry.
"Don't be late," he said over and over again. "Don't be late."

Two days after Henry bought Elias in 1847 from the white newlyweds passing through from Bath County, Elias found Celeste sitting
on the ground. He knew only Moses and the men in his cabin, but had
seen her from afar, limping here and there. She seemed to have been
playing with or helping two children who were now skipping away.
"Come on, Celeste," the children said. "I be there directly," she said.
She struggled to get to her feet and after many tries she was standing.
She stood quietly and unmoving for some time, looking down at her
feet covered by her long green frock. The children called to her but

she did not move. Finally she went off, taking one lumbering step after another. He watched the whole time but had not moved to help her. Escaping had been his only thought since he had come from Bath with the newlyweds who had argued with each other the whole way, and he didn't want to be touched by any other notion. He turned and thought he was getting away before she noticed him, but she had first sensed and then seen him and she would not forget it. She had not wanted his help, but she felt he was watching a show with a cripple woman and had enjoyed it and that was not right.

She had been bought for $387 a year or so before him, but as long as she had been on the plantation, Celeste had not been known by anyone to be a hurtful woman. She never said "Master" or "Mistress" to Henry or Caldonia; just "Mr." and "Ma'am," her small way of saying no to everything. She had the best heart, people said of Celeste. But over the next weeks she came to resent Elias for being a cripple woman watcher and could not stop herself from being mean to him whenever she could. He would be eating his dinner at the edge of a field off to himself and she would go out of her way to limp by him and work up as much dust as she could, dirtying his food. She liked to work a row opposite one he was in just to show others how slow he was. She told people he was a lazy somebody and she didn't mind if he heard her. When she walked down the lane and he was standing in her way, she limped faster and dared him not to move. "What you do to that woman," someone funned him after seeing Elias nearly run over, "for her to rue the day you was ever born?"

Toward the end of his second week on the Townsend plantation, Elias became ill, suffering headaches that hammered him senseless. He could not keep food in his stomach, and there were unaccountable blisters on the soles of his feet. At times, he had to lean over in a furrow to collect himself, as some rush of pain overwhelmed and seemed to want to tear him apart right where he stood. He knew that in order to slip away one night he had to be seen as reliable, but his work suffered with his sickness and Moses also took to calling him a lazy man. "You mighta bought a pig in a poke, Master," he told Henry one day. Elias would wake in the night and hear the wind counting off the days he had to live. "Better play. Better play," the wind told him, "cause ain't no more after today."

He had never been one to believe in root work, but he began to feel that Celeste was doing something to him and that it would lead to his death, a long way from freedom. He dreamed she had gotten her limp by wrestling with the devil. But she wasn't one for root work, and because she was the kind of woman she was, her resentment against him had actually dissipated after the third week. To her he had become just another man who couldn't stand to be around a cripple woman. By the fourth week, she would see him bent over in a furrow and feel sorry for him.

Then, toward the middle of the fifth week, he began to improve and the wind stopped talking to him. He had been weakened by the illness, however, and tried to restore himself by working harder and longer in the fields, often staying there long after Moses told him he was finished for the day. But even by the ninth and tenth weeks his body was not what it had been, and by the fourth month, he began to despair. He continued planning to run away, but he worried that he might not have the strength to run for miles, might not be able to turn and break the necks of any dogs chasing him.

In his fourth month there, he got up off his pallet about midnight and walked away, following the stars that pointed north. This was in the time when Sheriff John Skiffington's patrollers were getting used to their new jobs. Elias got about five miles from the Townsend place when he began losing his strength. He ate most of the hoe cakes he brought with him, thinking the problem was a body rebellious due to hunger. He stopped as often as he could to collect himself but each time he started up again, he was weaker than before. At about seven miles he was nearly reduced to crawling, and at the eighth mile he collapsed. He awoke, stretched out in the road, to hear a slow horse coming his way. Uncertain which way the horse was coming from, he began crawling toward the side of the road where tall grass waited. He parted the grass and made a place for himself and heard the horse come up and stop. It was William Robbins on Sir Guilderham. "Whatever you are, I know you are there," Robbins said. "Come out if you're nigger, and if you are white, tell me your name and I'll leave you to it."

Robbins waited for several minutes and then opened his coat and took out his single-shot pistol. "Then you are nigger and not white," he said. He fired once into the grass, grazing Elias's left thigh. Elias did not move and after a short while Robbins said, taking out another pistol, "I smell your blood all the way over here. If you don't want me to draw more of it, rise up and come to me." Robbins aimed and as he did, Elias got to his feet, his arms high in the air, his fingers spread out. It was not a full moon but it was bright enough for Robbins to see Elias's fingers wiggling nervously. The blood was flowing slowly down his leg.

"You free or slave?"

"Slave."

"And no pass. I can tell that just from the smell of fear in your blood. Who do you belong to?"

"Master Henry Townsend, sir." The "sir" was so he would not be shot again just out of pure meanness.

"Come here. What you out here cattin around for?"

"No, sir." Elias started to move but found his left leg mired in a puddle of blood and he had to pick his leg up to go forward. When he reached Robbins, the white man leaned down and punched him as hard as he could in the jaw and Elias fell back. Then he took two quick steps toward Robbins, thinking that if he killed the white man, there was no witness except the horse. But Robbins cocked the second gun and held it out. Elias stopped.

"I know Henry Townsend," Robbins said, "and if I have to pay for a dead one, then that is what I will do. Come here." He held the gun an inch from Elias's face and punched him again. Elias fell. "If you live to be a hundred, know not to run up on a white man."

The word seemed to go out among the slaves at Henry's place even before most of them had come out of their cabins: Somebody done got away. It was Sunday and Moses slept late and got the word last. People were happy for Elias. "Somebody's soul done flew away. Whooossh. . . . Feel that breeze from them wings. Lord almighty." Stamford could not place Elias's face and thought he was the dark-skinned fellow with a June-bug-sized mole on his left cheek until Delphie reminded him that Henry sold that man away because the man with the mole liked to fight everybody. "Was fightin from the time he got up till the time he shut his eyes. Would see his shadow pesterin after him and started hittin that. Po thing. Lord . . . Was fightin even you, Stamford," Delphie said. "Hmmp!" Stamford said. "He musta lost that fight then. Musta got his head knocked off and thas why he was sold off. Didn't have no head and couldn't work. Had to sell that fool for scrapple meat." Delphie said, "That ain't the way I member it." "Then you memberin wrong," Stamford said and held his fists out to her to show what the man with the mole had had to contend with. This was in the days when Stamford had another young woman to be with, in the days before Gloria. "Get outa my face with them things, man," Delphie said. The few children then on the Townsend place took much of their happiness from the adults and they began funning Stamford. The doomed Luke, then eleven, the boy who would be worked to death, shared a song he had learned from his mother—"I'm over here, I'm over there, I ain't nowhere . . ." Celeste heard about the runaway Elias as she was eating the last of her ash cakes. She did not like Elias but she, too, was happy for him. What she herself could not have she always wished for someone else, so her food went down well that morning. After he got the word, af-ter he ate his breakfast, Moses went up and told Henry, "Master, that new nigger's in the wind."

On Sundays, a preacher, a free man named Valtims Moffett, came

over and held services for the slaves, in the barn when it was cold and
out along the lane when the weather was nice. He would preach for
some fifteen minutes and then everyone would sing two or three
songs. The day Robbins caught Elias was a day of nice weather, not
too warm, though the preacher liked to say that every day was a good
day for God's word. The preacher was a large man who suffered with
gout and rheumatism, which, he was quick to tell people, "God put
upon me the same way he put the cross on our savior Jesus Christ."
Some mornings it took him more than an hour to get out of bed and
dressed. He had a wife and one slave to his name, but the wife, Helen,
was a tiny woman and so was their slave, Pauline, full sister to the
wife, and both of them together could do only so much with a large
man with a cross to bear. The preacher was quite late that Sunday
morning after Elias ran away, but he was not as late as he was the day
Henry was buried.

Moses had just told Henry that Elias was gone when they heard
Robbins's voice and they both went around the side of the house to
the front. Robbins had awakened that morning and not remembered
the encounter with Elias the night before, that he had taken Elias
back to his plantation and chained him to the back porch. His cook
came in and reminded him at the breakfast table.

Robbins now said to Henry, "Good mornin. Sweet good mornin.
Are you and Caldonia well?" Elias, chained, stood next to Robbins,
only inches from his booted foot in the stirrup.

"Yessir, Mr. Robbins, we well enough," Henry said.

"I have something of yours," Robbins said, and he kicked Elias
and the slave fell to the ground. "Picked him up on the road home last
night. He has a wound somewhere in his leg, but it won't kill him and
it won't amount to anything if you decide to sell him off one day. Less
he had a very noticeable limp." He laughed, a little joke between
them, because Robbins was even less inclined those days to sell a slave
and that was what he always advised Henry. He had said once,
"Niggers appreciate in value, so appreciate them."

"I see," Henry said. Moses was behind him. "Help him up, Moses. You wanna come in, Mr. Robbins." Moses picked Elias up by the shoulders and gave him a little bit of a smile and reminded Elias with the smile and his eyes that he never liked him.

"No, not today, Henry. Not today, but tell Caldonia I will come back this way soon. I promise." The land they stood on had once belonged to Robbins, sold to Henry at a price far cheaper than Robbins had ever sold anything, save the slaves Toby and his sister Mindy. Robbins looked once at the side of Elias's head and nodded to Henry. Henry told him good day. Robbins raised the reins up from his lap and pulled gently and the horse, in a slow and beautiful move of its grand head and neck, the glinting bit in its mouth a kind of accent to all that grandness, turned, and they left, prancing away down to the road, where they took off in a full gallop. The glint would stay forever in Elias's mind. The night his second child was born he would hold him, still wet from fighting into life, and the fire from the hearth would reflect off that wetness and that glint would come forward again until he blinked it away.

Henry went to Elias and slapped him. "This is a hurtful disappointment to me. What I'm gonna do with you? What in the hell I'm gonna do with you? If you want a hard life, I will oblige." "I will oblige" was a favorite phrase of Fern Elston's during her lessons, heard by Henry the first time as he sat with her in her parlor dominated by trees, a peach and a magnolia, she and her servants had managed to domesticate. Her husband the gambler had seen it done by foreign people in a Richmond whorehouse and brought the technique back to Manchester County. "Is that what you want?" Henry asked. "I will oblige you with a hard life." The trees in Fern's house disoriented most people, those used to the inside always being inside and the outside always being outside. People said nice things about the trees to Fern even as their minds were swirling. Those people were all free Negroes because white people never came to Fern's place. Henry had feared that Caldonia might want that done with their parlor.

"No, Marse." Elias was still chained, Robbins having forgotten that the chains belonged to him. Other slaves had come out and were watching. Celeste was just behind the first row of people and Stamford twisted his shoulder a bit so she could see.

"You sure don't act like it," Henry said. Once you own them, once you own even one, you will never be alone, Robbins had told Henry after Henry purchased Moses from him. Knowing how painful loneliness could be, having been separated as a child from Augustus and then Mildred, Henry had thought that a good thing, never to be alone, to always have someone. Henry said to Elias, "If you want a good life, I will oblige that, too." Fed by light streaming in from windows that went from the floor to a foot shy of the ceiling, the trees in Fern's parlor grew to a height of about eight or nine feet, then stopped, as if on command. The peaches born on the tree were very tiny, could fit on a man's thumb, and they were very sweet, too sweet for a pie or cobbler if the cook could manage to collect enough of them. The magnolia blossoms were also small, so beautiful that Fern's gambling husband said he would frame them if they were pictures.

"Moses," Henry said, "take him and chain him till I decide if he wants a good life or a bad life." Since the day was a good one and Valtims Moffett the preacher would hold the services in the lane, Moses chained Elias in the large barn. "You want a good life or a bad life?" Moses mocked and then left him.

His first hours in the stall were spent thinking how he could kill everyone around him, first everyone on the plantation, then everyone in the county, in Virginia. Colored and white. He tried not to move the chains because the sound of their rattling hurt his ears, spread a dryness throughout his mouth. He could stand comfortably enough, if he wanted to stand all the time facing that section of the barn wall, the one section that was without a hole through which he could see the outside. When Elias sat, he found he could twist himself a little away from the wall, but his hands were suspended about level with his face and it was impossible to lie down. For a long time he looked up at the rafters, at the sparrows coming and going to the nest they were building. Engaged in a simple task of living—take straw to the nest, go back for more. The sun came in on them but there was not much of it near where their nest was. He wondered if he would be there long enough for the birds to have eggs, then chicks, to see the chicks grow and then make their own nests. Take straw to the nest, go back for more. To see the grandchildren sparrows become parents. He could wring the neck of everyone on the plantation, it was just a matter of whether to start with Moses or the master. Moses's neck was thicker. The children's necks would be the hardest. But over and done with in a snap. He could close his eyes tight with them, with the children, and with the old people. The women would scream the loudest, but God, being the kind of God he was, would give him strength.

He was very tired, not having slept at Robbins's place. When he leaned his head forward and closed his eyes, his neck soon stiffened and he finally had to lean his head back as far as he could and accept what relief came with that. He closed his eyes but there was no sleep, not even the jittery dozing that had come at Robbins's place.

Not long before Moffett arrived, Elias opened his eyes and saw a boy watching him. When the boy saw him open his eyes, he came closer, asking, "You want some water?"

Elias closed his eyes again and did not answer because he did not want to spare anybody's neck.

"You want some water?"

He nodded without opening his eyes and he heard the boy leave. When he did not return, Elias thought he had been having fun with him, and he found some peace in that. He soon heard Moffett's preaching voice, the words indistinct. When he opened his eyes again, the boy was standing before him, a chipped, discarded porcelain cup in one hand and a large piece of hoe cake in the other. "The preacher here," the boy said with a smile, as if that was the news Elias most

needed to hear. "I useta hear him when I was over the other place."
Three days ago Henry had bought Lot Number Four, a group of three
slaves, and the boy had been one of them. Elias took the bread in his
hands and ate, and in between bites, the boy put the cup to his lips and
he drank.

"My name Luke," he said when there was no more water.

"I know," Elias said, looking at a fly alight on his hand and
edge toward the bread. The boy smiled and turned the cup upside
down and shook it. "I know." The boy stood and ran out and returned
quickly with more water. He sat before Elias and since the bread
was gone, Elias held the cup in his hands. "You want some more hoe
cake?" Luke said. The man shook his head. "I know a song bout
Jesus. I can sing it." Elias shook his head again. Moffett, Sunday after
Sunday, had but one theme—that heaven was nearer than anyone
realized and that one step away from the righteous path could take
heaven away forever. "Hang on," he liked to say, "just hang on,
cause heaven is right over there. See it. See it. Close your eyes and see
it." His ending words were that they should obey their masters
and mistresses, for heaven would not be theirs if they disobeyed. "One
day I want to sit with yall and eat peaches and cream in heaven.
I don't wanna have to lean over and look way way down and see
yall burnin in them fires of hell." Luke and Elias could not make
out his words and so they just listened to the way his babble came
into the barn and bounced around. The sparrows were no longer
flying, just chirping somewhere above their heads. Elias could see
them in his mind, arranging the straw and turning around and
around on it to make a place smooth enough to be a home to the eggs.
At last Luke said, "I was born on Marse Colfax place. . . . You know
that?"

Elias said, "I know. I know that." Dropping the cup into his lap, he
leaned his face into his hands and began to cry. On the worst days he
had ever had, he had always been able to see himself as one day living free. But now . . .

"Is all right," Luke said. "I'll sit with you. Is all right. I'ma sit with you till all them hants leave you alone. I ain't afraid of no hants."

Moffett, after the services, sat with Henry and Caldonia in their dining room, eating bread and cheese and a tea that was more honey than anything else. He claimed anything sweet eased his gout. Now and again in their lives Caldonia and Henry would go down to the services with the slaves but generally the sitting with Moffett would pass in their minds as a kind of service, as communion with God. After the meal, Moffett sat with his feet propped on a stool Zeddie the cook had brought in from the back for him. The stool, padded, was used for little else and had become known as the Reverend Moffett stool.

Henry said little, thinking about what he would do with Elias.

"You are away from us this day, Henry," Moffett said at one point. He had been paid the $1 for conducting the services the moment after he entered the house. In his early days of preaching, before the gout, he had been paid 3 cents for every slave he preached to, but the county had been wealthier then. Now, few white slaveowners employed him, many preferring to simply read to their servants out of the Bible. The few black slaveowners had begun to believe that their own salvation would flow down to their slaves; if they themselves went to church and led exemplary lives, then God would bless them and what they owned. And one day they would go to heaven, and so would their slaves. So why pay Moffett to help do what they could manage for nothing?

"He hasn't been sleeping well," Caldonia said. "I believe, Reverend Moffett, he works too hard and it shows with all those headaches. Sleepless nights. 'Rest up, Henry,' I'm always telling him. 'Rest up.' Perhaps you could supplement my words, Reverend Moffett. Remind him that God would not be happy to see us work ourselves to death." She and Henry had been married three years and seven months.

"He certainly wouldn't," Moffett said. "Laziness is one sin, Henry, but working too much is also a sin. Why do you think God put such emphasis on Sunday, on resting. Keep the Sabbath holy is just God's way of telling us not to overtax ourselves. Make God happy, Henry, and tax yourself just enough to pay your bill."

"Precisely," Caldonia said.

"I do," Henry said. "I do rest up. It's just that my wife doesn't see all the times that I do." Watching Moses tell him that Elias was gone, he had decided that a whipping would not be enough, that only an ear would do this time. He had just not decided if it should be the whole ear or only a piece, and if a piece, how big a piece?

"Oh, for goodness sakes, Henry!" Caldonia said. "You might get Reverend Moffett to accept that, but I know better."

Moffett shifted in his chair and put one foot over the other on the stool. He had two more services to conduct that day and he would be late for both. Henry used him because he remembered him from his days as a slave at William Robbins's, had liked to listen to him after his parents were gone into freedom and there was only Rita, his second mother, to care for him.

Moffett left.

Henry watched him ride off in his buggy and decided then that he would send for Oden Peoples, the Cherokee, the next day. He told Caldonia once they were back inside, in their parlor.

"That," she said, "seems too great a punishment, Henry. Too much for such a small crime." She was on the settee and he was at the window on the left side of the room.

"It ain't that small, Caldonia. It's a bad apple in the barrel, right down at the bottom, not even at the top where you can pick it and throw it away. Somethin gots to be done," he said. Sometimes he talked the way Fern had tried to teach him and sometimes he did not. He was especially "deviant and lazy," as she called it, when he was tired and uncertain. Caldonia sensed the exhaustion now and went to him, putting her arms around his back. Marriage, too, meant the end of loneliness, but Robbins had said nothing about that.

"Let him try one more time to do what's right, Henry."

"I cain't. I just cain't." As a boy at Robbins's plantation, he had known a man whose right ear had been cut off after he ran away a second time. When the man, Sam, wifeless, childless, was old and running was not so much on his mind anymore and he had time to gnaw on his unhappiness, he liked to grab small children to scare them, putting the earless side of his head close to the child's face until the child screamed to be let go. The wound had blossomed into a terrible mushroom of scar tissue and was as different from the other side of his face as heaven from hell. "Go find my ear!" the old man would holler as he shook them. "Go find my ear, I say, and be quick about it!" One boy had fainted. Another child's father had beat Sam but still he did not stop grabbing hold of children. Henry himself had been grabbed a few times, but one day, when he was twelve, he found himself not afraid anymore, wondered where the fear had gone as Sam pulled him closer to the side of his head and the mushroom once again threatened to open up and become large enough to pull him in. He was held long enough to study the brown smoothness of the scar that invited him to reach over and touch. Henry even had time to peer into the ear hole partly covered over with gray hair and brown smoothness and wonder how much sound such an ear could take in.

"Give him another day in the barn to reconsider," Caldonia said. She took her arms from around him and held them at her sides but still continued leaning into his back.

"A day too long a time, Caldonia."

As had been planned, they took an early supper at Fern Elston's. Her gambler of a husband, Ramsey, was there and had started to drink even before their guests had arrived. Ramsey was not drunk but as often happened with him, he turned combative in the middle of the meal and accused another guest of owing him money. That guest, Saunders Church, was there with his wife, Isabelle, two free colored people without a slave to their names. Saunders laughed at first, thinking Ramsey was trying to fun him.

"Ramsey," Fern said after her husband had asked for the money a third time, "let us leave financial matters until another day."

Henry had been silent the entire meal. He had not wanted to come but Caldonia had insisted, saying that it might raise his mood.

"I owe you nothin," Saunders said at last, seeing that Ramsey was not out to fun him. "I owe you nothin." It was true; the drinking often made Ramsey think the whole world owed him a debt. The three men and the three women were the entire supper party. Ramsey was at the head of his table.

"Why not leave off, Ramsey, just like Fern said," Henry said. "Saunders be your guest." He was sitting at Ramsey's left and Isabelle was sitting at Ramsey's right.

"I didn't ask some white man's nigger about living my life," Ramsey said. "You ask Robbins what to say this evening?"

Henry looked down at his lap and then reached over swiftly before Ramsey could move and held tight to Ramsey's throat, shook it a time or two and continued to hold on. Ramsey began to sink in his seat. He was a reddish black man but slowly, as Henry held tight, all color disappeared from his face and his mouth opened and closed ever so slowly, like that of a fish, as he tried to pull in what little bit of air he could. Ramsey was able to look down across the table to his wife. Their marriage was approaching the far side of the hill from where they had started out and Fern looked into his eyes and did not move.

"Henry, for God's sakes!" Caldonia said and took hold of his arm with both of hers. "Please, Henry!" Saunders got up and managed to pry Henry's hand from Ramsey's neck and Ramsey sank even deeper into his seat. Caldonia pulled Henry away and her husband sat in his seat and rested both hands on the edge of the table, on either side of his plate. Henry looked down to Fern and said, "I'm sorry to ruin such a good afternoon." Isabelle and Saunders and Caldonia tended to

Ramsey. Fern nodded and said, "I know you are, Henry. I know you are."

That day the Townsends and Valtims Moffett arrived back at their respective homes at about the same time. Moffett came up the short lane at his place and before he was even five yards from his little house he could hear his wife and her sister arguing. The dog was dead so there was no one to greet him. There was still a good bit of sun left and his body, oiled and fed by the long day, had enough energy and power to do some work. He took the carriage to the barn and went to his house, stood at the edge of the porch and listened. Their fighting had been going on for two months, since two days after he had slept with his sister-in-law. His unhappy wife had let it be known to her sister that she would not care if the sister slept with Moffett. But once the sister had done so, an unexpected rage took hold of the wife and the two would argue all day and late into the night.

Moffett stood and listened. He took a perverse delight in hearing them, was lulled into sleep by the sound of their fighting. He knew God was not pleased about that, but he felt he had many years of life ahead of him, despite his ailments, and so there would be time to force his knees to bend before God and ask his forgiveness. The women worked to please him, to show him that each was better for him and that the other should be cast out. Did God deny David and Solomon any less? Moffett went to the barn. He could still hear them from there. Soon the sun would be gone, and it would take with it his strength. He prepared the horse for the night and took up his plow. He emptied the money from his purse and counted out what he had earned—$4.50. Still in his Sunday preaching clothes, he took up the tools needed to sharpen the plow.

Henry and Caldonia retired early that night and he made love to her twice, forever seeking the son who might temper Augustus Townsend's heart. When it was done, he lay on his back and she rested on her side and put her arm across his chest. "What anyone said never mattered to me," she said after a time, thinking of what Ramsey the gambler had said. He was sweating and she put her tongue to the side of his face where the sweat poured down and caught some of it with the tip of her tongue.

"I know," he said.

"Put more armor round that heart of yours about such things," Caldonia said.

"I'm tryin," he said and smiled. "I spect I'll have the full armor by day after tomorrow." He closed his eyes and she pulled herself even closer and the sweating stopped and she closed her mouth. Sam, the man with one ear, lived on at the Robbins's plantation. He had a cabin to himself, which Robbins had permitted even after the overseer had said it would spoil him. "Once he learned right from wrong, he gave me good work," Robbins said to the overseer. Sam was still grabbing and frightening little children. The grown-ups knew it was a habit that they could do nothing about, so they tried to teach the children to avoid him. "Give him not even so much as a good mornin or a good night. Wave from way over yonder when he speak to you and be on your way."

On his way to the Townsend place on Tuesday morning, Oden Peoples the Cherokee met Sheriff John Skiffington and told him he had been hired by Henry after one of his slaves had run away. Skiffington had in his saddlebag a month-old letter from his cousin Counsel Skiffington in North Carolina. The letter swore by a woman in Amelia County who had a cure for stomach ailments, which John Skiffington had suffered from since he was a boy. Counsel had always

teased John about his "woman's stomach" but he had never thought
his cousin's pain was not real. John had set out for an overnight trip
to the woman in Amelia, but hearing about Elias running away,
he decided to go with Oden Peoples, one of his patrollers. A runaway slave was, in fact, a thief since he had stolen his master's
property—himself. They arrived about nine-thirty. Moses and one
other man took Elias from the field and Oden sliced off about a third
of his ear as everyone, including Henry, stood in the lane. Elias had
his head down all the while except when Oden pulled it up to get the
razor to do a better job. All of the lobe and then some. Oden always
carried a pouch with a pepper poultice, which he blended with vinegar and mustard and a little salt—a proven remedy to halt the bleeding of even those who seemed to have more blood than other men.
"The bleeders," Oden called them. Elias lowered his head again and
stood with his hands at his side, refusing to hold the poultice in place.
In the end, Oden had to tie the poultice on Elias's head with a rag
Moses brought from his cabin.

Henry told Moses to take everybody back to the field. And there
in the lane he paid Oden $1 for doing the job on Elias's ear. "You
think it'll hold," Henry said after he and Oden and Skiffington had
left the lane and were nearing Oden's saddleless horse and Skiffington's red mare. "I don't know," Oden said. "It depends on what
kinda heart he got in him. But," and he took the reins, "I'll come back
and do the rest of that ear and won't charge you."

Henry nodded.

Skiffington said, "I'll pass through when I return from Amelia to
make sure all is right. But you, Henry, have some responsibility. As
does everyone else with servants who get it into their head to run
away. You must be vigilant." Not long before, after he had hired the
patrollers, he told one white man whose slave had a habit of coming
and going as he pleased, "My men are not angels, able to fly above and
see wrong being committed and come down and turn the wrong into
right. They can only do so much. So you have to help and look out for
your servants, too."

"We'll see to him, Mr. Skiffington," Henry said.

Oden said of Elias, "If he runs again, the rest of the ear I'll do for nothin, but I will have to charge you for any work done on that other ear." He mounted. He took part of the horse's mane and ran his fingers through it, laid it to rest on the left side of the horse's neck. Skiffington mounted and said, "I ain't never seen a servant with both his ears gone." "I have," Oden said, "but it whatn't me that done it." Henry said, "That would be a shame. To have em both gone." Oden, being a Cherokee, wouldn't have merited a "Mr." if Henry had called him by name. "Yes, it would be," Oden said. "Just remember I gotta charge you for the other ear. Thas only fair. But I'll do the rest of that one for nothin. Won't cost you a cent."

Henry said nothing and both men rode out to the road and there they parted, Skiffington to Amelia with hope that the woman could help him and his stomach and Oden, his ponytail bouncing, home to rest after a night of patrolling. Oden would not have had his ear business if it had not been for the death of a slave in Amherst County. A white man had cut off the ear of his "habitual runaway," and the slave had bled to death. No one could understand what had happened— people had been cutting off ears or parts of ears for more than two centuries. In the seventeenth century throughout the Virginia colony even white indentured servants had had their ears cut off. But somehow the luck of the Amherst County man had run out and his $515 slave had died from the loss of blood. A few white people wanted him indicted for manslaughter, but the grand jury declined, finding that the man had suffered enough with the loss of his property.

People were spooked by what happened to the slave who bled to death, began to believe that even after two hundred years of doing it there might yet be a real science to cutting off ears, just as there was to hobbling a slave and butchering hogs in the fall. Promising good, efficient work and no dying, Oden had stepped forward after the death of the Amherst County slave, a twenty-seven-year-old left-handed man named Fred. Even after Oden took on the task, some masters continued to use the man's death as a way to frighten possible

runaways. "You mess up on me and you'll get what that nigger Fred
got. Then I'll throw your damn carcass to the hogs." That wasn't
true—hogs would eat just about anything, but Virginia hogs would
never eat human beings. By Skiffington's fourth year in office, Oden
practically had a monopoly on ear cutting in some five counties, not
including Manchester.

Luke slept beside Elias that Tuesday night after Oden cut off part
of his ear. Luke knew a boy who had known Fred and he thought
that if Elias should start bleeding during the night, he would be there
to help him, could run fast enough to get Loretta before Elias lost all
his blood. Elias told him at first that he didn't want a soul near him
and that he would kill him if the boy stayed. Luke said nothing and
made his pallet a few inches from where Elias was chained up.

Caldonia and Loretta came in the barn before either the man or
the boy went to sleep. Loretta removed Oden's poultice and put on her
own bandage, never saying a word during the whole time.

"Please, try to be good," Caldonia said before leaving. "Please,
try." The two women had knelt down to Elias and Loretta had
dropped Oden's poultice in the straw and Caldonia had picked it up.
There was not enough blood on it to worry about; one hour of her
monthlies produced more. The smell of the pepper was strong.
Caldonia said to Elias before standing up, "It is just as easy to do good
as it is to do bad." Elias stayed silent.

Caldonia looked down at Loretta tending to him and Luke looking
at the man and the woman. All of it, every single bit of it, was a horrible mess. These were the times that made her want to rethink the
road they were all going down. Such a long road for such a legacy, for
slaves. "My legacy," her mother Maude often said. "We must protect
the legacy."

Loretta stood and took the poultice from Caldonia. "I'll see bout
you in the mornin," Loretta said. They left the barn and Caldonia told
her to go on up to the house, that she wanted to visit a mite before re-

tiring. She often visited the people in the lane, and some of them were ashamed to have her come into the cabins, knowing the miracle of the house she lived in. "I'll come with you," Loretta said. Caldonia shook her head. She said, "Tell your master I'll be along directly." Caldonia turned away and went to the lane. Where there was light seeping from under a door she knocked and knocked again until someone opened or asked, "Who that there? Who that comin to my door?"

Some two weeks later, another Sunday, after Moffett had come and preached and gone, Elias came upon Celeste holding Luke in her arms. They were near the fields and the boy was sobbing. She looked up and saw Elias and was not happy to see him, remembering the way he must have watched her limping about.

"Luke, boy, whas the matter with you?" Elias said. For a brief moment he thought Celeste may have slapped him and then regretted what she had done. But the way her arms engulfed the boy told him that she had done him no harm. His time with the boy had put Luke as close as any human being could be to the man's heart. "Luke, boy, tell Elias whas wrong? Who hurt you? Tell Elias who it be?"

Celeste said, "I think he just missin his mama. A boy can miss his mama. A girl can miss her mama. I found him under that tree just cryin his heart out." She did not want Elias the watcher man to come any closer to them but he did and he put his hand over the boy's head and his hand was near one of her wrists. "Luke, I'll be your mama," she said. "I'll be all the mama I can be for you."

Soon, the boy quieted. Celeste looked at Elias's hand and then up at him. There was a storm coming, which was why Elias had gone looking for Luke. The boy liked to play in the rain and never cared that lightning could kill him. The rain came now, a teasing kind of rain, soft, intermittent drops. A thirsty sparrow could have leaned its head back and enjoyed the drops without any fear of drowning. Celeste looked at a large drop of rain on the back of Elias's hand covering Luke's head, watched as the one drop was joined by two others.

There was the sound of thunder but it was still far away, on the other side of the mountains. Celeste said, "We best get him out of this mess." She managed to look the man in the face. "Yes, we best get him out of it."

They, Celeste and Elias, continued to have next to nothing to say to each other after that, and Elias went back to planning on running away. Late in the night, after Moses had assured Henry that Elias had learned his lesson, Elias would test the waters and go out to the road and wait to see what might descend on him.

When he began to care for Celeste, he would never be able to say, only that he awoke one morning to a quietness and stillness in the world he had never known before. The birds were not singing, the fire in the hearth did not crackle, the mice did not come and go, and even the snorers he shared the cabin with slept in silence. It was at such a time that he had always imagined he would slip away to freedom, a time when all the world had their heads turned the other way. But he sat up on his pallet and listened to the nothing and wanted to be with her. Slowly, the world seemed to come back to its senses and the first thing he thought he heard was the sound of her limping down the lane, the hem of her frock swishing along the ground, the foot of her bad leg scraping along in that second before she lifted it.

When he tried to get close to her, to walk a little bit beside her, hoping that closeness would say what he did not have words for, she would hurry away, believing he only wanted to see her life with a terrible limp. He hurt, day after day, to see her move away. Then, late one evening, almost two months after Oden took the razor to his ear, after all the work of the day and the slaves were in those moments when they set their minds to sleep, he came to the cabin she shared with two other women and Elias tapped until one of the women came to the door. Celeste had brought Luke to live with her, but he was not there.

"Could you mind tellin Celeste I'd like a word with her?" Elias said to the woman.

The woman laughed but when she saw he wasn't going away, she turned and called to Celeste, "That Elias be wantin you."

It seemed a long time before she came to the door. He nodded and she nodded back.

"I just wanted a word with you, thas all," he said.

"All right," she said.

He looked her full in the face, the light from inside the cabin silhouetting her. "Why you all the time treatin me bad when all I wanna do is treat you good?"

"What that you say?"

"Why you all the time treatin me bad when all I wanna do is treat you good? Thas what I said."

"I ain't think I was treatin you no kinda bad way."

"Well, you was and all I'm askin is that you stop it."

She put one hand on the doorjamb to steady herself to come down the one step to him and he took her by the other arm. She said after a minute or so, "I didn't mean no harm by it."

He believed her and was again without words. He found them when he heard one of the women inside the cabin laugh at something the other woman said. "I be talkin to you, then. Tomorrow if thas all right with you. I be talkin to you tomorrow."

"Yes." She turned, a hand again on the doorjamb, and stepped up as he held her elbow. She went inside and closed the door.

A week later he was at her door again and she was in the doorway and he opened a little piece of a rag and presented a comb he had carved out of a piece of wood. The comb was rough, certainly one of the crudest and ugliest instruments in the history of the world. Not one tooth looked like another; some of the teeth were far too thick, but most of them were very thin, the result of his whittling away with the hope that he was approaching some kind of perfection. "Oh," Celeste said. "Oh, my." She took it and smiled. "My goodness gracious."

"It ain't much."

"It be the whole world. You givin it to me?"

"I am."

"Well, my goodness gracious." She tried to run the comb through her hair but the comb failed in its duty. "Oh, my," Celeste said as she struggled with it. Several teeth broke off. "Oh, my."

He reached up and taking her hand with the comb, they extricated it from her hair. "I done broke it," she said when they had pulled it away. "Dear Lord, I done broke it."

"Pay it no mind," Elias said.

"But you gave it to me, Elias." Aside from the food in her stomach and the clothes on her back and a little of nothing in a corner of her cabin, the comb was all she had. A child of three could have toted around all she owned all day long and not gotten tired.

"We can do another one." He reached up and picked out the comb's teeth that had broken off in her hair.

"But . . ."

"I'll make you a comb for every hair on your head."

She began to cry. "Thas easy to say today cause the sun be shinin. Tomorrow, maybe next week, there won't be no sun, and you won't be studyin no comb."

He said again, "I'll make you a comb for every hair on your head." He dropped the broken teeth onto the ground and she closed her hand tight over what was left of the comb.

She put her face into her other hand and cried. There had been a slave on the plantation she had come from who had come upon her in a field of corn and told her that a woman like her should be shot, like a horse with a broken leg. And she had cried then as well.

Elias put his arms around her, tentative, for this was the first time. He trembled and the trembling increased the closer she got to his body. He kissed the side of her head, near the hairline, and his lips met not only her skin and hair but a tooth from the comb that he had somehow missed.

They ate their supper together the next day at the edge of the field, and when he was done, he told her he had to speak to the master and he got up from beside her and walked out of the field and Moses didn't ask him what he was doing or where he was going. At the back of the house, he tapped at the door. Zeddie the cook opened it. "Zeddie, I got to speak with Master Henry. Can I speak with Master Henry, please?"

"I go tell him," Zeddie said. "You step in here." She opened the door wider and he came in, his first time in the house. He smelled what a tree smelled like when it was first cut into, the wood blood from the first wound of the ax. Elias shut the door. She returned in moments with their master and Henry said before he was fully into the kitchen, "What is it there, Elias?"

Elias looked at Zeddie, then said, "I be likin Celeste, Master, and I be likin her more as the day go by. That likin ain't gon stop tomorrow, as I can see."

"That so, Elias?"

"Yes, Master. I wanna marry her. I wanna be with her. There ain't nothin more I want sides that, cept to live." He had dreamed again last night that he had run away to freedom. He had been as safe as an angel at God's knee, safe on the road to freedom, and then he remembered that there was something way back in slavery that he had forgotten and so he ran back into slavery, passing millions who were running toward freedom. He searched the empty slave quarters for what he had forgotten and in the last cabin out of the hundreds he searched, he had come upon Celeste, without even one leg to stand on. She saw him and turned her face from him.

"And you be wantin me to say 'Yes' to this?"

"Master, I make her a good husband and I be a good worker every day God gimme strength. I would hate, Master, for us to be took apart after she my wife. It would feel bad for us to be sold apart. It would feel bad." Elias knew what he was saying and he knew that if his master blessed it all, he would never again dream of being on that road. "I would hate to lose a good wife and Celeste would hate to lose a good husband. We would hate bein separate."

"I want you happy, Elias. And I want to make Celeste happy. So you get back now and both yall be happy."

"Thank you, Master."

Zeddie had been stoking the fire in the stove and now she left off that and opened the door for Elias. He went out. Henry went through his house and came out the front door in time to see Elias walk down to the fields. Elias was the only human being about, and the way to the road was closer than the way to the fields. Henry went down the stairs and followed Elias, who went straight to the fields and took up his work, just as he had done before supper, which was now over for every slave in the field. Henry could see Celeste limping up the rows, limping and fast at work, and she was in one part of the fields and her husband-to-be was in another part. Elias did not look at her and she did not look at him. Moses waved to Henry and Henry waved back.

Henry stood watching Elias for some time, and in all that time Elias did not look at Celeste. His feelings were all the looking he needed, Henry realized. And he realized, too, that what was happening was better than chains. He had them together, bound one strong man to a woman with a twisted leg, and there was not a chain in sight. He could not wait to tell William Robbins. Henry went back the way he came, back to the house, and he put in his big book the day he had decided that Elias and Celeste would marry, wrote it in the flowing script that Fern Elston had taught him when he was twenty years old.

Moffett married them, and while he was away his sister-in-law beat her sister half to death. It took a little shifting around but Celeste and Elias got a cabin to themselves and brought Luke to live with them. Skiffington arrested Moffett's sister-in-law, but nothing came of it because her sister did not want her prosecuted. She went back home and the three of them went on as before.

The boy Luke was happy. When Shavis Merle, a white man with three slaves to his name, sought to hire Luke during the harvest, Elias told Henry he would go instead, for all the world knew how hard Merle could be. But Henry did not want to grant Elias two wishes in one year and he hired Luke out for $2 a week. Merle believed in feeding his workers plenty of food, but they gave it all back in the field, from sunup to sundown, and no one that year gave up more than Luke did. After Luke died in the field, Merle protested up and down about paying compensation, but William Robbins got him to pay Henry $100 for the boy. "Fair business is fair business," Robbins had to keep telling Merle. Moffett was early to the boy's funeral, which Merle attended, and Moffett said some words at the gravesite, but no one said more than Elias and at the last his new wife had to put her arms around him to bring an end to all the words.

4

*Curiosities South of the Border. String Tricks in a
Doomed City. A Child Departs from the Way.
The Education of Henry Townsend.*

Beginning in the mid-1870s and continuing throughout most of
the 1880s, a white man from Canada, Anderson Frazier, made
a good living in Boston publishing two-cent pamphlets about
America and its people, especially what he called their "peculiarities."
Most of what he published was gleaned from newspapers and magazines, but he rehashed everything in his pamphlets in a most colorful
way, delighting thousands of readers. He had come to America in
1872, having grown frustrated with what little he had in Canada. He
was the middle of seven children and did not want to go into the trad-
ing business that his father and his grandfather had established and
that his older brothers were so comfortable with. He was also tired of
what he saw as a certain Canadian ruggedness that had served the
country well in the days when Europeans set out to make the place
safe for white people; but he had come to believe that that once-
necessary ruggedness, most evident in his brothers, was becoming the
defining quality of the country. And he wished to be free of it. He did
not see Canada again until 1881. The country would be more or less
the way he had left it, but his family would be different, for the worse,
and there was a part of himself—as he sat in a kitchen full of nieces
and nephews talking to one of his sisters—that felt had he not gone

away, most of his family would have remained going down the fairly good path on which he last saw them.

Once he went into pamphlet publishing in Boston, he began traveling up and down the east coast of America, down to Washington, D.C., and all the way out to the middle of the country, gathering additional material for The Canadian Publishing Company. In 1879, he met in New York a young woman named Esther Sokoloff, who returned with him to Boston but who refused to marry him though she would never say why. He loved Esther more than he thought he could ever love an American, he wrote to a friend in Canada who could not read and had to get someone else to read Anderson's letters. During their first year and a half together she would leave him from time to time without a word and go back to her people in New York, refusing to see him when he came to that city. He once had a female intermediary go to her house to ask that she meet with him, and when Esther refused, Anderson decided to visit the America below Washington, D.C., an area of the country he had not been curious about before the pain that came with Esther.

It was in the South that Anderson came upon material he would later put in a new series of pamphlets he called *Curiosities and Oddities about Our Southern Neighbors.* The Economy of Cotton. Good Food Made from Next to Nothing. The Flora and Fauna. The Need for Storytelling. This series was Anderson's most successful, and nothing was more successful within that series than the 1883 pamphlet on free Negroes who had owned other Negroes before the War between the States. The pamphlet on slaveowning Negroes went through ten printings. Only seven of those particular pamphlets survived until the late twentieth century. Five of them were in the Library of Congress in 1994 when the remaining two pamphlets were sold as part of a collection of black memorabilia owned by a black man in Cleveland, Ohio. That collection, upon the man's death in 1994, sold for $1.7 million to an automobile manufacturer in Germany.

Anderson Frazier began the southern series just three months before Esther returned from New York one March day and told him she would not leave him again. He converted to Judaism two months later. He kept putting off the circumcision until his rabbi, a very short man with untamable hair, told Anderson he was in danger of abandoning his faith and his covenant with God. He and the rabbi sat in the rabbi's study. "God is all," the rabbi told him. He had known the rabbi for many years by then, had sought him out for advice and comfort the first time Esther returned to her people. Before Anderson had found the rabbi that first time, he had heard that a rabbi in the area had recently lost his son and daughter-in-law and four grandchildren in a fire. Anderson went to the man's house that first day seeking solace, not knowing that he was entering the home of the rabbi who had had the tragedy. Anderson thought that the deaths of six people had happened to another rabbi in another neighborhood.

So after the rabbi told him he was in danger of abandoning the covenant, Anderson was circumcised and then he was married.

The pamphlet on free Negroes who had owned other Negroes was twenty-seven pages, not including the six pages of drawings and maps. There were seven pages devoted to Henry Townsend and his widow Caldonia and her second husband, Louis Cartwright, the son of William Robbins. Cartwright was the last name Louis's mother, Philomena, had chosen for herself and her children. On one of those seven pages in the pamphlet there were two long paragraphs mentioning Fern Elston the teacher, who "herself had owned some Negroes," Anderson wrote.

Anderson met Fern one day in August 1881, had come up to her sitting on her porch with her glass of lemonade and large hat and asked her if he could speak with her. Fern had never been one to suffer white people and that condition had only worsened over time. "I suppose," she said, under the shade of a mulberry tree that was not as old as she was. "I suppose, if you will not take up too much of my time. We do not have time for the picayune, not you, and certainly not me." To Anderson, Fern could have been sixteen or thirty-nine or fifty-five or seventy-eight. He felt that as a journalist he should have been able to nail down her age without asking her. He never asked, and in his report for the pamphlet on free Negroes owning slaves he never mentioned age.

He came up to the porch of a pleasant house in a Negro neighborhood of pleasant houses. At first he thought that the dark-skinned man at the street corner had directed him to the wrong place because the woman he was seeing was surely a white woman, indeterminate age or not.

Once he was on the porch, she was cordial, and after he had been sitting more than half an hour, she offered him some lemonade. A man who had once been her slave and who was now the closest friend she had in the world brought the lemonade out to Anderson.

Anderson had first heard about free Negroes owning slaves only five months before and had thought that it was the oddest of all the oddities he had come upon. He said that to Fern.

"I don't know," he said near about eleven o'clock, "it would be for me like owning my own family, the people in my family." He had not long come back from seeing his family for the first time since leaving Canada in 1872. As he spoke to Fern, his siblings came into his head and he wished that he could be with them, that he had never left Canada the first time, and now a second time. The name of each sister and brother marched through his mind, slowly, so he had all the time in the world to trace each letter in their names with his mind's finger.

"Well, Mr. Frazier, it is not the same as owning people in your own family. It is not the same at all." Fern smoothed down her dress though it didn't need it. "You must not go away from this day and this place thinking that it is the same, because it is not." Whenever she looked at him, and it was rare that she did, her wide-brimmed hat would obscure part of her face. From the side, with her looking out into the street, he had a much better view. "All of us do only what the law and God tell us we can do. No one of us who believes in the law and God does more than that. Do you, Mr. Frazier? Do you do more than what is allowed by God and the law?"

"I try not to, Mrs. Elston."

"Well, there you are, Mr. Frazier. We are alike in that way. I did not own my family, and you must not tell people that I did. I did not. We did not. We owned . . ." She sighed, and her words seemed to come up through a throat much drier than only seconds before. "We owned slaves. It was what was done, and so that is what we did." She told him her last name was Elston, but that was her first husband's name. The world about her knew her by her third husband's last name. That husband was a blacksmith, a former slave, a pecan-colored man by whom she had had two children at a time when she thought her body could not do that for her. Her husband called her "Mama" and she called him "Papa." She said to Anderson, "We, not a single one of us Negroes, would have done what we were not allowed to do."

Fern looked down into the palm of her hand. Had Anderson not been white and a man, had the day not started out hot and gotten hotter, had she and her husband not quarreled that morning about such a trifle it did not deserve the name trifle, had the gambler not gone away to Baltimore a long time ago with one leg missing, had all of this not been so, Fern might have opened up to Anderson. *This is the truth as I know it in my heart.* Had the gambler left with both of his legs, had he just lost some tiny, tiny finger there on the outer reaches of one of his hands.

The names of his family members stayed with Anderson as he sat with Fern and it was a strange comfort. "Have you ever been homesick, Mrs. Elston?" Negroes, all of whom said good morning to her, walked by her house, up and down the dusty street of a little Virginia town where the railroad tracks said very clearly to the natives: All Negroes over here and all the white people over there. Anderson, not being a native, on his way to being a pious Jew, had gotten lost at first.

"No, I have endeavored to live beyond the control of such a malady," Fern said, waving away a fly. "Though I understand that it is not as debilitating and not as life-threatening as all the other illnesses. The ones they write about in books"—she turned to him—"and in pamphlets." She turned away again.

"No," Anderson said. "No, it is not as life-threatening. Indeed, it can be quite pleasant." He looked out at the ground before them, the grass, the trees on either side of the winding path that led up to her porch, the sunlight blanketing everything, and then he saw his brothers and sisters standing there side by side. He had heard three months before his visit to Canada that one of his sisters, Sheila, second from the left there in Fern's yard, had died. All his siblings now stood in Fern's summer yard in the heaviest of winter clothes, coats, boots, fur hats. It was snowing. His sisters and brothers were waving at him, one hand from each of them, and aside from the waving, they were very still, the way they would have been had they been posing for a photographer. "Yes, quite pleasant."

Fern turned to him, a man perhaps done in by the unsparing heat of the South. "I see," and she looked away. "I will have to take the word of a journalist."

A man passed the house and told Fern good morning, that it looked like another hot one.

"Did you get to taste those okras I sent over, Herbert?" she asked the man.

"Yessum," he said, raising his hat, "and I do preciate em. Adele fixed them up right nice. Just the way I like em. I'm gonna finish up that back fence a yours tomorrow. Adele wants to know when you comin by."

"Tell her I will see her soon. Please give my best to her. And, Herbert, there will be more okra to come. I can promise you that."

"And I thank you right on."

She and Anderson watched the man go down to the corner, look left and right, then go left. "I sometimes think I put too much faith in my garden," Fern said. "One day it will fail me and I will come to be known as a liar to one and all."

"Mrs. Elston, would you tell me about Mr. Townsend?"

She sipped from her lemonade but did not look back at him. She took a long time swallowing, and then she considered the glass when she was finished. Cold glasses of lemonade cry, she thought. Some poet should put that in a poem to his lady, unless the lady has already said it twice in one of her letters to him. "Henry or Augustus? I can say I knew Henry. I think I knew Henry very well. But I cannot say that I knew Augustus at all." Even as she spoke, she was trying to remember Augustus, but the memory of him was full of holes, the same as her memory of the one-legged gambler. *Such duty, such a wife.* In her life, she had not seen very much of Augustus, and most of what she retained came from the day she stood across from him at Henry's funeral. He was a handsome man, she said of Augustus. "I never leaned toward exaggeration," she said to Anderson. "So when I say he was a handsome man, he was indeed. Henry was, too, but he never got old enough to lose that boyish facade colored men have before they settle into being handsome and unafraid, before they learn that death is as near as a shadow and go about living their lives accordingly. When they learn that, they become more beautiful than even God could imagine, Mr. Frazier."

In addition to being William Robbins's groom, the boy Henry Townsend had been an apprentice to the boot- and shoemaker at the Robbins plantation. He became better than the man who taught him. "There ain't nothin else for me to put in his head, Master," the man, Timmons, told Robbins about two years before Augustus and Mildred bought their son's freedom. "He done ate up all I had and lookin round now for some more." It was not long after that that Robbins allowed Henry to measure him and had the boy make him boots for the first time. He was very pleased. "If Mrs. Robbins would permit,

Henry, I would sleep in them." This was shortly before he and his wife began sleeping in separate beds, she in a part of the mansion their daughter as a child called the East and he in what the daughter called the West.

As the days dwindled down to the time Henry's parents would take him into freedom, Robbins was surprised to know that he would miss the boy. He had not been so surprised about his feelings for a black human being since realizing that he loved Philomena. He had gotten used to seeing Henry standing in the lane, waiting as Robbins came back from some business or from visiting Philomena and their children. The boy had a calming way about him and stood with all the patience in the world as Robbins, often recovering from an episode of a storm in the head, made his slow way from the road to the lane and up to the house. Fathers waited that way for prodigal sons, Robbins once thought.

"Good mornin, Massa Robbins," the boy would say, for it was invariably morning when Robbins returned home.

"Mornin, Henry. How long have you been here?"

"Not so long," the boy would say, though he usually had been waiting for hours, starting in the dark, no matter what the weather. Robbins would make his way off the horse, and sometimes he needed help getting to his door. Once the man was inside, the boy would tend to the horse.

When Henry went into freedom, Robbins had the boy come back again and again to make boots and shoes for him and his male guests. Henry was, to be sure, not allowed to touch a white woman, but by using one of Robbins's female house slaves to measure their feet, he made the same for Robbins's wife, Ethel, his daughter, Patience, and for any women guests at the plantation. Such measurements done by slave women were not as perfect as he would have liked, and he soon learned to take their measurements and a sighting of the women's feet to come up with more exact ones. Robbins put Henry's name out wherever he went, and with Robbins's praise and the praise of the

guests returning to their homes, Henry became known for what one
guest from Lynchburg called "the kind of footwear God intended for
feet to have."

Henry began to accumulate money, which, along with some real
estate he would eventually get from Robbins, would be the foundation
of what he was and what he had the evening he died. It was Robbins
who taught him the value of money, the value of his labors, and
never to blink when he gave a price for his product. Many times he
traveled with Robbins as the white man worked to create what he had
once hoped to be an empire, "a little Virginia in big Virginia." In
Clarksburg once, Robbins was conversing with the master of the
house as Henry measured the man for a pair of riding boots. The man
became restless and kicked at Henry, saying the nigger was hurting
his feet. Robbins, a man with five pairs of Henry's boots by that time,
told Henry to go outside, and when he returned, the man, face red-
dened, was far more agreeable, but he never bought another thing
from Henry.

Augustus Townsend would have preferred that his son have nothing to do with the past, aside from visiting his slave friends at the
Robbins plantation, and he certainly would have preferred he have
nothing to do with the white man who had once owned him. But
Mildred made him see that the bigger Henry could make the world
he lived in, the freer he would be. "Them free papers he carry with
him all over the place don't carry anough freedom," she said to her
husband. With slavery behind him, she wanted her son to go about
and see what had always been denied him. That it was often Robbins
who took him about was a small price for them, and, besides, he was
the one who had limited his world in the first place. "All this takin
him about is just redeemin hisself in God's eyes," Mildred said.

At the end of two weeks or so of being with Robbins, Henry would
come back to his parents, his eyes gleaming and his heart eager to
share whatever part of Virginia he had been to. Mildred and Augustus, hearing their son's horse approach, would go out into the road

and wait for him to appear, as patient as Henry waiting for Robbins to come up the lane to the mansion. Robbins had told him to trust the Manchester National Bank and Henry would put part of what he earned there. The rest he and his father would, as soon as he was off his horse, bury in the backyard, covering it all with stones so the dog would not dig there. Their neighbors were all good and honest people but the world had strangers, too, and some of them had strayed from being good and honest. Then the three would walk the horse into the barn, settle it down, and come into the house, holding close to one another.

Henry went through his late teens that way.

The desire to live in Richmond had seized Philomena Cartwright when she was small, long before she became free. She was born on Robert Colfax's plantation, which was where Robbins first saw her when she was fourteen. When she was eight, Colfax purchased two slaves from a man traveling about the countryside selling off his property, human and otherwise, because he was going bankrupt. He aimed to make a new start in a new life, the man told Colfax, and he started that new life by giving Colfax a good price for the slaves. One of them was Sophie, a thirty-five-year-old woman who liked to tell the young Philomena what a grand place Richmond was, though in fact she had gotten no closer to Richmond than a dot called Goochland. In Richmond, Sophie said, the masters and their wives lived like kings and queens and had so much that their slaves lived like the everyday white masters and wives they saw around Manchester. The Richmond slaves had so much to eat that they were forever having to get new clothes as their bodies changed practically every week. There were Richmond slaves who themselves had slaves, and some of the slaves of slaves had slaves, Sophie said. And there were fireworks every night to celebrate anything under the sun, even a little child losing the first tooth or taking a first step. If it was a happy part of life,

Richmond would celebrate it. The stories about Richmond started when Philomena was eight, and they were still coming when Robbins saw her for the first time.

That day Robbins came up to Colfax's house on Sir Guilderham and saw the girl come down from the back of the house and walk down to the quarters. She had a load of laundry she was carrying on her head. He got off the horse and walked with the horse to the quarters, and he noted the cabin she went into. He often had to go to Richmond but he thought it as bad as Sodom.

He mentioned the girl to Colfax and within two weeks Colfax had sold her to him. Robbins had two children by a slave who lived with those children on a far cabin on his plantation but it had been nearly a year since he had been with her. Six months after his relationship with Philomena began, after he had put her in a house a little ways outside the town with a maid he brought in from his plantation, she told Robbins she wanted her mother and brother with her, and Robbins purchased them as well, though Colfax was not as generous with the price as he had been with Philomena. Robbins freed Philomena for her sixteenth birthday and several months later gave her her mother and brother. She had him purchase Sophie—who told stories about Richmond—two months after that, in her first month of being pregnant with Dora. Philomena's brother soon managed to run away with Sophie and Philomena proclaimed her ignorance about what they had been up to, and she said it in such a way that Robbins believed her. Robbins did everything he could to have them found and brought back but they had disappeared. He offered a bounty of $50 for each of them, and then a month later he raised it to $100 each, making the dollar amount the largest thing on the wanted posters. Philomena didn't seem to mind that she had lost two pieces of property. She told her mother that she believed they had ended up in Richmond, and some days she was happy for Sophie, having loved her for many years, but on other days she despised her for now having the life she herself wanted in Richmond. Would they, she wondered one day after Sophie had been gone a year, run out of fireworks before she herself could see Richmond?

The birth of Dora pulled Robbins even closer to Philomena than he could imagine. She called him "William" for the first time when the child was a week old and he did not correct her, came to enjoy the way his name flowed out of her mouth and seemed to swirl about in the air like some meaningless song before his brain registered and told him that was his name. He enjoyed being with her even when she was pouting and acting too much the child. "You don't be treatin me right, William. You just don't, William."

The need to be in Richmond returned strong with the birth of Louis, three years after Dora's. The need had never gone away but the birth of Dora had helped turn her into a woman who could bide her time; even devoid of fireworks, Sophie's Richmond was an eternal city and would wait for Philomena. But Louis's coming made her morose, and day by hard day, she turned over the care of the children to her mother and the maid, who was now her property as well.

She ran away to Richmond for the first time when Dora was six. Robbins sent his overseer to fetch her and that man found her sleeping in the streets, where she lived after she had used up what little money she had brought to Richmond. The overseer let it be known, in his indirect way, that he did not appreciate being used to haul back his employer's bed partner. The second time Philomena fled to Richmond she took her children and had more money than the first time. Dora was eight and Louis was six. Robbins himself went for them and took Henry, who was sixteen years old at the time. It was Henry's second time in Richmond.

At the end of a long day Robbins found the three in a boarding-house less than ten blocks from the Capitol, the same place Philomena had stayed in her first time in Richmond. The man and the woman who owned the place, people who had been born into freedom, opened the door and held their candles high to take in the face of the tall Robbins and told him which room upstairs he could find Philomena.

Robbins stood at the closed door for a long time and Henry stood less than two feet away, wanting, for the first time ever, not to be anywhere near the white man who had come to mean so much to him. At last Robbins turned and looked briefly at Henry in the dim hall. Henry held a lamp the owners of the house had given him but the smoking lamp was poor with light. "What is today, Henry?" "Wednesday, Mr. Robbins." "I see. And so far from midnight to make it Thursday." "Yessir. A good ways from midnight." Robbins opened the door.

Henry watched from the doorway, afraid to go and afraid to stay. Philomena was sitting on the side of the bed, one slipper on and the other across the room, and she did not look surprised to see Robbins. She was alone in the room and the two lamps there, one on the table beside the bed and the other atop the chiffarobe, gave abundant light to the room. Henry could see her face almost as well as he could have seen it under a midday sun.

"I don't wanna go back. You hear me, William? I don't wanna go back! Don't make me." He went to her and held her shoulders and she pulled away and fell back on the bed. "Where are the children?" Robbins asked and she managed, after a time, to raise her finger and flick it feebly toward the wall, toward the room on the other side of the wall. He looked at the wall as if he could see through it and into the other room and when he looked back at her he was angrier than the moment before. He picked her up by the shoulders and when she began to wiggle, he slapped her. She slapped him, the first time only a soft tap but the second had the force of a punch and it turned his head. He released one of her shoulders and showed her his fist, then he punched her and he immediately was sickened. She dropped her arms and fell back on the bed. Henry, seeing Philomena dissolve into nothing, screamed and Robbins then remembered he had not come alone.

Henry continued to scream until Robbins reached him and told him to be quiet. "Stop that! Stop that, I say!"

"But she dead," Henry said, looking around Robbins and pointing at the still Philomena.

"She ain't no more dead than you or me." Robbins held him gently by the throat. "Now hush that ruckus." Robbins went back to Philomena and Henry followed him. The man sat on the bed and held Philomena and shook her, and with each moment, the sickening subsided. Henry watched and said nothing. "Go find them children," Robbins said. "In the next room. Go find em and see to em." He watched Henry leave and wished he had not told him to go. I am in this nigger house, he thought, surrounded by niggers. He watched the pulsing vein in her neck, counting the beats. When the number was nearing 75, he closed his eyes but went on counting.

Henry did not see the partly opened door to the left leading to the room where the children were. He went out into the hall to the right, never thought to knock and simply pushed open the door and saw only darkness. He did not sense that the children were there and went to the door on the other side of Philomena's room and opened that door. Dora and Louis were in the bed and the girl was holding her brother. They had heard their mother shouting and then their father shouting and then they had heard Henry screaming.

He went to them and told them everything would be fine and, within a few minutes, they began to believe him. He had made their shoes, which were in a little pile in the corner. He gave them water and they drank as if it were the first in a very long time. This was the beginning of why Louis would get down into the hole without a second thought and dig for some while to help make Henry's grave. Without even knowing why, Henry began to sing to them and gradually Dora was able to let go of her brother.

Robbins found Henry kneeling beside the bed, still singing. Henry had found a piece of string from somewhere and with the string he was making and unmaking Jacob's Ladder, the one thing Rita, his second mother, had known how to do with string.

"I'm just a little somebody and I don't care a bit," he kept singing. "I'm just a little somebody and I don't care. A little somebody..." Robbins stood in the doorway and listened. "I'm just a little somebody and I don't care a bit." He wondered if his wife back home was asleep. Someone across the hall laughed and he remembered the laugh from a slave working in his fields. Robbins touched the door with his fist and watched it open wide and then wider.

Dora saw him first and bounded out of the bed and into his arms. He kissed her cheek. She held on to him until he took her back to the bed and put her down. He touched Louis's cheek, but the boy did not respond because Henry had given him the string and that was all the little boy knew for that moment.

"I want you to stay with em tonight, Henry," Robbins said, pulling the covers up to Dora's neck and blowing out the lamp on her side of the bed. "Stay with em and keep em peaceful. Just stay with em."

"Yessir."

He went to Louis's side of the bed and laid him down and pulled the covers up to his neck. "Yall listen to Henry," he told them. He took a few blankets piled on a chair and told Henry to lie beside the bed, and Henry took off the shoes he himself had made and he lay down and Robbins blew out the candle at Louis's side of the bed and left the room.

The owners of the boardinghouse were with Philomena when he returned to her room. The side of her face was bloating, turning purple with each moment, but he didn't know what color it was because the lamp on that side of the room had gone out. "I want somebody to attend to that," Robbins said to the husband and then repeated himself to the wife, nodding all the while in the direction of the injury. "We will," the woman said. "We will," the husband said. He went to the bed and thought for the first time that what he felt for Philomena might well doom him. His wife liked to retire early, but his daughter would stay on in the parlor to read or to keep up with her correspondence. The downstairs of his mansion his daughter called the South

and the upstairs she called the North. "Go to the East, Mama,"
Patience, the daughter, would say years later on that day Dora came
to the mansion. It was the day Patience thought William Robbins was
near death. "Go to the East and I will seek you out there. Please,
Mama. Please, sweetheart." Dora would be standing in the mansion
doorway. The two daughters had never seen each other before that
day. "Go to the East and I will seek you out, Mama."

Robbins knew Philomena would not be able to travel in the morning and he decided then that he would have to leave her. And he did
not want his children to see her face. He told the boardinghouse owners that he wanted to see that Philomena got back to Manchester. "I
see to it," the man said. "I got somebody and we see to it." Robbins
had no faith in the man's word but it would have to do. "She be ready
in a day or two," the woman said, holding Philomena's chin and inspecting the injury. Even as they all spoke and the man and the wife
tried to assure him that they would bring Philomena to him, he began to fear that he would not see her again. He looked at her and
could not take his eyes from her. He hoped that her love for their children would compel her back to Manchester. He dared not hope that
any love for him would do it.

He went back to the white hotel he had registered in earlier and
drank a good bit, though that had not been his intention when he first
entered the Negro boardinghouse. He awoke about eight, later than
he would have liked, and returned with his horse to the boardinghouse and was surprised to see that Henry had already made arrange-
ments for the trip. He had secured a surrey for himself and the two
children and for Philomena, since he had not known that she would
not be returning with them. The surrey would be pulled by the horse
Henry came in on and another horse he had gotten from a stable
nearby, using the name of William Robbins as currency because he
had come to Richmond with little money of his own. After seeing to
Philomena, Robbins found the children in their room, fed and rested
and full of giggles. He took them to Philomena, for the swelling in

her cheek had subsided, and then he took them out and down to the carriage. Philomena slept through their visit.

They left for Manchester near about ten o'clock. At five that day they stopped at a house close to Appomattox, about halfway to their destination, and at that house they stayed the night. The owner of the house, a white man of forty-nine then married to his fourth wife, who was the sister of his dead second wife, was used to much traffic on the road, had made a good life catering to it. He knew Robbins well enough to let him keep three Negroes in the room next to Robbins and he didn't charge him any extra for having Negroes in the place and not in the barn.

Henry drove the surrey the whole way to Manchester, Louis beside him and Dora in the back, a cloth doll for company, and for a good bit of the way Robbins rode Sir Guilderham beside them. Once, way on the other side of Appomattox, Dora looked out and up at him. He smiled at her and then, after about half a mile, told Henry to stop and he tied the horse to the back of the carriage and he got in with Dora and she moved without words into his arms. Robbins looked at the back of Henry's head, at the way Louis watched him, as if this was all a lesson he would later be tested on. Dora dozed and Robbins thought that this would be a good way for him to die, right there, on the road home with his children. The only thing to make it better would be to have his daughter Patience on the other side of him. Looking at the back of Henry absorbed in his work, it came to him like something he had long been avoiding, that the world would not be very good to the children he had had with Philomena, but whatever world it would be, he wanted Henry in it for them.

They arrived at the house he bought for Philomena a little after sundown of the second day of their trip. Philomena's mother was at the door, waiting. She had been seeing a man from a nearby planta- tion and he had just left after she fed him. That man liked the banjo, which he played for her all the time, but it had a strange sound be- cause it was missing a string. The children's grandmother came down to the surrey and made quite a fuss over the two children, whom she called her "little hushpuppies." Her daughter owned her but that didn't mean anything between them.

When Henry, at twenty, bought his first piece of land from Robbins, he told his parents right off. The land was miles from where they lived but a short ride from Robbins's plantation, though it was not connected. By the time he died he would own all the land between him and Robbins so that there was nothing separating what they owned. He had supper with Mildred and Augustus the day of the land sale. But the day he bought from Robbins his first slave, Moses, he did not go to their house and he did not go to them for a long time. He spent that first day of ownership with Robbins, and Moses and he and the white man planned where he would build his house. He did not have a wife, was not even courting anyone. When he told his parents about Moses, the house—which was to be half as large as Robbins's—was a third completed, and still he did not have a wife.

When the house was half done, Robbins, one afternoon in early fall, rode up on a horse sired by Sir Guilderham and stopped, watching Henry and Moses tussling in front of the unfinished house. Henry and Moses had not noticed him come up, and the dog, so used to seeing Robbins, had not bothered to bark.

"Henry," he said at last, still on the horse. "Henry, come here." He turned and rode away several yards and Henry came out, followed by Moses. When Robbins, still moving, turned his head to see Moses following, anger appeared on his face. He shouted to Moses, "I said 'Henry, come here.' If Ida wanted you, Ida said for you to come."

Moses stopped and Henry looked back at him. Robbins rode slowly on, then a bit faster, and Henry finally had to run to keep up. When Robbins had come to the road again, he stopped but did not turn around. When Henry reached Robbins, he could hardly catch his breath. He leaned over behind Robbins, his hands on his knees. "Yessir?" Henry kept saying. "Yessir?" Robbins still did not turn around and Henry went around to face him, putting a hand up to the horse's forehead, which was a good two feet higher than his own head.

"Yessir?"

"Who is that?" Robbins said, raising his gloved hand and pointing his thumb over his shoulder. "Who is that you playin with like children in the dirt?"

"That Moses. You know Moses, Mr. Robbins." Moses had been his slave for less than six months.

"I know you bought a slave from me to do what a slave is supposed to do. I know that much."

"Yessir."

"Henry," Robbins said, looking not at him but out to the other side of the road, "the law will protect you as a master to your slave, and it will not flinch when it protects you. That protection lasts from here"—and he pointed to an imaginary place in the road—"all the way to the death of that property"—and he pointed to a place a few feet from the first place. "But the law expects you to know what is master and what is slave. And it does not matter if you are not much more darker than your slave. The law is blind to that. You are the master and that is all the law wants to know. The law will come to you and stand behind you. But if you roll around and be a playmate to your property, and your property turns round and bites you, the law will come to you still, but it will not come with the full heart and all the deliberate speed that you will need. You will have failed in your part of the bargain. You will have pointed to the line that separates you from your property and told your property that the line does not matter." Henry pulled his hand down from the horse's forehead. "You are rollin round now, today, with property you have a slip of paper on. How will you act when you have ten slips of paper, fifty slips of paper? How will you act, Henry, when you have a hundred slips of paper? Will you still be rollin in the dirt with them?"

Robbins spurred the horse and said nothing more. Henry watched them, the man and the horse, and then looked over at Moses, who waved, ready to return to work. Moses, with a saw in his hand, did a little dance. Henry went to him.

"We can get in a good bit fore dark," Moses said and lifted the saw high above his head.

"We ain't workin no more today."

"What? But why not?"

"I said no more, Moses."

"But we got good light here. We got good day here, Massa."

Henry stepped to him, took the saw and slapped him once, and when the pain begin to set in on Moses's face, he slapped him again. "Why don't you never do what I tell you to do? Why is that, Moses?"

"I do. I always do what you tell me to do, Massa."

"Nigger, you don't. You never do."

Moses felt himself beginning to sink in the dirt. He lifted one foot and placed it elsewhere, hoping that would be better, but it wasn't. He wanted to move the other foot, but that would have been too much—as it was, moving the first foot was done without permission.

"You just do what I tell you from now on," Henry said. He dropped the saw on the ground. He bent down and picked it up and looked for a long time at the tool, at the teeth all in a row, at the way they marched finely up to the wooden handle. He dropped the saw again and looked down at it. "Go get my horse with the saddle on top of it," Henry said, still looking at the saw. "Go get my horse." "Yessir, I will." Moses soon came with the animal.

Henry mounted.

"I be back later. Maybe I be back tomorrow. But I want you here doin right when I get back, doin good." The horse walked off. Henry was many yards from his place when he remembered that he had left his hat, but the day had been a pleasant one and he figured he could get by without it. It was not many more feet beyond that point that he heard the sounds of Moses working. The birds of the day began to chirp, and in little more than a mile, the bird songs had replaced completely the sound of the man working behind him. Then, in little more than another quarter-mile, a mule was honking, joined by the lowing of a cow, and as he rode on farther, the crickets came in, and then the birds and the cow mooing and the crickets and the evening air all came together.

Moses finished the kitchen floor before he lay down to sleep. The darkness came on but he felt some need to complete the work and set up candles and a few lanterns about the room and worked on with their flickering help and with some inner sense of what should go where. It was a sense that would have served him somewhat even if he had toiled in perfect darkness. And gradually, as the evening and night went on, he forgot everything but what he was doing. There was not time and there was not darkness out there beyond the room. There was no empty stomach. There was only work. The sweat came down his face and he licked at the sweat that came near his mouth and drank it. When the work of that day—the thirty-third since the first nail was pounded into wood—was done, he ate some biscuits and three apples and drank all the water his body could hold. He went out to the cabin he and Henry had shared, and he knew that now the cabin would be his alone. Tomorrow, or whenever his master returned, they, he and Henry, could move through from the kitchen toward the front of the house. They might even make it to the beginning of the second floor, and in one of those rooms on the first floor, whether the completed dining room or the parlor, Henry would sleep. Moses stopped at the door of the cabin and looked up at the night. His grandmother, or a woman who told the world she was his grandmother before she was sold away, had tried to tell him about the stars ("Them stars can guide you"), but he had no head for the stars. Now he looked at them and he raised his hand to his eyes to shade them, just the way he would have done if it were the middle of the sunniest day. He was standing less than ten feet from the spot where he would die one morning.

Leaving Henry's place that day, Robbins went to Fern Elston's before going home to his wife and daughter. What had always surprised him was that he had never seen as many flaws in Henry as he
had seen in white men who had enough possessions in their lives to
bring on the envious wrath of the gods. Robbins had always believed
that the fewer flaws in a man, the fewer doors there were for the gods
to enter a man's life and pull him down to nothing. And not seeing as
many failings, Robbins had thought Henry would make a way for
himself where even some good and strong white men had faltered
and been ground back down to dust. But over the years he had seen
enough wrong in the way Henry sometimes conducted himself to
worry him. And no failing had worried him more since the day he
brought Henry into his life than wrestling around with the slave
Moses like some common nigger in from the field after a hard day.
How could anyone, white or not white, think that he could hold on to
his land and servants and his future if he thought himself no higher
than what he owned? The gods, the changeable gods, hated a man
with so much, but they hated more a man who did not appreciate how
high they had pulled him up from the dust.

Robbins arrived at Fern's and saw a servant and told that servant
to tell his mistress that he wanted to see her. Robbins did not dismount from his horse and had he not seen the servant he would have
remained on his horse, waiting until someone noticed he was there
and asked if he might be helped. Fern came out of her door and
stepped to the edge of the verandah and Robbins took off his hat but
still did not dismount. Fern did not come down the steps and so they
were more or less eye to eye.

"Fern, good day."

"Good day, Mr. Robbins."

"I have someone who needs to be educated, starting with writing
and whatnot. He can't even write his own name. He should know how

to do that and much else besides. He should know how to conduct himself in Virginia."

"I see," Fern said. She had not heard that he had any more children with Philomena Cartwright, so she thought that he had taken up with another colored woman and now the child of that coupling needed to be educated. She liked to take children at age four; the older they were after that, the more their heads had been filled with nonsense that her teaching could not extract.

"It's Henry Townsend. I think you know him."

She laughed, but when Robbins did not, she stopped. "The Henry I know is a man," she said. *"A man,"* and she made sure that he was looking at her when she repeated herself.

"That be him," Robbins said. "A far piece from being a boy. But he is coming into himself and I would not want to see him hurt by all that he does not know."

"A man does not learn very well, Mr. Robbins. Women, yes, because they are used to bending with whatever wind comes along. A woman, no matter the age, is always learning, always becoming. But a man, if you will pardon me, stops learning at fourteen or so. He shuts it all down, Mr. Robbins. A log is capable of learning more than a man. To teach a man would be a battle, a war, and I would lose."

"Not with Henry, Fern. He would be open to what you had to teach him. I would not come to you about any other Negro." He had paid her $20 a month to educate Dora and Louis. He had been tempted to have her come to his house and give private lessons to his white daughter, so pleased with what she had done with his black children, but there were some things his wife could not abide and that would have been another door for the gods to come through. Patience, that other daughter, had been educated well enough but not as well as Dora had been taught by Fern. "He would not be as obstinate or as thick as a log."

"The oldest child ever brought to me was ten years old," Fern said. "It was a war, but I prevailed. I was also a younger woman." She looked Robbins in the face, then looked to the side, beyond him out to the place where the gambler Jebediah Dickinson would camp. "So you send word to Henry Townsend to come by here at ten tomorrow morning. Any later than that and he will have failed the first lesson." She did not say that he himself should tell Henry for she knew he would not go and take a message from a woman not his equal to a man who was not his equal.

"Good," Robbins said. "Let us wait a week and see what price this will be."

"It will not be a child's price. I can practically teach children in my sleep."

"Tell him nothing about this and I will pay the price of a man. Even the price of three children," Robbins said. He put his hat back on his head. "Good day, Fern." He still wanted Henry in any world his black children would have to inhabit, but the wrestling around with Moses had shown him how unprepared Henry was. Fern would see that and she would do what had to be done. That August day the Canadian pamphlet writer Anderson Frazier came to visit, Fern said, "No, Henry never lived to be completely handsome. Augustus did, but his son fell short."

"Good day, Mr. Robbins," Fern said.

She watched him ride out to the road and turn to the left. She had heard from Maude, Caldonia's mother, that there might be something unnatural between him and Henry. Why else would a white man of his stature spend so much of his life with a young man he had once owned? Now she knew the unnatural was not it. Robbins had a fear in his eyes, the same fear a man would have sending his son out into the world to hunt for bear with only a favorite gun that had failed the father once too often.

She came down the steps of the verandah. Ramsey, her gambling husband, gone a week, had promised to return that day. Zeus, the slave she trusted most, came around the side of her house and asked what he could do for her. "The garden," she said, pointing her chin out in the direction of the azaleas. "I have not seen to my garden since yesterday." Zeus would be the man who would bring the lemonade out to Anderson Frazier that August day. Zeus would then be earning a salary from Fern and her blacksmith husband, called them his employers, though he would be, in fact, Fern's best friend.

"Yes, ma'am," Zeus said, glancing at the garden. He went to the shed for her gardening hat and all she would need to make it through.

The sound of Robbins's leaving was no more. She sighed and looked down to the road where the white man had gone. A month to teach him to write his name. No, perhaps two weeks. She was a great teacher and Augustus and Mildred were not thickheaded people, so maybe the going would not be as difficult as chopping a log with a dull ax. She came to the garden and seeing it made her heart beat faster. She had not bathed since her husband left, but her days of being so long from water were coming to an end, though she herself could not see the end. Zeus arrived with her equipment and he set the hat on her head and he did it so well that she did not need to adjust what he had done. "We must get us a new one of these, Mistress," he said of her hat. Her husband had accepted Zeus as part of a white man's gambling debt when Zeus was twelve years old. He had come with a name that she did not like and so she, then a new wife, had renamed him. Named him for a god she would have worshiped had she been the worshiping kind. Neither Fern nor Zeus could remember what his old name had been. Fern said now, "Oh, Zeus, this hat will do us for now. At least until the end of the month. And then you and I will see."

They went into the garden, avoiding the most fragile of what was growing. She herself did not bend down to the flowers but pointed to what she wanted done, what needed snipping, what needed pruning, and Zeus knelt down and made it right. He had a hat of his own and it was as old as the one Fern was wearing. He was never to retire from being employed by Fern and her blacksmith husband. On the day Anderson Frazier the pamphlet writer came to visit, Fern had been earlier that morning in her new garden, working on her knees beside Zeus, her employee. As she sat with Anderson on her porch, she noticed some dirt under one fingernail and silently chastised herself for missing what even a small child would have seen as she washed up.

Fern Elston had chosen not to follow her siblings and many of her cousins into a life of being white. She stayed in Manchester County where everyone knew what she was—a free Negro, though she was as white as any white person. Part of why she stayed was Ramsey Elston, a free Negro who came from north of Charlottesville. Had she gone anywhere else and passed as white, the color of her husband would have made her suspect. While he was quite light-skinned, he was not as light as she was and it was most evident that he was colored. She would have been a white woman in the rest of the world with a Negro husband, and that would have limited her world almost as much as their just living as a colored man and his colored wife. And being a white wife might have gotten her husband killed.

But it had never crossed Fern's mind to pass as white. Not caring very much for white people, she saw no reason to become one of them. She was known throughout Manchester as a formidable woman, and being educated had only piled more formidability on top of what she had been born with. Sheriff John Skiffington's patrollers came to dread seeing her if she was on the road after dark, which was rare for her.

In the early days of the patrollers, the first thing out of her mouth when they stopped her was "I will not abuse you in word or deed and I do not expect you to abuse me in word or deed. And I do not want my servant abused," the servant being whichever one of her slaves was driving her at the time. Then she would produce papers showing she was a free woman and that would be followed by a bill of sale for the slave. She waited patiently for them to look over the papers. Some of the patrollers could not read, and she was just as patient with them, waiting as the illiterate man made a show of pretending to read. She knew people were not born knowing how to read. She did not say "Good day" when they stopped her, and she did not say "Good-bye" when they let her go on her way. "Pass on," she would say to the servant.

If there was something "disagreeable" with the patrollers she would tell William Robbins, not Sheriff John Skiffington, about it the very next day. Once, a patroller, Harvey Travis, who could read, had been displeased with the coldness of her manner and had crumbled up the papers and thrown them in her lap. "Just git now," he said. "Pass on," she said to the servant, with the same tone she spoke when she had not been abused. She went to Robbins that next day. She had never gone around to the back door of a white person's home and she did not do it that day. The servant who drove her went to the back, found a slave who was washing clothes and told her that Mistress Fern would like a word with Master Robbins. By the time Fern's servant got back to her in the carriage, Robbins was coming down the stairs of the verandah.

"Mr. Robbins," she said, "I have had a disagreeable episode with one of the patrollers and I fear that if something is not done, there will be more episodes." She remained in the carriage the whole time as Robbins stood beside it. Both of them paid taxes to fund the patrollers but that was not something that would have meant anything to the patrollers.

He knew her well enough to know that she had not gone to Skiffington. "I will look into it, Fern. I will see what I can do."

"If you can do something, you will have my gratitude."

"Then I will work even harder to get something done."

No patroller ever abused her again. Always after that, when she saw the patrollers on the night road, she would stop and produce the papers even before they had asked. In time, all the patrollers came to know her and did not require the papers. But she pulled them out nevertheless. "We know who you are," they would say. She said nothing. And then, when it became clear that she never had to stop again in her life, she would still stop and do what she had been doing all along.

Ramsey Elston's gambling was making them poorer, though it was a poverty that the great majority of the county, white and free black, would have been very comfortable with. He did not gamble in the county. Instead, he would go at least two counties over to find white men sporting enough to gamble with a Negro. And he had to be sure that if he won, they would not be so resentful as to take their losses out on his hide, and then, after the beating, take their money back. He was often gone for three or four days, a week at the most, and in the early time of their marriage it was something she could bear. And, too, he usually won. The acreage that they had was producing, and then there was the money from relatives in Richmond and Petersburg. The money had been coming for years without there ever having been an agreement to it. A bank in Richmond or Petersburg would communicate with the one bank in Manchester and there would be money in Fern's account. She suspected that the relatives were sending it as Fern-you-keep-our-secret money, but the last thing she would have done was tell the world she had relatives who were passing. She knew them all, had played with some as children, slept beside them in their beds, but she no longer thought of them as people who had the same blood as hers.

Ramsey, especially in the days before the arrival of fellow gambler Jebediah Dickinson, would return and be the most attentive of husbands for weeks and weeks until the need to be around a table of money and cards and men and cigars took hold of him again. That gambling world two counties away tugged at him and she could see it in the way he lumbered through their home, the way he nudged the puppies out of his way with his foot. He needed to be back to that world, all of it, even the sight of that one servant whose one job it was to fan the cigar smoke away with a newspaper none of the gamblers had even bothered to read.

Fern was not a woman to wait for her husband at the window. But

she did pine for him. He would tell her the very day when he was coming back. "Don't wash," he would say before he left. "Don't you bathe
till I get back." This was hard for her in the beginning, for she had been
raised with the notion that the lack of cleanliness put one closer to
those laboring in the fields. "I need to bathe, Mr. Elston," she said. "I
want to bathe." "Do it after I get back." "But I will perspire all over myself in the meantime, all the way down to my poor ankles." "Sweat me
up a river, I don't care. I'll swim in it. Just don't bathe." She tried to
avoid her students at such times, for she had taught them, from Dora to
Caldonia, the same notion about cleanliness. Ramsey would come back,
generally in the late evening, and find her in their bedroom. "I have
been a dutiful wife, Mr. Elston." He would laugh. "And I a dutiful husband, Mrs. Elston," and she would believe him, night after night, until
Jebediah Dickinson came. Then Ramsey would start to undress her,
piece by slow piece, the one candle in the room wearing itself away
even faster now down to a nub. Long before he had finished undressing
her, she would grow heavy with wanting him and feel as if she would
drop to the floor, and that was when he would kiss her throat, making
the first contact with her skin, tasting for the first time the buildup of
salt. The kiss would revive her and she would live until she became
heavy once more and he had to kiss her throat again. "Have you bathed,
Mrs. Elston?" "I have not bathed, Mr. Elston," each word being such an
effort and yet so very necessary. "I have been a dutiful wife."

This was in the spring and early summer of their lives together.
There was a saying in that part of Virginia that candles burned
brighter in the spring and summer of a year because of how the wind
came down from the mountains and gave the flames more air to
breathe. Other people said no, that they had seen candles burn just as
brightly in the fall, and even in the winter when the air wasn't as nice.
Fern Elston subscribed to the latter notion.

The Elstons rarely had more than thirteen slaves, though the gambler Jebediah Dickinson, for the time he was there, would bring

the number to fourteen. Thirteen slaves were always enough to serve them in the house and to farm the few acres that would meet all their needs. The field slaves lived in quarters closer to their masters than any hands at any plantation or farm in Virginia. Why this was so, no one ever knew. There was certainly land enough to place them farther away. Those Elstons didn't have slaves, colored people said, they had neighbors who happened to be slaves.

Fern did not tell Anderson Frazier, the white man who wrote pamphlets, that Henry Townsend was the darkest student she ever had, but she did tell him that he was the first freed slave and was probably the brightest of all her students.

"It might be that his blood was untainted in some way," she said as the time neared noon that day with Anderson. She was prepared to give no answer if he asked what she meant by that, but Anderson said nothing. She listened to the word *untainted* echo in her head, thinking that it was the first time she had used it in a long time. "When he could read and write, I opened my library to him, but most of the books did not hold him the way I thought they might have. He was a man, of course, and not a child given to luxuriating. He read, enjoyed, and presented himself for the next one. He would take a book back to his land. Where he got the time to read, I do not know because the word I received was that he was working on the house all day long." That August day with Anderson, a man and a woman, hand in hand, walked by and she waved to them and the couple waved back. "Now and again some book would take a firm hold of him and he would talk about it for days. Do you know Milton, Mr. Frazier? Do you know *Paradise Lost*, Mr. Frazier?"

"I do, Mrs. Elston."

"So did Henry. 'Ain't that a thing to say' is what he said of the Devil who proclaimed that he would rather rule in hell than serve in heaven. He thought only a man who knew himself well could say such a thing, could turn his back on God with just finality. I tried to make him see what a horrible choice that was, but Henry had made up his mind about that and I could not turn him back. He loved Milton and he loved Thomas Gray. I am partial to neither, but I must reveal them to my students nevertheless." She turned to Anderson and tipped her head back somewhat so that her whole face was visible. She continued, "I could not break him of his diction. Sometimes he spoke the way I wanted him to speak, but there were so many times when he spoke the way a man had to speak who had been twenty years in the field. His own father spoke that way as well."

The day Robbins saw him wrestling with Moses, Henry Townsend reached his parents a little after seven that evening. Mildred and Augustus were awake and he was glad. He had stayed away and not told them about the purchase of Moses or that he had started building a house. Part of him just wanted to surprise them about the new house. Part of him had been afraid to tell them about Moses. But Henry was weary in the mind after what Robbins had said to him and thought that sharing the story of his house and Moses would be a good way to pass the evening before sleep. He found them at the kitchen table and Mildred stood and covered his face with kisses. Augustus was playing with one of the dogs, tugging gently at its ears. "Leave off now," he told the dog as he rose and the dog sidled away. Augustus and Henry kissed on the mouth, a habit born in those days when Henry and Robbins traveled about, a way of pulling Henry back into the family. The day of the wrestling the family had not been together in nearly two months.

They sat at the kitchen table. Mildred put a slice of apple pie before her son, then took it back and put a second slice on the plate right beside the first. As always, they were silent for very long moments. The time the three had spent apart in the early years had built up an awkwardness that came out in such moments: Augustus first being free and

working to free his wife and then mother and child living together as
slaves and then father and mother working to free Henry and then the
three of them together forging a life just when the sap was commenc-
ing to rise in the boy. But then, in the midst of the silence, Mildred or
Augustus would do some throat clearing and the words would flow
again among them.

"I'm workin on a house," Henry said in between chews on the second piece of pie. "I'm puttin up a house. A big house."

Mildred and Augustus looked at each other and smiled. "What
next, a wife?" Augustus asked.

"Maybe. Maybe. It's gonna be a good house, Papa. Even white
people will say, 'What a nice house that Henry Townsend got.' "

"Why ain't you tell me, Henry?" Augustus said. "You know I
woulda done all I could. I coulda come down there for you. Thas why
I'm here."

"I know, Papa. I just wanted to get anough of somethin for you
and Mama to make a fuss over. Maybe you can come in when we get
to that second story."

"Two floors," Mildred said. "Look out, Augustus, he's buildin
somethin bigger than what you got." She winked at her husband.
"When 'we' get to the second floor? Who this 'we' you talkin about?"

Henry put down his fork from the last of the pie. "Thas the other
part of the news. I got help."

Augustus shook his head in pleasant wonder. "Who you got? You
hired out Charles and Millard from over Colfax's plantation. They
good men with they hands, I haveta say. Good men and worth what
you gotta pay. Get your money out the backyard and do right by em.
And Colfax'll let em keep some of what they earn. That Charles could
use the money with him tryin to buy hisself away from Colfax. Is it
Buddy? Free Buddy, not Buddy thas from Dalford's plantation. I don't
know bout slave Buddy's work sometime. But free Buddy be somethin
else."

"No, Papa. I got my own man. I bought my own man. Bought him cheap from Master Robbins. Moses." The pie had made him drowsy and he was thinking how good it would be to go upstairs and fall asleep. "He a good worker. Lotta years in him. And Mr. Robbins lend me the rest of the men for the work."

Mildred and Augustus looked at each other and Mildred lowered her head.

Augustus stood up so quickly his chair tilted back and he reached around to catch it without taking his eyes from Henry. "You mean tell me you bought a man and he yours now? You done bought him and you didn't free that man? You *own* a man, Henry?"

"Yes. Well, yes, Papa," Henry looked from his father to his mother.

Mildred stood up, too. "Henry, why?" she said. "Why would you do that?" She went through her memory for the time, for the day, she and her husband told him all about what he should and should not do. No goin out into them woods without Papa or me knowin about it. No steppin foot out this house without them free papers, not even to go to the well or the privy. Say your prayers every night.

"Do what, Mama? What is it?"

Pick the blueberries close to the ground, son. Them the sweetest, I find. If a white man say the trees can talk, can dance, you just say yes right along, that you done seen em do it plenty of times. Don't look them people in the eye. You see a white woman ridin toward you, get way off the road and go stand behind a tree. The uglier the white woman, the farther you go and the broader the tree. But where, in all she taught her son, was it about thou shall own no one, havin been owned once your own self. Don't go back to Egypt after God done took you outa there.

"Don't you know the wrong of that, Henry?" Augustus said.

"Nobody never told me the wrong of that."

"Why should anybody haveta teach you the wrong, son?" Augustus said. "Ain't you got eyes to see it without me tellin you?"

"Henry," Mildred said, "why do things the same old bad way?"

"I ain't, Mama. I ain't."

Augustus said quietly, "I promised myself when I got this little bit of land that I would never suffer a slaveowner to set foot on it. Never." He put his hand momentarily to his mouth and then tugged at his beard. "Of all the human beins on God's earth I never once thought the first slaveowner I would tell to leave my place would be my own child. I never thought it would be you. Why did we ever buy you offa Robbins if you gon do this? Why trouble ourselves with you bein free, Henry? You could not have hurt me more if you had cut off my arms and my legs." Augustus walked out the room to the front door, meaning for Henry to follow. Mildred sat back down but soon stood up again.

"Papa, I ain't done nothin I ain't a right to. I ain't done nothin no white man wouldn't do. Papa, wait."

Mildred went to her son and put her hand to the back of his neck and rubbed it. "Augustus . . . ?" Henry followed his father and Mildred followed her son. "Papa. Papa, now wait now." In the front room, Augustus turned to Henry. "You best leave, and you best leave now," Augustus said. He opened the door.

"I ain't done nothin that any white man wouldn't do. I ain't broke no law. I ain't. You listen here." Beside the door, Augustus had several racks of walking sticks, one under the other, about ten in all. "Papa, just cause you didn't, that don't mean . . ." Augustus took down a stick, one with an array of squirrels chasing one another, head to tail, tail to head, a line of sleek creatures going around and around the stick all the way to the top where a perfect acorn was waiting, stem and all. Augustus slammed the stick down across Henry's shoulder and Henry crumpled to the floor. "Augustus, stop now!" Mildred shouted and knelt to her son. "Thas how a slave feel!" Augustus called down to him. "Thas just how every slave every day be feelin."

Henry squirmed out of his mother's arms and managed to get to his feet. He took the stick from his father. "Henry, no!" Mildred said. Henry, with two tries, broke the stick over his knee. "Thas how a master feels," he said and went out the door. Mildred followed him.

"Please, son. Please." He kept walking and on the steps he realized that he was still holding the pieces of the stick and turned around and handed them to his mother. "Henry. Wait, son." He went on to the barn. He had come to stay the night and so had made a place for his horse, but now he saddled it with what little moonlight found its way into the barn. The horse resisted. "Come!" Henry told it. "Come now!" His mother came out into the yard and watched him go away in the dark. For a long time she could hear the horse moving on what passed for a road out where they were and the sounds of his going away gave her an image of him in her mind that stayed with her for days.

The pain in his shoulder did not allow him to ride quickly and it took him some three hours to reach Robbins's place. Mildred and Augustus had wanted a place as far away from most white people as they could get. Henry feared that Robbins would not be home. He had thought he would simply sleep in the barn until morning. But Robbins was drinking alone on the verandah and neither man said a word as Henry came slowly up into the yard. The moon gave them good light. Robbins's horse was in the yard and raised his head from the grass to look at Henry. Henry dismounted. He led the white man's horse away, and after a bit, he returned to get his own horse.

When he returned, he stood in the yard, looking up at Robbins, who was drinking from a bottle, something Henry had never seen him do out in the open.

"May I come up and sit with you, Mr. Robbins?"

"Of course. Of course. I would no more deny you a seat than I would deny Louis." Robbins was one of the few white men who would not suffer from sitting across from a black man. Aside from the crickets and a sound from the odd creature of the night, their words were all there was. Henry sat on the top step. Robbins's wife was watching from a window up in the East. Robbins was not in his customary rocking chair, for the rocking had begun to pain his back. "I would offer you somethin, Henry, but there are some roads you'd best not go down. At least not now when you have all your senses."

"Yessir."

"Is today Tuesday, Henry?"

"Yessir, it be Tuesday. Least for a little bit more."

"Hmm ...," Robbins muttered and drank from the bottle, two quick sips. "My mother was born on a Tuesday, in a nice place just outside Charlottesville. I've always thought of Tuesday as my lucky day, even though I myself was born on a Thursday. I cannot go wrong on a Tuesday. I married on a Tuesday, though Mrs. Robbins would have preferred a Sunday."

"Yessir."

"Do you know what day your mother was born on, Henry?"

"No, Mr. Robbins, I don't."

"I got down the big book last week. Not my Bible. The other book. The book of all my servants and all else. No, maybe it wasn't last week. Maybe it was two weeks ago, or whenever it was you started in on your house. And I looked up her name. She has a Tuesday, Henry. Remember that. Marry on a Tuesday and you will be happy. You were born on a Friday, the book says. But pay that no mind."

Henry said he would pay it no mind.

"Are you happy with your house, Henry?" He could see Henry kneeling before the bed as he amused his children that night in Richmond. His children would be better for having Henry in their world, if he could just stop wrestling with niggers.

"Yessir, I am." He kept shifting to get the best relief for his pained shoulder.

"Don't settle for just a house and some land, boy. Take hold of it all. There are white men out there, Henry, who ain't got nothin. You might as well step in and take what they ain't takin. Why not? God is in his heaven and he don't care most of the time. The trick of life is to know when God does care and do all you need to do behind his back."

"Yessir."

"I know you have it in you to want, to want to take hold and pull it in for yourself, don't you, Henry?"

"I do, Mr. Robbins." He did not know how much he wanted until that moment.

"Then take it and let the world be damned, Henry."

Henry waited until then to tell Robbins he thought his shoulder was broken and that he might need some help moving from the steps.

Fern Elston said to Anderson Frazier the pamphlet man that day in August, "A woman born to teaching wakes in the morning desperate to be near her pupils. I was that way. I am that way. I have told my own children and my husband to put on my grave marker 'Mother' and 'Teacher.' That before all else, even my own name. And if the chiseler has room, to have him put 'Wife.' 'Wife' below my name. 'Dutiful Wife,' if he can manage it." She paused for some time, then returned to the subject of Henry Townsend. "I had nothing in mind beyond a pleasant afternoon and early evening when I invited Henry to supper with some of my former students. I believe it was a little less than a year since I began teaching him and he was still my student. He came in some woolen suit, much too warm for the day. I suspect that if you had taken a beater to that suit, the dust would have been enough to engulf him. I believe he himself was the owner of three servants by then. Perhaps four, one of them being a woman to cook for him. . . ."

"How did he acquit himself that evening, Mrs. Elston?" Anderson said.

"Quite well. Dora and Louis knew him, of course, adored him. He was a kind of older brother to them, so it was not going to be an uncomfortable gathering. Calvin, Caldonia's brother, took to him right away. Calvin had long been uneasy in his own person and so lived to put everyone else at ease. The two of them talked together most of the afternoon, into the evening. Then, toward the end, having sat across the table from her the whole time but never spoken to her, Henry said to Caldonia, 'I saw you ridin and sometime you keep your head down.' He didn't excuse himself from talking to Calvin and he didn't excuse himself to Frieda, to whom Caldonia was talking. Manners had not yet been one of my lessons with him. It would have been one of the first lessons with them, with children, of course, but in teaching a man, the fundamentals must change." She went on to describe the remainder of the evening. It was clear that it was one of her favorite memories.

Caldonia had looked across at Henry as if she had not noticed him before. "Oh," she said after he said he saw her riding. "You keep your head down and that ain't right," Henry said. He took the pepper shaker in his right hand, extended his arm before him and moved the arm from right to left. Everyone at the table was now watching him. The hand with the shaker moved smoothly, gracefully from the right to the left. "Thas how everybody else rides," Henry said. "Me and everybody else." Henry put the pepper shaker in his left hand, tipped it and moved his arm less gracefully from the left to the right. And as it moved, pepper poured out of the shaker onto Fern's white tablecloth. He said, "I'm sorry to say this, but thas how you ride." Henry did this with the shaker several times—going from right to left, the pepper shaker was upright, but going from left to right, the pepper flowed down. Fern thought there was something rather sad about the pepper falling, and it was all the sadder because it really didn't have to be that way. She said to Anderson, "This was his clumsy way of telling Caldonia she was losing something by not looking up."

In the end, Henry noticed the line of pepper on the tablecloth and looked at Fern. "I'm sorry," he said to her. "It is not the problem you think," Fern said. "Mr. Elston has done far more harm to my tablecloth."

Caldonia had not taken her eyes off Henry, and she finally smiled at him. "I will try to do better from now on," she said. "I know I will do better." Henry put the shaker back on the table and used his finger to sweep the pepper into a little pile.

Calvin, Caldonia's twin brother, said to her, "I've been telling you for years that you ride that way and you have never listened to me."

Her eyes were still on Henry and for the moment she had forgotten where Calvin was sitting. He was two people to the left of Henry, but Caldonia began looking to the right for him, not really focusing very well because her concentration was on Henry. "Well, dear brother," she said as her eyes went from the right to the left, trying to direct her words to her brother. "Dear brother, you never in all that time spoke to me as if my life depended upon what you were saying." Everyone laughed and Frieda said, "Touché."

Fern said to Anderson Frazier, "Caldonia's father was alive then, so he was there to give his permission to Henry's courting her. The mother's maid went about with them, as good girls did not go about alone with men they were not related to. Had her father been dead, I do not think her mother would have given permission, and Caldonia did not then have a mind to go against her mother."

"Why," Anderson asked, "would she not have given her permission?"

Fern was reminded again that he was white. If he were to come to know things about black people, about what skin was thought worthy and what skin was not, he would not learn them from her. "I don't know why," she said. "Maude, her mother, could be peculiar about certain things."

Henry's funeral lasted a little more than an hour. All the slaves he owned surrounded his family and friends and the hole where they put him. Because Valtims Moffett was late, they started without him. Not knowing when Moffett would arrive, Caldonia decided that there, at the end, God would not hold it against Henry Townsend for not having a proper conductor on his last train. Mildred spoke for a long time. She rambled and everyone knew that was fine and Caldonia had her arm through Mildred's the whole time. Fern sang a song about Jesus that she had learned as a child. She started to sing believing she still knew the words, but midway through the song her memory failed and she proceeded with words she made up. Augustus did not speak. Robbins, with Dora and Louis on either side, did not speak. A storm came into his head and he missed a good part of the service. This was Robbins's second colored funeral in less than a year. One of the first slaves he ever owned had died, had stood in the field, stopped working and slowly sank down and down to one knee, then the other knee. The slave was alone in his row, his full sack around his neck, and for a long time people worked on and did not notice that Michael had disappeared. "You make a soft place for me in the bye and bye, son," Mildred said at her son's grave, "and I'll be along directly."

Moses and Stamford and Elias filled in the hole. The people of the field had that day off, but the servants of the house worked very late caring for those who stayed to mourn and remember Henry. Robbins did not stay. He had come in on a horse, not in the surrey of the day before.

A fter the Richmond evening when Robbins hit her, Philomena Cartwright would not see the city again for many, many years. Her jaw did not heal properly and she could never eat hard food on that side of her mouth. The one time she threatened to flee and return to Richmond, Robbins told her he would sell her back into slavery. "You can't," she said. "You can't, William. I got my free papers." He told her that in a world where people believed in a God they could not see and pretended the wind was his voice, paper meant nothing, that it had only the power that he, Robbins, would give it. When she saw Richmond that third and final time, it was on a day not long after the Army of the North had burned most of it to the ground. She was forty-four years old then, and it had been thirty years since the day Robbins first saw her with the laundry on her head, practically skipping along, her mind full of what Sophie had been telling her about Richmond. The fires were still smoldering in Richmond when Philomena got there that last time, and she commented to Louis and Dora and Caldonia and her grandson, Robbins, that the fires on the ground were a poor substitute for fireworks in the air.

5

That Business Up in Arlington.
A Cow Borrows a Life from a Cat. The Known World.

Because Manchester County was mostly a tranquil place, there were months and months when Sheriff John Skiffington had no more to do than tell a drunk to go home, and often that drunk was Barnum Kinsey, one of his patrollers. Once or twice every few months Skiffington and his wife Winifred would accept an invitation for supper from a family, and perhaps stay a night or two when it was too far to return home the same day. They loved the companionship of others, especially Winifred, and, too, Skiffington knew the value of having voters know him as a good man and a good husband, separate from being the good face of the law. If they stayed with a family of means similar to their own, the supper might include couples from the same class and perhaps one, but generally only one, from William Robbins's class. They also stayed with people in Robbins's sphere, but when they ate with them, Skiffington and Winifred represented their class alone. As for the class that produced the patrollers, they were a hand-to-mouth people and invitations to anywhere were very rare.

In the spring of 1844, many white people in Manchester County remained uneasy about news from other places about slave "restless-ness" that had gone on a few years before. In the North, people called it slave uprisings, but in much of Virginia the word *uprisings* had an abolitionist undertone and was felt to be too strong for what many slaveowners preferred to characterize as "a family squabble," instigated by unknowns not part of the family. One of those who could not shake her uneasiness was a fifty-four-year-old cousin of Winifred's, Clara Martin. She lived in the most eastern part of Manchester, as far east as Augustus and Mildred Townsend lived in the west. Clara had a distant relative up in Arlington who had a neighbor whose slave cook had been caught, after many such meals, putting ground-up glass in the neighbor's food. The distant relative wrote to Clara that it was "especially heinous" because the neighbor had raised the cook, Epetha, from a pickaninny, taught her all there was to know about a kitchen, "up and down, and sideways." Clara read the letter over and over, trying to imagine how the glass could have been ground up so fine that the poor, trusting woman did not know what she was eating. Had she been served greens all those times, Clara wondered, and so was fooled into thinking that the glass was nothing more than grit because the greens hadn't been properly cleaned? Had she even once reprimanded the cook about unwashed greens? Was the glass still in her, tearing up her insides because, unlike real food, it did not know the right way to come out?

Clara Martin had but one slave to her name, fifty-five-year-old Ralph, a thin man with hair down to his shoulders who suffered with rheumatism throughout the winter. All through those months, hobbled, he moved through a world of thick molasses, suppressing a moan with each step. But come March, his bones, as he put it, got happy again. Ralph had been in her husband's family since his birth and had come along when she, at twenty, married "my dear sweet Mr. Martin." Her husband had been dead ten years, and their only child, a son, had gone to find an eternally elusive happiness in untamed California, "on the other side of the world," as Clara once put it in a letter to her Arlington relative. So for years Clara had lived alone, peacefully, with Ralph, who did the cooking, among other tasks, for her. Her nearest neighbor was a long walk away into another county. And then the slaves became restless in other Virginia counties, followed by that awful letter about a once faithful slave up in Arlington who didn't want to follow the usual recipes anymore.

That spring of 1844 on a Friday, Skiffington and Winifred went out to spend time with Clara. They left Minerva—then twelve and coming into her own—at home; Winifred, and even Skiffington, might think of her as a kind of daughter but everyone knew who was included in a supper invitation and who was not. There was but one prisoner in the jail, and Skiffington's father had agreed to feed and watch over him. The prisoner, an amiable Frenchman named Jean Broussard, had murdered his Scandinavian partner, the first murder of a white person in the county in twenty-six years. Broussard liked to talk. He liked to sing even more. Skiffington had grown tired of Broussard calling him "Monsieur Sheriff." Indicted only three days before Skiffington left for Clara's, Broussard had been waiting for Virginia authorities to find a judge to come out his way for a trial. Broussard said he was innocent, and he said American justice would ultimately proclaim it so.

By mid-morning of that Friday, Skiffington and Winifred had reached the plantation of Robert and Alfreda Colfax, a white family with ninety-seven slaves to their names, and it was there that they took a twelve-thirty dinner. Robert had a collection of antique European pistols that he loved to show anyone he felt was capable of enjoying them without letting envy intrude. His problem was that most men envied, so he could not show the pistols the way he wanted. Robbins, a good friend to Colfax, did not envy and they often enjoyed them together, sometimes well into the night. Skiffington also did not envy. Colfax's sons thought the pistols no more than toys. So he loved when Skiffington visited because they could, together, with such care, take down the pistols one by one from the cabinet Augustus Townsend had made and admire what some German or Italian had crafted a long time ago as if his life had depended upon it.

The Friday Skiffington and Winifred arrived about three o'clock, Clara Martin was standing in the yard, and Ralph came from around the back and took their horse and carriage. "Good mornin, Mr. Skiffington. Good mornin to you, Miss Skiffington," he said. His long hair was tied back with a rope.

Skiffington and Winifred said good afternoon. Ralph turned and looked at them, then nodded. "Yes. Yes, good noon," he said. Clara watched him lead the horse and carriage away and when he was gone, she gave Skiffington a knowing look. "What am I gonna do with him, John?" she said.

He smiled. "He's fine, Clara. A little slow, but he's fine." Skiffington had had his patrollers look in on her from time to time but that had not been enough. "John, she skittish as a colt," Barnum Kinsey told Skiffington after one visit. "And to tell you the truth, John, I ain't seen nothin for her to be skittish about. I looked but I couldn't find it."

They ate a little after five, with Ralph preparing the meal and then retiring to his room that had been built onto the kitchen not long after Clara had married. Clara picked at the food. Winifred and Skiffington ate heartily, hoping that their good appetites would show her that there was nothing to fear. She said nothing but Winifred could see that Clara had lost weight since the last time she saw her. Winifred had had an aunt who had wasted away to skin and bones but that had been from consumption and the woman had lived in Connecticut.

"I'd like you to talk to him," Clara said to Skiffington after supper. They were in the parlor. Ralph had appeared to take away the dishes and then disappeared again before bringing in coffee some fifteen minutes later. The rope was gone from his hair. Once, some five years before, he had come into the parlor and found Clara struggling to comb and brush her hair. "Oh, my goodness," she kept saying. "Better

I should have no hair at all than all this mess." "Now don't you say that, Miss Martin." "Well, it's just a mess, Ralph. It most certainly is." It had been raining all day and it was summer so his bones gave him nothing to complain about. "My sister," she said, "got the hair God shoulda given me. And she has never appreciated it, I must say. Wondrous red hair. A queen's hair. Not one day has she thanked God for that hair and yet he lets her keep it right on." "Yo sister got nothin on you, thas for sure, Miss Martin. Let me now, if that be fine with you," he said, standing behind her, touching the back of her hand. He had never touched her before in any deliberate way, only in some innocent, accidental way no witness would ever think anything about. Hesitantly, she raised her hand higher and after a few seconds she opened it and he took the brush. There had been thunder and lightning earlier in the day but now there was only rain, falling on the porch, tapping the window, watering the plants in the garden that had gone so long without. "Let me, if that be fine with you," and he gently worked through her hair. When the brush had done its work, he reached around without asking permission and took the comb, which had been resting in the very center of her lap. There were a few strands of hair in the comb and he took them out and they took their own time falling to the floor. She leaned back in the chair and closed her eyes, thinking, *Yo sister got nothin on you*. He spent an hour on it, brushing and combing and applying a little sweet oil, and before he was done, she had fallen asleep, which was unusual for her because she always said the bed was the only place where her body could sleep. She awoke hours later to find Ralph gone and her hair in plaits, soft to her fingers, callused and bony. She called his name, once and once again, and when she saw the candle, dancing with a feeble light, and became aware of a silence that seemed to have a kind of voice, she thought there was something wrong in calling him like that and so closed her mouth. She sighed and leaned back in the chair. She soon fell asleep again and stayed much of the night in the chair. The rain went on for another two days and he did her hair each of those days but never again after that. "That should do, Ralph," she said that final time. "That will do for now." "Yessum."

As they drank their coffee, Clara said again to Skiffington, "I'd like you to talk to him."

"Now what would I say to him, Clara?" Skiffington said.

"I don't know. Somethin sheriff like. Somethin a sheriff would say to a miscreant. A possible miscreant. 'I have my eyes on you, you possible miscreant.' "

Winifred laughed. She had been drinking coffee at that moment and now set the cup on the tiny table beside her. The laughter came from what Clara had said but also because the word *miscreant* reminded her of school days and spelling tests in Philadelphia. Her husband had been sheriff for about a year. He called her "Mrs. Skiffington," and she called him "Mr. Skiffington," except when he had displeased her or made her unhappy, and then he was "John" for days and days.

"It is all so very serious, John," Clara said. "It really is. You have no servants to speak of, only a child you have raised. But Ralph is not a child, and the world is changing from once upon a time."

"But you've known him for a very long time, haven't you?" Skiffington said.

Winifred turned to Skiffington. "Since before God sent the flood to Noah, probably."

Clara said, "Time has no meaning anymore, Winnie. Loyalty either. The world is turning upside down."

"Has he said something to you to make you afraid?" Skiffington said. "Something," and he winked at his wife, "something I could arrest him on."

"No, no, Lord no. There is just . . . ," and Clara held her hand out before her and fanned it a few times. "There is just the miasma. The miasma he and I have."

Winifred thought: *M-I-A-S-M-A.*

"What is that?" Skiffington asked. "What is that word?" It certainly wasn't one he had ever come across in the Bible.

"It's the air, Mr. Skiffington," Winifred said, then tapped her forefinger to her closed lips as she fought with her memory for a better meaning. "It's the atmosphere. It's the air."

"Bad air," Clara said. "Bad air."

"I'll go out to talk with him before I leave," Skiffington said.

"What will you say?" Clara said. "Don't say anything to hurt his feelings. Please don't say anything mean, John."

"Clara, either he is a miscreant or he isn't. I don't know what I'll say. None of it will come to me until I'm standing before him. But it won't be anything harsh because I think he's a good servant, and I have to tell you that or I wouldn't be honest with you. He's served you all these years and he will go on serving you, despite all the foolishness you hear from somewhere else."

Clara sighed. "A half a loaf is better than nothin."

"A slice of bread is better than nothing," Winifred said.

After the women had retired for the night, Skiffington remained in the parlor, reading the Bible, as he often did at home, after Winifred and Minerva had gone to bed. His father smoked a pipe at night before sleeping, and while the son had tried to take it up, he had not found the enjoyment his father had. It was a pity, he often thought, because the words of God sometimes put his mind in a turmoil that a pipe might calm.

He heard Ralph in the back and got up, placing the Bible open to his page on the chair. In the kitchen, Ralph was in the last stages of cleaning up before going to bed.

"Is there somethin I might get you this mornin, Mr. Skiffington?" he said as Skiffington stood in the doorway. "We got some more that pie you was so fond of. Put a nice little piece on a plate for you, send you off to sleep like a baby."

"No, Ralph. I just wanted to come in and say good night. I wanted to make sure everything was fine with you. I know caring for Miss

Clara can be a mighty chore. You have served her well and she knows that."

"Night? Good night?"

"Yes. I just wanted to say good night."

"Yessuh. Thank you. And good night, suh."

"Yes, well . . . Good night."

"And good night to you, suh. A good night." His hair was in the rope again. "No pie? It's fine pie if I say so myself."

"No, thank you. But good night. And thank you for a fine meal. For the pie, too."

"And thank you, too, suh. A good night. And good mornin when mornin comes."

"Good night." Skiffington left, the awkwardness still in the air. He went back to the parlor and picked up the Bible where he had left off. But that chapter was not what he felt he needed right then so he flipped through the book and settled on Job, after God had given him so much more, far more than what he had before God devastated his life.

He told Clara the next day that he had spoken with Ralph and that all was well, that she was not to worry anymore. "Worry bout rain for your garden, and don't go any higher on the worry ladder," he told her.

He had business with two patrollers—Harvey Travis and Clarence Wilford—several miles from her, and after dinner, near one o'clock, he set out on a horse Ralph saddled for him. The Saturday was cloudy but he was confident that he could get there and back before the rain, if rain there was.

When the group of patrollers were formed, Barnum Kinsey and Oden Peoples, brother-in-law to Harvey Travis, were the only patrollers who owned slaves. The patrollers were paid $8 a month, mostly from the tax on slaveowners, a levy of 5 cents a slave every other month. (The tax went to 10 cents a slave with the start of the War between the States, and it was enforced through most of 1863.) Barnum Kinsey was exempt from the tax for the time his one slave Jeff was alive, and Oden Peoples was never taxed.

Oden was a full-blooded Cherokee. He had four black slaves. One was his "mother-in-law." Another was his "wife," who was half-Cherokee herself, and the other two were their children. His wife had belonged to Oden's father, and so had the mother-in-law. When Oden took Tassock as his woman, the father threw in her mother because he thought Oden's woman might be lonely so far away from the village where she had been his slave. Oden's father liked to go about the world claiming he was a Cherokee chief, the leader of a thousand people, but that was not true, and people, black and white and Indian, would ridicule him about the lie, to his face and behind his back. "Chief Tell-A-Lie," they called him.

Oden's wife was half sister to a woman the patroller Harvey Travis had married. She, too, had been a slave, though full Cherokee, but Travis essentially bought her from Chief Tell-A-Lie and freed her, saying he would never marry a slave.

In so many ways, Travis became Skiffington's most difficult patroller. But Travis was good at what he did, and Skiffington saw him as a free-ranging cat who couldn't be tamed but who killed enough mice to make up for his lawlessness.

That cloudy Saturday after dinner at Clara's, Skiffington rode out because of a dispute Travis had with the patroller Clarence Wilford. Travis had a dying cow that he decided to sell to Clarence and his wife Beth Ann. Harvey got $15 and claimed to Clarence that the cow was a good milker, though in fact more milk fell from the sky than came from the cow. Clarence had eight children and they were getting to the point where they were forgetting what cow milk tasted like. Indeed, his three youngest had only tasted their mother's milk.

So Beth Ann and Clarence bought the cow and waited and waited for the milk to come. "I've never known drier teats," Clarence told his wife. That went on for weeks, with Clarence stewing and growing ever more angry with Harvey. It was so bad that during patrols they would argue and fight and no other patrollers wanted to work with them.

Then, a week before the Saturday John Skiffington showed up, Clarence came out of his house, determined to slaughter the cow and settle for the meat he could get. He knew the problem he would have, for his children had taken a liking to the cow, had even given the thing a number of pet names in the time she was with them. Clarence came out to the barn and found his wife Beth Ann on her haunches milking the cow. She looked up at him and her whole face was wet with tears. "Dear dear Jesus," she was saying. She was using the water bucket to catch the milk and as she milked with both hands, she was trying to dry the tears from her face with the sleeves of her blouse, lest the tears fall into the milk. "She was mooin out here and I just came in to see what was the matter."

Clarence went to his wife, kissed her cheek. "Call em," she said to him, speaking of the children. "Call em all in here." He stood up from her and stepped back once, twice, three times, then he turned his back and shot around to see if the milk was still there. As if she could read his mind, Beth Ann took one teat and aimed it at a cat standing to her side. The cat closed its eyes and opened its mouth and drank. Its tail had been in the air, but as it drank, the tail lowered and lowered until it was at last resting on the ground.

The children came in, the big ones carrying the little ones. They all drank from the bucket and when it was empty, their mother filled it again. Then she filled it twice more. Soon, the children, on the barn floor, lay down and fell asleep. Clarence sat beside his wife and after a time he put a hand, the one not stained with milk, to the back of his wife's head and rubbed her hair. The cow swung its tail and chewed its cud. It farted.

In the end, the parents had to carry all the children into the house to bed because the children did not want to rouse up and walk in. "You know what this means?" Beth Ann said as they carried in the last of the children. "Tell me?" he said. "It means we'll have to get a new water bucket."

Harvey Travis wanted the cow back because a cow flowing with milk was not what he had taken $15 for. Clarence had told Skiffington that he had been shot at twice and though he hadn't seen the shooter, he believed it was Harvey. Beth Ann sent word to Skiffington by patroller Barnum Kinsey: "We will kill him or he will kill us."

Skiffington got to Clarence's place and found Beth Ann with two of the children in the garden. Clarence was in the woods and she sent one of the children to fetch him. Skiffington sent the other child to get Harvey, then he and Beth Ann went into the barn so he could see the cow.

"I'm glad you're here, John," she said, clapping off the dirt from her hands. Skiffington knew her to be the more fiery of the two. "Maybe you can make some sense of this whole mess. I sure can't, and Clarence can make less sense than me." A few chickens scurried as they made their way to the barn. Her long black hair was slightly unkempt, and he saw that it would have taken only a few brush strokes to make it pleasing. The Wilfords were poor but not as poor as the family of Barnum Kinsey.

"I wouldn't wanna leave here, Beth Ann, without a full settlement."

"I want you to know I meant what I said about killin Harvey Travis. If it comes to him or the father of my children, I would not hesitate." Barnum had told Skiffington that word about killing had come from both man and wife. Now he knew that the wife was the sole author, and he could see why Clarence, a man who had craved peace all his life, would want a woman like Beth Ann as his wife.

The barn door was ajar and she forced it open with a hand and a foot.

The cow was scrawnier than Skiffington had imagined, dull yellow with brown spots the size of platters. Dull yellow eyes, too. Something Joseph might have dreamed up and warned Pharaoh about. All that week the Wilford children had been calling the cow Smiley.

When they came out of the barn, Clarence was coming upon them in a trot, sweating, and in little more than a minute, Harvey came over the rise with two of his boys and Clarence's boy that Skiffington had sent to get him. None of Travis's children favored him. They all looked like his Cherokee wife, though they were lighter than she was, and that light skin was Travis's only gift to them.

"You sell Clarence and Beth Ann that cow?" Skiffington asked Travis. Skiffington's dinner had not set well with him and he was now, suddenly, impatient.

"Yes, I did, John."

"Well, that should be the end of it, Harvey," Skiffington said. "The law is on Clarence's side. Square bargain. Clean deal."

"Now wait here a minute, John," Travis said. "Maybe I shoulda got to you first and pled my case, steada bein second to testify like I am."

"John, you can see what we had to wrestle with out here," Beth Ann said. "This kinda talk and bullets to keep em company."

"The only bullets were from your side." Travis looked at Skiffington. "Or are you to believe all her side on that too?"

"I take no side but the right one," Skiffington said to Travis, "and if you don't believe that then you can turn around and go home." He waited. "I ain't got time to waste on this cow business, Harvey. I don't want my patrollers actin like this." He and Harvey were now facing each other. Beth Ann knew enough about life to know when things

were dancing their way so she was quiet. Skiffington stepped to Travis
so they were but two feet apart. "You tell me this, Harvey: If that cow
had died a day after you sold it to him, a day after now. No, not a day,
not even a day. One hour after you sold it to him, just long enough for
Clarence to lead the thing from your place, over the rise to his place
so all them hooves are standing on his land and he owned it free and
clear and then it up and drop dead on him, would you give him his
money back? Would you think you sold him a dead cow and give him
his money back? Now would you?"

"I'd feel it was the right thing maybe, seein as how . . . I mean after all, the cow didn't live long enough . . ."

Skiffington was disappointed in the answer but he knew he should
not have been. He took Harvey's shoulder and they walked away from
everyone. "You sold him the cow, Harvey, and there ain't a thing I can
do. There ain't even nothing President Fillmore can do. You know
that if I thought there was something wrong, that if Beth Ann and
Clarence was wrong in any way, I would stand up for you. I would
move heaven and earth to make it right for you, Harvey. Do you understand me?"

"Yes, John, I do."

"I'm sorry. I don't want any more bad things between you two
men, not a one. Do you understand me, Harvey?"

"Yes, John, I do."

"I'll say this to you: Twice a week you send two of your chaps over
here with whatever they can carry to take back some milk. But only
two of them chaps, Harvey, and just twice a week. No return trips for
that day. One trip and that's all. And never you or your wife are to
come."

Travis wiped his mouth with his hand, then wiped his brow with
his sleeved arm. His eyes teared because he had gotten the worst of it
after setting out with a plan five weeks before that should have left
him on top with $15. He nodded.

"Stand here," Skiffington said and went back to Clarence and Beth Ann, who agreed to what he had told Harvey.

"John, am I gonna have any more trouble outa him, shootin trouble?" Beth Ann asked.

"Will this end, John?" Clarence said.

"There won't be no more. No more of this."

"By whose word then, John?" Beth Ann said. "His word or your word?"

"First his word, then backed up by my word," Skiffington said.

"Good," and she shook Skiffington's hand and then he shook her husband's hand.

Skiffington went back to Travis. "If things stay peaceful, then there might be more days with milk for you, Harvey, but that has to come from Clarence and Beth Ann. They can give you more days cause it's their property." Harvey nodded. He turned to leave. "And, Harvey, if someone shoots at Clarence again, I will come out to get you, and it will be a different world for you, your wife and your chaps."

Travis said nothing but shook Skiffington's hand and collected his children and went down and over the rise. He still had some of the $15 he had received for the cow, but it would not give him the pleasure he had known before he learned that the cow had another life. Skiffington watched him. Travis had a child on either side of him, both with their black Cherokee hair flowing and both almost as dark as their mother. One of Travis's children looked up and said something to Travis and Travis, before they all disappeared, looked down to answer the child, the man's head seeming to go down in small stages, heavy with bitterness. The boy nodded at whatever his father had told him.

R iding back to Clara's, he was surprised that it had gone well. He could tell by the way Harvey walked away holding his children by the hand that he would keep his word and there would be no more trouble with the cow. His stomach continued to bother him. He often told Winifred that he was a man coming apart at all his seams—bad stomach, bad teeth, a twitch in the left leg before falling to sleep. A twitch in the right to wake him during the night.

About midway back to Clara's, he decided to walk, seeing that there would be no rain and thinking the walk would ease his stomach. He sensed that Clara's horse was not one to saunter away so he dropped the reins and the horse followed behind him, like a dog. Then the sun came out brighter, then even brighter, and he stopped and took out his Bible from the saddlebag and sat down under a dogwood tree. Before he opened the Bible, he looked all around, at the way the sun poured down over two peach trees and over the hills. The baby's breath swayed every which way, and as he looked, he grew happier. This is what my God has given me, he thought.

He liked to think at such times that all the people in his life were as contented as he was but he knew the folly of that thought. Clara was good and Winifred and his father and even the child Minerva, growing every day beyond childhood. Maybe Barnum Kinsey the patroller had had a good night and had not awakened with a pained head from a night of drinking. A boy down the road from Skiffington had burned his leg at the fireplace and Skiffington hoped the boy was doing well. He and the boy liked to fish together; the boy knew how to be silent, which was something not easily taught to a child fisherman. He liked the boy very much but he longed for the day when he would have a child of his own.

Skiffington flipped through the pages of the Bible, wanting something to companion his mood. He came to the place in Genesis where two angels disguised as strangers are guests in Lot's house. The men in the town came to the house, wanting Lot to send out the strangers so that they could use them as they would use women. Lot sought to protect the strangers and offered the men his virgin daughters instead. It was one of the more disturbing passages in the Bible for Skiffington and he was tempted to pass on, to find his way to Psalms and Revelation or to Matthew, but he knew that Lot and the daughters and the angels posing as strangers were all part of God's plan. The angels blinded the men as they tried to storm Lot's house, and then, the next morning, the angels laid waste to the town. Skiffington looked up and followed a male cardinal as it flew from left to right and settled in one of the peach trees, a red spot on shimmering green. The female, dull brown, followed, alighting on a branch just above the male's head. Winifred had always felt such pity for Lot's wife and what happened to her, but Skiffington had no strong opinion either way about what happened to her.

So he read through the passage, and not for the second time, and not for the third, and not for the fourth. Then he moved on to Psalms, and after four of those he thought it best to get on to Clara's. The male cardinal was still there but the female had disappeared.

He never worked on Sunday, the Lord's day, but riding the carriage back to town with Winifred was far from work. After breakfast, Ralph had brought the carriage around and Skiffington and Winifred and Clara came out. "I be wishin yall good mornin," Ralph said before he disappeared behind the house. "It's a good day for a ride. A good day for whatever it is a soul want it to be."

"Yes," Winifred said, "a good day for everything."

Clara had been quiet the last evening and just as quiet that morning. Now, her arms folded across her breasts, she watched as Skiffington helped Winifred into the carriage and he came around, kissed her cheek and got in the carriage.

"I'll take your word that everything will be fine"—and she tipped her head in the direction of the back of the house where Ralph was. They, Clara and Ralph, would live another twenty-one years together. Long before then he became a free man because the War between the States came and found them. With freedom, Ralph got it into his head that he would go elsewhere. He had people in Washington, D.C. But

Clara cried and cried and said this old place, this old damn place wouldn't be the same if Ralph wasn't traipsing morning, noon and night all about on it. So he chose to stay; his kin in Washington had never been likable people anyway—one of them was a natural-born drunkard.

"You have my word," Skiffington said, taking the reins from Winifred. "You got that and more."

"John, I just don't know what I would do if Ralph ended up murdering me. What would I do, John?" And after that twenty-one years, Clara would die first, asleep in her bed, a knife under her pillow and another beside her in the bed, as close as a lover. Her hair flowed about her head, not done up but loose, the way she sometimes liked it when she slept, the way Ralph's hair was when it wasn't held back by the rope.

Skiffington smiled. "I would come out and arrest him. That's the first thing I would do."

On that Sunday, the day Skiffington and Winifred left, Clara had been eating Ralph's cooking for more than twenty-four years. But after that day, even though she knew no more about cooking than a bird sitting on a nest, she fixed her own meals and she sat across from him while he ate what he had prepared and looked at her and spoke about happy times as she ate what she had prepared.

"Mr. Skiffington would come out, arrest him and take him in to jail, Clara," Winifred said. "Quicker than you could say Jack Rabbit."

For some reason this seemed to ease Clara's mind more than anything else he or Winifred had said that weekend. She smiled and smiled and wouldn't let loose of the smile even as Skiffington took her cheek in his hand and tugged on it twice. The door to her bedroom was always locked. When she did not come down to fix her breakfast the day she died, Ralph went up and knocked. After more than half an hour of knocking and calling her name, he went out, his own breakfast getting cold on the kitchen table, and he walked two miles to the nearest farm, all the way into neighboring Hanover County, and brought back a white man and the white man's one-armed cousin and the two white men forced the door open. The door had been se-cured each night for years with two nails.

"Clara, we'll see you before long, surely before the end of June, unless you come into town," Winifred said.

"Good, you know how I look forward to Mr. and Mrs. Skiffington. The Skiffingtons have a place at my table anytime." Ralph would go to live with his people in Washington, for with Clara's death relatives materialized from high and low and he was then without a home. The relatives sold the land to William Robbins, which angered Robert Colfax. Ralph's people in Washington were not as bad as he had al-ways thought. The drunkard had found God a week after a Fourth of July and had said good-bye to the bottle for good.

They rode home sitting close in the carriage, her arm through his and Skiffington singing a few songs his mother sang to him when he was a child in North Carolina on his cousin Counsel's place. Then they talked for the first time about what life they wanted in Penn-sylvania in a few years when he left the job as the sheriff of Man-chester County. She wished to be close to relatives, particularly her sister, in Philadelphia. He wasn't awfully partial to Philadelphia, but doing a visit up there a year before, they had come upon a nice area around Darby, just outside Philadelphia. There was even a place for him to fish, a good place to teach a son how to be patient and silent and appreciate what God had done for them.

"Will your daddy come? I wouldn't like to think of him down here without us."

Skiffington smiled and Winifred leaned her head on his shoulder. "The South is all he knows, but he can fish for souls up there just as easy as he can down here," he said. His father had taken up evangel-ism but he was quiet about it, diplomatic, never wanting to force his religion down someone's throat unless they gave him permission.

"Yes, well, I have a feeling that he'll like the challenge of the peo-

ple in Pennsylvania," Winifred said. "If you present your case in just
the right way, they'll accept."

"Like you did with me."

She laughed and raised her head and looked at him. "I would say,
Mr. Skiffington, that it was the reverse of that. I was standing in one
spot and you walked over to me. I wasn't raised to live any other way."

He said nothing.

"And Minerva?" Winifred said.

"She would come, too, that is if she isn't grown and off on her own
when we leave." He could see Minerva, out in the back of their house,
near the chicken coop, reaching up to pick apples, the ones not quite
ripe and so best for a pie. "We can make a way for her in Pennsylvania.
And if she is grown, then there will be nothing to talk about. It will be
her life to do with as she pleases."

"I want her up there with me as well," Winifred said. "I would
hate to be home without her. I want everybody I love up there, like in
a big garden where we wouldn't want for anything."

"I think Adam and Eve might have taken that from us,"
Skiffington said. "And Pennsylvania may be as far from Eden as we
can get."

"Pooh."

"We'll make our own way. I give you my word."

"Then I take the pooh back." She held her hand out before her.
"Come back pooh." She opened her hand and then put it to her open
mouth and clamped her mouth shut. "There, pooh is back." A little
farther on she yawned and closed her eyes with her head against his
shoulder. He went back to singing. Soon she was asleep but he went
on singing anyway, just a mite softer than before.

Minerva was waiting at the gate when they pulled up. She waved
and they waved to her. She was almost as tall as Winifred. This
was before Skiffington began to think of her in a different way.

"Father Skiffington went to the jail to feed that man," Minerva said. Carl Skiffington, John's father, was not above working on Sunday, and besides, he said, feeding a prisoner was a necessity, not a task that could be put off until Monday. Minerva sailed up the front steps of the house and wrapped her arms around the post. She turned and opened the door and the three went in.

She, Minerva, was not a servant in the way the slaves all about her were, for they did not believe they owned her. She did serve, charged with cleaning the house, sharing the job of cooking the meals with Winifred. But they would not have called her a servant. Had she been able to walk away from them, knew north from south and east from west, Skiffington and Winifred would have gone after her, but it would not have been the way he and his patrollers would pursue an escaped slave. A child would have been lost and so parents do what must be done.

The world did not allow them to think "daughter," though Winifred was to say years later in Philadelphia that she was her daughter. "I must have my daughter back," she said to the printer making up the posters with Minerva's picture on them. "I must have my daughter back."

So she was a daughter and yet not a daughter. She was Minerva. Simply their Minerva. "Minerva, come here." "Minerva, how does this taste?" "Minerva, I'll get the cloth for your dress when I come home from the jail." "Minerva, what would I do without you?" To the white people in Manchester County, she was a kind of pet. "That's the sheriff's Minerva." "That's Mrs. Skiffington's Minerva." And everyone was happy with all of it. As for Minerva, she had known nothing else. "You done growed," Minerva's sister was to say years later in Philadelphia.

John Skiffington got to the jail about eight that Monday morning. "Ah ah, good morning, Monsieur Sheriff," Jean Broussard said as soon as Skiffington came in the door. "I have missed all of your company, though I must say your *père* is a charming and most adequate substitute. He says all the time that God is with me, but that is something I knew long ago. God is everywhere in America, especially here with me."

"Broussard, good morning."

"I do not want to rush the way the world goes, but I am beginning to think I will not be walking free before I am as old as your *père*."

"You say you are innocent, and if that is true, the law will see it and set you free."

"I *am* innocent. I *am* innocent, Monsieur Sheriff." Broussard had claimed all along that he had been defending himself when he killed his partner, a man from Finland or Norway or Sweden, depending upon the mood the partner was in when he was asked where he was from. When the partner was in a foul mood, he said he was from Sweden. He was Swedish the day he died.

"So much depends on when the circuit judge gets here to try your case," Skiffington said, hanging his coat on a rack near the door. Broussard's coat was the only other thing hanging, and it had been hanging there for two weeks. "He gets here, the jury hears you and the whole world belongs to you again. France and any place else you want to go." Skiffington went to his desk and sat, started looking for paper to petition, once more, for the circuit judge to come. The town had not had a need for a judge since a white man a year before was charged with wounding his wife. He was acquitted after the wife, a dressmaker and Robert Colfax's lover, testified that she had somehow shot herself in the back.

"Perhaps not France anymore. I love France. France gave me birth, but I am America now, Monsieur Sheriff. I raise the flag! I raise the flag high over my head and over all your heads, Monsieur Sheriff!"

"Good for you, Broussard. Good for all of us." A man from Culpeper had agreed to come down and defend him. Skiffington found a piece of paper for the petition, and in another drawer he found the list of questions that needed to be answered on the blank paper before someone in Richmond would say the judge could come. Each question had to be written down on the petition paper, followed by the answer. And each question from the list had to be written down even if there was no answer to it. *Nature of the Alleged Crime.*

"I am thinking that I will stay forever to live here, stay in this place and be happy." Broussard had been a citizen of the United States for three years. He had not seen France and his family since he left them eight years ago. He still planned to bring his family to America. Only his two oldest children even remembered what Broussard looked like. "Stay and pursue the happiness, heh, as be always the right of you and me." Broussard's wife had taken a lover two years after he left. The wife and every last one of Broussard's children were in love with the lover. It was a love from which Broussard would not have been able to retrieve them. "I sing America. I sing America happiness."

"Yes," Skiffington said, opening the ink jar, "pursue it to your heart's content." *Name of Alleged Victim or Victims.*

"I will bring my wife here and we will be strong like you and the Mrs. Skiffington. I will be Mr. Broussard and we will be Mr. and Mrs. Broussard. Have a house bigger than yours, Monsieur Sheriff. Do you have a big house, Monsieur Sheriff?" Broussard and his partner, Alm Jorgensen, had come to Manchester with two slaves to sell—Moses, the man who would become Henry Townsend's overseer, and a woman named Bessie. They had heard that Robert Colfax was looking for new slaves, but Colfax was not satisfied with how Broussard and Jorgensen had come about the slaves. "We got the people in Alexandria, goddamn the world," Jorgensen kept telling Colfax. He also told Colfax he was Finnish. But they had no bills of sale for Moses and Bessie, and because Broussard and Jorgensen were strangers, and foreigners to boot, Colfax sent them away.

"My house is big enough for me and my family is about all I can put in it. I told you you could call me John," Skiffington said.

"Yes yes. John, like me is a John, heh?" Broussard had planned to use his share of the money from the sale of Moses and Bessie to bring his wife and children over. After an evening of drinking, he and Jorgensen had fought on the porch of the boardinghouse where they were staying and the Swede had ended up dead.

The jail door opened and William Robbins walked in, followed by Henry Townsend, who was then twenty years old. Henry was a little more than a year from buying Moses, nearly three years from marrying Caldonia. More than half of his time was spent at Robbins's plantation, in a cabin separate from the slave quarters. He was a free man, a bootmaker and shoemaker, coming and going as he pleased, as long as he took his free papers with him.

"John," Robbins said. He reached across the desk and shook Skiffington's hand. The handshake was complete before Skiffington had fully risen.

"Bill."

"Good day," Broussard said, though he didn't know Robbins.

"John, we had a little nasty business with Henry here. Harvey Travis gave him bad treatment not two nights ago when he was leaving my place. He hit Henry once and might have done more if Barnum Kinsey hadn't stepped in to take Henry's side. Bad business, John, very bad business. Henry was only headin to his folks."

Henry had not moved from the door.

"Good day, Monsieur Bill." Broussard was at the bars, as he had been since Skiffington entered.

Robbins turned around. "It was Travis, right?" he asked Henry. "Yessir." "Travis," Robbins said to Skiffington.

"I just saw him Saturday, Bill. Saw Harvey on Saturday."

"About this here business?"

"No, another matter," Skiffington said. "I'll see him again this evening before the patrol. I'll speak to him." He knew of Henry, the boot and shoe Negro, had spoken a few times to him over the years. Skiffington and Winifred and Minerva would be at Henry's funeral. As he looked at Henry standing at the door, Skiffington recalled that he was the son of the furniture maker Augustus and the woman Mildred who, at the far end of the county, might as well be at the end of the world.

Broussard and Jorgensen had gotten the name of William Robbins from Colfax, and it was slowly occurring to Broussard that this was the man Colfax had said might be interested in purchasing Moses and Bessie. "Monsieur. Monsieur Bill, please a moment. Three moment."

"What?" Robbins said.

"Please, we have slaves for you. Two good humans for you." Skiffington explained.

"I didn't come here for no damn slaves," Robbins said to Broussard. He had heard about the Frenchman who had killed his own partner.

"Please. Please. I want to bring my wife and babies here and be America."

Skiffington and Robbins looked at each other and then Skiffington shrugged. Robbins looked for one second at Henry then said to Broussard, "Where is this property?"

"Sawyer has em back of his place, and what little money Broussard had for their upkeep is running out," Skiffington said. "He gets to live here free but I don't know what will become of them when the money runs out."

Robbins turned to Henry. "Go tell Mr. Sawyer to bring the property here, and tell him I want to get home before dinner."

"Yessir," Henry said and left.

"Good humans. The finer of the slaves," Broussard said.

"Plain 'finer' ain't good enough," Robbins said and turned from Skiffington and Broussard and looked out the window that faced the street. "Only the finest will get me out of the bed in the morning."

"Then finest it will be, Monsieur Bill."

Sawyer walked in the door first. He was a fat man and he was out of breath. Then came Moses who turned to help Bessie because there was something wrong with her foot. She was limping and winced with each step. They were without chains, him and her, but Sawyer was holding a pistol. Then came Henry who stayed at the door after everyone had walked into the room.

"See, see, Monsieur Bill. Finest humans."

Moses and Bessie looked at Broussard, then at Skiffington and finally over to Robbins, who had watched them come down the street. He already knew the woman would not do. The injury may not have been permanent, but he saw a kind of unsettling tilt to her walk, as if God had leaned her body just a bit to the side when he made her and bid her walk leaning just to the left for the rest of her life. And he could see that she had been crying and it had nothing to do with the foot. That, the crying, was also a permanent condition, he had decided.

Robbins stepped to Moses. "Take them things off," he said to Moses about the rags he was wearing. "Sir. Master Sir, this woman, her and me is together," Moses said. "Do what I said," Robbins said. In a moment Moses was naked. Robbins walked around him and after squeezing both his arms and legs and looking into his mouth, he said to Broussard, "How much?"

"Eight hundred dollars, Monsieur Bill."

Robbins said, "When I ask you a plain and simple question, I expect no less than a plain and simple answer." Henry shifted from one foot to the other. Broussard held tight to the bars.

Sawyer was still trying to catch his breath. He took out a rag and leaned against the wall. Skiffington had the only chair at his desk. He had been standing beside the desk, but now he took two steps and was in the chair. Sawyer wiped his face and the back of his neck. Skiffington picked up the list of questions. Now he would have to start all over again. *Nature of the Alleged Crime. Are there witnesses to the alleged crime? Can such witnesses be believed?*

"But, Monsieur Bill, they are finer human beings. Please, please, my beautiful wife is waiting."

"Sir, I have never known your wife, beautiful or otherwise, and she has never known me."

"Yes. Yes. Then seven hundred dollars, Monsieur Bill. And five hundred for the woman. Good prices. They come from Alexandria. You have heard of Alexandria. Alexandria, Virginia, has known for the humans it sells. Go to the Alexandria for the best humans to sell, people told me. Alexandria. Ancient like the Egypt."

Skiffington wrote. *Name of Alleged Victim or Victims. Name of Alleged Criminal or Criminals.*

Robbins said to Bessie about her rags, "Take them things out." Henry moved a half step back until the doorknob was in his back. "Please, Master Sir," Moses said, "we together, her and me. Don't pull us apart. We together." It was true that he and Bessie had come from Alexandria, where they first met in a holding pen. And now, after two months, he could not stand the thought of being away from her. "Please, master sir, she and me be family." Robbins ignored him. Bessie began crying again, and she went on crying as she disrobed. Robbins touched her the same as he had touched Moses. "Please . . ." Moses said. "If you say one more word to me," Robbins said to Moses, "I will buy you just to take you out in the street and shoot you. Just one more word."

Skiffington looked up from his papers. *I arrest you for the murder of this nigger right in front of my eyes.*

Robbins went to the bars and said to Broussard, "I will give you five hundred and twenty-five for the man and not a penny more. If you say anything but 'Yes,' I will leave."

"Yes, Monsieur Bill. Yes." Broussard took his hands from the bars and put them at his sides. "Yes, Monsieur."

"What am I gonna do with the woman, Bill?" Sawyer said.

"I don't know, Reese. I really don't know."

Where did the alleged crime occur? That was the easiest question of them all, and he wrote, "Manchester County, Virginia." *Date of the Alleged Crime.* He had forgotten the exact day of the murder and would have to ask Broussard. He knew that way down on the list was a question about witnesses. He would have to ask Broussard about that as well.

"We together, Massa," Moses said to Skiffington. "Me and Bessie together. She all I have in this world. We is one as a family."

"I know that," Skiffington said, trying to write. "Don't you think I know that?" It occurred to him that a white woman might pass the window and have her sensibilities offended by seeing a naked slave man and he stood and went to the window, as a kind of distraction for any woman passing.

"Please, now, we is one, her and me. We is one."

Skiffington saw Mrs. Otis strolling on the other side of the street. She stopped to pass the time of day with Mrs. Taylor, who was obviously in the family way. Mrs. Otis had the hand of her youngest child, a boy who had not developed as swiftly as her other children. Mrs. Taylor laughed at something Mrs. Otis said and put her gloved hand briefly to her mouth. She held her unfurled parasol down and to her side. The Otis boy was fascinated by it. Skiffington liked the Otis boy and thought that all he needed was a few years and he would be no different from any other boy his age. "Give him time," he said more than once to Mr. Otis. He would not say that to Mrs. Otis because she did not believe there was anything wrong with her boy. The boy reached for the parasol and Mrs. Taylor, knowing what he could do if he got hold of it, raised it up and out of his way. While Skiffington was hopeful about the boy's progress, he was not blind. There had to be a problem with a boy sucking three fingers at a time at twelve years old and afraid to leave his mother's side because the demons would eat his private parts. It was that boy, along with his older brother and a slave boy named Teacher, who would burst into flames in front of the dry goods store. The younger white boy first going into flames, then followed by his brother. The slave Teacher would go five minutes after that, just as a man with a bucket of water came running up the street.

Moses said once more that they were together and Sawyer told him to be quiet because he was hurting his ears. "I got only her, Massa. We family."

In moments they were all gone from the jail except Skiffington and his prisoner, who stayed quiet long enough for Skiffington to complete the petition. Then he signed his name and gave his title and ended by putting down the date.

"I will reward you for your assistance, Monsieur Sheriff," Broussard said after a time. He was on his cot and quite pleased with how things had gone, even though he had Bessie yet to sell.

"I want nothing, Broussard. They pay me for what I do here."

Broussard jumped up and came to the bars. "But no. No. I want to show how I appreciate." He pointed to the left wall where Skiffington had hung a map, a browned and yellowed woodcut of some eight feet by six feet. The map had been created by a German, Hans Waldseemuller, who lived in France three centuries before, according to a legend in the bottom right-hand corner. "I live where they make that beautiful map. I know who make them, Monsieur Sheriff, and I can get you better, bigger map. I can do it to show how I appreciate."

"That one will do fine," Skiffington said. A Russian who claimed to be a descendant of Waldseemuller had passed through the town and Skiffington had bought the map from him. He wanted it as a present for Winifred but she thought it too hideous to be in her house. Heading the legend were the words "The Known World." Skiffington suspected the Russian, a man with a white beard down to his stomach, was a Jew but he could not tell a Jew from any other white man.

"I get you better," Broussard said. "I get you better map, and more map of today. Map of today, how the world out together today, not yesterday, not long ago." The Russian had told Skiffington that it was the first time the word *America* had ever been put on a map. The land of North America on the map was smaller than it was in actuality, and where Florida should have been, there was nothing. South America seemed the right size, but it alone of the two continents was called "America." North America went nameless.

"I'm happy with what I got," Skiffington said. The map had come from the Russian in twelve parts, each weighing about three pounds, and Skiffington had had a time putting it together. He did it while Winifred and Minerva were away at Clara's, and when Winifred returned and told him she did not want it in her house, he had to dismantle it and reassemble it again in the jail.

"You see, Monsieur Sheriff," Broussard said. "I get you better. I get you more better map."

Jean Broussard was convicted of murder in the first degree and taken to Richmond and hanged. The ne'er-do-well brother-in-law of the prison warden managed to find in Richmond a Roman Catholic priest—a man who was at a time in his life when all the people in his dreams spoke Latin—and that priest, seeking to escape those dreams, stayed night and day with Broussard until the end. The $525 Broussard would have received for the sale of Moses was conveyed by Skiffington to Richmond, who conveyed it to Washington, D.C., who conveyed it to the French embassy. And in five months the money, now in francs, reached Broussard's widow. Mrs. Broussard never had a fixed idea of America, was never able to comprehend that America was a place of separate states and yet one country at the same time. And with that notion in her head, she was never to understand that the money came from the government of the Commonwealth of Virginia. She, along with her children and her lover, would always believe the money came from the government of the United States of America, and that it was payment for what the government had done to her husband, an American citizen.

The $385 for Bessie, who was sold two weeks after Moses to a blind man and his pious wife in Roanoke, went the same route from the county of Manchester, but somewhere between the county and the ship carrying mail along with discouraged and homesick immigrants returning to Europe, the $385 was lost, or simply taken. Someone enjoyed the money, but it was not the widow Broussard and her children and her lover in Saint-Etienne.

Perhaps it was just as well that Jean Broussard came to the end that he did in America. His family would never have separated from the lover; he would have had to come with them, or they would not have come at all. No, it was over for him in France. Someone had even accidentally broken Broussard's favorite mug. His family could have done worse than the man his wife took up with. The lover was, in his fashion, quite a religious man. And he was handy with a knife. He could carve out a man's heart in the time it took for that human machine to go from one beat to another; and with that same knife the lover was able to peel an apple, without sacrificing any of the apple meat, and present it fresh and whole to a waiting child.

If Alm Jorgensen the murdered man had any heirs, no one knew about them.

The records of the Jean Broussard trial, along with most of the judicial records of nineteenth-century Manchester County, were destroyed in a 1912 fire that killed ten people, including the Negro caretaker of the building where the records were kept, and five dogs and two horses. The Broussard trial took one day; actually, part of a day—the trial itself all that morning and the jury deliberations a portion of the summer afternoon. One of the jurors was a man who had studied the law at the College of William and Mary, where his father and grandfather had gone. When that man, Arthur Brindle, returned from the college to Manchester and began practicing, he found that the law was making him a poor man. So he went into dry goods and he made a good living. He suffered from sleepless nights most of his life, this merchant/lawyer did. He and his wife discovered that if he talked to her about his day before he tried going to sleep, he could manage to pull at least two hours of sleep from the night, which was better than the half hour he usually got when they did not talk. And so the night of the day he and the eleven other men convicted Jean Broussard, he lay beside his wife and told her about it. On the stand, Broussard, the merchant said, kept repeating that he was a proud and upstanding American citizen and that he would never hurt another proud and upstanding American citizen if he could help it. It was not this so much, this repetition of who he was, that hurt his case, the merchant said, yawning and listening to the quiet hum that was his ten children sleeping all about the house. It was not that the defense attorney from Culpeper kept telling the jurors Broussard's Scandinavian partner was not an actual American citizen, though that did not help his case either. It was the accent. The accent gave him "the stench of a dissembler." Everything Broussard said came out warped because of the accent, even when he spoke his own name. The jurors, the merchant told his wife, would have been able to accept why the partner was killed if Broussard had sat on the stand and told his whole story without an accent.

6

*A Frozen Cow and a Frozen Dog. A Cabin
in the Sky. The Taste of Freedom.*

On Sunday, the second day Henry Townsend had been in the ground, Maude Newman, his mother-in-law, came into her daughter's bedroom at the house Henry and Moses had built and sat on the side of Caldonia's bed, took her daughter's hand in one of hers, sighing all the while. "My poor widow child," Maude said. Only moments before, Loretta, Caldonia's maid, had asked her mistress if she wanted her to bring up something for Caldonia to eat or drink. Caldonia told Loretta that her mind was not on food or drink; it was all she could do, she said to the woman who had been with her most of her married life, to open her eyes and to breathe. Loretta said, "Yes, ma'am," knowing how true that must have been, and stepped back to watch Caldonia take her time to raise herself up in bed. Loretta had known of one woman's slave who was required to do virtually everything for her mistress, even to wipe the mistress's hind parts after every bowel movement. Caldonia had always been strong, choosing to do so much on her own, and Loretta had, over time, become more of a companion. "For all thas in her, she coulda been a slave," Loretta had funned once to Celeste, Elias's wife, knowing Celeste could keep secrets.

Once Caldonia was up in the bed and leaning back on the pillows, she stared at Loretta as if to ask what next did the world expect of her. Caldonia looked over at the open chiffarobe, whose door was broken and so would never close properly, looked at the black dress hanging there. It seemed to have its own life, so much life that it could have come down and walked over and placed itself over her body. Fastened itself. Her mother had worn the dress for only a month after Caldonia's father had died. "I cannot do any more time with this dress," Maude had said when she put it away. "Wearing black makes my skin itch. Mr. Newman was a man after God's own heart but why should I suffer now that he is sitting with our Lord?" And Maude's mourning had come to an end.

"My poor widow child," Maude said again.

"Mama, please. Please don't give me this today. Tomorrow. The day after tomorrow, but not today."

"The legacy is your future, Caldonia, and that can't wait. I wish it could, but no. All else can, but not the legacy." For Maude, the legacy meant slaves and land, the foundation of wealth. Her fear was that Caldonia, in her grief, would consider selling the slaves, along with the land, as if to accomplish some wish Henry, tied to the want and need of a material world, had been too afraid to try to fulfill in life. "I don't want you to be like your father, mired in so much grief he didn't know right from wrong."

"I learned from Henry not to let something like grief turn me from right to wrong, Mama." With those words she could see him, in her mother's garden saturated with the smell of honeysuckle, still wearing clothes too heavy for the season, talking about how he would be a master different from any other, the kind of shepherd master God had intended. He had been vague, talking of good food for his slaves, no whippings, short and happy days in the fields. A master looking down on them all like God on his throne looked down on him. He was a young shoemaker, a bootmaker, who more than a year before had completed the generous deal for Moses with William Robbins. But the words did not matter to Caldonia; she was young, unhappy with the courtship prospects all about her, and so even had he talked all afternoon of planting and harvesting tobacco, it would have been a serenade. This was more than a year after Augustus had broken his shoulder with the walking stick of an acorn and squirrels.

Caldonia considered her mother. Henry had been a good master, his widow decided, as good as they come. Yes, he sometimes had to ration the food he gave them. But that was not his fault—had God sent down more food, Henry would certainly have given it to them. Henry was only the middleman in that particular transaction. Yes, he had to have some slaves beaten, but those were the ones who would not do what was right and proper. Spare the rod . . . , the Bible warned. Her husband had done the best he could, and on Judgment Day his slaves would stand before God and testify to that fact.

"Henry taught me well," Caldonia said to her mother.

Caldonia lay back down in the bed and closed her eyes. What would his slaves have said that very day about the kind of master Henry had been? Would they be as generous as they would be on Judgment Day when it was all over and they could afford to be generous? She opened her eyes and Maude was smiling at her. In Fern Elston's class one day when Caldonia was ten, Calvin, her brother, had punched another child on the arm and the boy cried. "I didn't hit him all that hard, Mrs. Elston. I hit him with a soft lick, a baby lick. I didn't hurt him." Fern had come up to Calvin and slapped him and shook him by the shoulders until Calvin cried. "Why are you crying, Calvin? I just gave you a baby lick." When both boys had stopped crying, Fern said gently to Calvin, "The hitter can never be the judge. Only the receiver of the blow can tell you how hard it was, whether it would kill a man or make a baby just yawn."

"I have no doubt that Henry taught you all you need to know," Maude said and squeezed Caldonia's hand. "But like your father, you have too much melancholy in your blood for your own good." The death of his youngest child some thirteen years before had led Tilmon Newman to believe God wanted him to free his slaves, which numbered twelve at the time of the child's death. God, Tilmon told Maude, had failed to get his meaning across with the deaths of Tilmon's parents and his brothers—all of them in captivity—so he had started in on Tilmon's children to bring the lesson closer to home. "Ain't none a yall safe from God," Tilmon said, days after he buried his child, who had been four years old. "Not even you, Maude. He will come through every mountain to get at you."

Loretta now stepped away until her back was touching a bedroom wall. Then she edged herself so that she was all but enveloped by the shadow in the corner. She had to be near if Caldonia wanted her, but it would not do to have Maude think she was taking in every single word of the whatfors and whynots of their lives and making some strange sense of what was overheard. Some white mistresses did not care what their servants heard; they felt the servants had no more ability to hear and judge than the cups and saucers. And some, like Caldonia, saw few servants as confidants. But others, like Maude, felt God had pitted the world against them and no one could be more against them than property that could hear and speak and think. They would never make the mistake of believing a slave was no more than a cup or saucer. It seemed to Loretta that Maude rose each and every morning with the heat under her blood and a sword in both hands, and even her own children had to make known their loyalty to her all over again. Mistresses like that could be far more brutal on a slave, whether she owned the slave or not, and would do everything to separate a nosy slave from what little life she was used to. Years of serving with Caldonia might not mean anything to Maude. In a few moments, as the conversation continued, Loretta made her way unnoticed out into the hall.

"Mama, give me a little peace. My husband is not even cold. Just a little peace before you close me in with this. Moses is taking care of so much. And Calvin is here. I can mourn for just a bit more. Calvin is here."

"Calvin, Calvin," Maude said. "His blood has even more melancholy than yours. Leave it to him and your legacy will be out the door before morning." Caldonia slid down even more in the bed, withdrawing her hand from her mother's. "Don't be some little girl, Caldonia."

"I'm not being a little girl, Mama. I'm just being a poor widow child."

"I won't stand for any foolishness from you, Caldonia." Loretta stood where Caldonia and Maude could not see her but where she could see anyone coming up the stairs. "I won't go through this again." Tilmon Newman, like Augustus Townsend, had worked to purchase his own freedom. His plan had been to buy the freedom of all in his family, some four people, including his parents. But in the early days of his freedom, the young man had met Maude and married and they had started to build a life for themselves, a little land here, one or two slaves there. A child. Maude kept reminding him what a kind man his parents' master was and so his family's bondage was not the burden it was for many other slaves. "You were there," she said. "You know what kind of man Horace Green was. Your parents and your brothers will wait until we are good and set on our feet, until we have enough of everything so they can come into freedom and not want for anything." But in less than three years they all perished before he could buy them away: his mother drowned, his father was killed in a fight with another slave, his oldest brother died of food poisoning from a pig stolen from a neighboring farm, and his youngest brother, sent by his master to find a lost cow in a snowstorm, was discovered four days later, boy and cow huddled and frozen together. The boy and the beast had to be thawed out before they could be buried separately.

Caldonia sat up in bed again. "Mother, Henry worked too hard to give me all of this. I would not squander it away, not in any way you could imagine. I know my duty to what he left me. However much I am Papa's daughter, I am just as much your daughter."

"You must remember that it is so easy to go down into destitution."

Her own family had been free for generations but they had never had enough to buy even one slave. "I would not want that for you. A destitution brought on by grief." They looked at each other. "You should eat something, Caldonia."

"My heart is not in food, Mama."

"Put your heart into it, Caldonia. A little milk. A little bread. Try and put your heart into a little something." Tilmon Newman had planned to find a way to get all his slaves to freedom, had been in touch with a white man from South Carolina who thought they could load them all up and drive up to freedom. "We must go before God with no more than what babies come into the world with," Tilmon told Maude. But she had poisoned Tilmon before anything like that could happen. Arsenic pie. Arsenic coffee. Arsenic meat. The servants had thought she had gone mad wanting to do all the cooking for her husband. "He has done so much for me, so why shouldn't I tend to my husband from time to time?" she said to them. The arsenic devoured Tilmon, ate all the meat and muscle off his bones. "For the life of me," the white doctor said, "I can't find what's ailing him." Years later, Maude still had some arsenic left, kept it in a bottle in a corner beside her chest of drawers. The servants who cleaned that room thought it some remedy for Maude's frequent headaches. The house servants had never gone into the bottle when they had headaches for they all believed that what worked for Maude would never in a month of Sundays work for a slave.

"Some preserves on a piece of bread, then," Caldonia said.

Loretta was standing at the bed. "Some milk?" she said.

"Plain water. Cold, plain water, Loretta. Please."

Maude stood up. "And once she's eaten, Loretta, help her get dressed."

"Yessum."

"I always dress myself, Mama."

"You needn't go on with the old ways, Caldonia."

"They will do for now."

Loretta and Maude left together. Downstairs, Loretta went to the kitchen and Maude went out onto the verandah where she knew she would find Calvin.

"I hope you haven't been at her so early in the morning, Mama," Calvin said. He was leaning against a post and his arms were crossed. He had brought the white man from South Carolina to his father. "With all that legacy rigmarole. She shouldn't have to hear that so soon after burying Henry."

"Calvin, with each day of your life, you pull me deeper into misery," Maude said and stood at the other post. She realized after Tilmon was dead that her husband had known the South Carolina white man, the abolitionist, only because of her son. Within months of where they were that day, Maude would become terribly ill and would stay that way for years. Calvin would stay by her side, a kind of nurse to a mother who really didn't like him anymore. "For the life of me," the white doctor said to Calvin in the third year of his mother's illness, "I can't find what's ailing her."

"I'm sorry for that, Mama," Calvin now said to Maude. "For all the misery." It was getting harder and harder for him to think of a reason to remain in Virginia. He had, as he dug Henry's grave, thought that he would speak to Caldonia about freeing her slaves but he knew now that her mind was not going that way. And, too, his mother was formidable.

Maude came to him. "It's not your fault, Calvin. We are what God puts in us." She touched his arm and he looked at her briefly. "I do not want you to talk to Caldonia about selling her legacy. Telling her that she can be happy somewhere over yonder without all of it." He put a hand over hers, the one that was on his arm. "Don't try to put your dreams in her head."

"That was far from my mind, Mama."

Maude went back inside, then she returned in moments. "I want you to know that I have a legacy for you, whether you want it or not."

"I really don't." He waited for her to remind him that he lived in her house, which was run by slaves. Ate the food they prepared. Slept in a bed they made. Wore clothes they cleaned.

"Still. I have it, Calvin. With Caldonia on her own, I have no one but you to give it to. Everyone else is dead. I will leave it all to you. They may not allow me to take the legacy into heaven, so I will just leave it to you." She went back into the house.

L ater that morning, the slaves of the field went back to their labors. Only those under five years were exempt, cared for in Caldonia's kitchen by seven-year-old Delores. Some weeks, Tessie, Celeste and Elias's six-year-old, cared for the small children. Though it was Sunday, a day Henry always gave them to rest up from the other six, Moses the overseer decided on his own to put them back to work. Valtims Moffett came very early to preach to them and was surprised to see them in the field. He simply shouted out a few words to them as they labored and left without seeking payment. When Calvin—less than two hours after the slaves, including Celeste, four months pregnant, went to the fields—learned what Moses had done, he spoke with Caldonia and she said she wanted no work that day. Calvin went out and told everyone to come out of the fields and go back to their cabins. "Caldonia doesn't want you doing anything more on your own," Calvin told Moses. Moses disturbed him in a way he had never been able to understand and it pleased him to pull Moses down a peg. "Don't do anything without coming to her first. Or me." "Yessir, Mr. Calvin," Moses said. "I understand that now."

Calvin stood at the beginning of the lane and watched the slaves return in twos and threes, the children skipping ahead. He had worked hard to get to know all their names, as he knew the names of all the slaves at places he visited often. He called to people as they came his way, and most of them called or nodded or called him "Mister Calvin." The children were always shy around him and he wondered, again, what they might have been told about him and people like him.

"Now you tell Mistress not to worry," Stamford, the man who lived for young stuff, the man Gloria had turned away, was telling Calvin. "You tell Mistress Stamford said not to worry."

"No, don't let her worry, Massa," said Priscilla, Moses's wife. "It wouldn't do to have her worry her po self to death." The other slaves moved around the three; they knew how Stamford and Priscilla could be.

"You tell Mistress," Stamford said, "that Massa Henry went straight to heaven. He got to them gates and the Lord just opened em right up, said, 'Massa Henry, I been waitin so long for you. Just come right in. I got a special place for you, Massa Henry, right here sida me.' You tell Mistress that Stamford say that, Massa Calvin."

"I'll tell her," Calvin said, trying to remember if Caldonia knew all their names. Once, at twenty, he had gone to spend a week or so with a friend near Fredericksburg and they had met a man, a slave of a white man, on his way home as the evening came on. The slave knew Calvin's friend, a freed man whose family had had a slave but sold him because they could not afford to keep him. Calvin and his friend were drunk.

Alice came up and stuck her head between Priscilla and Stamford and chanted to Calvin, "Massa be dead. Massa be dead. Massa be dyin in the grave."

"How are you, Alice?" Calvin said. There had been something about the way the slave on the Fredericksburg road had so very readily taken off his hat for Calvin's friend and then for Calvin. "Hi you this evenin, Mister Ted?" the man had said to Calvin's friend before putting the hat back on. Calvin, as the friend and the man talked about nothing as the bats took off for the evening, had finally reached around and knocked the man's hat off his head. He did not know what had gotten into him. The drinking, he told himself later. He had always become meaner when he drank. He never saw the slave

again, and the best Calvin could offer as an apology was to never drink
again.

"Oh, gon way from here now, you. Take that mess on way from
here," Priscilla said to Alice, who drifted back and began hopping
away. "When that moon come?" she chanted. "When that moon
come? The sun wanna know when that moon come."

Calvin went back to the house. It was far from twelve o'clock and
he thought that there was a good bit of Sunday left for all of them to
enjoy. The man on the Fredericksburg road had been stunned, as had
Calvin's friend. "Just go on and hit me for doing that to you," Calvin
had said, his hands hard at his sides. "Hit me. Hit me with a good lick
for doing that to you." He knew the man would never have done that
and he hated himself for knowing why the man couldn't. If the man
had hit him a good one, Calvin would not have responded, would have
just let him beat him to the ground.

Calvin turned around from the walk to the house and looked at the
slaves disperse among the cabins and thought aloud so that anyone
within feet of him could have heard, "Our Henry is dead." He wished
that Louis was with him, though he knew nothing would have been
said or done. There was no solution for caring about the man with the
traveling eye. Maybe New York could help take away the love, along
with everything else. He got to the steps of the house and stopped,
counted each step for the first time. The feelings for Louis had been
there for some time, but it was two months ago that he knew it was
all hopeless and that to save himself he had best take himself some-
place else.

They had gone swimming at a creek, the way they had so often
as children after lessons at Fern Elston's. They had tired before long
and come out of the water, Louis following Calvin, and they lay down
on the bank, not five inches between them. Louis was talking about
some woman he was interested in, describing what all had first caught
his eye. That had long been his way with Calvin, to tell of this
and that he had an eye for. They were stretched out, and Calvin, on

his side, was looking at Louis, who was sitting up slightly on his el-
bows. Calvin had noticed a tiny pool of water and sweat that had collected in a small depression at the base of Louis's neck. The pool of
water stayed there for the longest, through all the talk about the
woman, with slight vibrations on the surface of the water as his
friend's words came up and out his mouth. Long before Louis was
done, Calvin had wanted to lean over and drink with his tongue from
the pool. He would have, just then with the final word, but Louis
turned his head slightly and all the water flowed down his chest.
Calvin stood up and said he wanted to go home. One day, he said to
himself, I will call New York my home and all of this will be a long
ways away. Even after the many years as Maude's nurse, he would
never see New York.

Calvin went up the stairs of Caldonia's house and lingered on the
verandah, standing at the post on the right. If he had reached over to
drink, he knew Louis would have tried to kill him right there. "New-
York," as he wrote it in a letter to a friend, would help. He knew no
one there, not a soul, unless the frozen dog counted. In his possessions
he had one of the first photographs ever taken of life in New York
City—a white family sitting all along their porch. They seemed to
live on a farm in that city and on either side of their house Calvin
could see trees and empty space rolling off and down into what appeared to be a valley, at least on the left side of the photograph. A few
of the faces blurred where the people had moved just as the picture
had been taken. In the front yard, alone, was a dog looking off to the
right. The dog was standing, its tail sticking straight out, as if ready
to go at the first word from someone on the porch. There was nothing
blurry about the dog. From the first second Calvin had seen the photograph he had been intrigued by what had caught the dog's attention
and frozen him forever. He had a very tiny hope that when he got to
New York he might be able to find the house and those people and
that dog and learn what had transfixed him. There was a whole world
off to the right that the photograph had not captured. Whatever it

was might be powerful enough, wonderful enough, to wait until Calvin could arrive and see it and know it for himself.

That Sunday Stamford left off from Priscilla and went to Cassandra, Delphie's daughter, to beg her once again to be his woman. Now that Gloria was cold on him, Stamford knew he needed some other young stuff to replace her. Winter would be there before he knew it. The man who told him at twelve that young stuff would help him survive slavery had had the ugliest mouth of teeth. But he seemed to have all the young stuff he could handle. "Young stuff," the man said once, "will drive you crazy if you let it. Tame that young stuff so it don't drive you crazy."

Stamford tapped at Cassandra's cabin door. "Cassandra, you in there?" A few months before he had opened it after knocking for some five minutes and Cassandra had come up to him and punched him in the face. He had tried to be patient since then but patience was not something he had ever picked up. "Cassandra, honey, you in there? It's me, Stamford." The cabin door opened and Cassandra was standing with both hands on her hips. Celeste looked down the lane at him from her door and shook her head. The story of his chasing Cassandra had gone from comical to sad and was now back to comical.

"I'm done hearin you, man? Leave off me now. I'm done hearin what you gotta say."

"Oh, sugar, now you know me. It's Stamford. It's your sweet Stamford."

She stepped back into the room and came back with a piece of wood. "If you don't leave off me, I'm gonna knock you upside the head. I mean it, Stamford."

"But, sugar, it's me, your sweet Stamford. You don't mean that."

She tapped him twice on the top of the head and the dust and dirt on the wood flew about and then settled on his head. "There your sugar," she said. "There all the sugar you gon get from me. Now take it and go on." She tapped him twice again and he stepped quickly back, just in time to avoid more dust and dirt settling on him. "That ain't a nice thing to do to your man, sugar."

He was back the next evening after Moses had released them all from the fields. He came later than usual, having waited until all was clear before he stole flowers from Caldonia's garden. "Sugar, I got somethin for you, sugar." He could hear Cassandra and Alice and Delphie in the cabin. He heard Cassandra tell one of the other women to go see what he wanted, and Alice flung open the door. Her eyes widened at the sight of the flowers, a few red roses and a couple of not very lively begonias. Alice began dancing about. "What is it, Alice? What he doin to you?" Cassandra said. She came to the door in time to see Alice support herself on the doorjamb, lean down and bite into the roses. She chewed and swallowed and went back for more as Stamford moved away.

"You girl, what you go and do that for? Lord have mercy?" he said. "Lord forgive her."

"Serve you right," Cassandra said. "Stealin and then wantin me to be in the stealin with you. Come on in here, Alice," and she closed the door.

What was left of the flowers was at the door at two in the morning when Alice came back from wandering. She brought them in and laid the little bundle beside the sleeping Cassandra on her pallet.

He might have come back again the next night but he had awakened disturbed the night he stole the flowers from a dream he could not remember. The dream went to pieces as soon as he sat up on his pallet, but what came into his head was the thought of his mother and father. He had not seen them in more than thirty-five years. He called out to them there in the dark and received no answer. He was forty years old. He sat on his pallet and began to think that he would never again have young stuff, that he would shrivel up and die alone in slavery. There in the dark he realized that he did not even remember his parents' names. Did they have names? he asked himself as the cabin rose and fell with the snoring of the two other men. Did they have names? They must have, he told himself. All God's children have names. God wouldn't allow it to be otherwise. If his parents did not have names, then maybe they had not existed, and so could not have created him. Maybe he had not even been born, but just appeared one day as a little boy and someone, seeing him alone and naked in some lane, had taken pity on him and given him a home. No mama, no papa, give that po boy a home.

Stamford lay back down and tried to find a comfortable spot on the straw. He turned and turned and finally settled for something on his side. It worried him that he could not remember their names. Maybe if he had thought of them more throughout his life. He closed his eyes and took his parents in his hands and put them all about the plantation where he had last seen them, his mother in his left hand and his father in his right hand. But that did not feel right and so he put his father in his left hand and his mother in his right hand, and that felt better. He set them outside the smokehouse, which had a hole in the roof in the back. "Hants come down that hole and take you to the devil," an older boy had once told him. Stamford was five and it had not been long since his parents had been sold away. "Say Jesus name three times and the hants gon leave you lone." "Jesus Jesus Jesus." "You gotta say it faster than that for the hants to leave you lone." "JesusJesusJesus." "That sound jus bout right."

Stamford set his mother and father down before the cabin they had shared with another woman, and still the names did not come. He left off for a moment to touch his navel and that told him that he had once been somebody's baby boy, been a part of a real live woman who had been with a real man. He had the navel and that was proof he had once belonged to a mother. In his mind, Stamford took up his parents again and put them in front of the master's big house, he put them in front of the master and the mistress, he put them in front of the master's children, big and redheaded and loud as three angry bulls. He put them in the fields, he put them in the sky, and at last he put them before the cemetery where there were no names. And that was it: His mother's name was June, and so he opened his right hand and let her go. His father's name did not come to him, try as he might to put him all about the plantation. Maybe God had slipped just that one time. Stamford slept, and just before dawn he awoke and said into the darkness, "Colter."

He went into a kind of mourning for his parents and did not go back to Cassandra. But he was afraid of death and so, after four days, he got it into his head that Gloria might take him back even though she said she did not want to have anything to do with him. He watched her go about her days, and on Thursday evening, after the fields, he sidled up to her coming back from Celeste and Elias's cabin and said, "Whatcha been doin, sugar?"

"Ain't none a your damn business."

"It be my business cause a what I feel for you."

"Well, be feelin it somewhere else, cause I don't want you feelin it here."

He was trying to be patient so he let her be for two days. At dinnertime Stamford found Gloria in a far part of the field she was working in, and she was eating with Clement, the last slave Henry had purchased before he died. "Whatcha you doin gettin with Gloria for?" he asked Clement.

Gloria laughed and that gave Clement license to ignore the older man. The two went on eating, some biscuit, some molasses.

"I done ask you what you doin with Gloria? She ain't with you."

"Look that way to me," Clement said.

"And look that way to me," Gloria said.

Stamford leaned over and pushed Clement's left shoulder. "You leave off now, Stamford, if you know whas good for you," Clement said.

"All right there now, Stamford," Gloria said, putting her food back in her pail.

"Leave me off, if you know what's good for you," Clement said. He shared the cabin with Stamford and they had always gotten along.

"Oh, I know whas good for me all right. Seem like the only person that don't know it is you." He pushed the shoulder again and Clement shoved the hand away. When he pushed again, Clement stood up.

"I'm gonna call Moses on you, Stamford," Gloria said, also rising. Stamford slapped Clement and Clement punched him in the face, first with one fist and then with the other. Gloria screamed and the other women near them began screaming, too. Stamford began falling with the second punch and all the screaming seemed to push him down more. Clement was upon him and began pummeling. "Leave me be is all I want," Clement said. "Just leave me be. Leave me in peace." Gloria ran to get Moses and Elias and the other men, and the women tried to pull Clement away from Stamford, who was now all blood and cuts and lying very still.

"Stamford," Celeste shouted, "don't you be dead!" and Tessie repeated what her mother had just said, word for word.

The women roused Stamford before the men arrived. Then four men carried Stamford back to his cabin and Moses, who was not one of the four, told everyone to get back to work. He did not want to carry the news to the house, to Caldonia: an overseer was supposed to handle all such little matters, as Henry had once told him. But when he got to the cabin and saw the condition Stamford was in, he knew he could not keep it from her. Celeste and Delphie followed him into the cabin and began tending to Stamford. "Lord, whas got into that old fool?" Delphie said. She was three years older than Stamford.

"Do what yall can to get him straight?" Moses told the women. "I be back."

Stamford was blinking and when he wasn't blinking, his eyes were focused on a spiderweb hanging in a corner of the ceiling. He wanted to tell the people touching him that the web was the hand of the hant, signaling that he was on his way. He opened his mouth and through the blood and loose teeth said to the web, "JesusJesus . . ."

Moses reached the house and saw a white man go up the stairs with a big book under his arm. At the back of the house Moses knocked and Bennett, the cook's husband, opened the door. "Stamford done got hurt," he told Bennett. "Somebody in here gotta know that." "He hurt bad?" Bennett said. He had been friends with Stamford. "Maybe dead bad," Moses said. Bennett said, "Dear Jesus. Lemme tell em up front."

The white man at the front door was from the Atlas Life, Casualty and Assurance Company, based in Hartford, Connecticut. His talking to Calvin at the door was what kept Bennett so long. Calvin eventually came back with Bennett and when Moses told him, Calvin went back and returned with Caldonia, followed by Maude, and Fern Elston. Calvin had told the Atlas man that his sister was not interested in insurance on her slaves. "He hurt bad, Mistress," Moses said to Caldonia, "far as I can see." Caldonia said for him to come with her and they all followed Caldonia back through the house, with Maude asking Moses twice if his shoes were clean and Caldonia telling her mother, "Leave him alone, Mama." Henry, following William Robbins's advice, had never taken out insurance on his slaves, and his widow, at least on that day, was now following her dead husband.

Maude and Fern stayed in the house and in no time Moses and Caldonia and Calvin were at Stamford's cabin. His mistress went to him and knelt at his pallet. The man from Atlas Life, Casualty and Assurance Company was out in the road in his buggy by then. The people in Hartford, Connecticut, had taught that a woman was more apt to buy insurance for her slaves than a man was.

"Stamford?" Caldonia said. "What all you got yourself into now?" She took the rag Celeste had and wiped the rest of the blood from the man's face. "Celeste, get me some more of these, please."

Loretta, who had healed many a soul on the plantation, came in

with a box of clean rags she used as bandages and knelt beside
Caldonia.

"What am I going to do with you?" Caldonia asked Stamford as
she took rags from Loretta's box. Stamford stopped blinking and was
concentrating on the spiderweb and trying to raise an arm to warn all
the people in the cabin. The hant be comin, the hant be comin, he
thought he was telling them. His eyes and cheeks were swelling
quickly; he didn't relate that to the punches he had taken. He felt the
swelling was from the power of the hant. The door to the cabin was
open and with the wind coming in, the web moved furiously. Look at
that hant, Stamford thought he was warning. You leave us be. We ain't
done nothin to you. JesusJesus . . .

After they had cleaned him up, he fell asleep. He woke at about
three and Delphie was there with some soup Caldonia had Zeddie the
cook bring down from the house. The door was closed as Delphie fed
him and somehow in the time he was asleep the spiderweb had been
blown away. His face was a swollen ball but Delphie managed to get
soup into him. He ate and kept thinking how saying Jesus fast had
worked. He had the cabin to himself that day and night, for Moses
sent Clement and the other man elsewhere to sleep. Delphie slept on
one of their pallets. Loretta came down three more times to check on
him—at seven o'clock, at ten o'clock and at five o'clock the next
morning. It was the ten o'clock tending to that told her he might yet
live. The five o'clock settled things once and for all.

No policy from Atlas would have paid Caldonia for the week and
a half Stamford was off from work. Policies for slaves injured
during work would not be issued for a few more weeks. (As it happened in the field, she might have been able to get away with calling
it a work-related injury, as long as the agent did not come and see
Stamford for himself.) Those work-injury policies would come about
because an agent in South Carolina would write to Hartford to tell

them that many of his clients were asking about insuring slaves hurt
while doing their jobs. Men and women were losing limbs, getting
sick from any number of ailments directly related to their jobs, the
agent said in his letter to Hartford, and his clients wanted some relief
for that. At the time of Stamford's beating, there was a policy, for a
premium of 25 cents a month, that would have paid Caldonia if he
had died. It would not have paid the price Henry paid for Stamford,
$450, because Stamford was now much older. But the money would
have gone a long way toward purchasing someone else, someone
stronger and no doubt more able to stand up for himself.

The Atlas man had come the day of the beating because Maude
had sent word to him that her newly widowed daughter needed all
the help she could get. Maude had policies on all her slaves. Riding
away that day, the Atlas man noted in his mind that next time he
would have to insist on seeing the mistress of the house and not settle on an answer from a male relative who did not know the benefits
of Atlas products. A negative response, the people in Hartford had
taught, was only the groundwork for a positive one.

Stamford did not go after Gloria again, or Cassandra. Though the
hant was gone from his cabin, he began to think that he was not
long for the world, that no young stuff would ever love him again. He
became most difficult and got into even more fights with men. He
even cursed children when an adult was not around to shoo him away.
The children in the lane started saying that he was a man who had
sworn off all human food. Stamford now ate only nails, they said,
rusty nails, and drank only muddy water, the muddier the better.

He met up with a slave from a neighboring plantation and that
man gave him from time to time a brew that the man claimed was
better than the whiskey white men drank. The basic ingredient of the
brew was potatoes that had been fermenting for months. There were
other things in it, mostly just what the man happened to find at

hand—leaves, dead insects, chicken feet, newspapers, dirty rags, brackish water. It all went into the brew. And for a while a body after drinking it would fall into a nice state, a place the brew man liked to call heaven on earth. The effect was brief and if the drinker did not go to sleep right away, a headache would come on that was worse than a tree falling on his head, for it was only men who drank the stuff.

A little more than three weeks after Clement beat him, Stamford came walking down to the lane. He had drunk some of the brew the day before and his head was paining him. His vision was blurry. It was Sunday afternoon and it was raining. He didn't remember where he had been, but he was heading now to Delphie's cabin. The muddy lane was empty except for Stamford and one of the three cats on the place who didn't mind being out in the rain.

He knocked on Delphie's door and she opened it before there was a need for a second knock.

"I been puttin my mind to studyin on why you and me don't get together," Stamford said. His head, though in pain, was clearer than it had been that morning, but it wasn't clear enough for him to know the entire difference between right and wrong.

Delphie said, "What?" She had helped him heal after the fight with Clement as best she could, and when she saw him take a turn toward something else, she had gone on about her business.

Stamford grinned. The road to young stuff takes you through the forest of wide grins, the man had advised when Stamford was twelve. But young stuff is worth it. Stamford grinned some more. "You and me. Us together. Me and you puttin up together and bein as one little family, is what I'm sayin." If he couldn't get young stuff, he would take what he could get. Winter would be there before he knew it.

Delphie stepped out of the cabin. She was not smiling because she was not very happy. Men like him never lived for very long. They died and were forgotten the week after the next. "I would not want that, Stamford. I would not want that at all."

"Sure you do. You sure do. I'm tellin you I got what ails you, honey.

Got that and more to spare." In the wintertime, the man had advised the boy, you can wrap yourself up in all that young stuff, and then you don't need to come out till springtime. Stay hibernatin like them bears. "Just gimme one chance to show you what I gots, honey. Just one chance."

Delphie looked up and down the lane. The rain was gentle right then, not hard, and she could see that just by how the sparse patches of grass did not lean and fuss when the rain hit them. Her eyes came back to Stamford and she realized that she pitied him more than she had ever pitied any human being. More than even a child lying dead and motherless in the road. She remembered what he called out in his dreams in the days after Clement beat him.

Stamford reached up and touched her breast. Now the titty, the man had advised the boy, is the real talker on a woman, you see what I mean. You have to tell it what you want even when that damn young stuff's mouth is saying something opposite a what you want. Talk to the titty first and the door will open just like that.

Delphie took his hand from her breast, firmly, and Stamford let it drop down to his side. His blood had soaked seven large rags. With his other hand Stamford wiped the rain from his face, but it was all for nothing because he was standing in the open and more rain quickly covered his face. Finally, he saw what she saw. The rain stopped for about ten seconds and, his mouth still locked in a grin, Stamford looked around to see what the new silence was all about. When he returned, she was waiting. "I would not ever be with you," she said. The rain came back. Delphie stepped closer to him and for just that moment he was hopeful, forgetting her words and taking in the smell of her. Delphie put her hands to his shoulders, held on to them, taking the full measure of him. "You too heavy a man for me to carry, Stamford. I done carried heavy men and I know how they can break your back. I ain't got but this one back and I don't want it broke again, least not before it can see fifty years." She stepped back, turned and went into her home. She was used to nursing people, trying to heal them, and so it was a long moment before she shut the door, and when she did shut it, it made no sound.

Stamford stepped fully out into the lane, into mud. The man, the adviser, was silent in his head. He walked absently away from where he was originally headed and trudged through the mud toward Caldonia's house. As the rain came harder, he understood that he was actually walking away from his own cabin and he turned around and through the heavy rain tried to make out just which cabin was his own. He went down the lane. The mud pulled at him. He walked on and gradually became aware of his surroundings. He passed Celeste and Elias's cabin. He stopped. It's rainin, he thought. Damn if it ain't rainin cats and dogs out here.

He stood there for a very long time, and the longer he stood, the more he sank. All the heart he had for living in the world began to leave him. He could feel the life running down his chest, his arms and legs, doing something for the ground that it had never been able to do for him. If God had asked him if he was ready right then, there would have been only one answer. "Just take me on home. Or spit me down to hell, I don't care anymore. Just take me away from this."

He stepped on, slowed down by the mud.

As he neared his cabin, another door opened and Delores, seven years old, came out of her place with a bucket in her hand. Once she hit the lane, with Stamford only three feet away, she slipped and fell into the mud.

"You gotdamn little fool," Stamford said, helping the child up. "What you doin out here in all this mess?"

"Goin to get some blueberries," Delores said. In one part of the world, way off to the right of the cabins, lightning came and went quickly before the man or the girl knew what had happened.

"What?" Stamford said. "Ain't you got the sense God gave you, girl?" If he knew her name, he had long ago forgotten it.

"I do," Delores said, "so you just leave me lone." She and Tessie, Celeste and Elias's oldest, were the only children in the lane who were not afraid of Stamford, did not care about his nails and muddy-water diet. "Just leave me be."

Stamford handed her the bucket. "Where in God's hell you goin in all this rain, girl?"

"I done told you: I'm huntin up blueberries," she said. Neither the man nor the girl noticed Delores's brother, four-year-old Patrick, standing in the doorway of their cabin. His sister had told him to stay inside with the door closed until she got back. "I'm goin to pick some blueberries," Delores said. "Now just leave me lone so I can go." She wiped the rain from her eyes and blinked up at Stamford.

"Blueberries?" He looked around at the cabins as if the blueberry patch was just a few steps away. "Where your mama?"

"Up at the house helpin out."

"Where your daddy?" Stamford asked.

"Over to the barn helpin with that sick horse."

"Lord, Lord," he said. "Hand me that damn thing. Give that bucket here."

"I need it for my blueberries. Me and my brother want blueberries." She looked at her cabin and saw her brother. "Ain't I told you to stay inside?" she hollered at Patrick, who hunched his shoulders, then stuck his tongue out at her, something his father had told him never to do. Patrick slammed the door shut.

"I'll get the damn blueberries and you just go in the house," Stamford said. The thunder and lightning were closer, and Stamford was now aware that there was more than rain about. He looked at the girl and the bucket. "I'll get the damn things." He knew he was going to die but he thought this little thing might provide him with a nothing stool way off in the corner of heaven that nobody cared about. That corner of heaven reserved for fools, people too stupid to come out of the rain. People got to that corner by heaven's back door.

"You promise?" Delores said.

"If I said it, I damn sure meant it. Now get on in the house fore you catch your death." The girl went inside.

Stamford emptied out what rain had collected in the bucket since the girl left her home. He walked toward where he knew the blueberries were, again the only person in the lane. He had heard of a poison plant one man had taken to get to the other side, but because Stamford had never thought he would want to die with all the young stuff on the earth, he had not taken note of what the plant was or where it could be found. A woman on one plantation in Amelia County had sharpened a stone and cut both her wrists. Bled out into the ground. He had heard that she was a real pretty woman so that must have been a waste of good stuff. Maybe she was a cripple like Celeste. Pretty was good. Cripple, not so good. The man, the adviser, was still silent in his head, and Stamford went beyond the lane out into a wide place not far from the useless woods where Moses went to be with himself. The thunder and lightning were now even closer, about two miles or so beyond where he believed the sweetest berries could be picked. Best hurry, he thought. Best get outa this weather. He wanted to die but he really didn't want to catch a cold to do it.

The patch he found was priceless, a hunk of ground that was partly on the plantation of the white people next door. Stamford didn't care. He climbed over the fence when he saw some he wanted. He worked steadily and was done in less than a half hour. He hefted the bucket. Yes, that would satisfy two babies' bellies until supper. He walked away from the patch, came back on the Townsend plantation. Soon the useless woods was on his right, and the lane and the cabins more than half a mile away. He was on a nice piece of open ground that some women said had the prettiest baby's breaths and morning glories. He had picked some when he was courting Gloria. Beautiful flowers in a man's sweaty hands. But they got the job done. Yessiree bob. Maybe he could kill her before he died. That would learn her. Send her ass to hell so she could sit on one of the devil's wobbly two-legged stools for the rest of eternity just so she could ponder what she done to him. Kill her and then sit on a rise himself and watch her suffer for the rest of eternity. Then he began to think that bad talk and children's blueberries didn't go together. The rain continued and the thunder and lightning came nearer.

He didn't pay much attention to the first crack of thunder, but the second one pulled his head around. He was in time to see the nearest tree in the woods shudder, stop, then shudder again. An oak tree. Moments later, he could see the first crow flying as if upside down, heading toward the ground, two or three feathers fluttering after the body. The second crow flying upside down told him it wasn't flying but death that had hold of them both. It took less time for him to blink the rain out of his eyes before the second crow joined the first on the ground, followed by more feathers. If they made a sound as they fell, the rain was too loud for him to hear it.

The top third of the oak tree was now a glorious blaze of yellow light, as though a million candles had been placed in it. The lightning had struck the birds and Stamford could see that it was now blazing up there at the top of the tree, hungry for some more. It occurred to him that the tree was very tall, and that if a man managed to climb up to the top, he could jump and die real good. Very slowly, as he watched, the lightning of the million candles came together to form one six-foot pulsating line of blue fire that he could see through the leaves and the branches. The lightning began to ease itself down the tree, staying close to the trunk as it burned everything in its way, leaves and limbs and branches and anything that might have made a home in the tree. Finally, the lightning stood at the base of the tree, still blue, still pulsating, still six feet.

Stamford set the bucket down and went toward the lightning, toward his death.

Before he had gone very far, he turned and looked at the bucket of blueberries, which was tilting because he had unknowingly put it on a small clump of dirt. If someone was to find it and know who should have it, then the bucket should sit up straight and be closer to the quarters, to the children. He went back and moved the bucket some ten feet closer to the quarters. The rain never let up.

The lightning had not moved, and as Stamford ran toward it, the lightning flowed down to the ground so that it was now a line of fire laid out across the grass, which did not burn. Stamford ran faster. When he was some five feet from the lightning and the woods, the lightning shot off away from him and stabbed itself into another tree, splitting that tree in half. Stamford arrived just in time to see the tree come apart and the two equal parts decide to go their separate ways. A punishing sadness took hold of him. Every day it was one damn thing after another.

The rain continued and the storm moved away from him, toward the cabins. The crows were at his feet. Stamford knelt. While the birds had fallen in deathly disarray, something had come along and laid them out nicely on the ground—feathers collected from all about and put back on their wings, their eyes closed, black bodies and wings glistening as though with life. Nothing burnt. They lay side by side, just as they must have perched side by side before death snuck up on them. They had never had such a pretty look in life, Stamford thought. And even if they came back to life, this, at that moment, was the best they would ever look. Now all they needed was for someone to come along and provide them each with a tiny coffin.

Stamford licked his fingers and rubbed them on each bird. "I just need a little to get me over to the other side," he said to the first crow. He closed his eyes and waited for death. He began talking to the second bird, "Now don't be stingy with what you got." He continued to rub his fingers on them and lick his hand. He talked to each bird separately, as if the history he had with one was distinct and different from the one he had with the other. To speak to them as a couple, as one unit, would be disrespectful to the history he shared with either. He continued licking his fingers and touching the birds, but neither bird seemed very interested in sharing its little piece of death. "Thas all right, old bird. I won't fault you," he said to the first crow. "I can understand that you just had anough for yourself," he said to the second bird. "I won't grudge you that." He felt something heavy and not rainlike fall on him and he touched the top of his head. He pulled down what he began to realize were the yolks of eggs. Then, bits of eggshells fell into his open hand, dull green pieces that were spotted dark brown. He looked up and more of the eggs and shells fell, along with twigs and sticks that had been the nest of the crows. He considered the shells and the yolks for quite some time, and all the while the rain continued. He looked about as if someone had called his name. Then he took some of the eggshells and tucked them under each of the birds' left wings. He rubbed the yolks over their bodies. And when he was done, the ground opened up and took the birds in. He cried.

This was the beginning of Stamford Crow Blueberry, the man who went on with his wife to found the Richmond Home for Colored Orphans. In 1909 the colored people in Richmond unofficially renamed a very long street for him and his wife, and year after year for decades those people petitioned the white people who ran the government of Richmond to make the name official. In 1987, after a renewed drive for renaming led by one of Delphie's great-granddaughters, the city of Richmond relented, and it put up new signs all along the way to prove that it was official.

Stamford walked back to the bucket of blueberries and knelt and immediately began to feel that maybe the bucket didn't have enough. But the children had been waiting a long time and he didn't want to disappoint them. He shook the bucket, thinking that might make it look fuller. It helped, but not by much. Maybe the boy might be fooled that it was a full bucket, but the girl knew things and she would know he had failed to bring a full bucket. His shoulders sagged, and the rain continued. He saw one blueberry rolling down a little hill in the bucket and he caught it. He held the berry between his fingers, began to squeeze it. It bled a little juice. The blueberry was now no good for any child and he regretted having squeezed it. Not to let it go to waste, he put it in his mouth. It wasn't bad but he could never make a life of eating the things—God had given him a head full of good teeth, but not a one of them was sweet. What the hell had happened to that full bucket? He chewed and swallowed the blueberry, and then he raised his eyes to see a cabin flying his way through the rainy air. It was not moving in any threatening way and so Stamford was not afraid. But he did stand up.

The cabin continued on and settled itself on the ground not ten feet from him. The door opened and Delores was standing in the doorway, her hands behind her back, quite pleased with herself in that way of little girls who had a secret they were dying to tell. She opened her mouth, her teeth and tongue stained blue, a girl happy with her blueberries. Her brother Patrick appeared beside her and he opened his blue mouth to show his happiness as well. Then, just like that, the boy shut the door hard. It wasn't a comment on Stamford: Despite what his sister always said about him, he didn't need to be told something three times. The cabin rose and rose and went back the way it had come. The closed door must have acted like a kind of eye because the cabin turned around so the door could see the way back to the quarters.

In 1987, the city of Richmond had just hired a young woman from Holy Cross College and that woman's first assignment was to design a sign that could contain the names of Mr. and Mrs. Blueberry. Delphie's great-granddaughter, who was on the city council, wanted both names on the street signs, not just something like "Blueberry Street." The black woman from Holy Cross did well, and the night of the day she completed her task, she called her mother in Washington, D.C., and read to her what she had managed to fit on one sign— Stamford and Delphie Crow Blueberry Street.

After he had given the bucket to Delores and Patrick, Stamford stood in the lane in the mud and the rain and counted the doors to the cabins where children lived. He left out the ones with infants because he knew they weren't old enough to bite down and enjoy blueberries. And he had never heard of a sugar tit laced with blueberries. He kept counting wrong and he had to do it over several times. Once that was done, he knew he had a new problem—how to find enough buckets for all those damn blueberries.

The rain stopped the next day, but it came back three days later. It was far worse and anyone walking in it felt the sting. "It was a very painful rain," Kim Woodford, an historian from Lynchburg College, wrote in 1952. The rain led to great flooding, and the Lynchburg historian noted, without hyperbole, that it may well have been the worst any county had suffered since Virginia became a state. Twenty-one human beings lost their lives, including eight adult slaves, five men and three women. All the children, whether white or black or Indian, free or in bondage, were spared. No one counted the livestock and the dogs and the cats that were killed because there were so many. The land was covered with animal bodies for weeks and weeks.

Three weeks to the day after Clement beat Stamford, the man from Atlas Life, Casualty and Assurance came back for the third time in his rented buggy and was told by Caldonia that she wanted no insurance. Maude was looking over her shoulder, sighing with displeasure.

"Good morning, Mrs. Townsend," the white man said to Caldonia before she sent him away, the big book in one hand and his hat in the other. It was his first chance to speak to her directly. "We are pained at your unfortunate loss. My company, Atlas Life, Casualty and Assurance, and all its employees send their everlasting condolences."

Caring for Stamford after he was beaten convinced Caldonia to try to put her grief aside as much as she could and get to the business of the plantation. She decided, after hearing from Celeste and Gloria and Clement, that Clement would not be punished. She sent word by Moses to Stamford that he was to mind what he was doing from now on. "No more fighting, from anyone," she told Moses,

though it was many days before Stamford obeyed, after the crows, after the blueberries and the cabin.

Moses did, on his own, require that Stamford and Clement work a
few hours on three Sundays. They could have appealed to Caldonia,
but they thought everything he did came on orders from her. The first
Sunday was one not long after Stamford had gone back to the fields
after the beating, and Elias worked for him after Celeste said she did
not think Stamford could do seven days in a row.

In the wake of the beating, Caldonia now had Moses come and
report to her each evening after all work was done. He stood in the
parlor and told her all that had happened during the day, from the
moment just after breakfast when he met the slaves in the lane until the moment in the evening when he told them their day was
done. At first, the report was over and done with in a matter of minutes. But as the days since Henry's death piled up, he would talk
longer and longer, for he had come to sense that Caldonia wanted
his words. Maude, and sometimes Fern, would peel away before he
was done, but Caldonia and Calvin listened to every word. And when
Caldonia was finally alone in the house and her mother and brother
and Fern had gone away, she continued to listen and his report became even longer, sometimes as much as an hour. Soon, he began
to leave off from talking about the work of the day and create stories
out of nothing about the slaves. Loretta sat in a chair in a corner,
knowing what was true and what was not but never telling her mistress.

The evening of the day Fern left, Caldonia told Moses to sit down.
He looked over at Loretta in her chair, and after a long minute's hesitation, he sat down. Caldonia told Loretta that she could retire for the
evening and Loretta left.

"You were here from the beginning, weren't you?" Caldonia said.

"Ma'am?"

"You were here with Henry in the beginning, from that first day?"

"Yessum, I was."

"What did you do?"

Moses took his eyes from his lap and began to invent some early days when they were building the house and there was not much on the land except what God had put there. Caldonia was at the edge of the settee, in her mourning dress. "Now Masta Henry always knowed what kinda house he wanted to build, Mistress. I don't even think he even knowed about you at that particular time, but he musta had some idea that you was out there somewhere waitin in your own kinda way, cause he set about buildin a house that you would want. He built it up from nothin. I was there but I wasn't there like he was there. He said to me that first day, he said, 'Moses, we gon start with the kitchen. A wife needs a place to fix her meals for her family. Thas where we gon start.' And he bent down and Masta drove in that first nail. Bam! That was a Monday, Mistress, cause Masta Henry didn't believe in startin somethin on a Sunday, God's day."

Caldonia, her hands clasped in her lap, leaned back and closed her eyes. The story about the first nail came a little more than a month after Henry had been in his grave. It was gospel among slaves that one of the quickest ways to hell was to tell lies about dead people, but Moses did not think about that as he spoke of the first nail, did not think about the dead needing the truth to be told about them. He did not think about it until that day Oden Peoples, the Cherokee patroller, said to the men around him about Moses, "Heft him on up here. I'll take him in. He ain't gon bleed for long."

Barnum Kinsey, the patroller and the poorest white man in Manchester County, was quite sober when he met up with Harvey Travis and Travis's brother-in-law, Oden Peoples, one night in early September a little more than five weeks after Henry Townsend died. Barnum had been sober for three and a half weeks, and he knew from experience that if he could survive the fourth—maybe even the fifth—week without drinking, he could move through the rest of the year without the craving that had often seized him in those first weeks, the craving that was gnawing at him even as he rode to meet up with Travis and Oden under the brightest moon he had seen in some time. After that fifth week of being sober, he would be able to look the craving full in the eye and say no and tell it to get on away from him. Then, with renewed strength, he could harvest whatever his land would give him that fall and for the rest of the year he could hire himself out so he and his family could make it with a little comfort through the winter.

He was desperately afraid of being without in the winter, saw the winter ahead as God's challenge for him to pick himself up from drink and walk on two legs without tottering. His grandfather, who had also been a drinker, had died in the winter, gone out for a drink and froze to death on the fourth-coldest night of that winter. Barnum's father had not been a drinker, so Barnum had been thinking for a long time that the curse tended to skip generations, for not one of his sons from his first marriage showed a need for the stuff. The boys from the second marriage had yet to smell themselves so drink wasn't yet a problem. As for the women through the generations in his family, the curse had avoided all of them, and they moved through the world unsoiled, their minds clear without a need for a challenge every winter God sent.

The three of them, Barnum, Travis and Oden, were nearing ten o'clock when Augustus Townsend came up the road on his wagon pulled by a mule who was as tired as his owner. The mule was older than the other one Augustus had and he didn't work him as much as the younger one, but every now and then he would take him out to show the mule that he still had faith in him. The mule and his man had delivered a chest and a chair and a walking stick to a man two counties away, a white man who had recently married off the last of his three daughters and so had a little money to spend on himself. "Make me happy with somethin," he had told Augustus, "before that next grandchild pops into my world." Augustus, as usual, had underestimated the time for the trip there and back and so he and the mule were about a day late getting home to his wife Mildred. Augustus had been thinking of Henry all day and all day he had been trying not to.

"Just hold up there," Travis told Augustus. "Just hold up there and show who you are." Augustus's wagon carried a lantern hoisted up from the seat. The mule liked having the light. It seemed to provide him some peace of mind as he went about his work. The lantern and the moon offered enough light for Travis to see Augustus was someone he had stopped so many times before.

Augustus stopped and brought out his free papers. He was too tired to talk, but he also knew words would be wasted on them, at least with the white man Travis and probably with the Cherokee Oden.

"Evenin, Augustus," Barnum said. Augustus had not seen him at first.

"Mr. Barnum, evenin. How your family?"

"They be good, as the Lord keeps them."

"This ain't no damn church social," Travis said, grabbing the free papers from Augustus. "This is the law's business." Travis could read and he held the papers up and borrowed light from Augustus's lantern as he turned the papers over and over. He did not read them, because he had read them many times before. You and me, Augustus thought watching the white man, know them word by word now. Unable to read himself, Augustus, early in his freedom, had given a free colored man a walking stick just to read the papers to him five times a day for two weeks and in the course of all the listening had memorized every word.

"They be good papers," Augustus said. "I've been a free man for a long time, Mr. Travis."

"You ain't free less me and the law say you free," Travis said.

"Now, Harvey, we been knowin Augustus many a year," Barnum said.

"Don't tell me what I know and don't know. You keep your potato trap shut. Tell what you know to the bottle if it has a mind to listen to you. Ain't that right, Oden?"

"I'll stand with you," Oden said, "if thas what you sayin. Barnum, John wouldn't want us to let just anybody pass just cause we done it many times before. That ain't legal."

Travis waved the papers about and said to Augustus, "I hate the way you just ride up and down these roads without a care, without a 'Yes sir, ain't it a good day, sir?' Without any kinda 'May I kiss your sweet ass today, sir.' "

"I'm only doin what I got a right to do," Augustus said.

Travis began eating the papers, starting at the bottom right corners, chewed the corners up and swallowed. "Thas what I think a your right to do anything you got a right to do."

"Now wait a minute," Augustus said. "You stop right now." He stood up in the wagon, the reins in his left hand. The mule had never moved since Augustus had stopped him.

Travis began to eat the rest of the papers, making a loud show of it, and when he was done eating, he licked his fingers. "You sho you know where them fingers been?" Oden said. Travis laughed and belched.

"Harvey, for God sakes, them papers belong to him," Barnum said. "What he gon do?" He looked beyond Augustus and saw something making its way toward them. He hoped it was Skiffington. "That ain't right, Harvey. This just ain't right."

Travis wiped his mouth with the back of his hand. "Right ain't got nothin to do with it," he said. "Best meal I've had in many Sundays." Some of the paper was stuck in his teeth and he sucked on his teeth, and the paper came easily away.

"I wouldn't wanna be you in the mornin when you have to shit that out," Oden said.

"I don't know," Travis said, "it might make for a smooth run off. Couldn't be no worse than what collard greens do to me."

A wagon twice as large as Augustus's came up to the four men.

Driving it was a large black man and beside him was a much smaller white man covered in beaver pelts. The heat of September didn't seem to bother him. In the back of the wagon were four black adults and a black child. The white man in the wagon took two beaver feet and sniffed them deeply. "There ain't nothin like the smell of Tennessee," he said.

"Darcy, Darcy," Travis said. "Where you goin? Off to get married again? You wear out women faster than I wear out my welcome."

"Just passin through with me and mine before your sheriff gets sight of me and puts too much of his snout in my business. John Skiffington shoulda been named John Sniffington." Darcy was forty-two, but with the unkempt beard that went to his knees and with much of his body covered in pelts, he could have gone for seventy-five.

Travis laughed and Oden followed. Barnum was silent. The child in the back of the wagon coughed.

"As it is, Darcy," Travis said, "I think you come along at just the right time. I didn't think you ever knew what time it was, but tonight, without knowin it, you look to be on time. God works in mysterious ways."

"Praise his name. I was born with a clock in my head," Darcy said. "Tick tock. Tick tock. Nighttime headin for more nighttime. Tick tock."

"Well, this ain't exactly what I had in mind when I stopped this nigger, but this here will do just the same," Travis said.

"Whatcha got for me, Harvey?"

"A nigger who didn't know what to do with his freedom. Thought it meant he was free."

"That one there," and Darcy pointed to Oden. Darcy laughed and elbowed the black man beside him. "It's been a long time since I sold an Indian. Maybe five months. Didn't bring me the money I was hopin. Remember that one, Stennis?" and he elbowed the black man again.

"Bought anough if I recall correctly, Masta," Stennis said.

"Well, I'll bow to your recall cause yours has always been better than mine. That clock in my head don't like to share it with no memory power. Selfish somebitch. I'll take the Indian and the nigger both."

"Not him," Travis said of Oden. "We's kin. We's family. You know Oden. I'm talkin bout the nigger in the wagon."

Barnum said to Darcy, "Mister, that Augustus Townsend is a free man. You can't buy him. Just leave him be."

Travis leaned over and pushed Barnum and spat at him. " 'That Augustus is a free man. That Augustus is a free man.' I liked you better when you was so likkered up you could barely stand, Barnum. You made more sense then. A nigger's for sale if I say he's for sale, and this one's for sale."

"Mister," Augustus said to Darcy, "I am a free man and been that way for a lotta years. Freed from Mr. William Robbins."

"Yes yes yes. Happy Christmas happy Christmas," Darcy said. "What you askin tonight, Harvey?"

"I tell you he's free," Barnum said.

"Gimme two hundred and I'll sleep good tonight," Travis said and pointed his pistol at Barnum.

"Damnit! Thas a month of good nights, Harvey. You tryin to turn me into your damn mattress and pillow."

"One hundred."

"Try twenty-five dollars. You got them two sayin he free, Harvey. That could be trouble for me down the line."

"Whoa, Darcy. This nigger makes furniture. He carves wood, and if you couldn't find wood, I'm sure he's got a good back for whatever else you need. Gimme that hundred."

"Still, he say he a free man, Harvey. Thas a risk for me. Thirty dollars."

Augustus took his reins and prepared to move away. Oden pulled out his pistol, looked a second at Travis and aimed the gun at Augustus. "You should stay. I think you should stay," Oden said. Augustus halted.

"Yes, stay," Travis said. "Barnum gon pull out the banjo and we'll have a good time. Now, Darcy, I got risks too. Fifty dollars, then. I'll settle for fifty."

"Hmm," Darcy said. "I must say you are a mountain of a negotiator. Stennis, could we stand to put fifty dollars in that man's pocket?"

"Don't ask that nigger bout white folks' business," Travis said.

"I live and die with Stennis," Darcy said. "Harvey, you don't know what all he's done for me."

"Marse," Stennis said, "we could stand fifty dollars but I don't think we could stand much more."

Travis shouted, "Seventy-five dollars! For the sake of God in his heaven, Darcy. Don't let your nigger cheat me. Don't let a nigger do white folks' business."

"Then fifty dollars it is," said Darcy, and he sniffed on the beaver feet again.

"Shit! Then ten dollars for the mule," Travis said.

"What mule?" Darcy said.

"That one right there." Someone in the back of the large wagon shifted and Augustus heard the chains move. The child coughed again.

"You can give me that for free, Harvey. I don't think that's much of a mule. Does he sing and dance in the moonlight?"

"Don't pee on me that way," Travis said. "You can say like you done in the past that I don't know nigger flesh. I'll leave you safe with that one, but I do know my mules and horses. I do know them, Darcy. I want ten dollars. I deserve ten dollars."

"All right, Harvey. But that mule had better hold up. He'd better be worth every penny, cause if he ain't I'm gonna sic the law on you." Darcy laughed and right away he was joined in the laughter by Stennis. Then Travis laughed, followed by Oden. Stennis reached down between his knees to the floor of the wagon and brought up a strongbox. He unlocked it with a key on a string around his neck, took out some coins and put them in a tiny sack and tossed the sack to Travis.

Darcy told Augustus to get down from the wagon and Augustus said no. "I'm a free man, mister."

"Yes yes yes. Happy Christmas happy Christmas. Now get down from there."

Augustus said he would not.

"Stennis," Darcy said, "why are we threatened on all sides by the incorrigible? Why do they threaten us every which way we turn? Have we displeased our God in some fashion?"

"I don't know, Marse. I done studied it and studied it and I still don't know."

"But, Stennis, you would agree that we are threatened on all sides?"

"Thas a true statement of what you talkin bout," Stennis said.

Travis holstered his pistol and dismounted and then Oden dismounted, still pointing the gun at Augustus. But before either of them was well settled on the ground, Stennis had jumped down from the wagon and over to Augustus in one effortless motion. He pulled Augustus from the wagon and began pummeling him.

"Don't bruise my fruit," Darcy said. Stennis and Travis dragged Augustus around to the back of Darcy's wagon and soon he was chained to the black man nearest the end of the wagon. Augustus wanted to say again that he was a free man, but he was in too much pain, and the words would not have come through anyway because his mouth was full of blood and no sooner had he spat some out, his mouth filled up again.

Stennis unharnessed Augustus's mule and tied it to the back of the wagon.

"I will now," Darcy said to Travis when he and Oden were back on their horses and Stennis was back on the wagon beside him, "I will now allow the wind to take me and mine away." Darcy pulled the pelts tighter around his neck. "Oh, to be in Tennessee. That is my dream, Stennis." "Thas mine, too." "I call on God to grant me my dream, Stennis." Their wagon had two horses and Stennis took up the reins and without a word the horses started going and the mule came along and as quick as anything the wagon had disappeared.

It was nearing eleven o'clock. Barnum looked down to where Augustus had gone and said, "You oughtna done that, Harvey. You know you shouldna. You know that and I know that." He turned to Oden. "Even Oden know that."

"I don't know no such thing," Oden said.

"Then you should. Both yall shouldna done that. Why?"

"That is not it," Travis said to Barnum. "It is not why he and I are doin it, but why you *aren't* doin it. That is the question for all time. Why a man, even somethin worthless like you, sees what is right and still refuses to do it." Travis hawked and spat in the road. He said, "That is all the question we ever need to ask." He was silent for a few moments. Then he said, "All right now," and he handed a $20 gold piece to Barnum and tossed another $20 piece to Oden, who had holstered his gun after getting back on his horse and was able to catch the money with both hands.

"I don't want it," Barnum said. "I won't have it." He handed the gold piece back to Travis.

"You'll take it and you'll like it," Travis said, taking out his pistol and again aiming it at Barnum. "You takin the nigger side now? Is that it? You steppin away from the white man and takin the nigger side? Thas what it is?"

"Yeah, thas what it is," Oden said. "Takin the nigger side against the white man?"

"I just don't want it, is all," Barnum said.

Travis rode up beside Barnum, heading south while Barnum was heading north. They were so close their thighs touched and the horses, uncomfortable being so close, began to twitch. Travis put his pistol to Barnum's temple. "I said you'll take it and like it." He put the money inside Barnum's shirt. "Happy Christmas happy Christmas," he said.

Barnum rode away.

"And not a word a thanks, huh, Barnum?" Travis shouted after him. "I should report you to Skiffington for not carryin your patrollin duties through to the end. Not a word a thanks, Oden."

"No," Oden said, "and not a good night either."

"We may as well shut the night down," Travis said. "We have found, tried and punished the one criminal out here tonight. The one true runaway out and about. We may as well shut down the night, Oden."

"May as well," and then Oden started up. "Give a greetin to Zara and the chaps for me, willya? Say I'm thinkin bout em."

"Yes. And a greetin to Tassock and them chaps for me," Travis said. "I'll see to the nigger's wagon. Good night."

Oden said, "Good night."

Travis watched him go away and after a few minutes he dismounted and used the fire from Augustus's lantern to set ablaze the straw in the back of the wagon that cushioned furniture on its way to new owners. When the fire was good and strong, Travis picked up kindling from the side of the road and threw it into the wagon. Then he mounted again and looked at the fire and did not move. He was determined to see the fire through to the end. The horse backed away as the fire grew hotter and Travis let him do it. After nearly an hour, Travis got off the animal, and walking with the reins in his hand, he stood at the fire. His horse was slightly uncomfortable but he turned and reassured it that everything was good and the animal calmed. It was the smartest beast he had ever known. He had taught it to back away when he said the word "Fire." And at the word "Water" it knew to come forward again. Now the horse stood silent behind him and Travis thought he could hear its heart beating in the quiet with just the crackling of the fire and the insects communicating with one another as the only other sounds in the world. Every now and again the breath of the horse would blow Travis's hair all about.

He stayed to the end with the fire, watched as the metal on the wagon dropped as all the supporting wood gave way. About one that morning, the fire began to fail, then, nearly an hour later, it went to its dying side, with just a few strong embers here and there. He dropped the reins and took up dirt from the road and poured it over what was left of the fire. Smoke rose, gray, feeble, almost pointless because it went up only a foot or so and then dissipated.

He had first come to know Augustus Townsend many years ago through a chair Augustus had made for a white man in the town of Manchester. The man weighed more than 400 pounds. "Over twenty-seven stones" was how the man put it. He was a bachelor, but that had nothing to do with his weight. Harvey Travis had gone to see the man one day about a woodcutting job. In the man's parlor was Augustus's chair, plain, not even painted, but smooth to the touch, and when the man sat in it, the chair did not complain, not one squeak. It just held up and did its job, waiting for the man to put on another 300 pounds. When the man left the room to get Travis's money, Travis examined the chair, looked all about it trying to discover its secret. The chair gave nothing. It was a very good chair. It was a chair worth stealing.

Now, as the fire from the wagon died out, Travis turned around and wiped both hands on his pants and took up the reins. He had taught the horse to bob his head once at the words "Good morning." "Good mornin," he said to the horse and he bobbed once. The horse had also been taught to bob twice at "Good afternoon," and with "Good evening" or "Good night," it would bob three times. Travis said "Good mornin" again but felt the need for far more and he continued saying it and the horse continued bobbing his head. Then, as if "Good mornin" was not enough, he went through again and again all the greetings of a day and a night and the horse kept bobbing until, at last, the animal, exhausted, confused, lowered its head and did not respond anymore. Travis stood for a long while and rubbed the horse's forehead. He had, as well, taught the horse to take him home.

It helped when the road was a straight one, straight as the crows flew. Otherwise, the horse sometimes went down a road that was not toward home. Travis mounted. "Take me home," he told the horse, who had just been through one of the longest days of his life. The horse took him home.

7

Job. Mongrels. Parting Shots.

Somewhere between the town of Tunck near the Waal River, the Netherlands, and Johnston County, North Carolina—where Counsel Skiffington, cousin to Sheriff John Skiffington, and his people had done well for three generations—Saskia Wilhelm, a newlywed, contracted smallpox, though she was never to be ill from it a day in her life. Married three months, she and her husband, Thorbecke, who also contracted the disease, took two months to get across Europe to England. Thorbecke was not a good man, would not make a good husband and father, something Saskia's father told her for the eleventh time a month before she ran off to marry Thorbecke. The love she had for Thorbecke, however; was a fevered one. Her mother had told her it would burn itself out if she gave it time, but Saskia disappeared with Thorbecke and the love only grew. After what happened to her with him, in Europe, in America, she would never love another human being in the same way.

The young man knew that along the Waal River he had a reputation worth nothing and during the trip across Europe he vowed, not to Saskia but to himself, that he would do better and one day return to Tunck and all the other towns along the Waal and have everyone say to his face how wrong they had been about him. He vowed this in

France, but was sent away because of various misdeeds, and he vowed it in England, but was sent away from there as well. His punishment would not be prison, the English decided, but the pain of never being able to enjoy England again. Thorbecke made the vow again on the ship to New York, where he and Saskia settled more than five years before Henry Townsend died. Thorbecke would live to be seventy-three, but he never returned to the Waal, and neither did Saskia, who lived to be seventy-one. They died in places ten thousand miles apart. She had no children when she died. Nothing had ever come along to tell her, as her mother and father might have told her, that there was a love beyond Thorbecke.

Saskia had a sense of her mistake midway on the journey to America. She could have returned to her people in Tunck, but she still felt for him and thought all along the way that she would never be forgiven, might even be told just to return to her husband. At first, Thorbecke worked as a fisherman along the Hudson River, but the captain and his crew got the notion that Thorbecke was bad luck and he was sent on his way. He went to peddling in New York City after that, clothes, trinkets, fruits and vegetables. He failed again, as he had a viperous temper and drove away customers. Soon he began to live on just what Saskia was making as a maid with the wealthy in the city. One of those families was the one in the photograph that Calvin Newman owned. The frozen dog in the picture was named Otto, after Saskia's own dog back in Tunck.

She did not make much as a maid. Room and board were part-of what she made, and that could not be turned into money for Thorbecke. He sent her into prostitution and then, after more than a year, he sold her to a man who took her and three other women, all of them from Europe, south, first to Philadelphia and, finally, to North Carolina, where that man's father and mother had a brothel. In that brothel, Saskia worked and put Thorbecke away, then she put her people and all of Tunck away.

It was there that Manfred Carlyle fell in love with her. By the time

they met, a little less than three years before Henry died, love was not
something Saskia cared about. She welcomed him each time he came,
told him all that he wanted to hear, and though he forgot during the
course of it that he was paying for the words, she did not. He came to
her often, forever desperate to be near her. "I made the trip here in
less time than I thought I would," he said once, his face sweaty and
red from the ride. "Then I will prepare your reward," Saskia said.

Carlyle was twenty years her senior, and he was one of Counsel
Skiffington's creditors. John Skiffington's cousin allowed Carlyle to
"air out" at his plantation from all the whiskey and sex at the brothel.
Counsel had always been pleased to accommodate a man he owed
money to and he told his overseer, Cameron Darr, to stay by Carlyle
and make him happy. In a little cottage at the northeast corner of
Counsel's plantation, Carlyle would air out, sleeping for some fourteen
hours a day. On what would be his last visit, Darr made him happy by
drinking with him. After the three days of airing out, Carlyle went
the twenty miles to his own place, to his family who were gray things
after his colorful time with Saskia. Like Thorbecke and Saskia,
Carlyle, too, would not suffer a day from smallpox, and his family and
his slaves were spared as well. On that last trip from Counsel's plantation, someone stole his horse while he peed down at a riverbank.
"That shoulda told me somethin," he told a friend months later, back
at the brothel.

Counsel Skiffington had suffered through three years of failed
crops and then, in the fourth year, the year Saskia arrived in
Johnston County, he began to prosper again. He considered it a good
year if each slave produced $250 worth of crops but for those three
terrible years, he got only $65 from each slave. The times had been so
hard that the house servants, people with flawless skin and hands that
had not known any blisters that mattered, were sent into the fields to
work with the hope that more hands could wring more from the land.

Carlyle was one of four creditors, only one of them a bank, and the creditors were kind to him during those years, though the bank sent a man out every other month to check on the health of the plantation. In that fourth year, the year of recovery, the profit from each slave was $300, and the bank man stopped coming. Counsel was on his way to an even better fifth year when, in the middle of a quiet night, Darr the overseer woke with a cough so loud that it woke Counsel's wife, Belle, in their mansion a quarter of a mile away. Her husband slept on, being the kind of man—as Belle noted once in a letter to her cousin-in-law Winifred Skiffington—who could sleep through Jesus knocking on the door. Darr's coughing woke the four Skiffington children, too, but Belle and two of the children's slaves managed to get them back to sleep. She told the servants to return to bed and she did the same, but found sleep elusive even after the overseer's coughing abated about an hour later.

There was no more coughing from Darr after that first night, but one slave after another began to fall ill with headaches, chills, nausea and an overwhelming pain in their backs and limbs. "They are not pretendin," the overseer told Counsel. "I would know pretendin and this ain't it." Darr, a man with five children, had very little beyond the life he had on the plantation, and he had so liked hearing Carlyle talk of all the places he had been and all the women who gave him heaven and how he settled at last on Saskia. Darr was not a drinking man but he had drunk that last time with Carlyle because it made his tales all the sweeter to hear, all the sweeter to remember. He told Counsel about the slaves not pretending a day or so before the dusty red spots began to appear on the slaves and on his own children. Counsel decided to bring in the white doctor, knowing that what the slaves had was not a one-week stumble on the way to a profitable fifth year.

The doctor diagnosed smallpox and quarantined the place and it wasn't long before word spread throughout the region that "A Child's Dream," as Belle had christened the plantation, was falling to pieces.

The man from the bank, fearing that his employer would make him go out to Counsel's even with the quarantine, quit his job.

By the time Manfred Carlyle had been home four weeks with his family, more than half of the slaves on Counsel's plantation had died, some sixty-two human beings, ranging in age from nine months to forty-nine years; that number included one-year-old Becky, who was teething but whose mother had nursed her as often as she could with the hope that the disease would pass on by her child; seventeen-year-old Nancy, who was days from marrying a man she thought she loved, a man with enough muscles for two men; thirty-nine-year-old Essie, who had just committed adultery for the eighth time; and twenty-nine-year-old Torry, who had a harelip but who had four days before he died swallowed whole two raw chicken gizzards, having been told by a root worker that they would cure his "affliction." Then, after those slaves perished, Darr's wife died, and so did three of their children. Ten more slaves died, and that same day the first of Counsel's children died, the oldest girl, freckle-faced Laura, who played the piano so well. In the three days that followed her death the disease swept up nearly all the rest of them, down to the youngest slave, ten-week-old Paula, whose mother had died in childbirth. Only Counsel remained, as healthy as the rainy evening his mother gave birth to him.

The animals would live, too, managing somehow to get by even with all their caregivers dead. The creditors, months and months later, would not get much for livestock from a place God had turned his back on. A buyer's place might be next if he bought a cow or a horse; if God could do that to Counsel Skiffington, one potential buyer noted, then what all would he do to poor me?

In the end, after Counsel had tried to drive the animals away, there was not much more than the land, and even that, more than a year later when creditors and others were brave enough to go on it, would be sold for a little less than 45 percent of what it was worth. Belle was the penultimate person to die, just hours before a slave, fifty-three-year-old Alba, wandered in delirium away from his cabin and sat down to death in front of Carlyle's airing-out cottage. With Belle's death, Counsel burned down the mansion. From the first death he had buried no one and all the people in his family, including the bodies of nine servants, were burned along with the building. He then went to the cottage where Carlyle had stayed and Darr's place, and he burned those structures down. The barns. The smokehouse. The blacksmith shop. Everything was burned to the ground. The cabins of the slaves, many with the bodies of the dead still in them, resisted the fire and most of them stayed up, scorched but ready for more tenants. The mud and cheap brick structures would be standing when the first creditor's accountant arrived to see what he had to deal with. Four months later, in Georgia, Counsel would take note of a two-door cabin built for two slave families, and it would come to him that the cabins on his land stayed up because they, like the two-door place, had close to nothing in them. Even God's mansion would burn easily if there were a piano in the parlor and 1,900 books in the library from floor to ceiling and wooden furniture that came from England and France and worlds beyond.

The crops would escape the fire and would thrive, tended by no one. The fields had not had such bounty in more than seven years. There would be no harvest in the usual sense, as no one came to reap what the slaves had sown. Had someone counted up what crops the fields had to give, it would have come to more than $325 a slave.

The fire at A Child's Dream burned for three days. Counsel left that second day, heavy with all the sorrow he would ever know, and went west in the county and then south, avoiding all human beings as best he could. He did not care, but it occurred to him in South Carolina that what he had done was a crime, since much of what he had belonged to others. He continued on, aimless, saddled with the memories of his loved ones and the end of a plantation that even men in Washington, D.C., knew about. He had kin in South Carolina, and Belle had people in Georgia, on the coast, but he decided not to go to those towns. Who could understand what had happened to him? And he had the cousin he had grown up with in Manchester County, Virginia, but he had always had so much more than John Skiffington had and Counsel had never missed a chance to let John know that. He could not see himself standing on John's doorstep, penniless, even though he sensed that John would have held his arms open wide and given him all he had. So he rode on, not even knowing that he just wanted some peace, and not knowing, until much later, that he wanted back all that he had lost.

About three months after he left his plantation, Counsel came to Chattahoochee, Georgia, south of Columbus, thinking that he was far enough away from the coast where some of Belle's relatives lived. He had ridden nearly every day except for a two-week stretch in Estill, South Carolina, where a rough cold had put him on his back. It was like no other cold he had ever had and he suspected that it was more, that the smallpox he was not even trying to outrun had finally caught up with him. He had brought some money from North Carolina and that afforded a place in a back room at an old couple's boardinghouse. He paid for a week's stay, thinking that by the end of that week, he would be dead. The old woman may have suspected what was in mind because she told him, on the third day as she fed him, that no one had ever died in her house and he would not be the first. He recovered and left their place in the night, taking the horse and the saddle that he had given them.

In Chattahoochee, a month after leaving Estill, illness found him again, just as he had hired himself to a man with a large-sized farm. The man had no slaves, only free Negroes he hired when he needed them. Counsel found himself strangely uncomfortable around blacks who toiled but were not slaves, people who came and went as they pleased. He said nothing, needing the money to be able to push on. He worked three days and then collapsed on the fourth day. "I am dying and there is nothing to be done," he said to the Negroes and the white farmer as they carried him from the field. "Then we'll find a place for you out yonder," the white man said, pointing to a cemetery that Counsel had passed by his first day there. He stayed in a room in the white man's house and was attended to mostly by Matilda, the black woman who cooked and cleaned for them. If she knew how to talk, she never said a word to him, not even good morning, not even good night. He began to recover, slowly, and day by day he cursed God for playing with him. "Make up your mind," he said to God. "I don't mind dying. I just want you to make up your mind."

Late one night, three weeks after he took ill, he waited until all were asleep in the house and took money from a desk in the man's parlor and saddled one of the man's horses and left. He wanted to go to Alabama and eventually make it to California. He knew nothing about California, only that it was very far from North Carolina. In November, in Carthage, Mississippi, he bought a pistol to replace the one he had not been able to find in the dark in the Estill farmhouse. That 1840 Allen pepperbox had belonged to his father and all through Alabama he had thought he might go back to the farmer and return the money so he would not have to be without his father's pistol. But so much more that had been his father's had been burned up in North Carolina and he realized, nearing Carthage, how foolish it was to dwell on a mere gun.

Outside of Merryville, Louisiana, in Beauregard Parish, he came to a wide expanse of land that seemed without end, parched grass and soil widening with cracks that were a foot or more in some places. The trees seemed not to have grown up out of the ground but to have been placed on the land, like pieces of furniture in a room. His horse, on his own, began to move slowly and Counsel felt the animal might at any moment decide to turn around and head back. He would have abided by that decision. Then, little by little, the land greened and cypress after cypress appeared and the horse moved ahead with more confidence. Counsel saw pelicans and thought he could smell the sea. But he still saw no sign of human beings.

The green land began to even out and at last he could see a house and a smaller structure in the distance, a place he might reach in two hours or so depending upon how fast his horse would go. He took his time, thinking what he saw was some trick of a tiring mind, and he came to the house in about an hour. But after riding for that hour, he was back in a desolate place again. The land seemed incapable of growing anything but sorrow, yet, as Counsel looked about, he could see that some effort had been made to farm. And in a few spots he saw some success, though he did not make out what was growing. The crops were about three feet high. The house was leaning to the right, and the barnlike building next to it was leaning to the left.

A mule came out of the barn and looked away from where Counsel and his horse were and then looked at Counsel and moseyed out to him. The mule nudged the horse in the nose and the horse nudged back.

Counsel had seen the smoke from the chimney about a half hour earlier and he dismounted and went up to the door. Before knocking, he took one last look about. Everything seemed better from the porch; it was a place that might well sustain a man and his family, if sustain was just all he ever wanted. Pelts and game, squirrel and rabbit and somewhat larger animals Counsel had never seen before, hung from the ceiling of the porch from end to end.

The door was ajar. He knocked once and a woman opened the door wide, looked at him as if she were deciding whether he deserved her smile. She didn't smile but turned to someone in the room and said, "It's somebody." Counsel found the woman attractive, especially after she moved her head and he saw the way her neck rose up to meet her hair. The beauty was fading and it was doing so at a fast pace. "Who somebody?" a man said.

A boy about twelve years old came to the door and told Counsel to

come in. He called the woman "Ma" and told her to close the damn
door after Counsel came in and she did so. A man was at a table in an
area that passed for the kitchen. The floor was hard-packed earth. The
room smelled heavily of smoke and the humidity hung thick. The
house was much bigger than it appeared from the outside, but it was
not a house of rooms but one giant one and each area seemed to have
a function as rooms in a normal house would. Beds far to the right,
stove and table in the back to the left, and near the front of the place
was a living area where two girls smaller than the boy were playing
on the floor with corncob dolls. Counsel could tell by the way one girl
was talking that it was not friendly play.

The man was eating at the table and said to Counsel, "I'm Hiram
Jinkins."

Counsel told him who he was and that he was passing through and
would appreciate a place to stay for the night, maybe a little something to eat. Jinkins pointed to a chair across the table from him and
indicated that Counsel should sit. The chair had one leg shorter than
the others and Counsel found it necessary to balance himself the
whole time. He had the feeling that the man would not want him to
move elsewhere. The only other empty chair was next to the man and
the boy sat in that one soon after Counsel sat down.

"That Meg," Hiram said, pointing to the woman who came up
and took away the empty metal pan that Hiram had been eating from.
"And this here Hiram number four," and nodded sideways to the boy.
Counsel said good day to them both. "You say you ain't ate?" Hiram
the man said. "That's right," Counsel said. "Well . . . ," and the
woman soon returned with the same metal pan, now brimming with
a stew that shared the pan with congealed grease. It had generous
portions of meat. Counsel was too hungry to ask what the meat was.
The woman set a spoon beside the pan. "Biscuits, too," the boy said to
his mother. "Don't forget the goddamn biscuits." Meg brought biscuits and Counsel ate. The girls were still playing in a far part of the
room and the one girl with the mean talk had quieted.

"Where you from?" the boy said. "You Louisiana stock?" While he looked to be about twelve, his voice was husky and in a dark room he might have gone for a man.

"Georgia," Counsel said, trying to remember all he could about the Estill farm.

The room was darkening as evening came on and Meg and the girls went about the place, lighting candles and two lanterns. The boy saw one of the girls with a lantern. He turned quickly in his chair and said, "Save the damn lanterns. You know better. Save the damn lanterns."

"Where he say?" the man asked the boy softly.

"Georgia. Where your damn ears?"

The man touched both his earlobes at once and said, "Where they always been."

"Well, act like it. He said Georgia clear as the damn day and you didn't even hear him. You closer to him than I am and you still didn't hear him." For the very first time ever, Counsel missed the evenings with his family, Laura playing the piano, Belle reading to the younger children. *Make up your mind, God, that's all I ask.*

"You can go eat shit, boy," the man said. "Pick up your goddamn spoon and eat shit."

"I'm doing anough of that already."

Hiram, the man, said, "What you do in Georgia, Mr. Skiffington? I can tell you know your way round books. I can tell that."

"How can you tell that?" Hiram, the boy, said. "How can you tell anything bout him when all he did was say his name and Georgia and come in here and eat our food? How can you say that, Pa?"

"Easy nough," the man said. Out of the corner of his eye Counsel could see Meg standing at the window. There was a draft from somewhere and the candle in that part of the room wavered and now and again, with the intermittent light, she seemed to disappear. The girls were talking but he had no idea where in the huge room they were. "What you do in Georgia?" the man said again.

"I did some farming. I even had a little store, sold some dry goods and whatnot."

"A man of everything," Hiram, the man, said. "I like men of everything."

"That ain't what he said, Pa. He ain't done everything and I don't know why you make it out to be so."

The man yawned. "I had three children die, then you come along," he said. He crossed his arms and said to Counsel, "We can put you up in the barn. You think you can live with that?"

"Yes," Counsel said. "And I'm thankful for that." He stood up.

"I just know you are," the boy said.

"Hiram," the father said, "see Mr. Skiffington gets settled in the barn. Show him where the shithouse is."

The boy said, "You see him get settled in the damn barn."

The man held a fist out to Counsel. "Three of em went on by." He opened one, two, three fingers. "Three of em and then he came along. God and his mysteries." He shook his head. "Meg, see that this man gets settled in the barn."

Meg had a candle and two blankets in her hands and led the way and Counsel followed to the barn, leading his horse. "You keep the candle," she said once she had pointed out an agreeable spot for him to bed down, "but please don't burn the place down. That would not do." "I'll be careful," he said as she left.

He saw that his horse was comfortable and he bedded down across from the mule that seemed to be pacing in its own stall. "Stop," Counsel said to the mule once he was settled. "Just stop that." The mule paused, seemed to consider what the man had said and then went back to pacing around. Counsel turned over on his side and pulled the blanket up to his ear. He was well into his sleep when he felt something touch his shoulder. He thought at first that the mule had wandered over and was nuzzling him, but the touching became more insistent and he reached for his pistol. He turned and cocked the gun. "Oh," Meg said and fell back with the sound of the gun.

"What? What you want?" Counsel said. He tried to make out her face in the dark, tried to remember what little of it he had seen during the evening, but all he could pull forward was the face of a woman in Alabama who passed him in her wagon with her belongings and her family.

Back on her knees, Meg raised the blanket and came in with him and began kissing his face. She pulled up her dress and put his hand between her legs. He wondered if the boy had come out of her. Finally, he laid her down and they continued kissing and he could hear the mule still pacing. His horse was silent. The woman pulled him on top of her and opened her legs wider, never once taking her lips from his. He was surprised to be inside her, as if all the touching and the kissing were not supposed to lead to that but to something quite innocent, something they could do at the table in front of the boy. In all the time she was there, the "Oh" was the only thing she said.

In the morning he lay awake for some time to get himself together. He heard the mule peeing in its stall. He knew right away that Meg coming to him was not a dream. That had sometimes been his problem with events since leaving North Carolina, the sense upon awaking that where he was was no more than a dream, that North Carolina was the real and nothing after that could be trusted. He looked over at his horse. It was staring out the broken barn door. If he lay for a while, Counsel had discovered, the world would right itself and he would know where he was and that it was North Carolina that couldn't be trusted.

As he came out of the barn, he looked at the side of the house and discerned that the dimensions were far smaller than the actual inside of the house. What he saw outside—the wall of no more than twenty feet—could not possibly hold all that he had seen inside last night. And the front of the house was no more than fifteen feet. The inside last night was easily seventy-five feet by fifty feet. Counsel thought he should go back to the barn and try to start the day all over again, but the thought of the boy made him want to get away.

He stood at the door to the house before knocking. He counted on the woman to keep their business to the two of them. She seemed the kind to know how to do that. He was still standing when the door opened and one of the little girls told him good morning. He said good morning and she said there was a little something to eat at the table.

Inside he saw the same seventy-five feet by fifty feet of the night before. The two Hirams were eating at the table and Meg stood behind the man. "Have a bit to chew," the father said and pointed at a pan across from him. Counsel took the same seat as the evening before. There was a lump of scrambled eggs and a slab of hard-cooked bacon sharing the pan with two large biscuits. Counsel sat and only then saw the gun beside the man's pan. It was about equal distance between the man's pan and the boy's pan, so it was difficult to tell who the gun belonged to. But to make it plain, the man put the gun in his lap and sucked once on his teeth.

"Sleep well?" the boy asked Counsel.

"It was better than most places," he said. "And I thank you for it." He had left his own gun out with the horse in the barn, and though he had walked in hungry, the food before him began to turn his stomach. He wondered: Does a bullet in the gut hurt more when the bullet doesn't have to mix it up with eggs and bacon and biscuits? Does it take longer to die on an empty stomach?

He had a good look at the woman. A dark blue knot sat right next to her left eye.

"We ain't got hotel fixins," the boy said.

"What he means is we aim to do right by strangers."

"I know what I mean, Pa. He know what I mean. I'm speakin Jesus' English."

The father continued, "You never know when a stranger is an angel, come to test which side of right and wrong you standin on. God still does that to people, no matter what some men, even preachers, might claim. He still sends out angels to test us. I don't want to fail."

"No," Counsel said. "I wouldn't want to fail either."

The father took up the gun and pointed at the food in front of Counsel. "Eat, eat," he said. "My wife slaved all mornin over that." He sat the gun beside his pan, much farther away this time from the boy's pan.

"I'm not all that hungry this morning," Counsel said. "Truth is, I just come in to say my good-byes."

"Oh, go on. Eat. I'm sure you hungry anough. Angel work must be hard work, I would think. Angels do all that hard work for God and the least we could do is feed em as we can." He had picked up the gun and said the last words tapping himself in the chest with the barrel. "I know *I* would be hungry if I was doin all that work."

"Listen," Counsel began.

"You sayin my wife's cookin ain't good anough for one a God's angels?"

"Thas exactly what I heard," the boy said. "You buckety-buck up here, sleep in our place and then turn your back on my ma's food. And you, Pa, I don't know why you call him some kinda angel."

Counsel said, "I just come in to thank you and say I have to be going. That's all I want to do." He stood up slowly and looked from the man to the woman, who did not appear unhappy at all, despite the bump on her face. "I just wanna get on my way, that's all I want." The chair, with the one bad leg, tipped over, and Counsel cursed it in his mind. "I just wanna be going." He stepped away, heading for the door, never turning his back on the man. The boy drank from a cup on the other side of his pan. It was milk and Counsel saw the white along the boy's upper lip. Where had they kept the cow all this time? he thought, taking more and more backward steps to the door. Where had the cow been? Where was the cow now? And the chickens for the eggs, where were the chickens? The pig for the bacon. "I just wanna leave in peace."

The man stood, without hurrying, as if Counsel was the last thing on his mind. "We'll be sorry to see you go, angel. But when you have to be about God's work, you have to be about God's work."

The boy said, "I should charge you for all you got. I should take every penny you owe. And then take your hide besides." He reached for the gun but the man turned away. "Don't you make me mad," he said to his father. "You know what happens when you make me mad."

Counsel opened the door and stepped out. Had she told the man and then enjoyed with her husband Counsel's discomfort, fear?

He got to the barn and saddled the horse and when he came out, the boy was on the porch, legs apart, both hands just inside the top of his britches. Counsel mounted and took a slow time leaving because he knew speed was one more thing in the world the boy didn't like.

He took all that day to cross into Texas. He no longer knew about California. There was so much of civilization in the east, near the Atlantic Ocean, so much certainty. Here, away from what he always knew, was a world he did not believe he could ever make peace with. He rode on and avoided towns, farms, any signs of people.

Three days after Louisiana, a forest appeared out of nowhere along about Georgetown, Texas, and he was happy to see it after so much flat sameness. Long before he reached the forest, he heard the thunder along the ground but he thought it some weather phenomenon—the sky sending a message down to the ground about the storm that was coming. In North Carolina he had once stood on his verandah as it rained, only to go down the steps and off a few yards to a spot where it wasn't raining. And many times there had been thunder and lightning while the snow fell. So he was used to the tricks of the weather. The trees of the forest seemed thick enough to provide a little shelter for him and the horse during the storm. The thunder on the ground grew louder as he approached the forest.

He was less than fifteen yards from the edge of the forest when

the dogs emerged from the trees, walking slowly, but moving with some purpose. It was a grand and strangely disciplined passel of mongrels. He couldn't see anything pure in the bunch, about twenty-five dogs in all. He was too near to them to run; it would not take them long to overtake him and the horse. First one dog noticed him, one in the middle of the pack, and then one at the edge of the group, and then all the rest took casual notice. When they had all cleared the forest, they sat down as one on their haunches. At some safe distance, he thought, he could have admired the wonder of them, the variety of colors and sizes, and the sense that they were sharing the same mind. They had stopped but the thunder on the ground went on. He eased his gun out of the holster and held it along with the reins. Perhaps just the sight of one or two of them dying would scare off the rest.

Something told him it would be best to continue on; perhaps they would credit him and the horse with some courage for not running away. He thought it odd that the horse had not shown one bit of hesitation or fear. He moved slowly into the pack and the dogs, row after row, rose and moved out of the way and then sat down after he had passed. He was well into the forest when the thunder grew louder, and he figured it was because the sounds were trapped under the canopy of trees. Then, as if they had been invisible and chose just that moment to reappear, there were ten men and women on horses facing him, and Counsel could see beyond them even more people and horses as well as six or seven wagons, all coming with ease through the forest the way they would go along a well-kept road. As he looked from face to face to face, the crowd of humans and horses slowed and stopped. His hand shook and the gun fell almost soundlessly to the forest floor. A black man, not three feet from Counsel, rode closer and leaned far down and swept up the gun and handed it to Counsel along with some of the wood sorrel the gun had fallen into.

The black man, on his right side, began speaking a foreign language and pointed to Counsel's coat pocket and his saddlebags. Counsel could make out a few English words but everything together

made no sense to him. Counsel shook the sorrel from the gun and rested it over the pommel. The black man kept on talking, and his talking, just above a whisper, was very loud in the forest, even with all the people and the animals. All the people and the horses seemed to have quieted just to listen to what he had to say. The man reached over and shook the hem of Counsel's coat and seemed disappointed that he didn't hear what he expected. Counsel used his gun to brush the man's hand away. A woman Counsel thought was Mexican rode up on a blond horse and stopped next to the black man and nodded to Counsel. He thought Mexican because she looked like a painting in one of his books back in his library in North Carolina.

"What that nigger saying?" Counsel said. "What's he talking?" He spoke to the woman but also directed his questions to a white man he noticed just behind the black man and to another white man who appeared on his left side. "What this nigger want from me?" he asked the white man on the left. "What's he talking?"

"He's talking American talk," the Mexican woman said, her face unsmiling as if to convey the seriousness of what the black man was saying.

He knew she was lying and he wanted her now to just go away.

"He is asking if you have any tobacco," the white man on the left said. "I take it you are not American or you would understand him." The man raised his hat by the crown and then let it drop back down on his head. "He's hard of hearing or he would start to discuss your calling him out of his name. His discussions can be painful, or so I'm told."

"Tell him I ain't got nothing for him." The black man shrugged, apparently because he understood what Counsel had said. He began riding past Counsel and then stopped and picked the last piece of wood sorrel from Counsel's gun. Would they all hang him from one of the trees if he up and shot the nigger right there? "Need a clean shooter," the black man said in the same clear way he had spoken all the other words. He went on by.

The white man on the left sounded to Counsel like someone who had some sense, despite the foolishness that had come out of his mouth. "I just wanna be on my way." Had he said that only an hour ago? A few days ago? Or was it the remnant of a conversation from a dream?

"We hold nobody back," the Mexican woman said and followed the black man.

"Not on purpose anyway," the white man behind her said.

Counsel started forward and people and their horses made way. He had underestimated the amount of people by half and as he moved on, he thought their numbers, with their horses and wagons, would never end. He turned around at one point and looked in the back of one wagon and saw two pregnant women, one white, one black, sitting up and staring at him. The black woman waved at him, but the white woman had a pout on her face; she had on a light green bonnet and one of the strings was in her mouth. He had seen a dark old man driving the wagon, not really a Negro, not really from any race that was recorded in any of the books in his destroyed library. As he looked between the pregnant women he saw a tiny blond-haired boy standing with his arms around the dark man's neck, hanging on for support. The boy turned and looked at him. Counsel wondered if the authorities knew about all these people. There was something wrong here and the government of Texas should be doing something about it.

When he turned from the wagon with the pregnant women, a boy smiling with perfect teeth was facing him. He knew the origins of this one from another of the destroyed books—someone from the Orient. It might be China, if the book had been telling him the truth. The boy was no more than fifteen, and his long and thick pigtail lay over his left shoulder with the ease of a coveted pet. The boy was in his way and Counsel stopped. The boy, his hand out, shifted slightly to the right side and Counsel continued, and as he passed, the boy's hand, never threatening, never harsh, paused at the ear of Counsel's horse and moved down the horse's neck, along Counsel's saddle and thigh and on out past the horse's rump, finally taking a gentle hold of the tail before letting horse and man go on. The boy had never stopped smiling, and the smile, more than the touch, was chilling to Counsel.

The people of one color or another and their horses flowed on past him, the ground thundering and the dappled sun coming down on them all. In the end, it did not seem that he and his horse were moving but were simply being carried forward by some counterforce the horses and wagons and people were creating as they went past him. He was in a river of them and he had no say in it. He closed his eyes.

"Better open your eyes or you'll fall off Texas." Counsel opened his eyes and saw a red-haired white woman looking at him. Beyond her he could see what he thought was the end of it all.

"I remember when you did that and fell off into Mississippi from Alabama." A blond-haired man appeared beside her. The hair seemed similar to that of the boy holding the nigger in the wagon, and Counsel, trying to make some sense of everything, thought the man might be father to that boy. The man and the woman were on black horses, though the woman's horse seemed to be turning blue as seconds went by.

"I did not," the woman said and gave a kick to the man's leg. "That was Jenny and her one eye." They were now in Counsel's way and he stopped again.

"You going farther into Texas?" the man asked Counsel.

"I have that plan." He felt that everything behind him, horses and people and wagons, had now stopped as if what he and the white woman and man were saying was more important than wherever they were going.

"Hmm," the woman said, "I've seen the rest of Texas and now I've seen you, and I don't think the two of you would marry well." Where was the law in Texas with all these people going about?

"You could join us," the white man said. Yes, Counsel decided, the little boy was his son. "We've seen Texas and we could tell what all you are missing. The rivers, the land, the dust. Before we're done telling you, you'll think you've been to every part of Texas."

"We're as good as picture books," the woman said.

"The only thing we ask is that you not hurt children," the man said.

"That's a hard one," the woman said, kicking the man again.

"I learned it. He can learn it."

"I want to see for myself," Counsel said and started up his horse again.

"You learned it after you learned not to lie anymore," the woman said and reached over and rubbed the back of her hand along the blond man's beard. He closed his eyes and smiled, and had he been a cat, he would have curled up and purred.

"No," the man said, opening his eyes, "that was Jenny that had the lying problem. Lying problem along with falling into Mississippi."

Counsel turned his horse to the right. "Texas," he said.

"Suit yourself," the man said.

"Suit everybody," the woman said, and as soon as she did the thunder of movement began and the white man and white woman parted and Counsel went between them. "Just don't lie and hurt the children. Jenny learned the hard way."

Counsel could see full sunlight for the first time since he had entered the forest, but after a few yards, he felt thunder coming from ahead and dozens of horses appeared. No people, just horses who seemed to be following all the people with the obedience of the dogs at the beginning of the forest. He went into the mix and closed his eyes. There was a sweet musty smell to all the horseflesh, and on another day, somewhere else, he could have enjoyed the wonder of them. A man behind him began to whistle. Maybe, Counsel thought, Texas was being emptied out of filth and it was now a better place for a man like him.

In five minutes or so, he was clear of everything and the land and the air belonged to him alone. But he could still hear the thundering and it stayed with him even as he put more distance between him and the pack. At a creek he stopped and he and the horse drank, and even after he had put his whole head in the water, the thundering remained. He and the horse walked across the creek, and on the other side he mounted, and they were fine for more than two miles. Then a thicket of vegetation came up. He dismounted and at first it went easy with just a few cuts here and there with his knife. He thought at any moment they would have a clearing again. But the vegetation continued and so did the thundering in his head. Counsel looked to the left and the right, hoping for a way to avoid the growth but there were just long lines of green that he felt would take days to pass. The horse began to balk. Counsel pulled on it and cut at the green with his knife.

"Come on," he told the horse, wondering if it might be sensing some snake lurking in the growth. "Come on." He released his reins and went ahead to cut a path. He returned for the horse and it seemed to be satisfied but as he moved on, still holding the reins and still cutting, the horse balked again. "I said come. I want you to come."

The horse began pulling him back. Counsel stopped, sweating, head full of thunder, chest heaving, and he looked the horse in the eyes. "Come," he said in as calm a voice as he could manage. "Come." He pulled out his pistol. "When I tell you to come, don't you think I mean it?" The horse did not move. "Come," he said, again calmly. He raised the pistol and shot the horse between the eyes. The horse sank on two knees and moaned and Counsel fired once more and the horse collapsed. Its breathing was heavy and he prepared to fire again but soon the breathing stopped. "Why is coming so hard?" he said to the horse.

In one of the destroyed books back home there had been a man in a dark place who commanded the power of a magic carpet. Counsel had sat one of his daughters on his knee and read stories to her. How easy it had all been for the man and his carpet.

He holstered his gun and all the thundering stopped for the first time since the entrance to the forest. A few flies appeared immedi-

ately above the horse. "What is it that you want of me?" Counsel
asked God. He sat down, less than four feet from the horse, and more
flies, bigger than any he had known in North Carolina, came to the
horse in a black cloud. He took off his hat and tried to wave them
away, but more came as if the waving had been a signal for them to
come. "What do you want me to do?" he asked God. "Tell me what it
is." He looked up and was surprised that the buzzards were circling so
soon. He shot at one but missed and no sooner had the sound of the
shot gone away than the buzzards began to land. Maybe it was not
Texas where he should be; maybe it was still full of niggers and people no one could identify because they weren't in books, and still full
of white women gone bad and white men letting them go bad. "You
tell me what to do and I will do it," he said to God. "Isn't that how it
has always worked? You say, I do. You say and I do." He thought of the
men in the large family Bible in the destroyed library who talked the
way he was talking now. Sometimes God heard and acted, took pity
on his creations, and sometimes he heard and ignored the creations
talking to him. His daughters had liked the stories in the Bible, the
Bible with their names and the days of their births written large and
in ink the general store man had said would last for generations.
"First," the man said, "the ink will note your children's birthdays,
and then it will note their marriage days. The ink will outlast you, Mr.
Skiffington." Counsel went on talking to God, and the buzzards came
down and joined the flies, all of them feasting on the horse and ignoring the man who still had some life in him.

8

Namesakes. Scheherazade.
Waiting for the End of the World.

From the day Fern Elston arrived when Henry Townsend died to the day she closed down her extended stay with Caldonia was a little more than five weeks, though she had returned home for periods of no more than a day or two. She lived some eight miles from Caldonia. Fern, like Maude, Caldonia's mother, and her brother Calvin, thought she could be of greater comfort and use to Caldonia if she were with her under the same roof, day by day. Fern knew how death and the mourning that followed could set a life adrift and how important it was for family and friends to guide a soul back to shore, back home. At the beginning of the fourth week, Fern could see that Caldonia had stood up in her boat, had placed her hand on the captain's shoulder to steady him and reassure all on board and was making up her mind about where it would be best to come ashore. "She had come from good people so I never feared for her," Fern told Frazier Anderson, the Canadian pamphlet writer that August day in 1881. "And you had been her teacher," Anderson added. She responded, ignoring the compliment, "I have been given credit when I should not have. And there have been times when I was denied the credit due me. But that is the fate of many a teacher, the good and the bad."

Maude was the first to return home. She might have stayed on longer but she knew that all the talk of legacy would have hardened Caldonia against what she was saying. And Maude was eager to get back to her lover, the one she had taken after her husband's murder. That lover, Clarke, a slave, had been left in charge of her place, and she trusted him perhaps as much as she trusted her own children. Clarke had taught himself to read and write, and Maude's trust flowed from the fact that he had, only weeks before the death of her husband, Tilmon Newman, come and told her what he was now able to do. She had not been left to find out on her own, to come upon him unexpectedly with his head in a book and Clarke hurriedly trying to explain it away by turning the book upside down and pretending he did not really know what he was doing. That had happened to a white couple, acquaintances of Maude's in Amelia County. It had frightened the white woman, seeing the incongruity of a nigger with a book, she told Maude after the slave, Victoria, had been whipped and told to forget what she knew. It frightened her more than walking into the barn and seeing a mule singing hymns or speaking the Lord's words, the woman told Maude.

"Do you know," Maude had said the first time she and Clarke had lain together, "that if I was a white woman, they would come in here and tear you from limb to limb?" "And what they gon do with you being colored?" he asked. Maude, delighted that she had taken such a step in her life, lay back, the sweat over her body still drying. "I suspect that since I own you, since I have the papers on you, they might do the same thing if I up and screamed. They wouldn't be as fast, I suppose, but they would come, Clarke." He said nothing.

Calvin followed his mother two days later, though he had very little to get back to. The place Maude owned had grown smaller and smaller over time as she rented portions of her land. She also rented out many of her slaves; each leased slave could bring in as much as $25 a year, and the renter was responsible for meals and upkeep while renting the slave, so just about all of the $25 was profit. Calvin was not an idle man, and he would work in the fields that remained alongside his mother's servants. But the toiling, even before Henry Townsend died, did not fulfill him as it had once. And when he returned home after Henry's death, he picked himself up and went out into the ever-decreasing fields only because he knew he would waste away otherwise. He would come to blame it all on slavery. Had he and Clara Martin, cousin to Winifred Skiffington, ever spoken, he might have understood her sense of miasma. A pain generated by the very air around him seeped into his bones and settled right next to the pain of silently caring for Louis.

Then Fern left. Her husband was at their place for all the time she had been away, abandoning his gambling sprees for the time being. But she had found, in her brief returns home, that he was becoming increasingly erratic and she could not depend on him to run things the way she knew they had to be run. Hers was not as large an estate as Caldonia's but, as she had told her students, size did not determine the vulnerability to rot. She had taught that the ruin of an empire could start not with rebellion in the farthest reaches of the empire, but in the attic or bedroom or the kitchen of the emperor's palace where he had allowed domestic chaos to fester and eventually bring down the palace, and with the palace the empire could follow. Her husband was not a man given to drink all the time, she said to Caldonia once, but he often acted with the irresponsibility of a drunkard. It would have been better if he were a drunkard, she continued, then at least he would have the benefit of the gaiety that came with drink.

Caldonia stood on the verandah and watched Fern go off, Loretta just behind her and to the left. They went inside and Caldonia read for much of the afternoon, then sewed with Loretta. Moses came that evening and told Caldonia about the first nail Henry had driven into a board in the kitchen, when the house was no more than a dream in his head.

The servant driving Fern home that day saw the man first and he told her there was someone up ahead in the road. It was nearing sundown, the sky afire with the red and the orange. The patrollers had already passed them, so Fern was assured that whoever it was was someone who had a legitimate reason to be in the road. "I can't make it out," Zeus the servant said to her. "It just a big somethin out there." "It" was big because the man was sitting on a horse, but with the dying sun behind the man making him a large silhouette, what Zeus could make out was a figure of one piece, not quite man and not quite horse.

"You be Miss Elston?" the man said, taking off his hat when they were near. He was a Negro and Fern could see with the last of the day's light that he was the color of a dark pecan.

"I be Jebediah Dickinson," the man said.

"Are you looking for me, Mr. Dickinson?" Fern said.

"I am, ma'am, and yet I ain't."

"I am tired, Mr. Dickinson, riddles are not what I want this time of the day."

"Your husband be owin me $500, and all I want is for him to pay so I can get where I need to be goin." Ramsey Elston, her husband, had left home the day before, the need to gamble having finally claimed him after so many weeks.

"I assume you have been up to the house and that Mr. Elston is not there. Beyond that, I cannot help you. Pass on," Fern said to Zeus, and he raised the reins but when the man began to speak, he dropped them again.

"A man would think that the debt of one be the debt of the other when two people are one and the same as man and wife." The man had not moved. He was more or less catty-corner to the road, though not in any threatening way, and Zeus could have gone through if his mistress had ordered it so. Jebediah's horse seemed the nervous sort, head forever up and down and tail wagging for all it was worth. The tail had been shortened but only Zeus, who was not around horses very much, noticed that.

"Is that so?" Fern said. Jebediah got down off the horse and came around to her and the horse's tail stopped wagging and, a few moments later, her head stopping bobbing. "You are quite mistaken, Mr. Dickinson. Whatever Mr. Elston does out in the world is his business. It has nothing to do with me, no more than what you do in the world is my business." *I have been a dutiful wife.*

"All I'm sayin, ma'am—"

"I do not care about all that you are saying. His debts are his own. If you are a gambler, and I assume that you are, you would know that." She wondered when Ramsey had started gambling with black people. She wondered if he still gambled with white people. "Pass on," she said to Zeus.

He was still there the next day and all the days after that for nearly a week. She came and went—once to Caldonia's—and he said nothing to her, just raised his hat at her going and raised it again at her coming back. In the night he was still out there, for she could make out a small fire. And there was movement, though that could just as easily have been a bear. The patrollers often came up to him and he pulled out his papers from inside his shirt and they would move on. Fern could see him from her window far up the path. She should not have been able to see him: she had wanted trees planted just before the entrance, trees that would now have been high enough to block him out. But Ramsey had always wanted the view unobstructed.

What he ate Fern did not know, and her slaves could not tell her. Seven days after he was there he knocked at her door. Zeus opened it and told Jebediah his mistress didn't like folks, slaves and Negro strangers like him, knocking at her front door. "Thas what they made the back door for," Zeus said. "Then what they make the front door for?" Jebediah asked. Zeus closed the door, gently, as if he didn't really want to make a fuss. In less than two minutes Fern came to the door, and Zeus, unsmiling, was behind her.

"Miss Elston, my horse be dyin on me, and I don't own a gun, so I can't put her outa her misery," Jebediah said. His hat was in front of his chest and he was holding it with both hands. "If I was strong anough, I could wring her neck, but that would take time and she would suffer and so would I. I have a knife, but thas about the same amount of sufferin for us both."

"Zeus," Fern said, "please ask Colley to come here. Tell Colley to bring the rifle and a pistol." When she married the second and third times, Zeus would be with her. Indeed, as she talked to Anderson Frazier that day in 1881, he was inside the house, occasionally looking through the curtains at the backs of their heads. He brought out lemonade to Anderson after Fern offered him some.

"Yessum," Zeus said.

"Are you planning to make that place out there your home, Mr. Dickinson?" she asked as they waited.

"Your husband been owin me $500, thas all there is to it."

She would have sighed but that was not in her nature. Sighing was an indication of surrender, of approaching helplessness. She folded her arms.

Zeus came around the side of the house, carrying a pistol, and he was followed by Colley, a man even larger than Jebediah. Colley had a rifle resting on his shoulder. The three men went out to the horse and after Jebediah said something to Colley, the man handed him the rifle and Jebediah shot the horse twice in the head and then handed the rifle back to Colley. Fern watched from the verandah and she could see how the horse simply disappeared in one, two seconds from her treeless view, leaving not one sign that it had ever been there except for a little bothersome dust. Zeus had just stood with his hands behind his back, the pistol in his left hand. They came back and Jebediah asked Fern for the loan of a shovel to bury the beast, and when he was done with the hole, Colley came out with another man and two mules and the three men and the two mules managed to drag the dead horse over and down into the hole. Dickinson covered the hole up. Zeus did not participate because all the work he ever did was in the house, except for a little puttering in Fern's garden.

Whenever Fern came out and back after that, she found Jebediah sitting on his saddle when he wasn't standing. He raised his hat as usual. And in all those days her husband never showed up or sent word about his whereabouts.

Oden Peoples, the Cherokee patroller, got tired of seeing Jebediah out there day in, day out and said so to Sheriff John Skiffington. That was the second week Jebediah was there. "Give him a little more time," Skiffington said. "I'll be patient with vagrancy but not till the end of my days." And so near the end of the second week, in broad open daylight when he wasn't supposed to be on patrol, Oden rode up to Jebediah and pointed his gun at him. Fern watched them from her window.

Jebediah raised his hands without any trouble. He must have said something about his being a free man because Oden shouted something long and hard at him. Oden was on his horse and he got down, never once taking the gun off Jebediah. He roped Jebediah's hands and waist, a rope of a good six feet, and then he got back up on his horse and he started riding, one hand holding the reins and the other holding the end of the rope that was chaining the walking Jebediah. He had holstered his gun because he felt he didn't need it anymore.

Fern came out to the road, with Zeus behind her, and they watched together. They watched them for a long time. It was more than ten miles into town but the woman and her slave couldn't see that far, only about a mile or more, and then the trees and the hills got in the way. She told Zeus to get someone to bring in Mr. Dickinson's saddle.

As far as anyone could remember, there had never been a colored man in the Manchester County jail. None of them, free or slave, had ever done anything to warrant a stay. The free men in Manchester knew the tenuousness of their lives and always endeavored to be upstanding; they knew they were slaves with just another title. Most crimes and misdemeanors by slaves were dealt with by their masters; they could even hang a slave if he killed another slave, but that would have been like throwing money down a well after the slave had already thrown the first load of money down, as William Robbins once told Skiffington.

Skiffington was most reluctant to put a Negro in a facility that would one day have to be used again by a white man, a white criminal. He resented Oden for putting him in that predicament. He could have chained Jebediah in Sawyer's barn out back, but Sawyer wanted an arm and a leg for everything, and Skiffington felt the law shouldn't have to pay that much. And, besides, the law mandated that the sheriff of a county have some control over a prisoner at all times, which wouldn't have been the case with Sawyer's barn. So he put Jebediah in the jail cell and decided that everyone would have to live with it.

Jebediah's free papers said he had been manumitted by Reverend Wilbur Mann of Danville, Virginia. The papers looked right, but Skiffington telegraphed the sheriff down Danville way that he had a suspect Negro and the sheriff telegraphed back that Jebediah was the property of Mann. "Rev. Coming," the telegram added. In four days Mann was at the jail. He arrived early one morning before Skiffington had even reached the jail and the sheriff found Mann looking in the window, laughing. The reverend was a tall man, very gaunt, and he had the prettiest long blond hair Skiffington had ever seen on a man.

"He belongs to me," Mann kept saying once they were inside. He produced a bill of sale that showed Jebediah was bought in Durham sixteen years before for $250.

"How he get that free paper?" Skiffington said.

Mann looked abashed. "He wrote em. He can read and write better than you and me." Mann took off his nice gray hat and set it with both hands on Skiffington's desk near the Bible. "That was my wife's doing, bless her name. I told her not to do something like that, but I could never say no to her. He was just a pup back then. She was sweet except for doing things I didn't approve of."

Jebediah, in the cell, was silent.

"You should make your wife stop doin work like that," Skiffington said. "She should know she shouldn't be doin that. She know what the law is about teaching slaves to read and write?"

"I know," Mann said. "But she dead now, been dead for two years, left us not long before this damn Jebediah here took off. Bless her name. I got me a real smart wife now—she can't read nor write so she can't teach anybody what she don't know." He told Skiffington that Dickinson was his first wife's maiden name. "Ain't that a kick in the head for you?" the preacher said.

"I don't know," Skiffington responded. "I'll just accept your word that it is."

"Well, it is. It's a big kick in the head," Mann said.

"If you didn't free him," Skiffington said, "how he get that free paper?"

"I told you he can read. He can read and write. Can do it better than I can, can't you, Jebediah? Can cipher like the dickens, too." He walked over to the bars. "Damn your soul to hell for causin me all this trouble." Jebediah still said nothing. "And why you wanna go and despoil my wife's good memory by usin her name to commit a crime with? Huh? You tell me that? Damn your soul."

"You can take him home anytime," Skiffington said.

"Lemme go out and get a little mouthful of somethin to eat. I brought my neighbor and he eatin now. We both can get him back where he belong."

"Fine, that's good with me."

Mann had turned to talk to Skiffington but now he went back to Jebediah. "I'm gonna whip your black hide till God tell me to stop, you hear me?" Jebediah stepped back and sat on the pallet on the floor. The cot for the white prisoners had been removed. "Yessiree, you rest up now cause I'm gon tan you good, boy. And then I'ma let you heal, give you time to grow another hide and then I'ma whip that one off you. Then let you grow another, then whip that one off. Go around despoilin my wife's good name and committin God knows what crimes. Thas all the work you ever gonna have to do again, Jebediah, just grow hides and watch me whip em off you." Mann took up his hat and then he leaned his head back a few degrees, patted down the front part of the blond hair and set the hat on his head with the same gentleness he would use to set the hat down in a hatbox. "I'll be back directly," he told Skiffington and went out the door.

As it happened, Ramsey Elston had returned home two nights before. He told his wife that he didn't know any Jebediah Dickinson, and if a Jebediah Dickinson didn't exist for him, then surely a $500 debt couldn't exist. Fern knew he was not telling her the truth. God's gift to Ramsey as he aged was easiness with lies. They were in their eleventh year of marriage. She had not been able to get Jebediah out of her mind since the day Oden rode away with him.

She had intended to go into town to inquire about Jebediah the day after her husband told her he did not know him, but Ramsey rose that first morning and was as sweet as ever. That evening he turned sour and she went to bed determined to go in and inquire about Jebediah. *I have been a dutiful wife.* She did not know about Mann and she arrived with Colley at the jail just about the time Mann must have been forking in his first mouthful of food at the table with his neighbor.

Skiffington told her the what-all about Jebediah and she sat in her surrey waiting for Mann to finish his meal. When he came back up the street he was followed by a white man just as tall as he was, but the man stayed outside the jail after Mann went in. Mann took off his hat again with both hands and placed it back on Skiffington's desk beside the Bible. Fern came in.

She told him she wanted to buy Jebediah. Right away he asked,

"How much?" When she told him $250, he did a little *click* with the side of his mouth to indicate he was displeased with the figure. "You cannot say he is very reliable, given his history," Fern said. "Paid $350 for him when he was a pup," Mann said. Skiffington had seen the bill of sale for $250 but he didn't contradict Mann. The only man of God whose word he trusted was his father's, and his father had been ordained by no human. Fern said $300. Mann walked to the cell where Jebediah was still sitting on the pallet. A sale was certainly going to be made that day and it was plain on Mann's face. What was also plain was the disappointment that he would not be able to do all he had been planning since he came up from Danville. Perhaps it was just as well, he thought, both hands on the bars of the cell, because just how many beatings could he manage before Jebediah keeled over and died on him. Fern and Mann said nothing for a few minutes, and finally Fern said $375, "a good profit for any man on any day." Mann agreed.

Mann and the white man he came with escorted Fern and her driver Colley and Jebediah back to her place. Jebediah was roped again and he sat in the front seat beside Colley, who never said a word to him. At Fern's place, Mann and the white man took Jebediah into the barn and there they chained him to a wall. "If he happens to get up and disappear during the night," Mann said before he and his companion left, "I am due my money." "I understand that," Fern said, "but I anticipate no disappearances." All this time Mann thought he was dealing with a white woman and he was never to know any different.

She told Colley to make sure Jebediah was comfortable, fed and blanketed, and he was as comfortable as he could be with less freedom to move about than he had in Skiffington's jail cell. Her husband, who had not been about when she came back with Jebediah, was brought out to the barn next day and right off Jebediah started ranting and raving.

"Where's my gotdamn money, Ramsey? You owe me five hundred dollars, and I want every gotdamn penny!" He strained against the chains and kicked straw up at Ramsey. "Let me loose, you hear!" he shouted to Fern.

"I don't know you and I know nothing about some five hundred dollars," Ramsey said, his feet apart and ignoring the straw that was settling on his boots. "Why you buy somethin that will give you nothing but trouble?" he said to his wife. Their parents had met and discussed their marriage before the two of them had ever laid eyes on each other. Ramsey had picked at his chicken the evening of their first meeting. She was not impressed with him and would not be for some time.

"Standin there with all the love in you now, huh?" Jebediah said to Ramsey. Colley had gone to Jebediah and whenever he would strain against the chains trying to reach Ramsey, Colley would take hold of the chains and pull him back. "There's a lot of people in Richmond and places that would be mighty surprised you had a damn wife." Then to Fern he said, "I didn't know he had a wife till he woke up screamin with that lovely cross the hall from me one night. Woke me up and woke a lotta other people up, too." Some straw had settled on Fern's dress and boots and she now began picking it all off. "I want my damn $500, Ramsey, and I want every penny now."

Ramsey left the barn. Fern left off picking off straw and stepped closer to Jebediah. "You will stay here until you learn some manners, until you learn you cannot get up and walk about like some free man."

"I am free," Jebediah said. "Mann ain't knowed what he talkin bout. I am free."

"The law does not say that." She had intended, only hours before, to free him, allow what she had paid for him to be a trade for what Ramsey owed him. She had expected Jebediah to go for that because he would be, after all, free and clear once and for all. But the knowledge of her husband's infidelity had come full and heavy and squatted down big in front of her, blocking everything else out. She resented her husband, and she resented the messenger, the companion to her husband. She was thirty-four years old. "This barn has been here many years, and it will stand many more with you in it if you cannot learn manners."

"Manners ain't what I need, lady. I need my money."

Fern said to Colley, "I don't want him going anywhere until he learns right from wrong, night from day."

"Yessum," Colley said and pulled three times on the chain.

"You and your gotdamn no-good husband can go to hell!" Jebediah shouted as she went out. "Y'hear me good. Both a yall can go straight to hell."

Jebediah stayed there four days and then he told Colley that he was ready to do what she paid for him to do and Colley and another man took Jebediah to the back of the house and Fern came out and down to him.

"I want no trouble. I want not one moment's trouble," Fern said.

"All right, all right," Jebediah said and she slapped him.

"I thought you said he had learned some manners," Fern said to Colley.

"He told me he had, Mistress. He told me that." Colley grabbed Jebediah by the neck and forced him to his knees. Ramsey had not gone away to gamble since he had returned while Jebediah was in the jail. He had not been in her bed since his first night back. She had not washed that day he came back; she had washed the night before she went in to buy Jebediah.

"Please tell him to let me up," Jebediah said. "I'm gonna do right. I told yall that."

He was a good worker, when he was there to work. For more than two weeks Fern had no trouble from him. Colley, who was as close to an overseer as the Elstons had, kept watch on Jebediah all the day and night long. Fern had alerted Skiffington that he might run, and the sheriff made sure his patrollers didn't retire for the night without knowing where Jebediah was. Everyone got used to his being a good worker. Then, near the end of the third week of doing what he was told, he would just saunter off. He didn't make a show of it. He would simply drop whatever they had him doing and walk away and go fishing, or he'd pick blueberries and gorge himself right at the spot where he picked them, or he would find a pasture to nap in, moving the cows away if they were in a spot he relished.

They would drag him back with little fuss, but he would be at it again, maybe not the next day or the day after but pretty soon.

With the fourth week he began going off in the night and returning before morning, seemingly with no trouble from the patrollers. Several slave women in the area knew his name and knew it well; he told one he was a preacher and had been called by God Almighty. For a week he walked by Alice and they would not say a word to each other but each time they waved as though they were passing in the marketplace. Then one night he said hello and she started in on her nonsense and he turned and started walking with her, listening to everything she said. He wanted to know how long she would keep it up and found that she could outlast his walking beside her.

What Fern and Ramsey were to discover was that he had somehow gotten hold of a piece of paper and made himself a pass and had been showing it to patrollers any night they found him on the road. He had been fortunate that he had not run into Oden Peoples. "This nigger," the paper said, "is on business for his owners, Ramsey and Fern Elston at the Elston Estate. He can be trusted to come back home." It was signed "Fern Elston," but it looked nothing like her signature because he had never seen it. The Elstons took that pass away from him, not knowing he had another signed "Ramsey Elston." On that one he was not just on "business" for the Elstons but "urgent business."

But the worst of it was that he started calling out whenever he was near the house that he wanted his money. "I ain't forget yall got my money. I ain't forgot what yall owe me. I want my five hundred dollars." In the night, before they took his passes away, he would say it. He said it on the way to the blueberries and he said it on the way to a nap. "I ain't forgot yall got my money." Ramsey came out one morning and shot his pistol over Jebediah's head, but that didn't stop him.

Then, three days after Ramsey returned to gambling, Fern came out and told him she wanted him to turn over a new leaf. She had Colley and two other men grab hold of Jebediah in front of the cabin he shared with one other unattached man. "This will all end today," Fern said. "I have been patient, but my patience is at an end. If you do not do right, I will have you in chains again."

Jebediah said, as she walked away, "If you was my woman you wouldn't be sleepin in that bed alone every night." She stopped but she didn't turn around. "Do you know how long it would take me to undo your hair and get them things off you? You know how long?" He must have known, with that heart and mind born in slavery, that he had gone way too far and he bowed his head. Without a word from Fern, the men released him and Jebediah took off his shirt and lay on his stomach on the ground. Fern never liked to flog slaves; for every whip mark on one slave's back, she estimated that his value came down $5. But there were some unforgivable matters in the world.

They whipped him twenty times, the last five having little effect because he had passed out at fifteen. He took a week to recover, was silent as he went about his work. And he didn't stray. A week after he went back to work he stepped on a plank with a rusty nail in the barn. He thought nothing of it at first, just doctored the wound with a little mud and some spiderwebs. But the wound festered, and in the end, they had to saw off Jebediah's right foot to save his life, or so the white doctor said.

He didn't move from the front of his cabin after that, except to go to the privy or to go in to eat and sleep. A little less than two weeks after they cut off his foot Fern came down and told him she would set him free. He said nothing, just went on listening to his phantom foot talking loud to him.

He came up with Colley to the house the next day, up and into the kitchen. He was on the crutches someone had fashioned for him. Fern was at the table, writing. When she was done, she blotted the paper and handed it to him. He read it and handed it back to her. "Ain't but one 'T' in *manumit*," he told her, "cept when you usin the pas tense." She had never written the word before. She wrote the paper again, then wrote another. Men were notorious for losing things. With all the human beings she would ever know in her life, he would be the only one she would come close to saying "I am sorry" to. She told none of this to Anderson Frazier, the pamphlet writer.

She offered him a place and a job on the estate, but he told her he had come to see Virginia as a demon state and he wanted no part of it. "If there was ocean water right out there," he said, "I'd jump in and swim all the way up to Baltimore just so I wouldn't have to walk on damn Virginia land."

She gave him a wagon and an old horse to travel on. And she gave him $50. "You and your no-good husband owe me $450 more and there ain't no way round it. I give yall the work I done and my foot for free."

He left, him and the wagon and the horse with all its years behind it. He met a lot of kindness on his way north because he had only that one foot, but no matter how many warm beds and full plates black and white people gave him and no matter how well they treated his horse, he never stopped thinking that he was moving through a demon state. He came to Washington, D.C., and settled for it, though it was Baltimore that he had had his heart set on. Fern's horse died six months after Jebediah hit Washington. He never bothered to go the forty miles to Baltimore to see if it was all he had dreamed. He named his first child, his only daughter, Maribelle, the name of the horse he had to shoot outside of Fern's place with Fern's rifle. He named his second child Jim, after the horse that had brought him to Washington. He caught his son one day writing "James" on his lessons and he told the boy without raising his voice that if he had wanted to name him James, that was what he would have done.

Caldonia and Moses had developed a routine with his coming to the house most of the working days and telling her what had gone on. There was rarely any real news but he related what he did say in some detail—how many shingles to repair the barn, the yields Caldonia might expect for each crop, what was fed to the slaves for dinner and supper, the number of pails of milk from each cow, how long it took to put up a new corncrib to replace the one a sleepwalking mule destroyed. Ultimately, the important thing was that the crops were rising well and that could have taken less than five minutes, but near the end of the recitation he added small bits about the lives of the slaves. One evening in early September, about the time Augustus Townsend was kidnapped and sold, Moses stood in the parlor, his hat in both hands. He had sweated much of the day and had waited in the back until he knew he was nice and dry. She told him to sit, and, as always, he hesitated since he was wearing what he wore in the fields. But he sat and at the end of the story of the workday he mentioned to Caldonia that Celeste's pregnancy was coming along fine and that Gloria had a lye burn and the left side of Radford's face was three times its normal size, toothache maybe, as Radford was known to chew on anything short of an anvil.

He was ready to go into another fanciful tale about Henry when Loretta came into the room and asked Caldonia if there was anything she could bring her and Caldonia said a tea biscuit and half a cup of coffee, more water than coffee, she added. Caldonia told her to bring Moses a biscuit.

There was a problem with someone stealing food from one or two cabins, Moses continued, but he had an idea who it was. "I got it in mind," he said, "that it might be some child. Twas mostly molasses that was taken." Caldonia had her head back and her eyes closed, which had been her way since the second evening. He had begun to feel that he could say anything and it would not matter.

"Do you know exactly who it might be?"

"I got my eye on Selma and Prince's little fella, Patrick. He could be in with Grant, Elias and Celeste's boy. Or Grant and Boyd. Every since that dream conniption, they been thick as fleas, sees one you see the other."

"The dream?" Loretta handed him two biscuits but he did not eat.

He told her about the boys sharing dreams and how they had grown close as a result. Celeste said the dreams were expected to end with the coming of fall, but Moses did not believe that was true. "They's badder than regular for little boys. They got the devil in em and he ain't gonna come out cause the season done changed."

"Do you think they are hungry?" Caldonia asked. "Could that be why they are stealing?" She was at the end of the settee again, dressed in black.

"Hungry?" For the most part, Henry had always allotted what he thought were enough provisions on Saturdays to each slave, including a pint of blackstrap molasses. Those provisions would decrease or increase according to his profit for a particular year; the pint of molasses had never changed and he believed it was enough for each slave, except for slaves with children. "Nome, I wouldn't say they be hungry. Marse Henry wouldn't let no slave be hungry if he could help it."

"I know he wouldn't," Caldonia said. She drank from her cup and then settled it with great care in her lap. His hand with the biscuits began to sweat and he put them in the other hand. He was not looking directly at her, but at a spot at the center of the settee.

"I know your boy Jamie is a large size, do you think he could be the culprit?" She gave a laugh to ease him in case he was hurt by her accusation.

"My boy? Jamie? Thievin? Well, he likes to eat and I can't say he don't, but he know I'd skin him alive if I caught him touchin what ain't hisn." With each word he had been taking his eyes from the spot at the center of the settee and moving toward her. He remembered the first time he saw her—a woman too thin to make any man a good wife.

"I see. It might be a good idea to increase the portion of molasses to a pint and a half," she said.

"Yessum, I'll start it this Saturday."

"Good. I'll see you tomorrow." She opened her eyes and raised up. Moses stood and said, "Good night, Missus."

He washed before he came the next evening, stood at the well and poured water over himself and scrubbed with his hands as Priscilla his wife watched, laughed. "Just gonna get all that dirt all over you again tomorrow."

"You just hush up," Moses said. He dried himself with the shirt he had worn into the field and put it back on.

"Can't go up to the house and let Loretta see how you been slavin in that field all day." Because Moses was not a good husband to her or much of a father to their child, Priscilla thought it not at all impossible that Loretta might be why he was going to the house so much. He was an overseer, after all, and though he was a field hand, he was a man of some power and any woman, even a woman of the house, might find it tempting to sway her hips in his direction. "No, we can't let Loretta see what we really is, day in, day out. Gotta clean some a that stink off first."

He slapped her. It was not a hard hit but she went to her knees nevertheless because the slap came with years of abuse and rejection. "Why you gotta treat me this way, Moses? Why you can't do right by me?"

"I do all the right I can do," he said.

Tessie, Celeste and Elias's girl, came by, leading Alice down to her cabin. "Little Marse be slappin. Little Marse be slappin. Little Marse got the slappin disease," Alice chanted.

"Why you cryin?" Tessie said.

"You just get on," Moses said to them. And to Priscilla, "You get on to that cabin."

She picked herself up and went down to the cabin. There were no secrets among the cabins and, much later, when the sheriff came to inquire about the disappearances, he would hear of how Moses would beat Priscilla. "We could all hear it," the children told Skiffington, though the adults said little to the white man. "It wasn't every night, but it was near bout every night. He would hit her and the walls they be shakin. Like this—boom boom boom." Priscilla reached her cabin and touched the door lightly and it opened to her, and the hearth fire her son had made for them lit her up and she went in and closed the door behind her. "And did he ever hurt that boy of his?" Skiffington would ask the children later. "Did he ever do harm to that Alice?" "He did it to everybody," Tessie would say, a statement confirmed by every child who could talk.

"Moses," Caldonia said after he had told her about the day, "how long did it take you and Henry to build this house?"

"How long, Missus?"

"Yes, how long? Weeks? Months?"

"I'd say maybe four months, every day workin. Yessum, many's the day we'd be workin away and he'd say, 'Moses, you think Miss Caldonia gon like this here room? You think her heart will be happy when she gets a look at this?' And I'd say, 'Yes, Marse Henry, she gon like this.' " Her head was leaning back again and if she remembered that the house had been completed long before Henry met her, she said nothing. "I see," she said after a time.

"Now I wants to say that there were some rooms that he wouldn't let me work on with him. There were rooms that he wanted to do all by hisself."

"Rooms?"

"This room, Missus. The parlor. He knowed there'd be days and days he'd want to be here alone with you, and I don't guess he wanted me to have a hand in it. And . . . and the sleepin room upstairs. He wanted that one to hisself. Thas just the way he was, Missus."

She could see the man she still loved working away. What had she been doing those days Henry was working here, when they did not yet know about each other? Had she been daydreaming about someone else, been planning the future with some other man she had passed on the road?

She dismissed him after nearly an hour and a half, their longest time together. Loretta was sitting in the hall when he left. Loretta rose from her chair and she and Moses did not speak and Loretta knocked at the slightly opened door to the parlor and he went down the hall toward the kitchen. He did not linger but he walked slower than he had usually done. In the kitchen he lied and told Bennett, Zeddie the cook's husband, that the missus wanted him to have another shirt and pair of britches. Had it been anyone else, a slave who was not the overseer and who had not been talking for many nights with their mistress, Bennett would have been suspicious. Bennett said he would have the clothes for him the next morning.

Moses found Elias on the stump, whittling a bird for his youngest child, Ellwood.

"We gotta meet that mule tomorrow mornin," Moses said. She had to have some man so why not him. "You best get some sleep." Dare he raise his eyes that high? Dare he, dare he? "I don't wanna have to come out here and tell you again."

Elias did not move. Moses, just before he opened his cabin door, said again, "We gotta meet that mule tomorrow mornin. You want me to tell her we got somebody down here who don't do what I tell him?"

Elias stood up and took the lamp inside with him. He carried it as carefully as he carried the bird and the carving knife. He had borrowed the lamp from Clement, who owned it together with Delphie and Cassandra. The lane was then dark and quiet and Moses stepped into his cabin. Priscilla had made him supper but he did not want it.

There were the last traces of the hearth fire and he sat at the side of their pallet and ate the tea biscuits. His wife and his son watched him. An hour after he went inside Alice wandered out, sniffed at each cabin door and went on her way. Her voice was hoarse from all the talk of the day but she chanted anyway. There were angels by the hundreds waiting for her songs.

Later, after the disappearances, Skiffington would question Elias the longest, and Elias, of all the adults, would hold nothing back. Celeste said the least. "I know nothin bout Moses and any of them," she said to Skiffington. "Don't say things to him, Elias," Celeste would say after Skiffington came to the lane the second time. "Please, don't, husband." "I got to," Elias said. They would be on their pallet, their children sleeping all around them. It would be cold outside that night and the fire in the hearth was going strong. "It's in my heart and I can't keep it there. Not for nobody can I keep it there." "Please, Elias . . ."

One day after Bennett gave him new pants and a shirt, Moses returned to the woods to be with himself for the first time since his master died. When it was done, he lay and watched the stars twinkling between the swaying leaves of the trees around him. The world was in the last days of summer and it gave off a fecundity that was pulling him into sleep. It was a moment of such peace that he said, in a whisper, that if he were to die now, he would not hate God for it. He was ready to get up and dress when he heard a twig break, and he knew right away that it was not an animal making its way, oblivious to him and what he was doing. He raised up on one elbow and waited. He was all too aware now that he was naked and he held his pants about his midsection. The weight of a human being released the broken twig and Moses heard the stick give out an almost imperceptible sigh. "Who out there?" he asked. "Priscilla? That you?"

He stood and dressed, and as he did he felt the person moving away. He went in the direction of the movement, then he ran.
When he was out of the woods, he was alone and there was nothing
but the crops and the crickets telling him things he did not want to
hear.

When he reached the lane, he found Alice in the middle of the
path, on her knees and praying. He said, "Get on home, you." She did
not acknowledge him. "Get home if you know whas good for you."
He came up behind her and toed her left thigh. "You hear me, girl?"
Whatever she was saying he could not understand, for it was more
gibberish than usual. "You get home or I'll put the strap to you." He
went on by and when he was at his door, he looked back and saw her
standing. She turned fully around once and stopped, and he knew that
it had been her in the woods. She came toward him and walked by,
disappeared into the area that would take her out to the road. He
heard her clearly now:

> I met a dead man layin in Massa lane
> Ask that dead man what his name
> He raised he bony head and took off his hat
> He told me this, he told me that.

It came into his head to go after her and strike her down, but when
he got to the clearing beyond the cabins she was gone. He still heard
the chanting but the more he stood there, the less certain he was
about what he was hearing—her actual chanting or the memory of
her chanting. And the sound of her voice seemed to come from everywhere.

He followed her the next night, resisted the need to go back to
the woods and hid behind the barn until he saw her leave her cabin.
Within minutes of her getting to the road, she had disappeared.
He went down the way he thought she had gone, and in several more
minutes, it occurred to him that he was farther from the Townsend

plantation than he had been in many years. He knew everything about the plantation but what was just beyond Caldonia's boundaries was alien to him. Moses looked about at the unfamiliarity and said quietly, "Alice? You there?" He called loudly. "Alice, you come here so I can see you. Come out here now, girl." The sound of galloping horses came from up ahead and he ran back toward the plantation, but he felt the horses coming closer and dove into a stand of bushes beside the road. The thick summer dust they riled covered him and the bushes and he felt himself choking. He buried his mouth in the bushes and bit down into thorny leaves, afraid that even with the noise of their galloping, the white men on the horses would hear him coughing dust. His mouth bled. The horses and their men passed, but when he had coughed out the dust and blood and got to the road again, he was not as sure which way was the plantation. He was at a crossroads of sorts and he shivered to know he had put himself there, that he had followed a woman whose neck should have been wrung long ago. He turned about. One road looked to be the correct one but when he looked at the other three, they seemed right as well. The stars and the moon were as bright as the night before but, as Elias was to say to Skiffington, he was "world stupid," and so the heavens meant nothing to him. "Sweet Jesus," he said, walking in the direction the horses had gone. But that direction produced a small stand of trees that he had not passed earlier. "Sweet Jesus."

He stood, trying to clear his head and spitting out blood. The sound of the horses and their patrollers was now a soft rumble along the ground. "Alice, come out here, I say." He heard a twig break along one road, a sound almost identical to that of the night before, and he went down that road.

He got to the plantation a half hour later, his mouth swelling from the bites of the thorns. At Alice's cabin he put both hands on the door, ready to push it in, and he knew immediately that she was inside, asleep or well on her way. He stepped back, out into the lane, and looked around. If her, then why not others who might have seen him in the woods? What would they think and what would they tell the mistress? Moses be alone out there in them woods, playin with hisself. No woman, no nothin, just hisself and hisself alone. They be talkin bout Alice, Missus, but Moses the one you gotta worry bout. Moses went toward his cabin. There were no windows on any cabin, for Henry would not have paid for the glass, but he felt their eyes watching him through the doors, through the walls. I see Moses walkin down the lane. I see Moses walkin down the lane. I see Moses layin in that lane. By the time he reached his own door, he could barely open his mouth. "Moses?" Priscilla said when he entered. She had been dreaming that she was in a strange house, not her cabin, not her mistress's house, and someone had knocked and she had gone to open the door and welcome the stranger to what she realized as she walked was her own house. "Welcome to my house," she told the stranger. Moses shut the cabin door and grunted once and Priscilla turned over and tried to go back to sleep.

By morning much of the swelling had gone down and he led the slaves out into the fields. Alice was no different than she was on any other day: a good worker who didn't sass and who seemed to go up and down a furrow in the time it took most people to turn around good. Occasionally, he would rise from his own work and look over at her, but, as always, she was in her own world. When the wind was right or when there were no songs from anyone, he could hear her: "*I'm gonna pick you. I'm gonna pick you. I'm gonna leave you be till you say my name just right.*"

That evening he changed and washed at the well and put on his new shirt and britches to report to Caldonia. The work of another day had gone well, he told her. He sat back in the chair and she asked him for the first time if he, too, wanted coffee. He said yes and Loretta brought him coffee in a cup that was identical to the one Caldonia had.

"I worry bout this Alice traipsin off every night," he said near the end of the meeting. "She might need lockin up every night just so them patrollers don't do somethin to her."

"The sheriff and his patrollers have said nothing to me. Has someone said something to you, Moses?"

"Why no, Missus. But she been doin this too long. A crazy woman be a disruption to peace and harmony, I'd say. Evbody else start wantin to act crazy, too."

"How long has she been doing this?"

"Since the day Marse Henry bought her."

"Then maybe she's as insane as she will ever get."

"Oh, she could get more crazy all right. I wouldn't put it pas her to get more crazy."

She set her cup on the little table beside her and leaned her head back and closed her eyes and was silent. He thought she was asleep but she unfolded her arms after several moments and rested her open hands on either side of her body. He followed her neck as it went down from her chin and disappeared into her blouse. She was still but her bosom rose and fell and he watched her for so long that he fell into the pattern of her bosom rising and falling. She had put on weight over the years. He had stood at his cabin door that first night she and Henry were married, had looked up at the house with only mild curiosity. Now he was only the distance of one jackrabbit hop from her, from all that Henry had been able to have any night of their life together.

"You won't forget him," she said at last.

"Ma'am?"

"You won't forget Henry Townsend, will you?"

"I'd sooner forget my own name, Missus."

"Good night, Moses. Tell Loretta to come in."

He waited as long as he could and then took the image of her on the settee with him out into the woods. He had not thought of a real woman, a woman he had met in the flesh, since the early days when he would come out there and think of Bessie, the woman Jean

Broussard and his Scandinavian partner had purchased along with Moses in Alexandria. Moses rose without lingering in the woods when he was done and listened for Alice.

When he got back to the lane, she was coming out of her cabin and he stepped into her path. She tried going around him but he followed her. "Leave me be or I'll send you to hell," he said and raised both fists to her face. "Oh, Marse, I'm just goin to feed my chickens," she said. "What?" Moses asked. "Whas that you say?" "I'm just goin to feed my chickens. Here little chick. There little chick, lemme feed you." He pushed her down as hard as he could. "I told you to leave me be." Alice began crying. "I told you to leave me be." He left her on the ground. Alice lay down all the way and spread her arms and legs and cried even harder.

Delphie came out and went to her. "Moses, whas this goin on? All right, child. I'm here. Moses, whas the matter with her? You know this ain't right."

"I told her to leave me be. You tell her leave me be or I'll kill her next time. I'll kill her down dead." He went home.

Delphie helped Alice to her feet. "You stay in tonight, all right?" Alice stopped crying once she was in the cabin, but an hour later she was back outside, sniffing at doors before setting off.

The next day was Sunday and he did not go out, but on Monday night he waited near the house and watched Alice emerge from the area of the cabins and walk with purpose to the road. The night was very warm and insects pestered him. He did not know how far he would follow but less than half a mile from the plantation he heard the horses galloping toward them. He stepped down into a ravine and could see her and the horses and their men many yards away. Alice lifted her frock and danced and tried to climb onto the horse with one man. The man pushed her away just as the horse reared up. The horses and the men charged off and Moses lay in the ravine until they were gone, closing his eyes and mouth and covering his nose from the dust.

When he raised up, Alice was walking away. Then she stopped
and looked around and cocked her head just so. She began chanting
again, softly at first, tentative. She stopped chanting several times to
listen and to take note of all around her. Each time she took up the
chant again, it was with less of the confidence of any previous nights.
He waited for more than an hour for her to return, and when she
didn't, he went home. And even after an hour waiting outside his
door, she did not appear. He went inside and felt some satisfaction as
he remembered how she had looked about and listened for him.
Maybe you could just be crazy by pretending to be crazy for a long,
long time. He lay down, and before he went to sleep he went through
his memory, trying to remember if there had been any slave who had
ever escaped from the Townsend plantation. There never had been.

He did not bring up Alice to Caldonia again. The patrollers would
take care of her one way or another, he thought. On Wednesday
evening the heat of the past few days subsided and Caldonia had
Loretta bring him cake along with the coffee. She asked that he tell
her again about Henry building the house, tell her about his constructing the parlor and the bedroom alone. "Tell me what he did,"
she said, leaning back and closing her eyes.

"Now I'm surprised this house didn't take years to put up, the way
Marse Henry went at it," Moses said. "Lookin at every nail, as I member. Weighin every board, every board of this very room. Missus, this
house will be standin the day Jesus returns to take us all home, thas
all the work Marse Henry put into it, all the time and care. I can see
him just like it was yesterday."

"Moses, you won't forget him, will you?" Before he could answer,
she leaned over and put her face in her hands, crying. He stood up.
Would Loretta hear and think he had harmed their mistress? He
looked at the door and it did not open. He listened, waiting for some
great stirring in the house, the converging of dozens on a slave who

had taken one step too many, and all he could hear was the house settling in one corner or another, and the sound of a woman crying and filling up the rest of the silence. He went slowly to her and knelt down. "I won't forget Marse Henry, Missus. I told you I wouldn't and I won't, not till I ain't here anymore." She continued crying, and then, as the house settled in other corners, he took her hand and opened the fist one finger at a time, ending with the thumb which had been encased in the other four fingers. He kissed the open hand and his world did not end. She pressed her hand to his face and when he looked up at her, she leaned down and kissed him, and still the world did not end.

They stood and held on to each other, and then, as if sharing the same thought, they separated and she put her hand to his chest, counting the beats of his heart. She was still crying. He touched the side of her face and told himself to leave, that that was enough for the evening. She had reached 109 in the beating of his heart when he went to the door and told Loretta that Missus wanted her and walked down the hall to the kitchen, to the back door.

The next night they stayed in their places. He had thought all that day she would not want him to return, but when he went to the back door and Loretta escorted him to the parlor and he saw her sitting just as she had the evening before, he lost the need to worry. That evening he weaved the most imaginative story yet about how Henry Townsend had tamed the land and made the place he would bring his bride to.

"I knowed the minute I laid eyes on you, Missus, that you was the one to make Marse Henry happy. He had this, that and the other but what he really needed was a somebody to set it all right, to shine on it and prettify it." He went on to create the history of his master, starting with the boy who had enough in his head for two boys. He was present at Henry's birth, he was there the day he was freed, he gave testimony of how all the best white people stretched out their feet and bid Henry to make them shoes and boots that they could walk to heaven in.

The next evening she cried again and he sat on the settee and held her. Then she allowed him to put her on his lap, with him filling every moment with words about Henry. The lovemaking would not happen for another week, with both of them still mostly clothed and the house very quiet, having done all the settling it would do for that day.

States of Decay. A Modest Proposal.
Why Georgians Are Smarter.

Darcy and Stennis and the people—including Augustus Townsend—they had stolen reached South Carolina in less than two weeks. Stennis had dumped the dead child, Abundance, on the side of the road long before they hit North Carolina, the child who had been coughing since Manchester. "We should bury that poor baby," the chained Augustus said as Stennis got back in the wagon after dropping the girl's body in the weeds. Augustus had held the dead child for miles, not wanting to believe she was dead. "Don't leave that poor baby out there like that." Darcy and Stennis had kidnapped Abundance Crawford, a free girl suffering from a cold, as she walked down a road outside of Fredericksburg in her new shoes. She would have turned nine years old in two more weeks.

"Should we bury her, Stennis?" Darcy said.

"Ain't got no shovel, Marse," Stennis said.

"I'll do it," Augustus said. "I'll dig her a grave with my hands. Just gimme some time."

The people in the back of the wagon with Augustus said they would help him dig a grave with their hands. Those people were two men and one woman. All of them, except for Augustus, would be sold before the wagon reached Georgia. The two men were Willis, a thirty-seven-year-old brick maker who had one leg shorter than the other, and Selby, a twenty-two-year-old baker who five weeks ago had married a woman whose hair went down two feet beyond her neck. Those two men had been free people, like Augustus. The woman was Sara Marshall, a twenty-nine-year-old seamstress whose master and mistress had given her their last name ten years before. "Don't bring shame to our name, Sara," they had said in a kind of ceremony in their kitchen. "Always bring honor to our name. The Marshall name stands for something in this land."

"Don't know bout no buryin, Marse," Stennis said of the child Abundance, "gettin them chains off and on. Watchin em so they don't run away. Lotta trouble for somethin that won't cause no more trouble in this world."

"Well," Darcy said, "if you don't know, how am I to know? Push on, Stennis. Push on."

In North Carolina, as they approached Roxboro, Augustus asked if Darcy might not send a telegram to Mildred, "my worryin wife," and let her know that he was alive. Darcy asked Augustus if he knew that sending a telegram would mean a loss for his pocket and told him that a careful man of business would try to cut down on losses as much as possible. A telegram was a loss, he said, adding that it was better that "poor Mildred" think he had just ascended to heaven due to his good nature. In Roxboro, Willis the brick maker shouted to a passing white man that he was free and had been kidnapped. Darcy grinned at the white man and said, "We done had this problem with him since Virginia." The man nodded.

It was in South Carolina, at Kingstree, at the Black River, that Augustus decided that he would do as little as he could to help his kidnappers, but beyond that he was helpless. By then, way before Kingstree, Selby the baker was gone for $310 and Sara Marshall was gone for $277 and an early-nineteenth-century pistol that Darcy was to learn only worked when it wanted to. Sara's buyer thought it amusing that she had a last name. "Shows her good breedin," Stennis said to the buyer. And there at Kingstree, Willis began to lean forward all the time, his chest over his thighs and his face in his hands. "We gon get outa this," Augustus kept telling him.

Darcy went up to a man in Kingstree as the man came out of his house. The house was on the only street in the place. "Might you be interested in some good nigger flesh," Darcy said and took the man back down to the end of the road and around to an alley where the wagon of people was. Darcy had the man by the elbow the whole time and the man had not protested. Stennis brought Augustus down from the wagon. Willis did not raise his face from his hands.

The man had the look of someone who did not have anything better to do at that moment. He said to Augustus, "Open your mouth." He himself did not own any slaves but had been to enough auctions to know that having a slave open his mouth was one of the first things a potential buyer did.

Augustus mumbled and put his open hand to the back of his ear. He mumbled some more.

"Why, hell, this nigger's deaf and dumb."

"The devil you say?" Darcy said.

"The devil he say, Marse?" Stennis said.

"I tell you he can't hear and he can't talk. Can you?" the man said to Augustus, who looked at him expressionless, his hand still to the back of his ear. "What kinda flesh you tryin to peddle, mister?"

"No no. He hear, he talk," Darcy said. "He was talkin and hearin in Virginia. He was talkin and hearin in North Carolina. He can hear and he can talk, I'm tellin you." Then, to Augustus, "Open your mouth and tell this white man howdy, tell him that it's a good goddamn afternoon."

Augustus mumbled and put the other hand to the back of his other ear. The white man looked from Augustus to Darcy and then to Stennis. "Well, it must not be a good goddamn afternoon cause he ain't tellin me so."

"He ain't deaf and dumb. You got my word on that," Darcy said. "Can't he talk, Stennis?"

"Yes, Master. He can talk. He can talk clear as a bird singin in the tree, clear as—"

"All right, Stennis, thas anough of that. I wouldn't lie to you, mister."

"I don't want a deaf-and-dumb nigger. I want a whole nigger, top to bottom."

The man turned to go and Darcy pulled at his sleeve. The man said, "Unhand me, sir, or I will hand you to God." Stennis grumbled loudly. Darcy stepped back and the man went away. Darcy said to Stennis, "You know better than to bark at a white man, even one thas an unwillin customer."

He turned on Augustus and poked him in the chest with two of his fingers. "What is the gallumpin about you, nigger? You ain't no more deaf and dumb than Stennis is. What is the gallumpin?" Augustus said nothing. "You done lost your hearin here in South Carolina, that it? Lost your tongue, too, huh? What did you lose in North Carolina? Your pecker? And Virginia, your brain, what little there is of it? And what it gonna be in Georgia? Your arms? And then your legs in Alabama and Mississippi, if we git that far? Just wastin away with every state we come to. That it?" Darcy looked at Stennis. "I bet if we got him to Texas, he'd be gone altogether, Stennis. Just a puff of nothin by the time we got to Texas. And wouldn't that be a shame? That would be a damn shame. Cause they don't pay a whole helluva lot for a ghost nigger in Texas."

"What we gon do?" Stennis said.

"We gon carry on, Stennis. We gon carry on till all the birds fall from the trees." He spat, then picked up the foot of one of the dead beavers hanging from his chest and inhaled it deeply. "Tennessee is a good place to be this time of the year, Stennis. The air will carry you along, wherever you wanna go." He dropped the beaver's foot and poked Augustus again. "And we gon sell this here nigger if I have to throw in my father and grandfather and his father with the bargain. Les go." Stennis yanked on Augustus's chain, picked him up and tossed him into the wagon. Darcy picked up another beaver foot and most of the leg and inhaled deeply again. "The air of Tennessee will cure all that ails you, Stennis."

"I can smell it from here, boss."

In Charleston they sold Willis for $325. Darcy would have gotten $400 but the white man and his wife, both schoolteachers, were suspicious of the papers Darcy had on Willis. Holding the papers, the woman said that her father had been in the slave business and so she knew that no price was eternal. "Three hundred and twenty-five," she said, and her husband repeated what she said. "I was a free man in Virginia," Willis said quietly to the teachers after the price had been agreed upon. Darcy laughed. "He keep saying that," Darcy said, snickering. "Virginia a beautiful place. We all feel free there. It's God's parlor, but he forgets this ain't Virginia." He was implying something unkind about South Carolina, but the teachers did not seem to notice. As Darcy and the teachers stood outside the bank and Darcy counted the money, Willis said to Augustus, "I be seein you. I be seein you in the bye and bye." Augustus said, "And I'll see you, Willis. I'll see you in the bye and bye. I promise."

In Winifred and John Skiffington's parlor there was a wondrous-looking bookcase, lovely oak, a lion's growling face at each edge of the top ends, three shelves, a secondhand item made by Augustus Townsend not long after Augustus bought his freedom. He had first thought he would keep it for himself and the family he would buy out of slavery, though none of them could read then. (He and Mildred would never learn to read.) He would keep it as a kind of symbol for his determination to get them. But then he realized that what he could get for the bookcase would bring his wife and child closer to him, so he put a price on it. Fifteen dollars. It had been originally sold to a man of two slaves who lost his sight and so, as he told Skiffington, lost his hunger and thirst for books. Skiffington bought it for five dollars.

Aside from the Bible, Skiffington was not much of a reader, which was not the case with Winifred. She had read so much, her husband once said, she could be a schoolteacher. All the shelves of that secondhand bookcase were full, primarily with books she had brought down from Philadelphia. Skiffington had asked that she not teach Minerva to read, but she had not been able to help herself. She had asked only that Minerva not let anyone see her reading.

Among Winifred's treasures on the first shelf of the bookcase were Shakespeare's complete plays in two volumes, a present from her parents, and Washington Irving's *Sketch Book*, a present from Skiffington when he asked her to marry him. Irving's book was in red leather, a beautiful second edition published in London in 1821. After supper the Skiffingtons, including John's father, would gather in the parlor and Winifred would pick something from the bookcase and read. Skiffington himself was partial to Irving's "Rip Van Winkle." "You'll wear it out, John," Winifred would say. "You will drain all the freshness out of it." To coax her, he would begin, "Rip Van Winkle, a posthumous writing of Diedrich Knickerbocker."

Skiffington thought of "old Rip" when he saw the man on the steps leading up from the street to the jail. The hair on the man's face was wild and quite abundant, and as Skiffington got closer he made out the eyes and nose and mouth poking through the hair. Only the hair told him it was a white man, because the skin was too dirty to bear witness to that. He could have been one of the mountain men who lived alone and came down every now and again just to hear human voices. The man stood up several yards before Skiffington got to the jail and he stood firm on his two feet, testifying that whatever the dirt and the hair said about him, there was a heart and a mind ready to say something different.

"John," Counsel Skiffington said.

Skiffington stopped with one foot on the steps and the other still in the street. He studied the man for more than a minute and when the man said his name again, Skiffington said, "Counsel, that you?"

He smiled and extended his hand. He had heard thirdhand that Counsel had fallen into the blaze he created at A Child's Dream in North Carolina just after he had shot himself in the head. The bank Counsel owed had actually started that story in its attempt to provide some conclusion to the whole Counsel Skiffington affair. Among dozens of burnt bodies, who would know that one wasn't the master of the plantation?

"It's me," Counsel said. "It's me and I think I can say that and mean it." They went on shaking hands and would have embraced but the cousins had never had that kind of love. Counsel had arrived late in the night with a man who had picked him up in Roanoke. The man was leading two wagonloads of goods—from cloth to bullets to books—to northern Virginia. Counsel had intended to accept free passage all the way to the man's destination, but the God he found in Texas told him he might as well stop and see what might happen with John Skiffington.

"Counsel, I took you for dead," Skiffington said. "Winifred and I took you and everybody for dead, that's what we heard."

"Everybody is, John. I suppose I was, too. But now I'm standing here and telling you I'm not."

"Let me take you home to Winifred, get you cleaned up."

"I don't think I'm fit to meet any womenkind," Counsel said. "Especially not one I'm related to."

"Mrs. Skiffington wouldn't mind."

"I would, John. I would," and Counsel remembered that the world had always called his wife "Mrs. Skiffington." "I would mind. Maybe if you could spare me something so I could put up at the boardinghouse, I might be presentable in a day or two. A bath, some meals, and I'll be a man ready for civilized society again."

"There's nothing wrong with you, but if the boardinghouse is what you want, then that is what I'll give you." They went two streets over and Skiffington paid for three nights at the boardinghouse.

He came by about noon and he and Counsel took dinner in the

house's small dining room. Counsel had bathed and shaved, and as he ate, the man John Skiffington loved but had had so much trouble with began to emerge. During the meal, Counsel said that he had been practically everywhere and now he did not know what to do with himself. By the end of the meal, Skiffington was asking Counsel if he wanted to be his deputy.

"You always struck me as a man who wanted the job all to himself," Counsel said, drinking coffee. "Or that's what I got from Belle reading Winifred's letters to me. John Skiffington could do everything alone."

"There gets to be more to be done. It wouldn't hurt to have someone standing sharp at my back. Family is good for that. Good for backing you up."

"I'll do whatever I can."

Counsel came to live in Skiffington's house, shared a room and bed with Carl Skiffington, John's father. Though he said nothing to anyone, Counsel thought himself entitled to the room that had always been Minerva's. He did not understand why a slave girl should be put above him. A slave he himself had once owned. He suspected that there was more between her and Skiffington and that her own room was just one thing the girl had managed to wheedle out of his cousin. He had seen other white men fall prey, so why not a man who claimed so much to walk with God? After his first month's pay, Counsel moved back to the boardinghouse, and the woman that owned the place charged him less than the other boarders, because he was the law and because he had suffered tragedies in North Carolina.

Mildred Townsend came out to the road in the morning and the evening every day after they took Augustus and waited for nearly a half hour. She knew that Augustus sometimes took on unexpected jobs when he was away from home and forgot to send word back to her that he would be home before long. At the end of each half hour she would raise her arms up high, her fingers extended, and she would feel Augustus's spirit flow into the tips of her fingers and she would know that he was on his way. She did not worry the first week or for most of the second week. "I'll give that man pure hell when he do show up," she said to their dog, who came out to the road with her and waited beside her the whole time. "And you help me, huh? You help me give him pure hell." She and Augustus had been married for more than thirty-five years, and she trusted him to be somewhere safe. She knew that with their only child gone, her husband would not do anything to put more suffering in her heart. It would be toward the end of that second week that she would go to Caldonia and they, with Fern Elston, would go to Skiffington, who would be away. But Counsel, his new deputy, would be there in the jail.

About a week after South Carolina, outside of McRae, Georgia, they camped and after Stennis had crushed up some food for Darcy, who had but two teeth in his head, Stennis fed Augustus and settled him down at an apple tree.

Augustus said to Stennis before he went to Darcy, "I owe you the same licks that you gave me back in Virginia. I want you to know I be owin you good."

"I spect everything cost somethin, even some licks from way back in Virginia."

"And when I come for you, you gon know it," Augustus said.

"I done figured that in the cost of my business, too."

"I wanna to go home," Augustus said. "I wanna go home and I think you know the way to help me."

"We all wanna go home."

"I want to go home."

Stennis noted that these were the first words Augustus had spoken since the deaf-mute stunt in South Carolina. "I see you back to talkin again."

"I ain't had nothin to say."

Stennis checked the chains again. "You have a good night."

"Let me just slip away," Augustus said.

"He would know that I the one that opened the door for you."

"Then come with me. We can go together. Us together."

"That ain't in my power."

"I say it is."

"It just ain't. He be my bread and butter. Jam, too."

"Back home," Augustus said, "I be my own bread and butter."

Stennis sighed. "I can see that." He stood up. "I can see that with my own two eyes."

Darcy shouted, "Stennis! Stennis! Where you at?"

"Over here, Marse." Stennis began walking away.

"Just let me slip away."

"Stennis!"

"Comin, Marse!"

"Well, come on then. Come here and rub my feet."

The morning after Caldonia Townsend made love to Moses her overseer for the first time, she woke about dawn and sat up in her bed and watched the sun come up. She had thought she would not sleep very well, but the night had been kind and she slept many hours without disturbance once sleep did arrive. She had had a dream just before waking of being in a house smaller than her own, a house she had to share with a thousand others. As she sat watching the sun she tried to remember more about the dream. Nothing came to her except the memory of someone in the dream saying that people in the attic were burning other people. The house Henry had built had no attic. She always slept with the curtains open, something Henry had gotten used to. Who else in this world could accept sleeping with the curtains open? she thought and raised her knees to her chin. She felt no guilt about Moses, which surprised her. Someone down in the fields, a woman, was singing. She soon realized that the woman was Celeste. It was not a sad song Celeste was singing and it was not a happy song, just melodious words to fill the silence that would otherwise be claimed by the songs of the birds. The room had been dark when she first opened her eyes, but as the sun rose and rose, it took Celeste's song and carried it with the light to every corner of the room, and little by little the stiffness of sleep went out of Caldonia and she stretched and yawned and wondered what in the end she would do about Moses. She did not think of him the way she thought of Henry Townsend the first morning after she met him. That morning she had gotten out of bed, afraid and weakened by the fear that she would not ever have the pleasure of seeing Henry again. Had she known that he had had similar feelings, she would have had the strength she had this morning as Celeste's song came to her one clear and undeniable word at a time.

She dressed and went out into the hall where the sun, even with a window at each end of the hall, was taking its time getting to. She heard Loretta stirring in her own room near the stairs but Caldonia did not knock and tell her maid to accompany her. In the kitchen, Zeddie the cook was at the stove and her husband Bennett was stacking wood in the wood box. "Missus," Zeddie said, "what can I get you for your breakfast?" "Nothing just yet," Caldonia said and opened the back door. "That air got a few teeth in it this mornin," Bennett said. "You want me to get you a coat?" "No, I'm fine," Caldonia said and went out and closed the door behind her.

The air did indeed have teeth in it, but she warmed as she walked to the cemetery with its one occupant. The mound of dirt had settled even more since her last visit. A tombstone had been ordered, but the man had said that it might take a month for it to be delivered. Standing at the foot of Henry's grave, she wished she had brought flowers from her garden. "Am I forgiven?" she said. The flowers from her last visit, just two days before, still had some vigor in them, and they were atop flowers from four days before that were browning and becoming one with the soil. "I still am your wife, so am I forgiven?"

Moses came to her that evening and she gave him no indication that he was to rise from the chair and come to her. So he talked of the slaves' work from the wing chair, hair combed and the not-so-new-anymore shirt and pants clinging to him because the sweat had come even before he had set one foot in the kitchen. He had hoped that by having her again they would cross an irrevocable threshold. But there were no tears and no hint that she wanted him, so he sat in sweat and fumbled through a recitation of their preparations for harvest. Had he not been her slave, he might have gotten up and went to her just on the authority of last night. But the sun did not rise very high in Moses's life, and it was only one day at a time and no one day was kin to the next.

"Tell Loretta to come in," Caldonia said and he got up and left the room. He had not been out and down the back steps when she regretted sending him away. What would have been the harm in letting him hold me? she thought as Loretta asked if she might want coffee and a little pie before she went to bed.

As arranged earlier, she had Fern, her brother Calvin, and Dora and Louis, William Robbins's children, to supper the following evening. Roasted chicken, one of Zeddie's specialties, and the pumpkin soup that Fern was fond of. Fern, who had now owned Jebediah Dickinson for some weeks, had little to say, which was unusual for the loquacious teacher among three of her former students who saw her as one of the primary influences in their lives. When she did speak, it was generally about her troubles with an "obstreperous" slave who insisted on calling himself Jebediah Dickinson, even though his former master said he was really just Jebediah and Jebediah alone. "Dickinson," the former master had said, "was stolen from my dead wife." Everyone at the table noted that Fern was not herself, but they passed it off because they loved her.

"With him there," she said after supper, "I feel as if I belong to him, that I am his property." The young people laughed to hear her say something so extraordinary. They were all members of a free Negro class that, while not having the power of some whites, had been brought up to believe that they were rulers waiting in the wings. They were much better than the majority of white people, and it was only a matter of time before those white people came to realize that.

"Why don't you sell him off?" Dora asked.

"I am afraid that all of Virginia knows him the way I know him and selling him would cost me more than I have already paid." That made no sense to the rest of them, and they blamed it on the fact that Fern had had a glass of port, which was also not like her.

"Sell him off down the river, as they say," Louis said.

"He would return," Fern said, "repeat himself like a bad meal. That is just my poor metaphor for the evening, dear Caldonia. It is not a statement about our grand evening this night. I trust you understand my state of mind, dear Caldonia."

"I do," Caldonia said. "Zeddie could not do wrong with food if she were blind and without hands."

"Precisely," Fern said.

"Mrs. Elston," Calvin said, "why not free him and send him on his way? Might that not be cheaper in the long run?"

"I have considered that. But I believe he has become a kind of debt inherited from my beloved husband. He is mine now and freeing him seems out of the question." She did not say that freeing a slave was not in her nature. Someone had once told her of a white woman in South Carolina who had freed her slaves after the death of her husband, and one of them had returned and killed the woman.

"Fern, it will sort itself out," Caldonia said. The oldest of the students, she had become a confidante of Fern's and she alone was allowed to call her by her first name. It was not a privilege the others coveted.

"I fear it will," Fern said and drank the last drop in her glass. "Have I had more port than I am allowed, dear Caldonia? Have I had my share?"

"In this house you are allowed all the port your soul can hold. You know that."

"One forgets when the mind becomes cluttered."

"Bennett?" Caldonia said.

Bennett appeared and filled Fern's glass. He went to Caldonia's side and whispered to her that Moses had been waiting in the kitchen "to tell you bout this and this."

She thought she might go to him and tell him she would see him tomorrow, but what Fern had been saying about the slave with two names entered her mind, and she told Bennett to tell Moses that the news of the day could wait unless there was something requiring her attention. She added that she was entertaining guests. Bennett delivered this in his own way, and Moses left for his cabin. Priscilla, his wife, said she had something for him to eat but he told her in as gentle a way as he could that he was not hungry and hoped that would be the end of it. She knew enough to read his mind, and she and her son sat before the hearth and played jack-a-rocks with their collection of pebbles. The boy had been improving, having found that if he threw the pebbles so that they bunched, he had a better chance of beating his mother. Moses, hearing them at play, was close to going out to the woods but he feared he was now sharing the place with Alice. Instead, he went to the equipment shed and sharpened hoes until the lantern light began to fail and his arms ached.

Fern's mood seemed to improve with the second glass of port, and there was no more talk of the slave Jebediah Dickinson. "I have," she began not long after Bennett had replaced the candles, "been receiving so many pamphlets about this abolition business. Where they get my name, I will never know."

"What do you think, Mrs. Elston?" Dora said.

"I realized all over again that if I were in bondage I would slash my master's throat on the first day. I wonder why they all have not risen up and done that." She sipped.

"The power of the state would crush them to dust," Louis said. He spoke, as always, not because he had any well-considered views on an issue, but to impress the women around him, and he was now at a point where the woman he most wanted to impress was Caldonia. He had come to Fern's classes after Caldonia had completed several years of her education, so she had not had much time to learn who he was. And Calvin had said little about him to her, so in many ways they were still strangers to each other. "The Commonwealth would put an end to it right quick."

"The state would hesitate," Calvin said. "It wouldn't want to lose its own people, so many fine white people, as well as all the people the state depends on to work the fields and do all the other work that helps make Virginia the great Commonwealth."

"Are you two men talking of war?" Dora said.

"Do you know it by some other name?" Louis said.

Dora laughed. "Slaves against masters. Try to place that image in your head, and then follow that with the image of all the slaves lying dead."

"I have," Fern said. "I have indeed." She was thinking of the boldness with which Jebediah walked away whenever he had a mind to. "The only question for us, around this blessed table, is which side should we choose. I suppose that is what those pamphlets want me to do. Choose my side."

"Have you?" Caldonia said.

"In my feeble way I believe I have," Fern said. "I do not think I would fare very well as a dressmaker's apprentice. 'Yessum' and 'Yessuh' do not come easily from my mouth. My hands, my body, they fear the dirt of the field."

"You could teach even more," Louis said. "You could teach all the time."

"The light of teaching is slowly going out for me."

"That comes from having bad pupils," Caldonia said and the five of them laughed. Fern thought she might have a third glass of port, but as she held the empty glass in her hand, the effects of the first two drinks took firm hold and she smiled at the glass and told herself that two would do for the evening. Since Jebediah arrived her husband had been staying home, but nothing was the same. *I am…I am this night a dutiful wife. This night…*

"I would leave all of this with any war," Calvin said.

"You wouldn't help out the precious slaves?" Louis said.

"Well, now that you say it, now that you put the matter out there, I think I would."

Caldonia laughed. "Do you think Mama would let you take up arms against her?" In their minds they all saw Maude—arms folded, foot tapping in an exasperated manner—and laughed.

"I would do it with her back turned." Calvin laughed.

"A bullet in your poor mama's back, Calvin, how nice?" Dora said.

"You said bullet. I love her too much to do anything more harmful than say no. Besides, my mother lives with a high brick wall at her back. Nothing could penetrate that." When his mother was ill for all those years, Calvin would sleep many nights on the floor beside her bed.

"Fine talk for an hour of digestion," Fern said. "What school taught all of you this?"

"A difficult establishment in Manchester, Virginia." Louis was looking across the table at his sister, and as he did his traveling eye caught hold of a floating piece of dust and followed it before he blinked.

Her guests slept there that night. In the morning, not long after breakfast, Caldonia and Calvin walked Dora and Louis out to the verandah, where Louis hugged her unexpectedly. "Your hospitality is without equal," he said, not at all trying to impress her. "The credit," Caldonia said, "goes to my guests." The day, much, much later, when Louis asked her to marry him, he would say he had feared asking because he did not think he was worthy. "We are all worthy of one another," Caldonia would say.

Dora and Louis rode off on their horses. Fern slept late and did not leave until late afternoon. Calvin stayed another night and so was there when Moses came that evening. Bennett came into the parlor to tell Caldonia her overseer was there. She rose.

"What is it?" Calvin asked.

"Nothing of consequence," she said, excusing herself and going ahead of Bennett out to the kitchen.

"Missus, I just wanted to let you know bout the day, is all," Moses said as soon as she entered. She did not dismiss Bennett.

"I am entertaining my brother," she said, walking up to within a foot of him. She wished to see him, her words and posture said, but this was the best she could do for now. "You can tell me all tomorrow evening. Now go home and get a good night's rest. I know how hard you work." He nodded and left.

"The responsibilities are coming in on you now, it seems," Calvin said when she returned.

"One by one," she said.

"You could be happy with me in New York. New land, new air. We could be happy there. The burdens would fall off our shoulders, Caldonia."

"Calvin, you have only yourself and whatever is on your back. I have the responsibility of so many people. Adults and children. I cannot choose not to have that. My husband has built something here, and now it is mine and I can't abandon that for a foreign land."

Calvin said nothing. He was in the chair Moses always sat in. He wanted to say that she could abandon all but by now he was losing faith in being able to persuade anyone of anything. She could not see any of those thirty or so human beings living as free people any more than he could see from Virginia all that the frozen dog in the New York photograph was seeing.

She did not want him to go the next day and she said so. She had found that with her people about—and she counted Fern and Dora and Louis in this—she was more capable of facing the world. He had business in Richmond, Calvin said, but when he returned, he would stay with her for a longer time.

She told Moses that evening she did not want to hear anything about the dull labors of the day and he sat trying to think up one more tale about Henry. She got up after a long time and sat on his lap, kissed him. She did not allow him to make love to her that evening, but when he came back the next evening, she did. "It has been hard without you," she said to him. "It was hard for me, Missus," he said. When he said that, they were done and partially clothed on the floor, and his words caused her to wonder if Virginia had a law forbidding such things between a colored woman and a colored man who was her slave. Was this a kind of miscegenation? she wondered. A white woman in Bristol had been whipped for such an offense, and her slave was hanged from a tree in what passed for the town square. Three hundred people had come to see it, the whipping and the hanging, the former in the morning and the latter in the afternoon. People brought their children, their infants, who slept through most of the activities. It had happened a year ago but the news had only recently arrived in Manchester.

"Are you going to come back tomorrow?" she asked after she had risen from the floor.

"Yes, ma'am. Yes, ma'am, I will."

He left and she said to herself in the moment before Loretta entered, "I love Moses. I love Moses with his one name." But when she saw Loretta, the words did not make as much sense. "I am ready for bed," she said, and that made the greatest of sense. Before going to bed, she washed her insides with vinegar and the soap her slaves made for everyone. Hers, however, was made with a dash of perfume that Loretta supplied to the soap makers. In Bristol, the authorities claimed the white woman had been with child. No word of mouth or the newspaper account said what had become of the child.

That evening was the first time Moses would think that his wife and child could not live in the same world with him and Caldonia. Had they made love in silence, as before, he would not have begun to think beyond himself. But she had spoken of tomorrow, and that meant more tomorrows after that. Where did a slave wife and a slave son fit in with a man who was on his way to being freed and then marrying a free woman? On his way to becoming Mr. Townsend?

He came down from Caldonia's house that evening and stood at the entrance to the lane. Where does a man put a family he does not need?

Alice came out of her cabin and if she was surprised to see him, she did not let on. But she did not chant, she did not dance.

"Where you goin?" he asked. He knew more about her than he knew even three weeks ago, and though she had acknowledged nothing, he felt that she was aware that she had less of the world than before. The night no longer just held her in her wanderings; it now held him following after her. Alice strode by him and he turned and took hold of her arm. "You answer me when I be talkin to you."

"Nowhere," she said. The simplicity of a clear answer hit them both and they said nothing until they heard Elias and Stamford laugh as they came from the barn and went to their cabins. Both men were carrying lanterns.

"Thas more like it," Moses said to Alice and released her. She went out to the path that would take her to the road.

He had expected her to take off that night and for her body to be delivered by the patrollers before morning, but she was at her cabin the next day.

The following evening he waited at her cabin door for her to come out. "I got a job for you," he said, "and if you do it right, you won't have to be nobody's slave no more." He had not made love to Caldonia that evening but his sky went up very high.

She wanted to chant, but the angels might not understand what she was saying with this overseer as her witness. *I met a dead man layin in Massa lane....* Maybe if she lifted her arms now, they would reward her for all that singing in the past and raise her up up to freedom. *A* man....*A dead man is what it is....How could you forget that dead man?* All her singing must be worth something. If she lifted her arms and wiggled her fingers, the angels might see her even in the dark with that overseer and pick her up like she was just somebody's June bug. *I met a dead woman laying way out there all the way in my dead Massa's lane....*

Moses said, "You go on, cause I got my eye on you. Got both my eyes on you." He watched her go. "That mule be waitin for you in the mornin," he said.

It was true, she thought as she stepped tentative feet onto the road, that the world had had eyes to see her, and even if the angels did take her now, the world would just reach up and pull her back. *They don't want you there, girl, so just come on back to us....* She did not go far that night and turned around not long after passing the crossroads. The lane was all quiet but it was not as quiet as on all the other nights when her voice had been hoarse and her feet tired from all the walking and dancing. She entered her cabin and waited inside for the sound of it all coming to an end. Maybe if she had cared enough about everyone; maybe if she had shared; maybe if she had even believed that Delphie and Cassandra would want to go and sing to the angels with her. Nothing came but the sounds of her own heart and she went down to her knees and crawled to her pallet a few feet away from those of Delphie and Cassandra. Maybe she had waited far too long, and in waiting the train and the people had waved as they went by her. Who knew that there had never been enough time? Who knew that God had parceled out time the way Bennett and Moses parceled out the meal and flour and molasses? *Thas gotta last so yall be careful how you eat....* On the last plantation she had been on, a woman had jumped into the well, vowing to swim her way home. And she had done it, too, without a blessing from a mule kick. Why had she held back in just walking home? Now, that mule might want to take back his kick. *You ain't usin it, now give it here....*

Two mornings later, Thursday, Caldonia told Loretta, who was to tell Zeddie, that she would supper with Moses in the kitchen. Loretta was not a woman to ask her mistress to repeat anything she said, but Zeddie wanted to know if Loretta was going around with ears too dirty to hear right. Loretta funned no one and when Zeddie saw she had the same face as on every morning, she said, "Tell her I get everything ready for her and the overseer."

The meal was over and done with rather quickly because they did not talk. He had never sat at a table such as that one and had a full plate put before him. He had not known what to do and she saw this and took him away from the table.

They did not make love but he went back to the lane with the same amount of joy. He knocked at Alice's cabin and took her outside, over to the side of the barn, and told her he was setting her free, that he had the power to do it. She said nothing and he laughed because he knew she was thinking this was an overseer's trick. "You just be ready to go on Saturday night. Ain't that a good time to go, Saturday? With all that lazy Sunday to go? Well, ain't it?"

"I don't know bout goin nowhere," she said. "I'm just Alice on Marse Henry's plantation, thas all I know. Marse Henry and Missus Caldonia Townsend in Manchester County, Virginia."

He laughed again. "Henry dead. I put him in the ground myself and covered him up." She could see that he was not the man fumbling and hugging himself in the forest, just one more sad sight as she mapped her way again and again through the night. No slave, not even the overseer, spoke the master's name without calling him the master first, and Moses was doing that and not caring who in the night could hear him. Then he said, "And I want you to take my wife and boy with you," and she began to feel that he was not just trying to trick her.

"Take Priscilla and Jamie? Take em, too?" The boy was fat and the woman was weighed down with worshiping her husband and her mistress.

He nodded. "Just take em along with you. Don't say you don't know what you doin. You ain't foolin me goin all over Robin Hood's barn, girl. I know you. I know what you been up to."

"I ain't been up to nothin. I'm just Alice, I told you. Over here on Marse Henry's plantation in Manchester County, Virginia." No one ever again drank out of the well the woman dove into to swim home. It had been the one used by the white people, and even after they had their new one dug, they wouldn't let the Negroes use the well the slave woman swam home in. Every slave on the place wanted to taste the water that gave a woman the power of a fish, but the white people bricked over the well. Some said they poisoned the water before they did it.

"You listen after my words or I'll see to it you never run around like you been doin."

That night Moses told his family that he was sending them into freedom and that he would soon follow. "I don't know how to get to freedom," Priscilla said. "Me neither," the boy said.

"Alice'll take you, and yall can make a place for me." Moses stood just inside the closed door.

"Alice? What is Alice, Moses? What is she? Her left hand would get lost tryin to find her right hand. What can Alice do?" Priscilla had been preparing to feed the hearth fire when her husband entered. Now she stood up with the wood pieces in her arms. The fire first wavered, then leaned toward the woman as wind came down the chimney and moved toward the bottom of the door.

"She knows more than you think, woman. She does. Now you just gon haveta trust me on this, Priscilla. You gon haveta trust that I can get yall to the other side."

Priscilla said, "Lord, Moses, why you throwin us away like this?"

"It ain't that," Moses said. "I'm makin the way good for yall on this side, thas all I'm tryin to do." Priscilla trembled and the wood fell from her arms. "Just trust Alice to know what to do," he said.

"Why can't you just come on with us now, Moses?" There was a chasm and he was telling her that it was an easy thing for her to jump, that she should simply make the jump to this freedom thing that wouldn't even include him at first. He was not a good husband but he was all she had. Some women had no husbands or husbands off on another plantation, not right by them every night, breathing and fighting with the world in their sleep.

"Pa, you be comin long later?" Jamie said.

"I be there," Moses said.

They said no more, but all the next day Priscilla tarried in her furrows and so Moses had to go to her and tell her to do right by her work. "I don't wanna get after you again," he said.

More than a mile from the plantation, that Saturday night, the four of them came to a stretch of woods that ended three miles later on William Robbins's plantation. Alice had said nothing to Moses, but Saturday was a day many of the patrollers were liable to have been drinking. She did not know it but the sheriff paid them on Saturday, and while he didn't forbid it, he didn't like them working on Sundays, the Lord's day, a day of rest. So the patrollers tended to start their Sundays way before Saturday midnight.

In the woods, Priscilla began crying. "Moses, why can't you come now? Please, Moses, please."

Alice stepped up to her and slapped Priscilla twice. Moses said nothing and Jamie said nothing. Who was this new woman, who was this Alice acting like this in the night? She said, "You just stop all that cryin right now. I won't have it. Not one tear ever watered my thirst, and it won't water yours neither. So stop it all right now."

"It ain't so bad, Mama," Jamie said. "We can make it. See." And the boy ran off for several yards and returned, then ran back and returned again. He stood running in place. "We can make it, Mama."

"Heed that boy," Alice said to Priscilla. "You better heed that boy. Moses, you hold off tellin long as you can." In the dark of the woods, they could not see faces straight on, so the only way anyone could see a person was to stare at something just to the side. Only then did a face come clear. Alice looked at the tree next to Moses. "If they say they see you on the other side, then they know better than I do."

To look at Alice, he looked at his son beside her. "Then I'll see yall."

"Bye, Pa."

"Moses," Priscilla said, "don't you forget me."

Alice took Priscilla by the hand and the three disappeared into the woods, and no amount of looking left or right could give Moses a picture of them. He heard what he thought was them, but he had heard the same sounds when alone with himself in that other woods. When there was quiet, he began to wonder what would happen if they were caught. *Moses helped us do it. . . .* He looked behind him, and the sounds started up again. *Moses, why would you do this when I trusted you? Why would you take our future and just throw it away?* He clenched and unclenched his hands. He knew the way back home, but could he reach them way out there somewhere and still find his way back? *Oh, Moses, why? We had this and that and this and that, so why, Moses?* He followed them, walking at first, then running, one arm before him to keep the low-hanging branches from hitting him in the face.

He waited until just after the noon hour to report to the house. His heart had beat furiously all night and he had hoped for relief as the sun rose, but the heart refused. In the kitchen, he told Caldonia, as Loretta and Zeddie and Bennett looked on, that Priscilla and the boy had left sometime during the night while he was sleeping. He had gone to Alice's cabin, he said, and found that she had not returned from her wandering.

Caldonia was not worried and told him the patrollers would come upon them and return them. "They had wandered off," she said. Alice was just crazy enough to have gotten lost.

When there was no sign of them by nightfall, she told Bennett she wanted him to go to the sheriff the next day, Monday, and report the "disappearance" of three slaves. Escaping was in a very distant part of her mind, given the three people—and no man—involved, but perhaps some harm had come to them. Patrollers may have taken advantage of the women and killed them all to cover the crime. But why kill them if the crime was only rape? Raping a slave would not bring the law down on them. In many minds, raping a slave was not even a crime. Killing property was the greater crime. She wrote Bennett a pass, then she wrote a letter explaining to Sheriff Skiffington what she knew. She told Moses to keep an eye on everyone until the matter could be straightened out. At first she put some blame on him since his wife and child were two of the missing, but her disappointment did not last very long.

Bennett found Skiffington talking to Counsel in front of the jail, and the more Bennett added to what was in the letter, the more Skiffington suspected Moses of something. He didn't know a great deal about the Townsend place and faulted himself as sheriff of the whole realm. He left Counsel and rode out with Bennett to the plantation. He had faith in his patrollers, that they would not let three pieces of property get by them. So the slaves were somewhere in the county. If alive, they could be back before sundown. And if dead, it could be wolves or bears or mountain lions.

Bennett took care of Skiffington's horse and Zeddie led him into the parlor where Caldonia stood when he entered the room. He took off his hat and said, as he had at the funeral, that he was sorry about her husband.

"I don't know where they could have gotten to," Caldonia said. No one sat.

"I understand the Alice one wasn't comfortable in her own head."

"No, and Priscilla would no more leave this plantation than I would, sheriff."

"How much were they worth?"

"Pardon?"

"How much were the three slaves worth? How much would you get if you were to sell them? On the market."

"Oh, I don't know. My husband would have known just like that, but I can't say I kept up with such matters. I'm sorry."

"It doesn't matter very much. How long that overseer and her been married?"

"I'd say about ten years," Caldonia said. It was the first time she had fully realized that she had been making love to another woman's husband. Priscilla had always been there and yet she had been on the other side of the earth, married to a different man.

"Ten years is a long time," Skiffington said. Caldonia said nothing but looked slightly puzzled. When he asked about Moses, she offered to have him brought to the house but he told her he would go out to meet him.

Heading to the fields, he remembered the slave man and woman in his office, the man being sold that day to William Robbins and the woman being sold days later to someone else. We are together, the slave man kept saying. *We are one....* He came to a small rise that led down to the fields and could not make out the overseer because he was not on a horse looking down, but was just one among the working slaves. He went down the rise and called out that he wanted to see Moses. Moses rose up from the furrow and made his way to Skiffington.

Moses took off his hat and said good morning to Skiffington and the sheriff said good morning.

"You know where they might be?"

"No, sir. I woke yesterday and they was gone, all three just gone."

"Were they there when you went to sleep?" More and more of the day Moses was sold in the jail was coming back to Skiffington.

"Yes, sir. But that Alice tend to wander, bein not in one piece the way she was. No harm by that. No harm by all that walkin about and such like. And sometimes my Priscilla and Jamie would just go to keep her company. They thought the world of Alice." Elias would put a lie to most of that on Skiffington's second visit. Moses continued building a story that Elias and others would tear down with just a few questions from Skiffington.

Finally, Skiffington told him to go on back to work and Moses set his hat on his head and returned. Skiffington would not remember in

a few days who told him that Moses and his mistress had supper—
"just like some man and his wife be eatin"—just before the slaves disappeared. He would remember that no one would ever report seeing
buzzards in the sky to evidence killing by wolves or bears. He became
convinced that the three were dead and that someone had had to put
the dead in the ground to deprive the buzzards. He watched Moses,
who overcame the need to turn and look back at the sheriff, and
Skiffington knew any slave would want to leave the field and never
return. It was in watching Moses walk away that he began to suspect
him of murder. He could not understand why until he heard he had
had supper with Caldonia. But why kill when all that was required
was for him to step out of the cabin door, wipe his hands clean of a
wife and child, and step through the house door? And why hurt a
child and a woman not of her own mind?

He watched as Moses went back to the row he had been in and
picked up his bag and became one with all around him, the land and
its bounty and the slaves leaning over and picking and stepping. The
crows hovered above them. Skiffington could see that the birds were
high enough to avoid a hand but not high enough to escape a thrown
stone. Moses had looked him straight in the eye the whole time, not
once blinking or looking away. There was a reason God had made
telling the truth one of his commandments; lying had the power to be
a high wall to hide all the other transgressions. Skiffington considered
Caldonia. He had heard of that white woman in Bristol who had slept
with her slave. Bad business. But what the coloreds like Caldonia and
Moses did among themselves was no crime in itself. Killing a slave for
no reason was always a crime, before man, before God.

Two days later, evening, Skiffington heard a commotion out on the
street and came to see what it was.

"Hey, John," Barnum Kinsey, the patroller, said from atop his
horse, the old thing his father-in-law had given him. Even before he

reached him, Skiffington could tell that Barnum had been drinking, and he had drunk a lot. It had been more than two weeks since Augustus Townsend had been sold back into slavery. Barnum's wife had had many sorrows but she had never regretted marrying him.

"Barnum?" Skiffington said.

The dry goods merchant had been trying unsuccessfully to shoo Barnum away from in front of his establishment but now that Skiffington was there, he left to close up for the night. Once the merchant went inside, the street was empty except for the two men, the horse Barnum was on, Skiffington's tethered horse and a dog across the street that had lost its way.

"Hey, John. Nice evenin, huh?"

"Not a bad one, Barnum. You headin home?"

"Yes, John, I reckon I will. Soon. But I do have my patrollin." He was quiet for a time, and while he was the dog got up from its haunches and went west. "I wanted to tell you somethin, and I have been workin my mind so the words will tumble out in a straight line. You know how that can be, John."

"I do, Barnum. Just set them words one by one and they'll do fine and we'll get where we got to go."

"Harvey Travis and Oden Peoples took Augustus Townsend and sold him. Harvey ate his free papers up, and then he sold him away, John. Thas all there is to it."

"Sold Augustus? When was this?"

"Days ago maybe. Maybe a week. Time and me not friends anymore so a day can be like a month. Or a minute." Barnum belched and seemed to be sobering with each word he spoke. "Man's name was Darcy, that slave speculator you told us to look out for. Sold him for more money than I see at one time. Sold his mule, too, John. Sold that man's mule. Had niggers in the back that he was probably tryin to sell. No tellin who they belong to."

"Tellin me sooner might have done some good, Barnum. Sellin a free man is a crime and you should be there to stop it."

"I know, John. I know all about that. You ain't tellin me nothin I don't already know." The dog came back and stood in the middle of the street, then looked around. It trotted east. Barnum belched again. He shifted in the saddle. "I wish I was braver, John. I wish I was as brave as you."

"You are, Barnum, and one day people will know that."

"I wonder. I wonder." He leaned forward. "Now I don't want you to take me tellin you all this as my becomin a nigger kisser or somethin like that. It ain't that. You know me, John. But they sold that Augustus and they sold his mule." It was twilight and the stars were quite evident in the sky. The moon, still low, was behind Skiffington and only Barnum could see it.

"I know you, Barnum."

"But he was a free and clear man, and the law said so. Augustus never hurt me, never said bad to me. What Harvey done was wrong. But tellin you don't put me on the nigger side. I'm still on the white man side, John. I'm still standin with the white. God help me if you believe somethin else about me." He shifted in the saddle once more. The moon was just above the horizon now, a large, dusty orange point, but Barnum did not raise his head high enough to see it. "It's just that there should be a way for a body to say what is without somebody sayin he standin on the nigger side. A body should be able to stand under some . . . some kinda light and declare what he knows without retribution. There should be some kinda lantern, John, that we can stand under and say, 'I know what I know and what I know is God's truth,' and then come from under the light and nobody make any big commotion bout what he said. He could say it and just get on about his business, and nobody would say, 'He be stickin up for the nigger, he be stickin up for them Indians.' The lantern of truth wouldn't low them to say that. There should be that kinda light, John. I regret what happened to Augustus."

"Yes, Barnum, I know." The merchant came out of the store and tipped his hat to Skiffington and Skiffington nodded and the merchant went home.

"A man could stand under that light and talk the truth. You could hold the lantern with the light right from where you standin, John. Hold it so I could stand under it. And when nobody was talkin, was tellin the truth bout what they know, you could keep the lantern in the jail, John. Keep it safe in the jail, John." Barnum closed his eyes, took off his hat, opened his eyes and studied the brim. "But don't keep the lantern too near the bars, John, cause you don't want the criminals touchin it and what not. You should write the president, you should write the delegate, and have em pass a law to have that lantern in every jail in the United States of America. I would back that law. God knows I would. I really would, John."

"I would, too, Barnum," Skiffington said. Barnum put his hat back on. "Now I want you to go home now. I don't want you patrollin tonight. You rest up. You go home to Mrs. Kinsey and the chaps. Go straight home." The dog came back and went west and did not return that night.

"I will, John. I'll go home to Mrs. Kinsey and the chaps." Barnum could see a burning lamp on the table he and his family had their meals on. He saw two more on the mantelpiece, and when he turned around in that room, he saw his wife, and the two lamps on the mantelpiece were reflected in her eyes. "I will, John." Days before he and his family left the county forever, one of his sons, Matthew, found a map of America in a two-year-old newspaper. Matthew showed his father where they were going, took his father's finger and traced the route from Virginia to Missouri. "A long way," Barnum said. "Yep," the boy said.

"Here," Skiffington said, "stand there a little bit." He went into the jail and returned with a small burlap sack no bigger than a puppy's head. "Some sweets for them chaps, Barnum. Some horehound. A little peppermint for the chaps."

"I appreciate that, John."

"You go straight home now, Barnum." He watched Barnum ride away. The candy had been for Winifred and Minerva, and maybe his father if he happened to be in the house. Now that the merchant was gone Skiffington would not be able to buy more until tomorrow. As for himself, his stomach did not permit him to have a sweet tooth.

The next morning he told Winifred that he might have to stay the night at Robbins's place and she was not to worry. He then went to the telegraph office and sent long telegrams about Darcy and the wagon to sheriffs between Manchester and the North Carolina border. He knew what Darcy looked like and he mentioned the beaver pelts and that he was traveling with a Negro who may or may not be a slave. He also mentioned Augustus Townsend, "a free man and upstanding citizen of Manchester County." "You sure you wanna say all this?" the telegraph man asked him. "I'm sure. Send every word. The county will pay." "I ain't worried about that, John."

He went to the jail and told Counsel that he would be gone the rest of the day and that he was to handle matters until he returned the next day. "Want me along?" Counsel said. Skiffington said, "I think I can manage alone. Just keep it even here, will you, Counsel?"

He rode as hard as he could. He wondered why Mildred or no one else had come to him about Augustus being taken. He hit William Robbins's place about one and could have used a good meal, but he went on. If he himself had been colored and had been somehow sold off, he would want someone to let a colored Winifred know, to let her know that there was hope for her. He passed the remains of Augustus's wagon that Travis had burned but he didn't know that it was what was left of Augustus. Toward three he reached Mildred's place and knocked at the door but got no answer. She was not in the barn nor in the little workshop Augustus had set up next to the barn. He found her in the back, coming in from her garden. The dog was with her, and it went up to Skiffington and sniffed and then went on toward the house.

He took off his hat. "Mildred . . ."

"My husband dead, sheriff?" She had a basket of tomatoes and she sat it down and wiped the sweat from one side of her face, and as she wiped the other side, she said, "Is my husband gone?"

"No, not as I know. He was sold by a speculator." There were still people in the county who believed tomatoes were poisonous but Mildred and Skiffington did not believe that.

"How can you sell a free man, sheriff?"

"Outside the law, Mildred. You go outside the law."

"Outside. Inside. Outside. Inside." She picked up her basket. "I don't think Augustus was outside it. That wouldna been Augustus."

"I will try to find him, Mildred, and bring him home to you. It is a crime what happened and the law will stand by that."

"I know it will."

"Why didn't you tell me he was missing?"

She had been picking over the tomatoes and looked up quickly at him. "Me and Caldonia and Fern went to the jail and your deputy say he gon tell you all about it. He told me he was gonna let you know that Augustus was missin."

He did not like telling Negroes about the failings of other white people, but he said, "He told me nothing, Mildred. I only heard of this last night."

"From him? This late from him?"

"No, Barnum Kinsey told me." He could see Counsel sitting at his desk, cleaning his gun and whistling. "I knew nothing, I can promise you that."

"None a that matters anymore, sheriff." She went by him and to the back door. The dog wanted to go in and she opened it for him and turned to Skiffington. The door shut on its own. "I had faith that he would come home. He could sometimes get caught up in fixin somethin and lose time and be late for days and days. I let that be cause I always knew he was safe. But your comin here is somethin else. I would rather have waited months for him to just ride on in then have you come here like this with what's just plain bad news."

"We will do what we can, Mildred."

"I have a feelin it don't matter anymore, sheriff. Nobody cares. Your deputy didn't seem to care."

"The law cares, Mildred. The law always cares."

She looked at him and he blinked because he knew that she was closer to what was true than he was. "The law cares," he said again. Mildred said nothing more and opened the door and went in. Skiffington put on his hat and went around the house and back to his horse. The horse was eating grass and Skiffington had to pull him away. He led him to the water trough, but that was not what the horse wanted so Skiffington let him eat grass again.

Mildred had come through the house and was now on the porch. "Augustus would not forgive me if I didn't ask if you wanted a mouthful to eat."

"No, I won't trouble you no more," Skiffington said. "I need to get back before it gets too late." He thought of the pretty tomatoes; maybe there was bread, too. "I appreciate the offer."

"Wouldn't be no trouble. I got plenty."

"I will sit and pass the time when I bring you good news about your husband," he said. "The next time."

She told him good day and went back into the house. The dog had been watching but did not move from the threshold.

Skiffington did not stop at the Robbins place on his way back to the town, but he did stop twice to read from his Bible. He had begun to think of Minerva again and he wanted the Bible to help him put it out of his heart. He didn't sit down. He just stood in the road and read from the book while the horse, both times, wandered about. It had had its fill of grass at Mildred's and so went here and there with the curiosity of a child. He read and read but could not concentrate.

Three weeks before, the morning after Minerva's fifteenth birthday, Skiffington, going out to work, had seen her getting dressed in her room. She had apparently gone to dump her slops and had returned to finish dressing and left the door ajar, the way she had been doing it since a little girl. In the instant he saw her, her nightgown was pulled tight around her and the fullness of her body, from her breasts to her knees, showed through. She did not see him and he left without saying anything, but she had been on his mind ever since. He knew many a white man who had taken black women as their own, and among those men, he would have been thought normal. But he saw himself living in the company of God, who had married him to Winifred, and he believed God would abandon him if he took Minerva. And Winifred would discover what he had done, even if Minerva never said a word.

He put off reading the Bible as it was doing him no good and got to the jail about seven that night and the place was dark until he lit the lanterns. There were no messages from Counsel and so he suspected the day had gone without event. He had been uncertain about Counsel from the beginning. Now his faith in him had crumbled further. He brushed down his horse and left him in the barn in the back and walked home. Minerva was sitting in the porch swing and she waved to him and he felt all over again that feeling he had had the morning he saw her after her birthday. What good had all the praying done? Why should a man feel this way about someone who was like a daughter to his heart? "Howdy," he said. She said, "You hungry?" "No. Where is Winifred?" "Inside sewing." He went in and was suddenly pulled down by the weight of the day and the long ride. The tomatoes in Mildred's basket were large and quite ripe. He would have liked one at that moment, but he knew his stomach would protest. The weight of the day pulled him down to Winifred in her chair and he sat on the floor beside her. She put her sewing in her lap. "I think your stomach could use something to eat," she said. "No. Nothing." "I say yes, Mr. Skiffington." "Let me start with a little milk," he said. "Fine," she said. "Milk, then all the rest."

He washed up. There was still the possibility of some word from the sheriffs all down the line. There was still that. But as he drank more and more of the milk, that hope went away. How could he punish Counsel and Harvey and Oden? He put the glass down and thought how a few sliced tomatoes with some salt and vinegar would give him whatever he needed now. A few sliced tomatoes laid out as pretty as you please on one of Winifred's precious plates.

He went to the boardinghouse and stepped into Counsel's room without knocking and found the owner sitting on Counsel's bed. She had her shoes off and though she was clothed otherwise, she put her hand up to her neck, which was fully covered. She told Skiffington that Counsel was out in the back tending to his business. She put on her shoes and followed him downstairs.

Counsel was coming out of the privy. "John."

"You get word that that freed man Augustus Townsend was missing?" Skiffington said before his cousin could close the privy door. "Counsel, you tell his wife and his daughter-in-law that you was going to tell me he was missing and then not tell me?"

"Augustus?"

"Augustus Townsend is the man's name."

"I might have heard, John, and just forgot. Niggers have stories about such from here until the end of time. Who can believe them?" The owner of the boardinghouse was standing up the three steps at the doorway. There was some light behind her in the kitchen but the light was not strong and it made her a poor silhouette. "You go on in now, Thomasina," Counsel said. She turned away. The woman said, "I'll be upstairs if you need me, Counsel." The amount she charged him for room and board was nearly nothing now. She was a good woman, but she could not one day give him children and stand beside him the way Belle had stood beside him. She always cried and trembled after they made love. A woman long dry coming back to life. He had saved some money by being nice to her but not enough to buy what God had taken from him in North Carolina. "Besides, John, they were three niggers talking about another nigger. I thought you hired me to look after white people."

"You were hired for the law's sake." It was not adultery, whatever there was between his cousin and the boardinghouse woman, Skiffington thought. The fornication sin was on their souls alone, but he felt the

lying about Augustus was on his head as well because he had brought
Counsel in. Had vouched for him before God. "I won't have this keeping things from me about the people in this county. You have but one
more time to do this. You hear me, Counsel?"

"I hear you, John. I still say——"

Skiffington walked away.

He rode out of the town and a little more than an hour later found
Harvey Travis and Oden Peoples riding and talking loud on the dark
road. The rules said there should be three of them but Skiffington
didn't notice.

"You men sell that freed man Augustus Townsend back into
slavery?"

Travis laughed but Oden was silent. "John, who put that pickle in
your ear?" Travis said. "Who would do such a thing to you, John?"

"Tell me if you did it, Harvey? You and Oden."

"Why, hell no, John. I ain't gotta do that kinda thing. Ain't that
right, Oden?"

"Thas true, sheriff."

"Who would tell you that, John? Barnum Kinsey?"

This, Skiffington thought, was the man who tried to sell a dead
cow and then wanted it back when the cow returned to life. But this
was also the man who had caught three of Robert Colfax's slaves trying to escape. He and Oden put fear into anyone trying to escape.

"John, don't put stock in what Barnum says."

"I don't want to hear anything like this about yall again." He
thought of Joseph and his brothers: *For they did unto thee evil: and
now, we pray thee, forgive the trespass of the servants of God of thy
father.* And Augustus Townsend could still be found and brought back
to his wife and home. God still had the power to do that. "If I hear
something like this again——"

"Well, you know you won't, John, and thas all there is to it."

He did not go home pleased with himself. He had been pleased
when Colfax praised him to Williams Robbins and some others. He

got to town and wanted to just keep on riding, but he could not put his horse through that. He asked for God's guidance. He dreamed of Minerva that night. He was walking through a field and crows were flying above him all during the walk and he came to a tent in the desert, the opening flapping in the wind. He knew she was inside, waiting for him, because he could hear her crying, and he was ready to go in but he stood observing the flapping of the opening. The tent was a faded blue that shouldn't have caught anyone's eye but he could not move from it. Then the wind stopped and it still flapped, and then when the wind came up again, the opening was still.

He wrote to Richmond the next day, telling the authorities that the Commonwealth of Virginia should be aware of a slave speculator who was selling free Negroes back into slavery. On a separate sheet of paper he answered the questions from the usual form about the alleged crime, the alleged victim or victims, and the alleged perpetrator or perpetrators. When he started writing, there had been certainty that selling Augustus Townsend was a crime, but he became less certain not long before he had to sign his name under all the answers. Had Virginia, in fact, declared such a sale a crime? Could the cord of a man born into slavery ever be cut forever and completely, even if he had been free for some years? Was he not doomed by virtue of the color of his skin? And what would he do with Travis and Oden with only Barnum to stand and say a crime had been committed? The word of a white man against those of another white man and an Indian. Barnum's word against Travis's would be something of a fair fight; Barnum was a drunkard but Travis was known to be a cheat and a brute. The dead-cow episode had been widely discussed. But Travis's word had help from Oden's word, which was worth only half since he was an Indian. But that half was a half Barnum did not have. Skiffington put the sheet with answers in a drawer and expanded on the letter.

He wrote, as always, to a Harry Sanderson, who was a kind of liaison at the Capitol and was generally helpful when Skiffington needed a circuit judge to come by and preside over a matter. "I have the Governor's ear," Sanderson wrote in a curious aside in one letter. Now, Skiffington said, something was amiss with the man Darcy but he needed help in determining what that something was. He wanted to know what the law wanted him to do.

Two days later, in response to one of his telegrams, he heard from a sheriff near the North Carolina border. Darcy had passed through, he said. There had been no trouble, "air undisturbed" was how he put it, but after Darcy left the county the sheriff had discovered a dead Negro child on the side of the road, "not a member of our community, as far as we can tell."

He got a letter from Sanderson three days after that. A crime had indeed been committed, he wrote, and Sanderson included material he had copied from books saying so. Skiffington heard from Richmond again four days later. In handwriting he did not recognize, a Graciela Sanderson let him know that her husband, Harry, was dead and that she was now charged with keeping up his correspondence. He read the eight-page letter twice but he found nothing in it about what Virginia was doing about the crime of selling free Negroes. The widow told him about her husband, how she had met him when he vacationed in Italy, how he had wooed her, brought her to America after their wedding, and made her a happy woman in Richmond, "where the Governor is in residence." She closed the letter with two paragraphs about the recent "discouraging" weather in Richmond, and then she asked Skiffington if she should return to her home in Italy, "where the sun is not as spiteful," or remain in the Capitol where her children and grandchildren were prospering. "I am despondent and I await some answer from you about what I should do."

He would get more letters from her over the next few days but there would not be time to write her back.

A t Hazlehurst, Georgia, just beyond the Altamaha River, Darcy and Stennis met a man outside a saloon. The man was somewhat tipsy but quite alert and he had a Negro beside him. It was evening but there was enough light for the white man to see Augustus in the back of the wagon.

"He's good flesh," Darcy said.

"Good flesh," Stennis said.

"I ain't in the business for no slave right now," the man said, one hand on the floor of the wagon.

Darcy said, "Four hundred dollars. Just four hundred, it don't get any better than that."

The man hiccuped. "Anything can get better on another day." The Negro with the white man had stayed near the saloon but now he came down to the street and looked up at Augustus and they nodded at each other.

"Not with this it don't," said Darcy. "Four hundred dollars is all I'm asking and I'll go home tonight and cry bout how you cheated me with that."

"That price seems a bit much to me," the man said.

"Not from where I'm standin and I'm standin in good boots. I paid five hundred dollars for this nigger up in Virginia."

"We a whole lot smarter about our money in Georgia."

"Yes, you are," Darcy said. "You certainly are. Why, just the other week when I was up in North Carolina, I said to a gentleman and his gracious and hospitable wife—I said, 'You can't beat the Georgia people for their knowledge and intelligence. You can't beat it with a stick.' And they agreed."

"Two sticks," said Stennis. "Three sticks. Four sticks."

"Why, I said, Georgia done give us our best president yet."

"What?" the man said. "What president?" He seemed to sober up.

"I said you can't beat the Georgia folks for what they gave and give and will continue to give this country, startin with that fine president."

"What? What kinda president you be talkin about?" He put the other hand on the wagon's floor, then shook Augustus's chain. "What damn president you talkin about?"

"Why, the president of the United States, of course. What other kind of president is there?"

"No other kind," Stennis said.

"There ain't been no Georgia president of the United States far as I know." He hiccuped. "I ain't heard of one yet."

Augustus and the Negro with the white man had not taken their eyes from each other.

"Why sure, there has been, sir. He was a fine president, too. What was his name, Stennis?"

"Lemme see. Whatn't that President Bentley? I think it was."

"Yes, President Bentley fom Georgia. Hooray for President Bentley. Hooray! Hooray!"

"I tell you there ain't been no damn president from Georgia."

"There ain't?" Darcy said. "There ain't? Well, there damn well should have been. And I'll tell you somethin—there will be a president from Georgia and real soon."

"Yes," Stennis said. "There will be. There will be five at least, as far as I can tell. Maybe ten. Maybe ten. There'll be ten if I have anything to do bout it. Could go to be twenty or thirty."

"All right, Stennis, thas anough of that. You see, mister," and Darcy took his hand. "I'm tryin to give you a good bargain in this here nigger. Just four hundred and fifty. Thas all I'm askin."

"I thought you said four hundred dollars a minute ago."

"Did I? Did I say that? Well, it jus goes to show how valuable this nigger gets every minute that goes by. Lordy lordy! Why, in another hour this nigger be so valuable you couldn't buy him if you was the king of England."

"I have to be going," the man said, "I got the queen of England waiting for me."

"Please, sir," Darcy said. "Maybe three hundred and fifty, and I'll be crying in my soup tonight about that."

"No." The man began walking away. Darcy followed him and Stennis followed. The Negro stayed with Augustus.

"Three hundred? Two hundred and fifty. Two hundred." Darcy tugged at the man's sleeve.

"No. Come along, Belton," he said to the Negro, but the slave did not move.

"Please. Two hundred dollars. What you want me to do, give him away?"

"That would be a good notion. Come on, Belton," and both men disappeared around a corner.

"Damn damn damn," Darcy said, looking at the space the man had just occupied. "You think I was too hard with the bargainin, Stennis."

"No, Master, I think you was right on the money."

"Hmm. Well, we best get to beddin down with this fella. I hate to think about headin into Florida. I don't see good luck in Florida, but tomorrow is another day."

"And another dollar, Marse."

A Plea Before the Honorable Court. Thirsty Ground.
Are Mules Really Smarter Than Horses?

The day Skiffington first came out to Caldonia's place about Alice and Priscilla and Jamie disappearing, Moses had expected to eat supper again with Caldonia that night, but she was not hungry and the dinner meal would be the only one of her day. She had thought all that day that the three would return before nightfall, finding it difficult to believe that two women and a boy would leave what she and Henry had made. A man perhaps, someone like Elias or Clement, not a madwoman and a woman who seemed to adore her. She had informed Skiffington as a kind of courtesy to the law, but when he showed up and stood before her, the whole matter of the disappearances became more important than the nuisance she figured it to be. It was as if one of her bulls had escaped and before a servant could find and bring him back, he had not just run through someone's fields but run over a child or two. A simple misdemeanor correctable with money had become a felony. What saved her was that she was the victim.

Moses told her in the parlor that all had gone well even without Alice and Priscilla and Jamie. The harvest would be good. She reached her hand out to him, wanting him to sit beside her.

"Where do you think they are?" she asked. She had looked in Henry's big book after Skiffington's visit and estimated that the three might fetch as much as $1,400, depending upon the potential someone might see in a chubby boy and a woman who could work but might wander off on occasion. "Do you think something has happened to them?"

"No, ma'am," Moses said. Feeling Skiffington's eyes on him after he returned to work, he had wondered how long before everyone got over that the three would not be coming back, before they all got on to other business.

He put his arm around her but she said she was tired, and when he did not withdraw, she pulled away. They sat for several more minutes before she said again she was tired and needed Loretta and he got up and left.

She went to bed soon after, but could not sleep and got up around two and stood at the window and imagined the three of them coming up the walk, exhausted and glad to be home. What would Henry say of the mess that had come to this place? If three more left tomorrow and then three more and then three more, there would be no one before long but her and Zeddie and Bennett and Loretta. Would Moses be there? Would he go, too? She found solace in the way Skiffington had arrived so promptly. He took what was happening seriously and there was hope in that. She was tempted to go out to Henry's grave but did not want to go stumbling in the dark out to the cemetery. Waking everyone on such a personal mission.

There was a gentle knock at the door and a momentary fear seized her that it might be Moses. The door opened and Loretta stood with a candle. "I knowed you would be up and not sleepin," Loretta said. Would Loretta ever leave her? Which group of three would she be among? Henry had paid $450 for her, the big book had told her that morning. "I can feel when the house ain't settin right."

"Even if I can't sleep, you should be," Caldonia said.

"You want me to bring you somethin?" Loretta did not know all that went on behind the closed parlor door, but she knew that it was probably not good for either the woman or the man.

"Please find something for me in that satchel of yours, Loretta."

Within five minutes Loretta returned with a drink and Caldonia drank all of it. She got into bed. Loretta sat on the side of the bed. They did not speak. The man Loretta would eventually marry would want to know why she didn't take his last name, why she wanted no last name at all. "Is that what marryin you gon be?" she asked him. "Question after question every day for the rest of my life? Huh? Is that it?" The man she would marry was a free man who had spent much of his life on the sea. He had been talking to a man one extraordinarily calm day on the sea, and over that man's shoulder he had seen two other conversing sailors simply disappear, become nothing in only the time it took to end one sentence to the man and begin another. The sailors were not in the sea and they were nowhere on the ship. "No," the man would say to Loretta, "I won't ask you no more questions."

"I worry," Caldonia said, the drink making its way through her system.

"Shouldn't worry," Loretta said. The captain and the sailors on the ship came to attribute the disappearances to one more mystery in their sea lives. The man Loretta would marry did not have very much heart for the sea after that. When his new bride asked him not to ask her so many questions, it was an easy thing to do.

Caldonia covered her mouth as she yawned. Loretta got up and straightened the covers and took up the candle and before she was out the door Caldonia was sleeping.

The next day Moses worked everyone, even the children, until well after dark. Delphie called out at last that they were all hungry and very tired and Moses should mind what he was doing. "We can't even see what we be doin," she said. "All this work just goin to waste cause we gon have to do it right tomorrow."

Moses relented. He stood in the middle of the field and watched them trudge away. He had the reins of a mule and the mule, seeing everyone else leave, started following them. Absently, Moses went with the mule. He had heard someone say after dinner that day that his family had hated him so much that they would rather be whipped and killed by the patrollers than suffer under him. Just yall wait, he had thought, just yall wait till this whole mess is done.

He put the mule up and went to the house, still in the clothes and the sweat of the fields. Caldonia found his appearance endearing. She herself went and brought him some cheese and bread and coffee and watched him eat until a grin slowly spread across his face. "I needed that," he said at the end.

"Why do you work so hard when you are the one in charge?" she asked. She took the tray from his lap and set it on the tiny table beside his chair. She pulled the perfumed handkerchief from under her sleeve and dabbed at the corners of his mouth and he was uncomfortable with an act that was so far removed from sex, but when she was done and had folded the handkerchief and placed it atop the tray, he was sorry the act was over. "I know overseers who sit on their horses and look over everyone else."

"Wouldn't know how to do it any other way," he said and realized very soon how inadequate was the answer. But his inability to explain was also endearing. Her talking brought more of the same discomfort, and he was afraid that in not knowing the right answer, he might somehow give a wrong answer. "I was sick on my back last year, and I musta hurt more from the not workin than the sick. My wife say it's in the blood." He did not pause at the mention of Priscilla, but it came back to her that the three were missing, and for the first time, with the words "my wife," she had a momentary thought that he might be involved. He held his hands out before him as if they could do a better job of explaining than his words. She took his hands in hers and felt the hardness of aged leather. They were smaller than those of Henry, who used to massage his hands with horse liniment.

She patted his hands and put one on each of his knees. "I been workin since I was three years old, just draggin that cotton sack along," he said, speaking in a way he had not spoken since the first days with Priscilla, "maybe even before that if I could member back that far," and he looked down at his lap. "The body commences to turn to the work the way you bend a tree and make it grow whichever way you got a mind to. It don't know no better. You know, Missus, there's horses that you can work and work and they keep on workin till they drop dead. Your average mule won't really do that, but your average horse will. The mule be smarter." She was afraid that he would share more and she stood up and hoped that that would bring it to an end, but he went on to tell her that certain work songs made the work a little easier but that there were others, depending upon the time of day, that dragged a body down, so "you just gotta be careful with your songs and your hummin and whatnot." Henry sang as she curled up in his arms. Moses noticed she was standing and stood. He was quiet and she kissed him, for no other reason than that he was now silent. When she withdrew, he realized he should go. He wanted sex because he needed to be able to walk through that back door again without knocking.

Skiffington came the following day to tell Caldonia that no one in the county had seen Alice and Priscilla and Jamie. He had found her going in after being in the garden and they talked on the verandah, a light sheen of sweat about her face.

"It's a mystery," he said, "and the law doesn't like these kinds of mysteries."

"I don't either," Caldonia said. "Do you think they could just have escaped from the county?"

He held his hat down at his side and thought of Travis and Oden selling Augustus. He did not believe they would sell three more Negroes so soon after Augustus and after he had warned them. And, too, he had a strong sense that whatever had happened, Moses was involved. "I am beginning to see that as a possibility," he said, raising his hat and running his hand along the brim. When she was younger, Minerva had put on one of his hats and he and Winifred had laughed, and so had his father. She was still nine. "They have escaped or—and you have to see this as being possible—they are dead somewhere."

"Why not just hiding out?"

He brushed at the brim. "I have had my people look in every spot in this county, and unless they have taken to living in tree trunks or beneath the earth, then . . ."

She wondered if the three slaves would have been covered under policies from Atlas Life, Casualty and Assurance. Payment for escaped slaves.

"I have to go see Mildred Townsend," he said. "I will say you said howdy if that is fine by you."

"Yes. Yes," Caldonia said. "Please tell her I will be out tomorrow. And you have heard nothing about Augustus?" He shook his head. "It might be the same people grabbed my three that grabbed Augustus."

"I have considered that," he said, "but those rascals are long gone. It would be months before they could come back through. He went south. If yours escaped, they went north unless the stars and the sun confused them, and they went in another direction." He put on his hat. "I'll be going, Caldonia. Want to ask a few things of your servants before I do, though."

"Yes," she said. "Have a good day, sheriff."

"And you, Caldonia." She went inside.

He walked his horse to the fields and looked for a long time until he found Moses among the other slaves. Moses saw him after a time but did not acknowledge him and kept on working. Skiffington got on his horse. He was beginning to feel that matters were getting beyond his control and that if he did not soon corral it all, he and all he had built up would be lost Augustus. Three slaves very possibly murdered. That was how it started with Gilly Patterson, a failure to corral and then

William Robbins's loss of confidence in him. He had once asked God if wanting Robbins's confidence in him put him in a bad light with God, and the answer came back no.

He saw a child returning from a privy to the fields and asked her if she knew the three missing slaves and she said she did. Tessie, Celeste and Elias's girl, seemed to take a while to answer and he thought she was thinking of some kind of untruth when she was really wondering why he would ask that when the answer was as easy as telling him her name. He also asked who lived in the cabin next to Moses and she told him Elias and Celeste and their children. He told her to go tell Elias he wanted to see him. She told him Elias was her father. "Tell your daddy to come here." Elias had nothing much to say but five days later he did, and his wife begged him to keep it to himself but he said he couldn't hold it in. Had it been anyone else, he would have held his tongue, he told Celeste. "Try to hold it then for me," she said back.

Skiffington knocked at Mildred's door and heard the dog bark. She invited him in but he knew he had no good news and so did not want to take up too much of her time. He said, "I am always in a hurry to get, and this is another one of those days."

"My husband still gone," she said.

"Yes, Mildred. I can say no more than that."

"I thank you for the trip."

He spent the night at William Robbins's place and blamed his angry stomach the next morning on the tough chicken—unusual for the Robbins table—they fed him for supper. Had they somehow riled up the bird before they wrung the neck? Angered up the meat?

At supper, Robbins had said, "John, I want to set a five-hundred-dollar bounty on the head of that speculator that took Augustus Townsend. I will pay that to whoever brings him to me or to you. Do I need to say it doesn't matter if he is dead when they bring him?"

"I think when a man sees that five-hundred-dollar number, he will think 'dead' without the poster saying it."

"Good," Robbins said and ate heartily of the chicken, of the corn, of everything on the table, and as Skiffington put his face in the bowl of water the next morning, he was grateful that Robbins had not asked about the three slaves. But that would not have been Robbins's way—he gave a man a while to prove if he could do the job. The slaves had been gone not a week.

On his way back to town, he stopped at Caldonia's plantation and went to the fields and sat on his horse until Moses knew that he was there. The courteous thing would have been to let the mistress of the plantation know he was about but he did not think Caldonia would mind. He stayed so long he had time to bring out his Bible and read from it, still sitting on his horse. His stomach calmed down.

That evening Caldonia allowed Moses to make love to her for the first time since the three slaves went missing. He had wanted a night with her in her bed and he told her that, but she just lay in his arms on the floor afterward and said nothing. Then he asked, "When you gonna free me?"

"What?"

"I say when you gonna free me?" She withdrew from him and stood up. "I thought you was supposed to free me." He could not be her husband without first being free, not a proper husband anyway with authority over everyone and everything. There were free colored women married to slaves, but they did not have land and slaves.

"Please, Moses . . ." Neither word of mouth nor the newspaper said how many times the Bristol white woman had been whipped for lying with her slave. Had the white woman been forced by the slave, forced over and over again? Would that have mitigated the punishment? He forced me down and had his way with me, your honorable honor of the court, shouldn't that be worth five fewer lashings? And, too, your honorable court, am I not still white? "Please, Moses, I don't want to talk about this." Freeing him had been on her mind but she had never put a day and a time to it.

"I want some free papers," he said, and then added, "Missus." He got up and put himself together. She herself was already buttoned up. He thought there was more to ask about, but Loretta knocked at the door and came in after Caldonia said, "Yes." Moses left in a quiet rage.

Celeste told Elias about six the next morning that she was not feeling all that well. She was some six months pregnant. "A little digestion trouble maybe," she said. "You know how your babies get about this time: wantin to see the world fore we know it's time."

"I'll tell Moses you can't work."

"Maybe I can make it," Celeste said.

"Mama, you can't make it?" Tessie asked.

"Ain't a thing to worry about, baby."

Everyone was in the lane and Moses opened the cabin door wanting to know why Elias and his family were lingering.

Celeste was nearest him and she said she was moving a little slow.

"I want you out in them fields long with evbody else," Moses said. He took Celeste by the arm.

"Now wait here," Elias shouted and hit Moses's arm with his fist and the overseer released Celeste. "Don't touch my wife. Moses, I done told you she ain't got it in her today. I'll do her share, maybe Sunday, maybe nighttime. I done told you she ain't got it in her. Let her be." He stood between his wife and Moses. This was part of why it would be so much easier to talk to Skiffington later.

"Ain't nobody doin nobody share but they own."

"Ask mistress if I can do her share. Ask her."

"We done spoke on it last night," Moses said, taking one step back. "We talk on this all the time. What you been thinkin, huh?" He took another step back and was at the door and people were looking in from the lane and he knew they were looking. "I ask her, she ask me, and we settle this here thing bout evbody workin before the sun even come up. What you been thinkin, huh?"

"Elias, I be fine," Celeste said. "You see. I be fine." She put her hand on his shoulder and he turned to her. She had combed her hair before the pain came on and he could see how her hair, on either side of the part, had fallen in line with the will of the comb. "What you think? You marry a weak somebody? I'm here. I'm here." She went around him and said to Moses, "I'm comin. I'm on my way." Elias had earlier taken Ellwood, his youngest, and the other children under five up to the house and now Tessie and Grant followed their mother. She left the two men standing in the room and went out and joined the others as they made their way to the fields. May and Gloria walked on either side of her and took her hands. It was a bright day, as much sun as anyone would want, the kind of day some people would pray for.

Celeste was fine until after dinner. She returned to her half-completed furrow and as soon as she bent over, the pain of the early morning came back and she sank to her knees. She screamed and clawed at the plants until she took hold of one, uprooted it and squeezed. "Dear, Jesus, take this away," she said of the pain. Before Elias could reach her, the baby in her was coming. He was down to her, holding her, when the baby arrived and settled in a bloody puddle in the furrow, still connected to her mother. The women came to Celeste and told Elias to step away, step on away. Celeste's children came to her as well but two men picked them up and took them away. Celeste fainted. "Step back, Elias," Delphie told him. "Step back, I say." "Leave her be," he said to Delphie, crying and believing in some insane way that by holding his wife he could make all things right.

Delphie took hold of Elias's neck with both hands and shook him and he released Celeste and Gloria held Celeste but not at all in the way Elias had been holding her. The ground had not had rain in a few days and so was quite ready for the bloody puddle.

In the end, Elias picked her up and carried her back to the cabin. She woke along the way and did not know where she was or, for a moment, remember what had happened. She did know that the sun was full in her face and that so much sun meant she might not have any rainwater to wash her hair.

He laid her on the pallet in the cabin and no sooner had Gloria and Delphie came in to see to her and change her clothes than Elias thought of Moses. "I'm gonna kill him," he said, the words coming like a hiss.

"What you goin on about, husband?" Celeste said. "What all you goin on about?"

Elias stood up. "I'm gonna hurt him like no man's been hurt before." Delphie rushed to the door and closed it and put a hand up to Elias's chest. "Ain't no place out there you needs to be now," she said. "Leave him there. Please, Elias, leave him."

"You move, Delphie. I don't wanna hurt you to get at him. You move now." He was not shouting. He had heard Tessie at his door and he wanted his daughter to know from a calm voice that her father was coming. In his mind, he could see her standing beside Grant, and he could also see Grant looking up at his sister as she called first to her mother and then to her father. He had forgotten that little Ellwood was up at the house. A calm voice was what his daughter needed. "I been knowin you a long time," he said to Delphie, "but you gonna make me go through you and I don't wanna do that."

"Husband, come over here," Celeste said and tried to raise herself up on her elbow. Gloria gently pushed her down. "Stay," Gloria said.

Delphie put her hand at Elias's throat, the more to gain his attention, and said, "Leave this mess be right now." "Husband, I want you to come over here. Ain't you listenin to me, husband?"

Out in the field Moses was in just about the same spot as when Celeste fell. He was waiting for the right time to tell all to go back to work. Clement, the man who had stolen Gloria from Stamford, had gone up to the house not long after Elias carried Celeste away. Now, as

Moses worked out the words in his head, Caldonia was moving to Celeste's cabin, and Loretta was following her. Loretta had forgotten to bring the satchel of bandages and root medicines.

Caldonia tried to open the door but when it wouldn't budge, she called Celeste by name, then she called Elias. "They inside," Tessie said. Delphie opened the door with one hand and held the other arm out to keep Elias back. "Moses made her lose her baby," she said to Caldonia. Delphie remained at the door and Elias lowered his shoulders and Delphie said to Tessie and Grant, "Your mama and daddy need yall to stay here for now." Before the children could speak, Delphie closed the door.

"This ain't over, Delphie," Elias said as Caldonia and Loretta knelt to his wife. "This ain't over by a little bit." "I ain't never said it was, Elias," Delphie said.

Moses stayed away that evening and the next evening the house was quiet as he came up to the back. He knocked and waited until Zeddie came and let him in. "She be in the parlor," Zeddie said and Moses took off his hat and went on through. He was wearing his good pants but had not bothered to wash as he sensed there was no use.

Loretta was standing at the window and Caldonia was in the middle of the settee. "Why would you put a woman in the family way in danger, Moses?" Caldonia said.

"She playactin," he said. "They all playact sometime. I ain't never seen a one that don't playact sometime." Loretta's back was to him and he spoke some of his words to her back and some of them to the grandfather clock next to the window.

"She lost her child, Moses. Don't you know that?" Caldonia said.

"I heard that," he said.

"You let me know from now on when somebody talks about feeling bad. You come to me first."

"That could make things bad all round. Real bad." He wanted to say her name but they were not alone. This is me, he wanted to tell her. It's me you sayin all this to.

Loretta turned from the window. Whatever she had been watching was no longer of interest. She unfolded her arms. This could have been my husband, she thought, and I could have been his wife. Married, one together. Would she now have been wherever Priscilla and Alice were, out in God knew where with her child?

"I don't have any more to say, Moses. This is a disappointment. I don't have any more tonight." Loretta took two steps, signaling Moses that he was to leave.

He went out the back door but did not go to the cabins. He stood many yards from them, watching the smoke rise from all the chimneys except his own. He heard a hum and thought it might be all the evening conversations rising as one above the cabins and making a noise to the universe. A hearty laugh drifted out of the lane but by the time it reached him there was no life in it. He wanted to go out to the woods and be with himself, something he had not done in days, but he would have had to go down through the lane and he did not want to see any faces seeing his own. There was a long way around but he chose not to take it.

After he had been standing there nearly two hours, the life along the lane quieted and he went down and into his cabin. There were no sounds from the cabin next to his, from Celeste and Elias's cabin. Moses took off his shoes. He sat with his back against the door in the dark. About three o'clock he just leaned over and fell asleep across the doorway. Not long after he did that, Elias came and tried to push the door in, but finding it barred, he went back to his cabin.

The next evening Moses came in the back door without knocking, just opened it and went by Bennett and Zeddie sitting at the kitchen table, and walked into the parlor where Caldonia was standing talking to Loretta.

"I needs to talk to you," he said. "I needs to."

"What?" Caldonia said.

He pointed at Loretta. "You leave."

"Wait, Moses. You wait," Caldonia said. Loretta walked around him to the door and Moses stepped closer to Caldonia.

"Why you got me waitin round like this, like I'm somebody's child? Why ain't you done freed me?" He raised his fist into the air between them. "Why you doin this?" He took one more step and as he did, Loretta took her time and put her arm around his neck, a knife in her hand pressing into his throat so that he had to lower his foot in mid-stride.

"I ain't foolin with you," Loretta said. He had seen her, too, once upon a time before he eventually married Priscilla, but had always thought that a house woman was beyond him. What would she have seen in him? But Priscilla had toiled in the same fields he toiled in. Such a better match. "I ain't foolin with you, Moses."

He and Caldonia were watching each other. He trembled and saw himself back in the woods, naked and on his back. The night birds were watching and Alice was watching. He could hear Priscilla approaching, loudly, stepping on first one twig after another. He lowered his head and the knife was closer than before.

When he was gone, Loretta got a pistol and gave one to Bennett. Loretta wanted to go out and find the patrollers, to have them take Moses away, but Caldonia told her he would be himself by morning. "Henry's death," she said finally, "has unsettled all of us." Before going to see Celeste that night, Loretta, on her own, had Clement come up and stay the night at the back door. "Be careful," Gloria told him before he left.

Moses could feel that the world had changed even before he came to his feet the next morning. When he opened the door they were all waiting for him to lead them off to the fields. Celeste and Elias were not there, as Loretta had told Elias to stay with his wife and that Zeddie would bring them food. The slaves of the field were murmuring, like they did on any other day, but he knew it was all different and felt a dryness throughout his mouth.

He went up to the back door at about eight that evening and Loretta was there and told him their mistress was not up to hearing him that evening. "Tomorrow'll do," she said and raised the pistol so that it was inches from his face.

"I got plenty to say to her," he said. "I got somethin to say."

"It'll wait. Where's it goin?" she said and Bennett came up behind her. "It ain't goin nowhere."

He left and stood where he had the evening before, waiting for the life in the lane to quiet so he could go home. Being in the woods did not cross his mind. Being out there was good only when he could come back to something that was not pain every second. It had been more than a whole day since he had eaten, he realized, but he was not hungry. And this thought came to him at about the same time as Celeste was standing over her husband as he fluffed the straw in their pallet. Their children were now sleeping and the hearth was throwing out the last of the day's light and heat. They, the entire family, had gone earlier for the first time to the new grave of the baby Lucinda, and they were all weighed down by the agony of the visit. When Elias was finished with the pallet, he reached up to his wife's hand and put it to his cheek and then helped settle her on their bed. "I wonder," she said for the first time ever, "I wonder if Moses done ate yet."

He could hear them gathering out in the lane before the first rooster crowed. Someone knocked once at his door and called his name, but he did not answer. He was sitting with his back against the door, just as he had the first night. And, as with that night, he sat there not to bar anyone but because that was as far as he went once he entered the cabin. Someone called him again. A woman sang:

Come on outa there, Mr. Moses man
Come on out and lead us to the Promise Land

People laughed, even the children. "Mr. Overseer, is you here? Mr. Overseer, is you there?" The woman sang again. Moses thought, Could anyone plant a row of cotton with that song? "Leave him be," a man said. He thought it might be Elias but the more he considered it, the more Moses realized it could be any of the men. Then he could hear them walk away to the fields, the first morning in a year that he had not been among them. Would they know that that bottomland had to be left alone for at least another five days? He had eaten a good pinch of the dirt two days ago and it just wasn't ready yet; a good rain was what it really needed, and then you could go at it all you want. But not now, not today ... "I'm countin on you to run this place," Henry had told him after the plantation had four slaves and three more were due to arrive any day from the neighboring county. "You be the boss of this place. There's my word, then my wife's word, and then there's your word." "Yessir, Marse Henry." His master had opened the big book one day to make some notation and pointed at some words in it, saying, "Thas you, Moses. That says, 'Overseer Moses Townsend.' "

There was quiet. This, he thought, is what this place be soundin like when not a soul be around. He got up and peed into the fireless hearth. He sat again at the door. His cabin was dark except for the thick line of light at the bottom of the door, the line broken in the middle by his body. Priscilla had had a time keeping the wind from getting under that door. "It's a wonder we don't all freeze to death, Moses. Can't you get me some more rags for that door?" Priscilla hadn't been such a bad wife. Lord knows if he and that Loretta had been together, he would have had to kill her by now. Pullin a gun and a knife on him like that. Yes, he would have had to kill her by now. Or she would have killed him. One or the other. Did those words really say "Overseer Moses Townsend"? Maybe they just said this man belongs to me always and always. And after I'm gone, he belongs to my wife, Mrs. Caldonia Townsend. Don't you see my brand right there on his hindpots?

Something pecked at the door. He heard the flapping of wings and a rooster crowed and Moses wondered who was supposed to be watching the chickens. The rooster pecked again. "Go way," Moses said. "Go way from that door." His voice just seemed to encourage the bird and he crowed once more. No, Priscilla hadn't been such a bad wife. And the boy could have turned out right with just a little more time. A little less fat. The rooster pecked. "You want me to come out there and wring your neck? Thas what you want?" Then the quiet returned.

What all had he ever really asked for in this life, such as it was? He could have done better for the place than Henry Townsend. People would have said, "That Marse Moses, he got somethin magic in him to make that plantation like it is. I did time over to Marse Robbins and Marse So-and-So and Marse Everybody-Else. Did time in all those places and they ain't got half the magic Marse Moses got. It's another Eden, the preacher say, and I can't say no more than that."

He sat there all that day, dozing and talking to himself, and then he listened to everyone return from the fields, listened to Elias and Celeste and their family next door preparing their supper. The children were loud in their laughter. Well now, you can't blame them. They just bein little chaps, is all. Who in this world can blame chaps? About eight-thirty Celeste tapped at his door. "I got a little somethin for you to eat, Moses. You open and take this now, Moses." He could hear her standing on the other side of the door, could see her as full and clear as if she were standing before him, leaning just a little bit to the left because of that bad leg, her hair combed with one of those many combs her husband had made for her. "Moses?" He had witnessed that slave saying to her one day that she should be shot like a lame horse, had seen her cry. Had she cried because of what the slave said or because she had seen him standing there and seen him turn away from her? Where was that slave now? You listen here—just take back every damn word you said to this poor woman. Take it back or this overseer will whip you till you raw. This woman gon be in the family way one day and she don't need that kinda talk. "Moses, just open this door one little bit and take this here nourishment. You need some nourishment, Moses."

She went away and came back about an hour later, then a half hour after that. Not long before midnight, he stood up and opened the door and stepped out, stepped right into the food Celeste had finally left at the door. He knelt down to it and ate the bread and the meat and put the corn on the cob in the pocket of the pants Bennett had long ago given him. Once standing again, he thought about the corn some more and the way the pants had felt when he had first worn them and he took the corn out of his pocket and knelt again and set it on the empty metal pan. He hoped she would not hold his leaving the corn against him. He stood up and thought he saw Alice coming out of her cabin, singing. *I met a dead man layin in Massa lane. Ask that dead man what his name....* Now that was a song a man could plow a field with all day long. *He raised he bony head and took off his hat. He told me this, he told me that....* Just the proper rhythm. Up this row and down another.

Loretta was at the parlor window when he went out to the road. She did not wonder what he was doing or where he was going, but she did set the pistol on the table beside her. Morning would be time enough for her to put it back in the cabinet.

He went the way he had seen Alice go one of those times he had followed her. And when he reached crossroads, he took the way he thought she would go. It was a clear way, that road, one that would allow him to see the patrollers long before they would see him. He thought that was one of the most important things. He did not know enough about the world to know he was going south. He could have found his way around Caldonia's plantation with no eyes and even no hands to touch familiar trees, but where he was walking now was not that place. The other three roads had bends and turns in them and he

didn't think Alice would have ever taken them. Why, he asked himself after he was well on the road, why would that dead man have his
hat on in that road like that? It just didn't make any sense at all. It was
a good song to work by, but that was all it was good for.

He had left the door ajar and Elias used both hands to push it open
all the way the next morning. Elias hunched his shoulders to the
little gathering when he came out. People were still coming out of
their cabins and Elias used that time to take the empty pan to his
cabin and then he walked up to the house and asked Bennett if he had
seen Moses, told him the overseer hadn't come to work that day or the
day before.

Elias came back from the house and told everyone that it looked
like Moses had run away. Some people went to work, others went back
to their cabins. Gloria and Clement slipped away amid the confusion
of the morning. Bennett came down about eight that morning and
told Elias to get everyone out to the fields and then he went into
town to find the sheriff to tell him that the Townsend plantation had
a runaway overseer on their hands. It would be late that day, after
Skiffington had come and gone, that anyone would notice Gloria and
Clement were not about. They would never be seen again.

"Don't tell them a thing," Celeste said to Elias after Bennett had
gone. "Don't send them to no fields. Don't send them nowhere. If she
want them workin so much, let her come out here and do it herself."

They were in their cabin, their children playing just outside the
door. The doll he had made for his daughter rested in the center of
her little pallet, next to their sleeping youngest, Ellwood.

"Don't do her work for her, Elias. Please, don't do it." He went to
her and took her in his arms. It was a good day outside where their
babies were playing; it was the kind of day made for running away. A
good strong man without a family could run all the way to freedom
and stand on the other side, his arms high above his head, and cuss out

the patrollers and the masters and the sheriff, just cuss them out all day and get up the next day and do it again before getting on with the life God meant for him. Yes, a good strong man could do. He kissed the top of Celeste's head.

Their children had been joined by others and one child screamed playfully, "Stop pushin me down. That hurt." "I told you I was comin," a child said. "I told you I was comin so look out the way."

"Everything'll be all right," Elias said, and as soon as he had said that, she took herself from his arms. "Now, Celeste, you listen to me." He was thinking: *When they bring Moses back, Moses will see how the world went on without him.* Elias took his wife's hand. It was not much, a day or even a week of good work to throw in the overseer's face; it was not worth a baby's life or his wife's sorrow, but it was what he had.

"It ain't right," Celeste said. "It just ain't right to go and do what they bought you for. Why make it easy?"

"Now watch and see how far this here rock goes," a girl outside shouted. "See. See." "Oh, that ain't nothin," a boy challenged. "I can make mine go clean over there." "You just showin off, is all." "Cause I got somethin to show off about."

Elias said, "Is this here thing gon grow up to be somethin bad tween me and you, honey?" Their son ran in and put his arms around Elias's waist. "Come watch me run," Grant said. Elias said, "Just answer me about if this here thing gon grow up bad tween me and you?"

Celeste was near tears. She looked through the tears at the boy. "Come watch me run, Daddy," the boy said. Elias saw her shake her head no. She was thinking, Not now, Grant, when she shook her head, but Elias thought she was saying no to that thing growing up bad between them, and so he was relieved. "I gotta go work," Elias told his son. "I watch you later, son." He felt himself in charge of the place now, and that meant his family, certainly not the children, would not have to slave away. "Well, I'll watch for a minute," he told the boy, "but a minute all I got." He said to Celeste, "You just rest up."

He left the cabin and she followed him to the door. Grant ran off and back and his father clapped and their daughter Tessie came forward with the other children and they all shouted to Elias that they could do it all so much better. The boy said no, no, not better than me. Elias told the children that they were not to come to the fields that day and he led the adults away. Grant came to Celeste and swung her arm about as if it were a rope hanging from a tree and then returned to the other children.

She limped out to the lane and looked back to make sure Ellwood was still sleeping. The children ran by, then ran back the other way. It was like Sunday. The rooster that had been pecking at Moses's door scurried to the side when the children ran his way and it would have run into her place but she shooed him away. "You get along home," she said. She was thinking that such a lovely day could only mean that they would kill poor Moses when they found him. The God of that Bible, being who he was, never gave a slave a good day without wanting something big in return.

Skiffington knew the moment he saw Bennett that the man had come about the overseer. What crime had he committed now? The sheriff had just come out of the general store and saw Bennett riding up in the wagon. He noticed that Bennett rode mostly with his eyes not on the road before him but down on the mule's head and harness. William Robbins had come by the jail the evening before, inquiring of him—and Counsel—about their progress on finding Caldonia's three slaves and Augustus Townsend. Robbins had brought Louis, but his son did no more than stand near the door as the white man let the sheriff and his deputy know that escaping slaves jeopardized practically everything they all had. "Bill," Skiffington had said, "you're not telling me anything I haven't thought about a thousand times."

Bennett made to get out of the wagon, but Skiffington told him to tell whatever it was from the seat. Bennett looked momentarily forlorn, as if his message would lose its urgency if he had to tell from the wagon. And as Skiffington watched him ride away, he saw that the man was not used to riding a wagon, just in the way he let the mule ride all over the road. No doubt, he thought as he continued to watch Bennett go away, if he knew nothing about driving a mule, he knew nothing about riding a horse.

Someone walking on the other side of the street called out good morning and Skiffington raised his hat out of habit. He and Winifred and his father and Minerva should have been in Pennsylvania long ago. He should have been an American citizen doing well in Pennsylvania, where Benjamin Franklin had lived. He should have been on the bank of a nice river, showing his son how to make a living just from God's bounty. And Minerva should have been out, out with some Pennsylvania Negro, out so that he would not think about her in a way a father should not think about a daughter. Out and about, Minerva should be, so that he would not think, as he had the day before, that once, just once, would not hurt anyone, would not disturb anything that mattered. Shhh ... Don't tell Winifred, and don't tell God. Shhh ... He saw that Bennett had stopped for something crossing the road. He seemed to be standing there for a long time and Skiffington wondered what could take so long to cross a road. Just once ... Is that what Eve said to Adam, or did Adam say that to her? And if it was just once, would God allow him to see Pennsylvania?

Bennett started up again and Skiffington went down the steps to the road, the dust rising almost imperceptibly as he set both feet down. A good rain would do us all some good. He looked over his shoulder. The door to the jail was open just a bit, but it did not matter because he had no prisoners that day. Someone else bid him good morning and he raised his hat again. He went left, headed for the boardinghouse, to get Counsel and tell him that he and the patrollers were failing with the primary reasons they had been hired. Four slaves from one plantation. Who could live with that? And one of those slaves had murdered the other three. But four were still gone, four had disappeared from the books. He stopped in the street and realized that the boardinghouse was in the other direction. And if he moved to Pennsylvania and Winifred gave him a daughter, and not a son, would he think of her the way he had been thinking of Minerva?

He turned around and headed down the way he had come. Slaves, Minerva, and now Counsel coming in later and later, sleeping up with that boardinghouse woman like he was a young dog who had never known a woman in his life. Everything was coming apart. "How you this morning, John?" His only job was to pull it all back together again, make it whole and right the same way God had given it to him. "John, tell Winifred Mrs. Harris so appreciated what she did for her. Tell her that for me, will you?" Mrs. Harris was a stutterer. Go and stutter no more, for I have led you out of the stuttering valley into this place I will give you and all your generations. Count them. . . . Sit here by the road and count them like leaves on a tree. . . .

Three days later Skiffington was standing in nearly the same spot as the morning Bennett came to tell him about Moses running off. "Mr. Sheriff," Bennett said, "Missus want me to tell you that her Clement and her Gloria done gone, too. Just up and went away. She want me to come tell you that." Bennett again had trouble maneuvering the wagon around. "Why don't you just ride a horse like every other man?" Skiffington asked him, counting up the numbers of missing slaves. "Well, sir," Bennett said, considering the reins in his hands, "a horse ain't nearly as smart as a mule, the way I hear it."

Just as Bennett managed to turn the wagon around, Counsel rode up the other way and Skiffington lit into him about what a lazy man he was becoming. Counsel said nothing but got off his horse and tied him to the post and went into the jail. Skiffington followed him, all the while calling him a lazy deputy, so loud that even after they were in the jail, people along the street could hear the sheriff, which was not like their sheriff, and the mule and Bennett could hear him as they rode out of town.

That was Tuesday.

11

A Mule Stands Up. Of Cadavers and Kisses and Keys.
An American Poet Speaks of Poland and Mortality.

There was once a generally well-liked white man in Georgia, near Valdosta, quite a wealthy man with his slaves and his land and his money and his history. This man, Morris Calhenny, suffered from a crushing melancholy, particularly on days when it rained. He would get on his horse, the mare that he used only on rainy days, and would ride and ride until he reached some peace with himself. The peace, to be sure, never lasted, but there wasn't anything Morris could do about any of it.

There was as well a black man, Beau, in that place near Valdosta, Georgia. His last name was also Calhenny, but only because all Morris's slaves had his last name. When they, Beau and Morris, had been boys, they were almost as close as brothers, and Morris would seek out Beau when the melancholy hit because Beau never asked why he suffered like that, why Morris couldn't just get up and walk away from whatever was bothering him. Beau just stayed by his side until things got a bit better.

When the two reached the age of fourteen, there was the inevitable parting and they never came back together in the same way. But many times when they were adults, Beau remembered how the sad days would take a hold of Morris and he would take one of

Morris's horses without asking anyone and go out in the rain in search
of his master. The two of them would ride for a long time until Beau
would ask Morris, "You done had anough?" The question always
came at the right moment, even with the rain still coming, and Morris
would nod his head and say, "I done had enough." Then they would
go slowly back to the barn, the one that housed only the Calhenny
horses, and then Morris would go into his big house and Beau would
go to his cabin where his family was waiting to ask what he was doing out in all that rain.

On one rainy day, Beau and Morris rode out to the eastern edge of
Morris's land and they sat their horses and looked down across the hill
to the line where the white man's land ended. On a back road not on
his property, they saw a young white woman trying to get a white
mule to stand up from the muddy road. The mule had been pulling a
wagon in the rain, and it wasn't clear to Beau or Morris whether the
animal had sat down because it was tired of working or because it just
liked sitting down in the rain.

The white woman was named Hope Martin, but only Beau knew
that. Though white, she was not in Morris's class.

"You want me to go down and help her?" Beau asked Morris.

"No," Morris said, "give her a little time."

The woman at first seemed to be talking to the mule, trying to
convince it that it should get up so they could continue. The mule
didn't move. Finally, Hope went to the back of the wagon and took
out several apples from a covered basket. She sat down in the road in
front of the mule and ate an apple as she fed first one and then another to the mule. She got more apples several times from the wagon.
The rain did not let up and the black man and the white man on the
horses did not move.

After some thirty minutes of eating apples, the mule stood up but
Hope still sat in the mud, taking her time as she ate her fourth apple.
Seeing Hope sitting there, the animal became restless, its tail swish-
ing and its head going up and down, first one front hoof stamping the

mud, then the other. After fifteen or more minutes of this, Hope stood and stretched, the rain still coming on. She said something to the mule and pointed up the road to where they had to go. The mule started moving even before she got back on board.

"What's her name?" Morris asked Beau as they watched the woman and the mule and the wagon go up the hill without any trouble.

Beau told him who she was, that she had come down from north Georgia to take care of her aunt and her ailing uncle. Both aunt and uncle were very old people, not long for the world. "She'd make some man a good wife," Beau said, putting an end to the woman's history.

He would not have said this if he didn't think his master was already thinking it.

"You done had anough?" Beau said.

"I think I have," Morris said.

Morris was father to a young man—the only white child he would ever have—with a wonderfully complicated mind. On the day they saw Hope and the mule in the rain, that child, Wilson, had been a year and some months in Washington, D.C., at the medical school of George Washington University. Wilson had learned a great deal at that university and his mind would have contained even more but well into his second year the cadavers began to talk to Wilson, and what they said made far more sense than what his professors were saying. The professors, being gods, did not like to share their heaven with anyone, dead or alive, and they sent the young man home in the middle of his second year.

Even before the professors had sent Wilson back home, his father had been thinking that he wanted Hope as his son's wife. Though she came from a different place in life, Morris felt that she could be cleaned off, made wholesome, the way an apple fallen into mud could be cleaned up and eaten. Morris had an emissary go to her and her relatives and tell them he wanted to see her, but the woman never came to him, and in the end Hope married another young man, Hillard Uster, poor except for the nice parcel of land he had inherited from his parents. Hillard was not as handsome as she was beautiful but Hope thought she could live with that, and indeed she did.

Their marriage angered Morris, and he was still angry when his son came home from Washington, D.C., for good and tried to tell Morris and his mother what the cadavers had been saying to him. The father and his son talked late into the nights, and there were many times when what the cadavers said began to make sense to the father. In the morning, though, Morris would have more clarity and he would blame many people—but especially Hope and Hillard—for all the things the dead people were putting in his son's head. Morris told people in that part of Georgia that Hope and Hillard were to suffer alone and everyone was forbidden to help them. And that was how it was for a long time.

The Usters' children were small and weak of bone and lung and the inherited land was left mostly to Hope and Hillard alone to try to make a living. Then, in 1855, Hillard managed to save about $53 and met a black man named Stennis and his white master, Darcy, who feared taking one last piece of property into Florida, where he had never known good luck. Hillard used the money to buy that human property from Darcy.

That day in September, Darcy and Stennis said good-bye to Augustus Townsend, who said nothing, and he watched them ride away in the wagon that had held up all the way from Virginia. They had sold Augustus's mule back in North Carolina. Augustus stood on the edge of Hillard's field, free of his chains for the first time since Manchester County. Hillard held a rifle. On either side of the white man was a boy. On the porch of the tiny house Hope was holding a baby. On either side of her was a little girl.

"I don't want no trouble outa you," Hillard said to Augustus. Darcy had said that Augustus, still new to Georgia, might be testy for a few days. "I don't want no trouble."

"I won't be nothin but trouble," Augustus said, looking around, getting his bearings.

"We got a nigger just like evbody else, Pa?" the boy on Hillard's right said.

"Hush."

"I just wanna go home and then I'll be outa your way."

Hillard raised his rifle, pointed it at Augustus. "Then you and me will have trouble."

"We gon have trouble, Pa," the boy on the left said.

"Hush," Hillard said. He raised the rifle higher, up to Augustus's face. "I just want you to work, like you suppose to."

"I done done all the work I suppose to do."

"I wanna feed my family and I'll do anything to make that happen. I just wanna feed my family. Thas all there is to it."

"I know family. I know all about family. But, mister, you can't raise your family on my back," and Augustus, noting where the sun was, turned and headed north.

"Our nigger goin, Pa?" the first boy said.

"Hush."

Augustus was a few yards away when Hillard said, "You come back here. You better come here. I'm tellin you to come back here." Augustus continued on.

"Stop, you," the second boy hollered. "You stop."

"Hilly?" Hope called from the porch. "Hilly, what is goin on?"

Her husband raised the rifle and fired a shot into Augustus's left shoulder. Augustus stopped, looked at the ground, and lifted his head again. The blood took its time spreading all over the top of the shirt, then spread down and all about, down some more to the top of his pants. Augustus lowered his head and fell to the ground. Hope screamed.

Hillard and the boys ran to Augustus. The girls on the porch ran as well, and so did Hope, but with the baby in her arms she was not as fast as the girls were.

"I told you to stop. All I wanted was for you to stop."

Augustus was on his back and he looked up at the man and at the boys. He didn't look at the girls and the woman with the baby because by the time they got there his eyes were closed, which helped with the pain.

"I told you to stop, dammit! Nigger, all I wanted was for you to stop."

Augustus heard him and he wanted to say that that was the biggest lie he had ever heard in his life, but he was dying and words were precious.

Hope and her family—except for the baby, who was put for the moment on the ground where Augustus fell—managed to get him to the barn, which is where Hillard had intended for Augustus to live when he wasn't working. Hope stayed with him most of the day and the evening and a good part of the night. Hillard did not come out to him, and the woman said to Augustus at one point, "I hope you won't hold his not comin out against him." There was a brave man in the neighborhood, a healer of sorts, a man not afraid of Morris Calhenny, and that man came out and tried to get the bullet out of Augustus, but the bullet was stubborn, having found a home.

When Augustus Townsend died in Georgia near the Florida line, he rose up above the barn where he had died, up above the trees and the crumbling smokehouse and the little family house nearby, and he walked away quick-like, toward Virginia. He discovered that when people were above it all they walked faster, as much as a hundred times faster than when they were confined to the earth. And so he reached Virginia in little or no time. He came to the house he had built for his family, for Mildred his wife and Henry his son, and he opened and went through the door. He thought she might be at the kitchen table, unable to sleep and drinking something to ease her mind. But he did not find his wife there. Augustus went upstairs and found Mildred sleeping in their bed. He looked at her for a long time, certainly as long as it would have taken him, walking up above it all, to walk to Canada and beyond. Then he went to the bed, leaned over and kissed her left breast.

The kiss went through the breast, through skin and bone, and came to the cage that protected the heart. Now the kiss, like so many kisses, had all manner of keys, but it, like so many kisses, was forgetful, and it could not find the right key to the cage. So in the end, frustrated, desperate, the kiss squeezed through the bars and kissed Mildred's heart. She woke immediately and she knew her husband was gone forever. All breath went and she was seized with such a pain that she had to come to her feet. But the room and the house were not big enough to contain her pain and she stumbled out of the room, out and down the stairs, out through the door that Augustus, as usual, had left open. The dog watched her from the hearth. Only in the yard could she begin to breathe again. And breath brought tears. She fell to her knees, out in the open yard, in her nightclothes, something Augustus would not have approved of.

Augustus died on Wednesday.

Skiffington had slept little since the day Bennett came to tell him about Moses. The Thursday after Augustus was killed had brought on a small toothache that became overwhelming by midday Friday. He lay in bed beside Winifred that Friday night only to avoid her pestering him about not getting enough sleep; he lay and listened to her quiet sleeping, thinking about where Moses could hide in his county and shifting now and again as the toothache hounded him into Saturday morning.

He had been berating Counsel and the patrollers all week, and he had them all out most of the days and the nights to search for the man he began calling the murdering runaway. "Which is the worst," Harvey Travis the patroller joked behind Skiffington's back, "the murdering or the running away?" The bloodhounds in Manchester seemed most ineffectual, "couldn't find stink on a skunk," Oden Peoples complained, and more dogs were brought in from other counties. But they failed as well. The patrollers and the dogs concentrated on places to the east of the town, the places that were the closest to the north. By that Saturday they were searching not only for Moses but Gloria and Clement as well. "Somebody," Travis said, "should close the gate at her place, or teach her how to own a slave. A man dies and a woman runs his place into the ground."

Skiffington spent the days chewing bark that a slave, a root worker down the street, said would give him some relief for his toothache. She had peered into his mouth on Tuesday and told him there wasn't much she could do for his suffering. "I do believe," she said looking from one tooth to another, "that that pain is bringin you down and you just gotta pull it out. Just take it by the root and yank and yank till there ain't nothin left." They hadn't bothered going inside to where she lived and she used the dying sunlight to investigate his mouth. "Open just so, Mr. Sheriff." She touched the bad tooth with the end of a piece of bark and he shrank away in pain. He thought all the talk of yanking was her way of saying she could perform the task. But she told him, after pulling him back to her and closing his mouth with both her hands, that the mouth wasn't something she liked to spend time thinking about. "You got a back ache, you got a heart ache, you got a foot ache, I can help you. But I don't like to go to the mouth. Too far away from what I know bout helpin people. Too near the brain." He came on Wednesday and offered her a fifty-cent piece to pull out the tooth but she said no and put the money back in his hand. Her master allowed her to do extra work for people so she could buy her freedom. On that Wednesday she had saved up $113 after three years of work. The price her master had quoted for her freedom was $350. "I can't touch your mouth, Mr. Sheriff. I might hurt you more than I can help you."

That Wednesday he went, again, with Counsel out to the farthest

eastern edge of the county, out to where his cousin-in-law Clara
Martin lived, then crossed into the neighboring county, knowing that
the sheriff there would understand his encroachment. On the way
back, Counsel complained about all the riding and said they should
spend the night at Clara's, but Skiffington wanted to get back to
Winifred.

Fern came with Dora and Louis on Thursday to see Caldonia. After
Robbins heard about the escaping slaves, he sent them to Caldonia
to see what help she might be. Robbins told no one except Louis that
he no longer had faith in Skiffington. Along the way to Caldonia, the
young people had paid a courtesy visit to Fern, and she had decided
to accompany them. It would be good to be away from Jebediah
Dickinson, the gambler. Weeks and weeks later, when he was on the
road to Baltimore, she would send Zeus into Manchester every day to
ask about the mail. She promised God that if she ever heard from
Jebediah she would send him the remaining $450 he said her husband
owed him.

They had an early supper and Caldonia excused herself and rose
from the table afterwards and told her guests that since the escape of
the overseer she had been visiting the quarters each evening, "to ease
my mind." She did nothing during the visits but walk with Loretta
from one end of the lane to the other, as if her presence might prevent still one more slave from running away. She had put the day-to-
day running of the plantation in Elias's hands. When she asked him
Thursday morning in the parlor if he knew if others might escape,
Elias looked first at Loretta and said that was a question for God. That
morning, after Elias went to the fields, she sent word to Maude, her
mother, to come to her, that she needed her near.

Her guests, including Fern, decided to come with her late that
Thursday afternoon. Carrying a lantern even though there was still
sufficient sunlight, Loretta walked two paces behind the group. Elias

had freed the slaves early from the fields and most everyone was home eating their supper. So the lane was empty when they first entered, but Elias came out and then Delphie and Cassandra came out of their cabin. Celeste came to the door but did not cross her threshold. "Howdy, Tessie. Howdy, Celeste," Caldonia said. Celeste only nodded.

"Hi you, Missus?" Tessie said. She was carrying her doll because her brothers had been playing with it more than she was comfortable with.

"I am well," Caldonia said. "And you, Celeste?"

"Fine, Missus."

"That's such a pretty doll," Fern said.

"My daddy made it for me," Tessie said. She would repeat those words just before she died, a little less than ninety years later. Her father had been on her mind all that dying morning, and she asked one of her great-grandchildren to go to the attic and find the doll.

"Your daddy got the touch," Louis said.

"Yes, Marse, he do."

Elias was in the lane and said good evening to everyone, nodding finally to Loretta. Ellwood, Elias's youngest, crawled up behind Celeste in the doorway and she picked him up. She heard Louis say that he was going out to search for Moses and the others and Elias said that if Moses was still gone come Sunday, he would join the search. Elias had asked Delphie to cut a lock of the dead baby's hair before she put her into the ground, and he carried that hair in a piece of cloth pinned inside his shirt. Celeste then heard Elias say to Louis that Moses was world-stupid, the same words he had spoken to Skiffington, and that Moses did not know north from south unless somebody told him and even then he wasn't real sure. The two men laughed. Caldonia said nothing and felt Loretta at her back.

Celeste shifted Ellwood in her arms. Tessie and Grant were on either side of her, clinging to her frock, and the four of them watched together. A bloodhound from another county, who had wandered into the neighborhood of the lane three days ago, rested beside Grant.

Celeste did not know what she was going to do with Elias. She loved him, and no matter what there would be no way to get around that. Everything else that came their way—even his hatred of Moses— would have to do battle with her love for him. She could only hope that Elias would find his way back to what he had been.

She saw Elias say something she could not hear, but she noted Louis and Fern laughing in response. Dora and Caldonia were holding hands, the way she and Cassandra often did, the way she did with May, the way she used to do with Gloria. How so very different the world would be if Elias did not love her, too. But she knew that he did love her, even if some things in their days and nights blinded him to it.

Elias turned and looked for a very long time at his wife. Wife, trust me, his eyes said, and I will get us, yours and mine, out of this. Then Elias looked at his two oldest children, at Tessie and Grant. They looked at their father. He held his hand out and they flowed to him. Ellwood the baby clung to Celeste and then he began to wiggle, want-ing to be let down to the ground. Elias looked once more at Celeste. Wife, wife . . . She lowered her eyes from him and then took them away from him, took them off down the lane that was now becoming crowded with people, then out down to where the sun tended to come up in the morning. The generations of Celeste and Elias Freemen would be legion in Virginia.

Ellwood continued to wiggle and when his mother put him down, he soon began to pull on her frock, wanting her to pick him up again. "See, see," she said. "See, you don't always want what you think you want. See. Why don't you listen to me sometime?" The baby looked up, pleading: I done learned my lesson. Pick me up again. His mother tapped the foot of her good leg. No, the foot said. No lesson could stick in the head if it was only a few seconds long. She tapped on. The bloodhound beside them was gnawing on a bone that he would keep even when a child came along later and offered something bigger and better. Ellwood extended both hands up to Celeste and she re-lented. Once up again, Ellwood put his arms around her neck. "Mr.

Blueberry," Ellwood Freemen would say more than twenty years later
to Stamford Crow Blueberry in Richmond, "I have come to fulfill my
duty, just as I gave you my word that I would. I have come to teach for
you and the chaps." Ellwood the baby, back in his mother's arms,
looked around and sighed. His mother kissed his neck and said,
"Maybe next time you'll listen to me." In 1993 the University of
Virginia Press would publish a 415-page book by a white woman,
Marcia H. Shia, documenting that every ninety-seventh person in the
Commonwealth of Virginia was kin, by blood or by marriage, to the
line that started with Celeste and Elias Freemen.

Stamford now came from behind Celeste and tickled her shoulder.
The baby Ellwood and Celeste and Stamford looked at the gathering
of people just beyond them in the lane. People came out of their cabins to Caldonia not so much because she was the mistress but because
she had not long ago suffered a death. They all knew death, even the
very young who had yet to lose someone. Ellwood the baby saw
Stamford and reached for him. Only weeks ago the man and the baby
did not even know the other existed, but then Stamford had seen the
cabin in the sky. Ellwood grabbed for him, needing him, and Stamford
took him in his arms. The baby studied Stamford and as his hands
reached for the man's face, Stamford teased and pulled it back, his
mouth beginning to open to say the words the baby wanted. Stamford
was still a year away from first kissing Delphie.

"Lord, I wish we could get some better days," Celeste said to
Stamford. "I'm tired a this mess of a weather. I really am. I wish the
Lord would reach down in that big bag a days of his and pull us out
some good-weather days that would last and last. Some nice and
plump days layin over there in the corner right next to day fore yesterday. God could give us some nice days, Stamford, if he had a mind
to. He could even lend em to us. By now he should know we a people
that take care a things and we'd hand em back just the way he give
em to us."

Celeste was practically talking to herself now because Stamford and the baby were in a world of their own. The baby's hands had reached the man's face and he was tapping every feature of it, doing everything that was necessary for the man to say the words the baby had come to expect in their brief history together. Stamford's mouth opened more and more. "You here early this mornin," Stamford Crow Blueberry would say to Ellwood Freemen that day some twenty years later in Richmond. Ellwood would be walking up the street with the reins of his horse in his hand, and Stamford would be walking with a baby resting on his shoulder, the newest member of the Richmond Home for Colored Orphans. Mother and father killed in a fire. Walking and singing to the baby in the morning seemed to calm the infant for the rest of the day. Ellwood Freemen would say, "I have come to fulfill my duty, just as I promised, Mr. Blueberry. Is that to be one of my pupils?" Stamford would shake his hand, nodding. Ellwood said, "You look as if you didn't believe I would keep my word." "Oh," Stamford said, "I whatn't worried. I know where your mama and papa live. I know where I could find them to tell em that their boy didn't keep his word." Ellwood told him he had to tend to some business elsewhere in Richmond and would return shortly to set-tle in at the home for orphans. He got on his horse and rode slowly out to the main street, the street that would be named for Stamford Blueberry and his wife Delphie. Blueberry, with the new orphan on his shoulder, followed. He watched Ellwood take his time going off and Stamford that day would realize for the first time just how far they had come. He would have cried as he had that day after the ground opened up and took the dead crows, but he had in his arms a baby new to being an orphan. Stamford, it don't matter now, he told himself, watching Ellwood and the horse saunter away. It don't matter now. The day and the sun all about him told that was true. It mattered not how long he had wandered in the wilderness, how long they had kept him in chains, how long he had helped them and kept himself in his own chains; none of that mattered now. He patted the baby's back, turned around and went back to the Richmond Home for Colored

Orphans. No, it did not matter. It mattered only that those kind of chains were gone and that he had crawled out into the clearing and was able to stand up on his hind legs and look around and appreciate the difference between then and now, even on the awful Richmond days when the now came dressed as the then. Behind him, as he walked back, was the very corner where more than a hundred years later they would put that first street sign—STAMFORD AND DELPHIE CROW BLUEBERRY STREET.

The baby Ellwood had now finished the ritual of touching every feature of Stamford's face. Celeste said, "Maybe a lotta days is too much to wish for. Maybe just two or three in a row." The baby Ellwood now waited and the reward came and Stamford opened his mouth and sang the way he would just before Ellwood came up the street that Richmond day with his horse trailing behind—

> *Mama's little biddy baby gon git it all real sweet*
> *Mama's little biddy gon git it all nice and sweet...*

The glee spread throughout the baby's body. He began clapping his hands, not as any sort of applause but because there was so much happiness in his body that this was the only way he could release some of it.

Celeste looked down the lane, where there was now a larger crowd, her husband and two children among them. The little twins named Henry and Caldonia came tottering out of their cabin and Loretta lowered the lantern just a bit so that all might get a better look at the children. As she brought the lantern down, the shadows of the twins that had been resting on the ground behind them grew and grew so that by the time everyone had a good look at the babies, the shadows were as tall as the children.

Celeste learned the next day, Friday, that Caldonia, with a recommendation from Louis, had made Elias overseer. The two men would become close over the next days.

That Friday, too, Ray Topps, the man from Atlas Life, Casualty and Assurance Company returned and had no trouble getting in to see Caldonia. He came with Maude. A widower with nine children, including three unable to walk and one unable to see or hear, a man who had failed at his patent medicine business, Topps had many papers, which he was eager to show Caldonia. All the papers had the name of the company spelled "Aetlas." "Unfortunately," he explained, sitting next to her on the settee, "there seems to have been an abundance of *E*'s at this particular printer's. But I assure you we have always been known as Atlas and we always will be. Your children will know us as that, and so will your grandchildren. Their children will know the same." For the moment, with all the talk of children, he forgot he was talking to a childless widow. "You get the meaning I'm trying to convey to you, Mrs. Townsend," he said, seeing his mistake. And Caldonia said that she did.

Topps told her that for 15 cents a head every two months, her property, each working slave over five years old, would be protected from just about everything God could think up: Getting kicked in the head by a mule while working a field. Dying from tainted food—as long as a doctor could certify the food was not simply rancid and that any normal person could have eaten it and not have the same death visited upon him. Breaking a neck in a well after falling down in it while cleaning it out. Getting bit by a snake of one foot or longer while working in the fields or the barn or the smokehouse or the tobacco barn or the corncrib; said snake, alive or dead, with suitably missing fang or fangs, would have to be produced to collect on the policy. Slave death by mad dogs in fall, winter or spring was compensable; canine madness in the summer was an "ordinary act of God," to be expected, so the policy was mute about that season. Nothing came from the loss of an arm or of one or both eyes, because such losses were not the best indicia of how much work a slave could still perform. Being hurt in any fashion by duly authorized slave catchers was compensable as long as the slave had not been running away; no monies for a runaway or obedient slave harmed or killed by "amateur" slave catchers not recognized by the law. Being killed or injured by a neighbor while walking across a neighbor's property while on some errand "of consequence" for the master or the mistress or their issue. No money for a slave hurt or killed by someone while said slave was visiting his family on another plantation. Being accidentally shot while assisting the master/mistress/their issue while hunting or while traveling with said people as long as travel was of three days duration or longer. Being struck by lightning while working in the field as long as recuperation was less than three days and as long as the slave had not been given sufficient warning that lightning was about to strike. Death by lightning was not compensable; such deaths were simply another "ordinary act of God" that "the Company, in its wisdom, could not reward."

For a total of just one dollar every month Caldonia would receive three-fifths the value of any runaway slave who was not caught within two months. Topps stated that a separate policy to protect against "plain old natural death" was 10 cents a head every other month, but Caldonia decided to stay with just the 15 cents policies, "for now." Fern Elston had stopped listening and left the room long before Maude began to point out that most of the slaves in the cemeteries in Manchester County had died while working, so there was no use insuring for ordinary dying. She also noted that most of the slave chaps who had died of natural causes were too young to be covered. "That is a fact," Maude said with some authority.

"So," Topps said as he finalized everything, "there will be no protection at this time on the perishment of your human property." "Perishment," or natural death, was a word the people at Atlas used very often, and no one used it more than the widowed Topps, who saw himself as one day ascending to an important position at the home office in Hartford, Connecticut, and looking down over the land and dispensing wisdom learned from years toiling in the wilderness of the uninsured. The word *perishment* had been thought up by a man at the Hartford office to try to convey the fragility of human life, especially that of slaves, and to try to get across to a customer the utter need for Atlas's policies on those lives, slave or otherwise. The man at the Hartford headquarters, who had never seen an American slave except in newspapers and magazines, was something of a poet and had brought over two books of his poems when he emigrated from Poland. At about the time he came up with the word *perishment,* a publisher in Bridgeport, Connecticut, had agreed to publish the books but felt that one of them was "too suffused with the weave" of Poland. "Forget Poland," the publisher wrote the poet. "I can't even find the damn thing on my map." He promised to publish both books if the perishment poet could reweave the Polish one, and the poet was thinking it over at the time Henry Townsend died. There was no money in either book, the Bridgeport publisher wrote the poet, but there was the promise of glory and remembrance and the adoration of a public hungry for the real truth of America. It was well known, even by a foreigner in an insurance fortress miles away in Hartford, that from his cubbyhole of an office in Bridgeport the publisher was as good as his word.

All of Caldonia's guests, except her mother, would stay until Sunday, when Elias and Louis went out to search for Moses and Gloria and Clement. Only the former overseer would be found.

12

Sunday. Barnum Kinsey in Missouri.
Finding a Lost Loved One.

That morning, Sunday, Skiffington woke with the first real idea of where Moses was. He remembered what Elias had said about the runaway being "world-stupid." It was as clear as anything and he wondered why God had not put the notion into his head before. Maybe, he thought as he sat on the side of the bed and watched the sun at his feet, he himself had put Mildred Townsend's place beyond consideration because he had not been able to bring Augustus back to her. And, too, the place was on the way south, the opposite of where a runaway slave might want to be. But God, working in his own time, had now put in his head the notion of where the murderer was. Skiffington had a feeling, based on what he knew about crime and criminals, that Moses was still there, but he sensed that if he did not get to Mildred's place soon, the escaped slave would be gone. And he also had a feeling, somewhat fainter than the first, that if Moses had killed his own woman and boy and the madwoman Alice, then he might have killed Mildred, simply because killing was now in his blood.

That Sunday, too, he awoke with the same toothache that had claimed him for many days. He had had some relief the day before but now it was back, a throbbing and insistent lump of pain bedded down on the left side of his face. He told himself he could live with it. Monday would be too late to go after the slave Moses and the other two. Still on the side of the bed, he lowered his head and prayed. His wife was downstairs with Minerva and his father. There would be no time for church services today. Ordinarily, he would have gone to get the tooth pulled at the undertaker, who doubled as the town dentist, but the undertaker had been three days in Charleston, caring for a bachelor brother who had no wife or slaves to do the looking after. Skiffington could have gone to the white doctor, but he and the doctor had not spoken in four years. The doctor had complained for a long time to Skiffington that the sheriff's Shetland sheepdog had been killing the doctor's chickens. With no sheep to run after, the doctor told Winifred, the dog had been taking it out on his chickens. Skiffington had believed that he had trained the dog well and the doctor should look elsewhere in the neighborhood for the culprit. "Suspect" was the way Skiffington had put it.

Then, one mild Monday morning after Skiffington had gone off to the jail, the doctor stepped out into his backyard and saw the dog walking casually toward his chicken coop. The dog turned and, almost mesmerized, looked for the longest into the doctor's eyes, long enough for the doctor to call to his slave for his pistol. He shot the dog four times, twice in the head and twice in the body. Then he had his slave pick up the corpse and throw it into Skiffington's yard.

Skiffington now dressed and left the house without a meal. He didn't tell Winifred about the toothache because she would have fussed some more. He found Counsel in the jail cleaning his gun, and the sight of his cousin working away on a Sunday angered him. He had told him about being in the jail on Sunday when there wasn't a prisoner but Counsel was hardheaded. Counsel was whistling a tune and Skiffington, stepping two feet into the office, thought the words that went with the tune were probably dirty ones.

"Best get ready," Skiffington said. "We goin."

"Where?"

"Out to get that runaway Moses." He was moving as gingerly as he could because movement upset the mess on the side of his face. He was not looking forward to the long ride, the bouncing about, but he had a sworn duty and he did not want to trust Counsel or the patrollers out there with a murderer. No doubt Augustus and Mildred had guns. He took his rifle from the rack.

By ten-thirty they were well out of the town of Manchester. It was a very hot day and they moved into what his father Carl often called "the teeth of the sun." Counsel was chewing tobacco, a habit he had picked up in Alabama, and now and again, he would spit ahead into the dusty road to see how far the spit would skip. They didn't talk much, and when they did, it was mostly Counsel just saying something to break the silence between them. And when he wasn't talking or spitting into the road, he was whistling the tune which surely had dirty words to go with it.

Skiffington did say, about halfway to William Robbins's plantation, that Counsel should try to drop the tobacco habit. He talked through clenched teeth to keep as little air as possible from getting in and knocking against the ornery nerves of the tooth.

"I've never seen anything wrong with it," Counsel said, making still one more note in his mental book about the shit way his cousin saw the world. "Just a little habit that God don't mind."

"If you pile up enough habits," Skiffington said, "you soon have enough for a real sin. Then you have trouble."

The unsparing sun put a greater burden on the men and their horses and they arrived at Robbins's about twelve-thirty, a little later than Skiffington had wanted. Robbins was not there but Mrs. Robbins and Patience her daughter made them at home. Mrs. Robbins had a dinner prepared for them. Skiffington wanted only soup, lukewarm and as close to a broth as the cook could manage. Patience said as they ate, "John, you and Counsel should just rest up here today and go out tomorrow." Patience reminded Counsel of Belle, his wife, when she was young.

Four years and one month from that day, William Robbins would suffer a stroke. This was at a time when his wife had already turned beastly sour because she lived in a house with a man who could not love her anymore. Not satisfied with the reports about her father's condition that she received second- and thirdhand, Dora would decide she could not wait any longer and went to her father's plantation after he had been in his sickbed for three weeks. Her brother, Louis, told her not to go, but she had more of her father in her than he did. Neither child had ever been to the plantation before.

Patience said to Skiffington, "Stay on here through the night, John. The rest will do you both some good. And your tooth'll thank you for the rest."

Dabbing at his mustache with his napkin, Skiffington said to Patience, "I wish I could stay, Miss Patience, but my business will not wait." He complimented her and Mrs. Robbins on the soup and finished the whole bowl.

That day four years later, Dora would knock on the front door of her father's mansion and Patience, the half-sister she had never met, would open it. Behind Patience was her mother. "I would like to see Mr. Robbins, please," Dora said, not contracting the "I would" into "I'd," something Fern Elston would have been proud of. Dora had not ridden out on a horse and was in a green dress her father had bought in Charlottesville. She had brought herself in a carriage. Her bonnet was yellow, and the untied strings at either side of the bonnet hung down two inches or so, reminding Patience of a sunburnt face she had not seen in the mirror for many years.

Except for Dora being darker and younger, the two women were identical. Negroes would say that on the day God made Patience, he knew he wanted to make another just like her. God really didn't want to wait for the day Robbins and Philomena would conceive Dora, so he made her right then because he knew he wouldn't be in that same state of mind when Dora came along years later. So he made Dora and put her in the left pocket of his shirt, to be brought out when she was ready to be conceived. Being in the left pocket was necessary, Negroes said, because heaven with all those happy people could sometimes get rowdy, especially on Saturday nights.

"I have come to see Mr. Robbins," Dora said. Patience opened the door wider. She knew almost immediately that standing before her was the only other person who loved William Robbins the way she did. She had been carrying the weight of his illness alone, and as she stood there, she felt the burden grow less and less. The servants had helped her but not because they loved her father. And her mother had stopped loving him and would not lift a finger to help.

Patience would turn to her mother and say, "Please, sweetheart, go to the East," the daughter's name for that part of the mansion where her mother now lived, where the mother and daughter had played hide-and-go-seek when Patience was a child. "Go to the East and I will come for you before long. Please do this for me." Her mother left, and Patience said to Dora, "Come. Please, come." And as a servant closed the door, both women took up their skirts and went to the West.

"Yes, John," Mrs. Robbins said to Skiffington, "please, stay the night. Sunday is for rest."

"I wish I could."

After the dinner, a servant made up a horseradish poultice and Skiffington and that slave fixed it to his jaw and he and Counsel were back on the road by two-thirty.

The poultice worked for a good hour but its powers seemed to fail as the sun got lower to the horizon. "Don't trust nigger medicine," Counsel said. "I didn't," Skiffington hissed. "Just be quiet about it now."

There was a little more than four hours before sunset when they neared on Mildred Townsend's place. They waited many yards away, Skiffington believing he might hear something of Moses. "We might as well go on in and take him," Counsel said. Skiffington said, "Just sit and listen." In the end, Mildred's dog came out to the road and barked at them and Skiffington decided to finish the job. They rode up to the house and Mildred opened her door and pointed her rifle at them.

"Come to tell me what I already know bout my husband, sheriff?" she said. "Come to tell me what God done already said." The dog was peering from around the side of the house and every time Mildred would say something, the dog would get bold and bark twice, then wait for more words from Mildred. Finally, the dog went and stood beside Mildred.

Her rifle told Skiffington once and for all that Moses was there.

"Mildred, you know why we are here."

"I know no such thing, Sheriff Skiffington."

"Surrender the property," he said, leaning on his pommel. "Just surrender the property and all of this will be over, Mildred." He could not remember if he had ever spoken her name before and for a moment he questioned the entire day because he thought he had gotten her name wrong. Was her name really Mildred? "Just surrender him on up."

"No more."

"Listen to what I'm saying to you, Mildred." He tried to remember her husband's name, to make some connection, but he could not remember the man's name. "I want you to surrender the property."

"No more. No more men from here. No more men from anywhere. Not one more."

"You just do what the sheriff says," Counsel said. "Surrender the goddamn property, like he said."

Skiffington turned to him. "How many times have I told you not to take the name of the Lord in vain? How many times, Counsel?" He had opened his mouth too much and the air came in and pounded the tooth's nerves.

Counsel said nothing; he thought it was just like John not to know when he was working on his side.

Skiffington turned back to Mildred. "I have not come all this way to be denied." The nerves all about the tooth pounded back, and Skiffington forced his words through a nearly closed mouth. "I have not come all this way to be denied by a . . . by a nigger. Do you hear me, Mildred? No nigger will stand between me and my duty." He closed his mouth completely to collect himself, and a minute later he spoke again. "I have a right to do what is right, and no nigger can stand and oppose that right." He had always tried to be civil, so why was she making him uncivil? Counsel did not move but kept his eyes on Mildred. "I have a duty to uphold," Skiffington said. "That's all there is to it."

Now Counsel said, "We have a duty to uphold."

Skiffington was glad that Counsel had spoken to reaffirm why they were there. He eased his rifle out of the sheaf, his finger on the trigger. "Surrender the property," Counsel said, and Skiffington made a quick movement to pull the rifle the rest of the way out of the sheaf and as he did, the rifle fired.

The shot first hit one of Mildred's knuckles, splintering it, and then traveled on into her chest, sending her back into the house some two feet, her gun falling loudly in the doorway and scaring the dog, who trotted to the back of the house. As soon as the shot blew Mildred's heart to bits, she was immediately standing in that doorway. It was late at night and she had been somewhere she could not remember. She went into the dark house and up the stairs and found the door to Henry's room open. Caldonia was beside him in the bed and she told Mildred that Henry had had a hard time going to sleep but now he was resting quite well. Henry did not stir as his mother looked down on him and Mildred was grateful for that. She left the room and found Augustus in their bed, also asleep, and she got in and made herself comfortable in his arms. The wind was coming through the window just the way she liked it. Good sleepin weather, she always said.

But where in the world had she been? Had she been in the garden? Had she been to the well? She closed her eyes and pulled Augustus's arm closer about her and closed her eyes. She could not remember if she had left the front door open. It did not matter because all their neighbors were good people.

Skiffington and Counsel were silent for a very long time and Skiffington prayed, but once again, the words failed him. Counsel looked at Skiffington, who dropped his rifle, and in the time it took for the rifle to reach the ground, Skiffington's horse took a few steps away from Counsel and his horse. "What have I asked except civility and righteousness?" Skiffington said. "John?" Counsel said. "John?" "I rise in the morning," Skiffington continued without hearing Counsel, "and I asked nothing of that nigger, except what is proper and right. No more than that do I ask of any nigger. No more. Who can say I asked for more, Counsel? Name that person this moment who says I asked for more than civility and righteousness for righteousness' sake. That person has no name because that person does not live. Are civility and righteousness so dear that I cannot have them?" Counsel said, "John? Do you hear me, John?"

"Counsel, I want you to go in there and bring that murderin nigger out here so we can take him to his owner, to his right and proper owner. This has gone on long enough. Every bit of this has gone on long enough."

"John?"

"Do what I say, Counsel. Uphold the law the way you have been sworn to do, the way we have been sworn to do. Go in and bring that murderer out here. Do what I say or you will be in a wrath of trouble. Act, damn you!"

Counsel dismounted and took out his pistol. He should marry the boardinghouse woman and turn his back forever on being somebody's deputy, especially deputy to a man he knew he was better than. He stood a foot or more from Mildred's body and raised his head high and higher to avoid seeing her. Skiffington said, "Counsel, we cannot leave her there like that. I know who that woman is. I know her name. I know her husband." Counsel held up one foot to step around Mildred but as he did he realized he might step into blood, so he had to look down. Her eyes were not closed and he asked God why he hadn't done that one small favor for him and closed them. He took a giant step past her. He went through the first floor and his eye caught the green curtain on the side window blowing prettily from a breeze he hadn't enjoyed out in the front. That was the nature of houses, good breezes from the side and hellish nothing coming in the front and back. He went out to the kitchen. It was such a clean house that no one would have thought a nigger lived there. A bowl of apples sat on the table, and one of them was tilted so that the long stem was pointing directly at Counsel, a kind of suggestion that it should be eaten first. The dog cowered at the back door and when he turned and saw Counsel, the dog began peeing. He opened his mouth to bark but there was no sound. Counsel looked at the dog for nearly a minute, then he went and opened the door for it, and after he had shut it, he thought for the first time since entering the home that he was in the house with a man who had murdered three people. He gripped the pistol tighter.

"Counsel! What are you doing? Bring him out!"

Counsel went back through the kitchen, staying to the side of the front room to avoid Skiffington seeing him. The problem was that the boardinghouse woman was not wealthy. Near the stairs he noticed the rack of walking sticks and found it impossible not to admire them. He reached up and touched one and turned it to better see what Augustus Townsend had carved. If the boardinghouse woman wasn't barren, he might get one child out of her. One boy was all he needed. Up and down the stick were houses, each amazingly different from the others, big and small houses, foreign houses like in the books in the burned library in North Carolina. Where had a nigger seen such things? The beauty of the walking stick kept him there, and, as if to release its hold on him, he tapped the most foreign-looking of the houses with the barrel of his gun and then looked toward the stairs.

The boardinghouse woman said she was thirty-seven, but the lines on her upper lip seemed to tell him something much older.

"Counsel!"

"I'm going to look upstairs now, John."

"Then do it and bring him!"

The stairs did not creak. One more strange thing about the nature of houses—some creaked, some did not, and there wasn't any use thinking you could say which was which just by looking at them. A two-story nothing in Mississippi had stairs that didn't make a sound. His destroyed house was one of the finest in North Carolina, in the South, and all the stairs in it had creaked, even the ones going up from the kitchen in the back that were used mostly by the servants and his children. All of them people of light feet.

On the second floor he looked in each room and as he neared the last, Mildred and Augustus's bedroom, his disappointment grew. If the slave was not here, there would be no living with John's rage. He stood in the middle of the couple's bedroom and cursed. "Counsel! We can't leave Mildred laying there like that." Counsel opened the top drawer of the dresser beside the door and moved things around with the barrel of his gun and then he heard a clinking. In the folds of a small bolt of yellow cloth he found five twenty-dollar gold pieces. He laughed and looked around, then laughed some more and put the money in his pocket. He went through the rest of the drawers, tore the bed apart, stamped on the floor to see what boards might be covering some hiding place. He found no more gold, but he knew there was more, knew that those two niggers had been out here with a white man's riches. He looked again around the room, but now with a new eye, the eye of a man who knew salvation and deliverance were very close by. He needed time to search the house, the land, and he did not have that time right then. "Counsel!" There might or might not be enough to share with another man, but he did not want to risk telling Skiffington. His cousin might say it was not theirs to have. There might well be enough to get him where he was before the devastation in North Carolina. No, it would be best not to tell John. What does God's monkey John Skiffington know about money and need and the loss of family?

He went down the stairs and tried to keep the coins from making a sound and stood at Mildred's head.

"Where is he, Counsel?"

Somehow, Counsel found it an odd question and he answered, without thinking, in an odd way: "I found him not." He put his pistol in his holster and reached down and picked up Mildred's rifle, now as bloody as the floor around her, and pointed it at Skiffington. "Stand back, Counsel. You best stand back and away." Counsel fired into Skiffington's chest, and though Skiffington leaned forward only a few inches, Counsel could see the wound was a mortal one. But because John Skiffington was a large man, Counsel Skiffington shot him again. The second shot singed the ear of Skiffington's horse before it entered the man and the horse reared up, but the man's weight seemed to force it down and the horse, once back on the ground, shook its head over and over and Skiffington slid to the side, trying to hold on because something told him that holding on was the only way he could be saved.

Skiffington was entering the house he had taken his bride to. He ran up the stairs because he felt there was something important he had to do. He found himself in a very long hall and he ran down the hall, looking in all the open rooms and wanting to stop but knowing he did not have time. He passed them all, from the one with his mother cooking his supper to the one with his father talking to Barnum Kinsey. Minerva sewing. Winifred in her nightgown with her arms open to him. But he did not stop. At the very end of the hall there was a Bible tilting forward, a Bible some three feet taller than he was. He got to it in time to keep it from falling over, his hands reaching to prop it up, his open left hand on the O in *Holy* and his open right hand on the second B in *Bible*.

Counsel had not moved. He was thinking of how he would explain everything to everyone, and it was a simple matter in his mind—the Negro woman had shot his cousin and the sheriff had shot her in return, before he, Counsel, could even raise his gun. And he would be right—it was to be a simple case for everyone and most of them accepted his word.

Skiffington fell. His horse tried to step away from him once he hit the ground, but it could not go far because Skiffington's right foot was caught in the stirrup, and so the horse was caught between wanting to be away from a dead man and wanting to be near its master. Counsel reached back and dropped the rifle, then wiped his hands on the parts of Mildred's clothing that were not bloody. At the sound of the rifle hitting the floor Skiffington's horse stopped moving. Counsel's horse had remained in its place all along, moving not one inch. Counsel heard the stairs creak and looked over to see a Negro watching him, his hands up. Counsel took out his pistol and waved him over with the gun. "You the Moses we've been looking for?" Counsel said. Moses came over, nodding his head all the while. "Where are the other two?" Counsel asked, meaning Gloria and Clement, and Moses said he didn't know about any other two, that he was alone, he and Mildred. So, Counsel thought, he had been hiding somewhere secret and that made him happy because it meant there were places where the gold could be.

The idea that Moses had killed Priscilla his wife and his son Jamie and the madwoman Alice died with John Skiffington, and that was where it stayed for many years.

Counsel said to Moses, "Are you sure you're alone?"

"Yessir." Moses looked over at Mildred and it was all he could do to stop from going to her. She had asked him not one question, just gave him a home. "We," she had said, "will find a way to get you out of this here mess."

"Open your mouth," Counsel said. Moses did and Counsel stuck his pistol far back into the man's throat and Moses tried to wiggle away but Counsel stayed with him. He took Moses by the shirtfront and held him. "I don't want to kill two in one day but I'm not above doing it." Moses coughed around the pistol. "You keep everything you know just as locked in as your words are locked in right now. You hear what I say?" Moses, in pain, gagging, nodded his head as much as he could. "If you ever say a word, I will shoot you down like a dog. And you can see right here that that's something I will do."

This nigger, Counsel decided, has never killed anyone. What had John been thinking?

Counsel withdrew the gun and motioned Moses to the door, and Moses bent down to Mildred, touched her bloody hair. Moses stood back up. Counsel, seeing his victory approaching after all those years, began to feel generous. He said to Moses, "Tell her good-bye in any way you see fit." The dead woman, after all, had opened the door to that golden victory. Was there a prayer Job had offered to God after he put his servant back a million times better than Job had been before the devastation? Thank you, O Lord. I cannot forget what I once had, but I will not resent you so much when I think of those old days and my dead loved ones.

"I don't wanna leave Miss Mildred out here on the floor like this, Mister," Moses said.

Counsel sighed and shrugged his shoulders. Moses bent down again to Mildred. In less than a half hour, when Counsel began to realize that he did not have all the time in the world, he would regret the generosity. But now he holstered the pistol and stepped out onto the porch. He didn't care about the rifle beside Mildred because all the power it had was now soaking in John Skiffington.

In less than two hours, many miles down the road from where Mildred and Augustus Townsend had lived, Counsel on his horse would come upon Elias and Louis, the bastard son of William Robbins and future husband to Caldonia Townsend. Counsel would also come upon the patrollers Barnum Kinsey, Harvey Travis and Oden Peoples, a full Cherokee man. All of those men would be on horses. Counsel was to greet them with the appropriate grieving face of a man who just had his relative killed. Tied to the pommel of Counsel's horse would be a rope that led back some five feet to the tied hands of Moses, the slave and former overseer, who alone would be walking.

After Counsel told them what had happened at Mildred's, Travis would say over and over, "John is dead. Is that what you tellin me? John is dead." When he had accepted what Counsel said, Travis said to the gathering, "We can't bring John back, but we have right here the reason for this whole mess," and he would point to Moses. "We have a nigger here who got it into his head that it was proper for him to run away. He got it into his head and now the sheriff of this county is dead. A good and upstanding sheriff. I say we make it so he never gets it into his head to stroll away again."

"What are you meaning?" Louis said. He was a Negro but the white men and Oden all knew that he was William Robbins's Negro, which made him special.

"Fix him right here in the road," Travis said, looking at Moses. "Let him remember every day what he done to John Skiffington. Fix him so he won't run again."

Louis said, "That slave does not belong to you for yall to do with as you please. He is not your property. He is not yours."

Travis said, "He is the reason our John is dead. That makes him everybody's property."

"Sure he belongs to us," Counsel said. "Would we be out here in this hot sun if he hadn't decided he had a right to run away?"

"Just leave him be," Louis said. Barnum was silent; something in his heart told him there were many lies about what Counsel said. But John was dead and that was the one big truth. Elias was also silent. He was sitting on a gray mare, which Caldonia said came with his new position as overseer. Celeste had said nothing to him that morning. Less than an hour later on that road, as the group of men and horses moved toward Caldonia's place, Elias would falter and be unable to ride. As he fell farther and farther behind, Louis, surprised at how close they had

become in the last few days, would go back to him, dismount and help
Elias off his horse, and both men would walk with the reins in their
hands, Louis telling Elias all the while that they should take all the
time they needed. "There's no hurry now." At that point in the road,
most of the day was behind all the horses and their men, as was the sun.

Moses, still behind Counsel and his horse, said to the white men
and to Louis, "Please, yall, don't hurt me like that. Please." He called
out to Elias, "Please, don't let em hurt me. Please, tell em to let me
be, Elias."

Elias could see Celeste standing in their cabin doorway, waiting for
him. He needed Celeste now. He needed Celeste to tell him right and
point him toward home. How had he come to forget just where he was
in the world? He worried at that moment that something would happen to him on that road with the white men raging and that he would
never see his family again. After Moses, Elias knew he would be next,
and then Louis, the son of a black woman. And if they needed more,
the white men would jump on the Indian, who wasn't as white as he
always thought he was.

Counsel and Travis and Oden got off their horses. Moses turned to
run but Counsel took the rope he had tied Moses with and pulled him
back. Barnum, on his horse, said, "He ain't the one that hurt John. He
ain't the one. And besides, it look like he done learned his lesson."
Oden looked at Travis and the two men laughed.

With Counsel and Travis holding the still-tied Moses, Oden bent
down and put his knife, in two swift back and forth motions, through
Moses's Achilles' tendon. "Please," Moses kept saying, "let me be." He
tried to get Elias's attention, and he tried to get Louis's attention.
"Please let me be." Moments after the cutting, Oden applied his
blood-stopping poultice to Moses's wound and the slave collapsed,
screaming in agony.

Barnum rode away, rode toward his home and his family. There
was not anything in Virginia for him anymore. He had been treading
water all his life in Virginia—not enough water to drown him, but

just enough to always keep his feet and britches wet. He was many miles away before he heard Moses stop screaming.

Hobbling anyone left a mark in the dirt for someone to always take note of, and that would be the case with Moses. A person knowing anything about the science of hobbling wouldn't take note of the mark in the road for very long. But a person ignorant of the science of hobbling might well bend down and wonder for the longest why a barefoot man would walk full on one foot and then tiptoe along forever on the other foot.

Back in Mildred's house two hours earlier, Moses said some words over her body but he knew what he was saying was not enough. He had never really listened all the way to a funeral speech and so was at a loss to say the proper thing. Had I only listened, he berated himself as he cleared the kitchen table of everything. He put the bowl of apples on a chair and took off the tablecloth. He knew he was grateful to her and so as he worked he thanked Mildred for helping him and then he picked up her body and laid her out on the table. He closed Mildred's eyes. A slower death would have given her all the time she needed to lie down and close her own eyes. Moses covered her body with the tablecloth and began thinking of more words to say. "You know, Moses," she had said only the day before, "I love a good tablecloth. I would rather have a good tablecloth over a good quilt any day. The bed could go naked for all I care, but I got to have my tablecloth for my meals."

Not long after John Skiffington's murder, Barnum Kinsey took his family to Missouri, where his wife had people. Barnum died not long after they crossed the Mississippi River, in a town called Hollinger. His oldest child from his second marriage, Matthew, stayed up all the night before he was buried, putting his father's history on a wooden tombstone. He began with his father's name on the first line, and on the next, he put the years of his father's coming and going. Then all the things he knew his father had been. Husband. Father. Farmer. Grandfather. Patroller. Tobacco Man. Tree Maker. The letters of the words got smaller and smaller as the boy, not quite twelve, neared the bottom of the wood because he had never made a headstone for anyone before so he had not compensated for all that he would have to put on it. The boy filled up the whole piece of wood and at the end of the last line he put a period. His father's grave would remain, but the wooden marker would not last out the year. The boy knew better than to put a period at the end of such a sentence. Something that was not even a true and proper sentence, with subject aplenty, but no verb to pull it all together. A sentence, Matthew's teacher back in Virginia had tried to drum into his thick Kinsey head, could live without a subject, but it could not live without a verb.

At Mildred's house the day she died, Counsel stepped out onto her porch and looked but once at his cousin's body and took out his tobacco and paper and rolled a cigarette. He had no more chewing tobacco. John Skiffington's foot finally came out of the stirrup and Counsel watched as John's horse began to walk away. Counsel wondered if the beast knew the way home, or would some bear ultimately come upon him drinking at a stream and take him down. He heard just a little movement from Moses inside the house. He should have picked up the dead woman's gun after all. The nigger could take it and hit him upside the head. Knowing this was possible, Counsel turned fully toward the doorway so he could be ready. All the gold would mean that he could buy a giant tombstone for John's grave, one as large as the man himself had been. He envisioned a tombstone so big that wild and insane men would come down from their lairs in the Virginia mountains and worship at the tombstone, thinking it stood over the grave of someone who had been a god.

On the road some two hours later, after Oden had hobbled Moses, he got back up on his horse. He looked down at the man writhing on

the ground and at his own handiwork. Moses certainly could not walk
back home now and Oden extended his arm down. He had gone out
without a saddle that day. Oden said, "He won't bleed for long. Heft
him on up here." Everyone, except Elias, helped Moses up onto the
back of Oden's horse. Louis trembled to see Moses in pain. By rights,
Oden could have made Elias the slave carry Moses, but he didn't like
the evil that seemed to be building in Elias. He might have been able
to make Louis carry him if he hadn't been William Robbins's son. So
it was just as well that he chose to carry Moses and not make a fuss
about it. "Heft him up. I'll take him in. He ain't gon bleed for long,"
Oden said, though no one could hear him above Moses's cries. Oden
would never put his knife to a man again. It was one thing to cut a
man, collect money for a job well done and go home and sup with his
family. It was another to ride a long way with the man at his back, ag-
onizing all the way in Oden's ear, the man's arms around Oden's waist
because the man had a fear, even in his great pain, of falling off the
horse.

After Moses covered Mildred's body with the tablecloth, he stepped
onto her porch and got his first good look at the body of John
Skiffington in the yard. He had no words for the dead man because he
could not think of one good thing Skiffington had ever done for him.
There would be plenty of people to mourn him, Moses thought, maybe
even just as many as would mourn Mildred. Counsel looked at Moses,
stepped onto the ground and put out his cigarette in the dirt. There was
no use chancing a fire before he could get out all the gold.

Counsel Skiffington did not find any more gold at Mildred's place.
The five twenty-dollar pieces were all there was. For weeks, he went
out to her place alone and dug all about her land, then, as he felt time
was running out, he got the help of Oden and Travis. A split treasure
was better than none, and he could get away with giving the Indian
less than he would have to share with the white man. They found hid-

den compartments in the house that they did not know were designed
to hide slaves for the Underground Railroad. In their frustration, they
burned the house down, but Counsel kept many things, including the
walking sticks. But the law eventually made him give everything he
had taken to Caldonia Townsend. For years and years, Counsel fought
for the land in the legal arena. He used a theory cooked up by Arthur
Brindle, the dry goods merchant who had once been a lawyer, and
claimed that there was some basis for him to have the property because his cousin had been murdered there. He enlisted the help of
Robert Colfax, but the law went to Caldonia's side. He married the
boardinghouse woman. They had no children.

William Robbins would enter the legal fray over the Townsend
estate because he felt it rightly belonged to Caldonia, who was to
become his son Louis's wife. Robbins and Colfax had not been getting
along since Robbins bought the widow Clara Martin's place from
her heirs, a piece of land Colfax had long coveted. The end of the
friendship of the two wealthiest men in the county affected just about
everyone in Manchester as white people took sides and sought alliances
in neighboring counties. Four white people were ultimately murdered
over the dispute, one of them on Robbins's side, his wife's brother, and
the other three on Colfax's side, including two cousins. Over time the
bad blood helped to tear apart the county, so that by the fire of 1912,
when all the judicial records of the county were destroyed, the town of
Manchester was the county seat to nobody. Manchester became the
only county in the history of the Commonwealth of Virginia to be di-
vided and swallowed up by other counties, by Amherst County, by
Nelson County, by Amelia County, by Hanover County.... "The
County of Manchester," a University of Virginia historian wrote as he
borrowed from the Bible, "was torn asunder." The historian called it
"the greatest disappearance of land" in the Commonwealth since large
western sections of Virginia, historically known as "The Mother of
States," were taken to form eight other states, including Michigan,
Illinois, Minnesota, West Virginia, and Wisconsin.

The men who kidnapped and sold Augustus Townsend—the white man Darcy and his slave Stennis—were caught without incident near Virginia's border with North Carolina. They were riding in a brand-new covered wagon. In the back of the wagon were two children, a boy and a girl, both stolen from their free parents. The children were Spencer and Mandy Wallace. Mandy would go on to become the first black woman to receive a Ph.D. in literature from Yale University. Also in the new wagon were two adult sisters, slaves, who had been taken one evening on their way home from the funeral of a third sister at a nearby plantation. Those sisters, Carolyn and Eva, might not have been on the road to get themselves kidnapped if the owner of their dead sister had not decided that her funeral should be in the late afternoon, after most of the work in the fields was done, so as to maybe cut down on the length of another colored funeral.

Stennis and Darcy were tried and sentenced, Darcy to five years in the penitentiary, and Stennis to ten years. Darcy spent his time at the same prison where the murderer Jean Broussard had met his end. Stennis would have gone to a prison for Negroes in Petersburg, but the day before Stennis was to enter, the authorities decided better use might be made of him if he was sold to help pay the families of the slaves they had kidnapped and sold. He had a colorful history and was bought and sold five times in six weeks. Only the owners of slaves were compensated, all of them white; those people the government could find were paid $15 for each stolen adult slave and $10 for each stolen slave child. All the money left over, some $130, was put in the Virginia treasury.

There was nothing the Commonwealth of Virginia could do about the stolen loved ones of freed people, since such people really didn't have a money value in the eyes of the law. So they received nothing but an earnest letter of apology from a dreamy-eyed assistant to the governor. The government acknowledged that it had failed to protect the loved ones and for that it was sorry, the assistant wrote.

Stennis was finally sold for $950 to a white man, a Kentuckian.

On the way there, Stennis asked if Kentucky was anywhere near Tennessee. "Next door," his new master said, "but we in Kentucky stays to ourselves." Stennis, driving the wagon, went on and on about how the air from Tennessee wouldn't have that far to travel to get to him in Kentucky. At the last, his new owner had had enough. He took out the pistol he had tucked in his coat and told Stennis to stop the wagon. He put the pistol to Stennis's temple and said, "I'm tired of your yappin so you best shut up right here and now. The people of Kentucky don't care one whit for a nigger woodpecker."

On Mildred's porch the afternoon she died, Moses looked at Counsel putting out his cigarette in the yard. He said to Moses, "You done your business?" Moses looked one last time at Mildred's covered body. Just before Moses came out, Counsel had been talking to God and God was answering back. God said, Job, I have not forgotten you. I heard you crying out there. You have been my worthy and loyal servant, and I have not forgotten you, Job. I will do what is right by you. I will put you back where I found you. I promise. "Your business done here?" Counsel asked Moses.

Moses nodded. He shut the door to Mildred's house.

"Then you ready?" Counsel said.

"Yes, I be ready," Moses said, not offering a "Master" or even a "Mister," but just saying again, "I be ready." Counsel didn't notice that he wasn't getting a "Master" or a "Mister." They both looked at Skiffington's body. Moses thought the white man would want to take the dead white man with them. He informed Counsel that Mildred's place did not have a wagon to carry the dead man. Skiffington's horse had wandered off.

"That so?" Counsel said about the missing wagon. He had never intended to take Skiffington with them. There would be time enough to come back and get him. "That so?" Moses nodded. "If you've done all your business in there, we may as well leave. So les you and me go,"

Counsel said as Moses walked toward him and held out his hands to be roped and tied.

Three years and nine months after John Skiffington was killed, Minerva Skiffington, the young woman who had been like a daughter to him, came out of a butcher shop eight blocks from the Philadelphia town hall and turned left. It was, as usual, a day of crowds. She lifted the tea towel over that morning's purchases in her basket with the notion that she was forgetting something. She made her way to the druggist for the soap she and Winifred Skiffington, John's widow, liked. Her skin had thrived once freed of the lye-based soap that was the standard in Virginia. They lived with Winifred's sister, who herself was a widow, and with John's father, Carl.

At the corner, one block from the druggist, Minerva stepped without looking into the street and was nearly knocked over by a white man on a horse. "Watch how you step!" the man shouted. Minerva screamed and was pulled back in time by someone behind her. She turned around to see a very dark black man a head and a half taller than she was. "You could get killed," the young man said. He was the darkest handsome man she had ever seen. "You could get killed by a horse," he said and let go of her shoulders. "Go on with all care," he said and she nodded. "Take all care." He raised his hat good-bye and stepped around her and went across the street and down the block.

Watching him blend into the crowd, Minerva crossed, and as she did, a pack of three dogs, smelling the purchases from the butcher, began following her. She walked right past the druggist, and near the end of that block, the black man turned around and she stopped and the dogs behind her stopped. She followed the man for one more block. The dogs continued to follow her. The dogs knew that people made mistakes and that at any moment the basket could become vulnerable.

The man turned around again just three blocks before the town hall and seemed only half surprised to see her. He came toward her and she bent to set the basket on the ground. The dogs came closer and she noticed them and pulled the tea towel away to make it easier for them. The man walked to her and people passed on either side of them. "Afraid of all them horses?" he said. "I'm not afraid of any horses," she said, "or anything like that."

She began telling him her story and he took her to the house where he lived with his parents and two sisters, one younger than Minerva and one older. Three days later the man saw a poster on a building and a similar one just two blocks away. He took the second poster to Minerva, to the room she had been sharing with the younger of his sisters. Minerva read the poster again and again. The next day she and the man went to the constabulary to tell the authorities that she was not missing and that she was not dead. She was, she said, nothing more than a free woman in Philadelphia, Pennsylvania.

The black man and his family would try for the longest to get her to go to Winifred to explain her new life but Minerva refused.

The posters read: "Lost Or Harmed In Some Unknown Way On The Streets Of This City—A Precious Loved One." They gave Minerva's name, height, age, everything needed to identify her. A daguerreotype of Winifred and Minerva had been taken not long after they came to Philadelphia, both women sitting side by side in the photographer's studio. The poster reproduced that portion of the photograph that contained Minerva. But at the bottom of the posters, like some kind of afterthought, in words much smaller than everything else on the poster, was the line "Will Answer To The Name Minnie." And so Minerva did not see Winifred Skiffington again for a very long time.

It was the "Will Answer To," of course, that had done it. Winifred had meant no bad thing by the words. With what little money she had, she hired a printer—an enlightened white immigrant from Savannah, Georgia—to make up the posters and put them up all about Philadelphia, "where any eye could see," she had instructed the printer. She had meant only love with all the words, for she loved Minerva more than she loved any other human being in the world. But John Skiffington's widow had been fifteen years in the South, in Manchester County, Virginia, and people down there just talked that way. She and the printer from Savannah would have told anyone that they didn't mean any harm by it.

April 12, 1861
The City of Washington

My Dearest and Most Loved Sister,
I take pen in hand to-day to write you not more than a fortnight after I
have arrived in a City that will either send me back in defeat to Virginia
or will give me more Life than my Soul can contain. I may be able to post-
pone forever my need to be in New-York. My thoughts have been on you
and Louis, as they have been since the long ago day you married. My
promise to return to be with you when your child is born remains stead-
fast, no matter how much Life this City affords me.

    The City is one mud hole after another, and there is filth as far as the
eye can see. Virginia green has been reduced to a memory. It has only
been in the past three days that I have summoned enough courage to go
much beyond the five square blocks that make up what I have come to call
my habitat. I am staying close to Home because the streets (I have trained
myself to refrain from calling them roads), particularly after dark, are
not safe for any man, even the ruffians have a hard time of it, and while
I am prepared to use my pistol, I would rather hold it back just yet. Aside
from the fear of man unleashed, there is also the general fear of such a
large metropolis, and I am more than afraid of being lost in the City.

    My Accommodations are more than adequate, certainly far more
than those some Immigrants must endure. How I came by those Accom-

modations is an interesting story, and I trust that you have the time, and the fortitude, to read how I came to be situated where I am.

The friend whose name Louis gave me has been dead for a year, I learned to my disappointment. I was told there might be lodging at a Hotel on C Street. I was also told that while Senators and Congressmen lodged there, it was hospitable to people of our Race because that was the way the owners and proprietors wanted it. The door facing C Street took me into the Saloon, which is on the first floor of the Hotel. While the people of renown in this City take to hard drink by one in the afternoon, I satisfied myself with a lemon drink at the bar. As I neared the end of my drink, I took on more courage and looked about. The room was empty save myself and two other gentlemen, one a man of our Race at a table in the corner.

I could see people coming and going from a room next to the saloon. I assumed it was the dining area of the establishment. I drank the last of my courage and decided to investigate that particular room. It was indeed a dining room, a rather large one with more than 30 tables, but I discovered that that was not why people were coming and going, Dear Sister. The dinner hours were over and supper was still a time away.

No, people were viewing an enormous wall hanging, a grand piece of art that is part tapestry, part painting, and part clay structure—all in one exquisite Creation, hanging silent and yet songful on the Eastern wall. It is, my Dear Caldonia, a kind of map of life of the County of Manchester, Virginia. But a "map" is such a poor word for such a wondrous thing. It is a map of life made with every kind of art man has ever thought to represent himself. Yes, clay. Yes, paint. Yes, cloth. There are no people on this "map," just all the houses and barns and roads and cemeteries and wells in our Manchester. It is what God sees when He looks down on Manchester. At the bottom right-hand corner of this Creation there were but two stitched words. Alice Night.

I stood transfixed. At about two-thirty there were few people in the dining room, only those preparing the table for the evening meals. I stepped closer to this Vision, which was held away from all by a blue rope of hemp. I raised my hand to it, not to touch but to try to feel more of what was emanating. Someone behind me said quietly, "Please, do not touch." I turned and saw Moses's Priscilla. Her hands were confidently behind her back, her clothing impeccable. I knew in those few seconds that whatever she had been in Virginia, she was that no more.

It was then that I noticed over her shoulder another Creation of the same materials, paint, clay and cloth. I had been so captivated by the living map of the County that I had not turned to see the other Wonder on the opposite wall.

"How have you been, Calvin?" Priscilla inquired. She had no fear in her words that I might have come to take her back. Her words conveyed only what she had said, a need to know my condition.

I responded, "I have tried to be well, Priscilla. I have tried very hard."

I could still see over her shoulder that other Creation. Priscilla saw it in my eyes and moved aside. This Creation may well be even more miraculous than the one of the County. This one is about your home, Caldonia. It is your plantation, and again, it is what God sees when He looks down. There is nothing missing, not a cabin, not a barn, not a chicken, not a horse. Not a single person is missing. I suspect that if I were to count the blades of grass, the number would be correct as it was once when the creator of this work knew that world. And again, in the bottom right-hand corner are the stitched words "Alice Night."

In this massive miracle on the Western wall, you, Caldonia, are standing before your house with Loretta, Zeddie and Bennett. As I said, all the cabins are there, and standing before them are the people who lived in them ere Alice, Priscilla and Jamie disappeared. Except for those three, every single person is there, standing and waiting as if for a painter and his easel to come along and capture them in the glory of the day. Each person's face, including yours, is raised up as though to look in the very eyes of God. I look at all the faces and I am more than glad now that I knew the name and face of everyone there at your home. The dead in the cemetery have risen from there and they, too, stand at the cabins where they once lived. So the slave cemetery is just plain ground now, grass and nothing else. It is empty, even of the tiniest infants, who rest alive and well in their mothers' arms.

In the cemetery where our Henry is buried, he stands by his grave, but that grave is covered with flowers as though he still inhabits it.

There are matters in my memory that I did not know were there until I saw them on that wall. I must tell you, dear Caldonia, that I sank to my knees. When I was able to collect myself, I stood and found not only Priscilla watching me but Alice as well.

I spoke to Alice thus: "I hope you have been well." What I feared most at that moment is what I still fear: that they would remember my history, that I, no matter what I had always said to the contrary, owned people of our Race. I feared that they would send me away, and even as I write you now, I am still afraid.

Alice responded to me, "I been good as God keeps me."

I am "laboring" here now, at the Hotel, the Restaurant, and the Saloon, trying to make myself as indispensable as possible and yet trying to stay out of the way, lest someone remember my history and they cast me out. I would be sick unto death if I were sent away. After years of being a nurse to Mother, my work here is not taxing. I am happy when I get up in the morning and I am happy when I lay my head down at night.

All that is here is owned by Alice, Priscilla and all the people who work here, many of them, to be sure, runaways. My room is on the top floor of the hotel where everyone lives. It is a nice room and it fits me well. Jamie comes and goes as a student in a school for colored children. He is as fine a young man as any father or mother could want.

I will close for now and pray that you and Louis are well. When you are able to write, recall my fear of being cast out and please write my name on the envelope as humbly as you possibly can.

> I remain
> Forever
> Your Brother
> Calvin

Caldonia read the letter over and over for days, relieved that Calvin had negotiated the state of Virginia and arrived safely in Washington. She shared it with Louis, who warned her that she would wear out the paper with all the reading and folding and unfolding. "By then," she told him, "I will have memorized every word and will be ready for the next letter."

Omitting Calvin's mention of him, Caldonia even read it at Henry's grave, knowing that her first husband had been fond of Calvin. She was returning to the house that evening and was up the back stairs when she saw down at the lane Moses limping back to his cabin. Her heart stopped. Even years after their last encounter, her heart stopped.

Moses did not look her way. She found it difficult to move after seeing him.

Moses went into his dark cabin and did not light a lamp. Within the hour Tessie and Grant, Celeste and Elias's children, brought him supper, lighting their way with a lamp brought from home. He rarely bothered to fix his own meals anymore. Sometimes he ate what the children brought and sometimes he just went to sleep without eating, the food only inches from his head.

That evening Caldonia read Calvin's letter at Henry's grave, Moses did eat. In the morning, the children returned with breakfast.

He had once tried to remember the names of Celeste's children who brought him food, but there seemed to be so many that he gave up. He remembered that once upon a time he himself had had a child. A boy. Who was too fat for his own good. He did know that the meals came from Celeste and he kept her in his prayers. Celeste, to be sure, would always have the limp, but her husband and her children never noticed until someone from the outside happened to point it out to them. "Why yo mama be limpin and everything?" "What limp?"

Celeste's children always came to Moses with a baby, who looked with fascination at Moses on his pallet. Moses could barely move in the mornings, the result, he would always think, of the times he spent with himself in the damp woods. He liked knowing the baby was there, though he had no power to turn and engage it in play or conversation. He lay on his back and kept his arm over his eyes, as if to protect them from some great light.

"How he doin?" Celeste would ask Tessie or Grant or one of her other children when they returned.

"He looked fine, Mama. But I think the light be hurtin his eyes."

"And how be that fire in the hearth?"

Tessie would usually say that she had a time trying to light the fire. "Mama, it just don't wanna do right, that fire."

"Well," Celeste would say, "I'll get your daddy to take a look at it. He's the handiest man alive with fires and such."

Her meals to Moses would be until the end. Celeste was never to close down her days, even after Moses had died, without thinking aloud at least once to everyone and yet to no one in particular, "I wonder if Moses done ate yet."

Insights,
Interviews
& More

An Interview with
Edward P. Jones

Throughout The Known World, *you intersperse your fictional account with historical records and data about Manchester County, Virginia. Are these records factual? What was your intent in incorporating them into your novel?*

The county and town of Manchester, Virginia, and every human being in those places, are products of my imagination. Other counties and towns—Amelia County, Charlottesville, et cetera—are real but were employed merely to give some heft and believability to the creation of Manchester and its people. The same is obviously true of real, historical people—President Fillmore, for example.

The census records I made up for Manchester were, again, simply to make the reader feel that the town and the county and the people lived and breathed in central Virginia once upon a time before the county was "swallowed up" by surrounding counties. Saying that the census of 1840 shows that there were so many black people, so many white people there, et cetera, affords a hard background of numbers and dates that makes the foreground of the characters and what they go through more real.

How unusual was it for free blacks to serve as slaveholders in the South? How did the idea come to you to write a novel that dealt with this issue?

I don't have any hard data but I'm quite certain that the number of black slave owners was quite small in relation to white slave owners. The fact that many people—even many black

Edward P. Jones

66 When you are raised by a woman who had it hard ... you develop the belief that they can 'make a way out of no way.' 99

people—didn't know such people existed is perhaps proof of how few there were. In addition, as I note in the novel, husbands purchased wives and parents purchased children, and so their neighbors may have come to know the people purchased not as slaves—as property—but as family members. Finally, owning a slave was not a cheap proposition, and the economic status of most blacks back then didn't lend itself to owning a human being.

....

Women in The Known World *wield roles of extraordinary power, whether assuming the typically male responsibilities of the plantation, like Caldonia Townsend; educating the illiterate, like Fern Elston; inspiring violence, passion, and grief, like Celeste and Minerva; or creating art that transcends the brutal realities of slavery, like Alice Night. How important was it to you to give voice to women's experiences of slavery in this work?*

I didn't set out with any agenda. When you are raised by a woman who had it hard and you are sensitive to how hard a life she had, you don't necessarily look around and think of women as fragile creatures, whether slave or otherwise. You develop the belief that they can "make a way out of no way." The hardy women of today had predecessors, I'm sure. It would have been insane for me, of course, to write a novel about a black woman who was president of the U.S. in 1855, or even a senator. But a black woman who becomes the head of a plantation due to the premature death of her husband who was helped along the way by the wealthiest white man in the county—that is believable. It is also believable that Fern Elston could make part of her living by teaching free black children; there were educated black women back then, and not all of them would choose to stay in the shadows, especially one with Fern's temperament. And no doubt there had to be people like Celeste who tried in their small way to fight something they were forced to live under; perhaps she, of them all, understood how Moses got to be that way—*He was not born hating the world,* she would have said. And I suppose Alice would have said that as well, had she not been so focused on escaping alone.

▶

3

An Interview with Edward P. Jones *(continued)*

Your account of antebellum Manchester County, Virginia, is by no means linear; you weave different strands of the story together and return to them at various phases of the novel. Why did you choose this format for your book?

I always thought I had a linear story. Something happened between the time I began the real work in January 2002 of taking it all out of my head and when I finished months later. It might be that because I, as the "god" of the people in the book, could see their first days and their last days and all that was in between, and those people did not have linear lives as I saw all that they had lived. What Tessie the child did one day in 1855 would have some meaning for her fifty, seventy-five years later. She might not be able to look back and see that moment, but her creator could. That, perhaps, is why she says something about the doll her father made for her to Caldonia and Fern in September 1855 that she will repeat on her deathbed, some ninety years later; she might not even remember the first time she uttered those words, but I can't afford to forget if I'm trying to tell the truth.

There is a touch of the supernatural in events such as the spontaneous combustions of the Otis boys and the slave Teacher, the cow with the endless supply of milk, the transformative experiences of Stamford with the crows and the lightning, and the details of cadavers "talking" to Wilson and Morris Calhenny. How do you explain these incidents in the larger scope of your novel?

I was raised among a people who believe that if a person is killed on a city street, the blood of that person will show up on that spot every time it rains. Even years and years later. I was raised to believe that one's hair should be taken from combs and brushes and burned—my mother did it in an ashtray—because the hair could somehow get out into the world where birds could find it, make a nest of the hair, and give the person headaches. Those people believed you shouldn't rest your hands on the top of your head because it will shorten your mother's life.

Given all that, it's easy to create a situation where lightning runs away from a man because the lightning doesn't think it's time for the man to die. The cow with all the milk came from hearing law school friends talk in the 1970s about a court case where a man sued his neighbor to get back a cow he had sold him after the cow began producing milk again. So the supernatural events are just another way of telling the story by someone who grew up thinking the universe did weird things all the time.

....

You open and close The Known World *with the figure of Moses, the overseer of Henry and Caldonia Townsend's land. In what ways is his odyssey central to your novel?*

Moses became another symbol of what slavery had done. I have no doubt that when Moses was standing naked in John Skiffington's jail and saying that he and Bessie were "one," were "family," that he was not the man who years later was bitter and grasping and wanted, as he put it, to get rid of his family now that they stood in his way of becoming Caldonia's husband. Slavery did things to everyone; some were able to transcend, as with Celeste, and others succumbed.

....

What are some of your favorite books and authors? Which writers have most influenced your work?

Black fiction writers, including Ann Petry, Paul Laurence Dunbar, Richard Wright, Gwendolyn Brooks. The Southern writers (black and white), including Faulkner. And others such as Chekhov and James Joyce, who was the primary inspiration for my collection of stories *Lost in the City.* ◡

5

The Known World
Dramatis Personae

TOWNSEND PLANTATION

Henry Townsend Plantation owner, son of Augustus and Mildred, husband of Caldonia

Caldonia Townsend Henry's wife, twin sister of Calvin, daughter of Maude

Loretta Caldonia's personal maid

Zeddie The Townsend cook

Bennett Zeddie's husband

Moses Henry Townsend's overseer and first slave

Priscilla Moses's wife

Jamie Son of Moses and Priscilla

Elias Slave husband of Celeste

Celeste Crippled slave

Tessie, Grant, and Ellwood Elias and Celeste's children

Alice Henry's wandering slave, believed to have been kicked by a mule

Stamford Slave, pursuer of young women

Gloria Twenty-six-year-old whom Stamford pursues

Delphie Mother of Cassandra, Alice's roommate

Cassandra Daughter of Delphie, also known as "Cassie"

MANCHESTER COUNTY

Augustus Townsend Father of Henry, husband of Mildred

Mildred Townsend Mother of Henry, wife of Augustus

Fern Elston Free black woman, wife of Ramsey, teacher to free black children

> ...husbands purchased wives and parents purchased children, and so their neighbors may have come to know the people purchased not as slaves— as property— but as family members.

Ramsey Elston Fern Elston's gambling husband

Zeus Fern Elston's most-trusted slave

John Skiffington Sheriff of Manchester County, husband of Winifred

Winifred Skiffington Wife of John Skiffington

Minerva Skiffington The Skiffington's "maid," a "wedding present" from Counsel and Belle Skiffington to Winifred

Clara Martin Cousin of Winifred Skiffington

Ralph Clara's slave

William Robbins Plantation owner and the most powerful man in Manchester, with 113 slaves

Ethel Robbins Wife of William Robbins

Patience Robbins Daughter of William and Ethel

Philomena Cartwright William Robbins's mistress, mother of Louis and Dora

Dora Cartwright Eldest child of William Robbins and Philomena

Louis Cartwright Youngest child of William Robbins and Philomena

Barnum Kinsey County slave patroller and the poorest white man in the county

Oden Peoples Cherokee slave patroller, brother-in-law to Harvey Travis

Harvey Travis County slave patroller, married to a Cherokee

Calvin Newman Twin brother of Caldonia Townsend, son of Maude

Maude Newman Mother of Caldonia and Calvin

Robert Colfax A prominent Manchester landowner

Anderson Frazier White man from Canada who published the pamphlet series *Curiosities and Oddities about Our Southern Neighbors*

Jebediah Dickinson Gambler, runaway slave

Valtims Moffett Preacher

BEYOND MANCHESTER

Counsel Skiffington North Carolina cousin of John Skiffington

Belle Skiffington Wide of Counsel Skiffington

Darcy Slave "speculator"

Stennis Slave of Darcy

The Girl Who
Raised Pigeons

A Short Story from Edward P. Jones's
PEN/Hemingway Award Winner, *Lost
in the City*

HER FATHER WOULD SAY YEARS LATER that
she had dreamed that part of it, that she had
never gone out through the kitchen window at
two or three in the morning to visit the birds.
By that time in his life he would have so many
notions about himself set in concrete. And
having always believed that he slept lightly, he
would not want to think that a girl of nine or
ten could walk by him at such an hour in the
night without his waking and asking of the
dark, Who is it? What's the matter?

But the night visits were not dreams, and
they remained forever as vivid to her as the
memory of the way the pigeons' iridescent
necklaces flirted with light. The visits would
begin not with any compulsion in her sleeping
mind to visit, but with the simple need to pee
or to get a drink of water. In the dark, she went
barefoot out of her room, past her father in
the front room conversing in his sleep, across
the kitchen and through the kitchen window,
out over the roof a few steps to the coop. It
could be winter, it could be summer, but the
most she ever got was something she called
pigeon silence. Sometimes she had the urge to
unlatch the door and go into the coop, or, at
the very least, to try to reach through the wire
and the wooden slats to stroke a wing or a
breast, to share whatever the silence seemed to
conceal. But she always kept her hands to
herself, and after a few minutes, as if relieved,
she would go back to her bed and visit the
birds again in sleep.

> ❝ In the dark,
> she went barefoot
> out of her room,
> past her father in
> the front room
> conversing in his
> sleep, across the
> kitchen and
> through the
> kitchen window,
> out over the roof
> a few steps to the
> coop. ❞

· · ·

What Betsy Ann Morgan and her father Robert did agree on was that the pigeons began with the barber Miles Patterson. Her father had known Miles long before the girl was born, before the thought to marry her mother had even crossed his mind. The barber lived in a gingerbread brown house with his old parents only a few doors down from the barbershop he owned on the corner of 3rd and L streets, Northwest. On some Sundays, after Betsy Ann had come back from church with Miss Jenny, Robert, as he believed his wife would have done, would take his daughter out to visit with relatives and friends in the neighborhoods just beyond Myrtle Street, Northeast, where father and daughter lived.

One Sunday, when Betsy Ann was eight years old, the barber asked her again if she wanted to see his pigeons, "my children." He had first asked her some three years before. The girl had been eager to see them then, imagining she would see the same frightened creatures who waddled and flew away whenever she chased them on sidewalks and in parks. The men and the girl had gone into the backyard, and the pigeons, in a furious greeting, had flown up and about the barber. "Oh, my babies," he said, making kissing sounds. "Daddy's here." In an instant, Miles's head was surrounded by a colorful flutter of pigeon life. The birds settled on his head and his shoulders and along his thick, extended arms, and some of the birds looked down meanly at her. Betsy Ann screamed, sending the birds back into a flutter, which made her scream even louder. And still screaming, she ran back into the house. The men found her in the kitchen, her head buried in the lap of Miles's mother, her arms tight around the waist of the old woman, who had been sitting at the table having Sunday lunch with her husband.

"Buster," Miles's mother said to him, "you shouldn't scare your company like this. This child's bout to have a heart attack."

Three years later Betsy Ann said yes again to seeing the birds. In the backyard, there was again the same fluttering chaos, but this time the sight of the wings and bodies settling about Miles intrigued her and she drew closer until she was a foot or so away, looking up at them and stretching out her arm as she saw Miles doing. "Oh, my babies," the barber said. "Your daddy's here." One of the birds landed on Betsy Ann's shoulder and another in the palm of her hand. The gray one in her hand looked dead at Betsy Ann, blinked, then swiveled his head and gave the girl a different view of a radiant black necklace. "They tickle," she said to her father, who stood back. ▶

The Girl Who Raised Pigeons *(continued)*
. . .

For weeks and weeks after that Sunday, Betsy Ann pestered her father about getting pigeons for her. And the more he told her no, that it was impossible, the more she wanted them. He warned her that he would not do anything to help her care for them, he warned her that all the bird-work meant she would not ever again have time to play with her friends, he warned her about all the do-do the pigeons would let loose. But she remained a bulldog about it, and he knew that she was not often a bulldog about anything. In the end he retreated to the fact that they were only renters in Jenny and Walter Creed's house.

"Miss Jenny likes birds," the girl said. "Mr. Creed likes birds, too."

"People may like birds, but nobody in the world likes pigeons."

"Cept Mr. Miles," she said.

"Don't make judgments bout things with what you know bout Miles." Miles Patterson, a bachelor and, some women said, a virgin, was fifty-six years old and for the most part knew no more about the world than what he could experience in newspapers or on the radio and in his own neighborhood, beyond which he rarely ventured. "There's ain't nothing out there in the great beyond for me," Miles would say to people who talked with excitement about visiting such and such a place.

It was not difficult for the girl to convince Miss Jenny, though the old woman made it known that "pigeons carry all them diseases, child." But there were few things Jenny Creed would deny Betsy Ann. The girl was known by all the world to be a good and obedient child. And in Miss Jenny's eyes, a child's good reputation amounted to an assent from God on most things.

For years after he relented, Robert Morgan would rise every morning before his daughter, go out onto the roof, and peer into the coop he had constructed for her, looking for dead pigeons. At such a time in the morning, there would be only fragments of first light, falling in long, hopeful slivers over the birds and their house. Sometimes he would stare absently into the coop for a long time, because being half-asleep, his mind would forget why he was there. The murmuring pigeons, as they did with most of the world, would stare back, with looks more of curiosity than of fear or anticipation or welcome. He thought that by getting there in the morning before his daughter, he could spare her the sight and pain of any dead birds. His plan had always been to put any dead birds he found into a burlap sack, take them down to his taxicab, and dispose of them on his way to work. He never intended to tell her about such birds, and it never occurred to him that she would know every pigeon in the coop and would wonder, perhaps even worry, about a missing bird.

They lived in the apartment Jenny and Walter Creed had made out of the upstairs in their Myrtle Street house. Miss Jenny had known Clara, Robert's wife, practically all of Clara's life. But their relationship had become little more than hellos and good-byes as they passed in the street before Miss Jenny came upon Clara and Robert one rainy Saturday in the library park at Mt. Vernon Square. Miss Jenny had come out of Hahn's shoe store, crossed New York Avenue, and was going up 7th Street. At first, Miss Jenny thought the young man and woman, soaked through to the skin, sitting on the park bench under a blue umbrella, were feebleminded or straightout crazy. As she came closer, she could hear them laughing, and the young man was swinging the umbrella back and forth over their heads, so that the rain would fall first upon her and then upon himself.

"Ain't you William and Alice Hobson baby girl?" Miss Jenny asked Clara.

"Yes, ma'am." She stood and Robert stood as well, now holding the umbrella fully over Clara's head.

"Is everything all right, child?" Miss Jenny's glasses were spotted with mist, and she took them off and stepped closer, keeping safely to the side where Clara was.

"Yes, ma'am. He—" She pushed Robert and began to laugh. "We came out of Peoples and he wouldn't let me have none a the umbrella. He let me get wet, so I took the umbrella and let him have some of his own medicine."

Robert said nothing. He was standing out of the range of the umbrella and he was getting soaked all over again.

"We gonna get married, Miss Jenny," she said, as if that explained everything, and she stuck out her hand with her ring. "From Castleberg's," she said. Miss Jenny took Clara's hand and held it close to her face.

"Oh oh," she said again and again, pulling Clara's hand still closer.

"This Robert," Clara said. "My"—and she turned to look at him—"fiancé." She uttered the word with a certain crispness: It was clear that before Robert Morgan, *fiancé* was a word she had perhaps never uttered in her life.

Robert and Miss Jenny shook hands. "You gonna give her double pneumonia even before she take your name," she said.

The couple learned the next week that the place above Miss Jenny was vacant and the following Sunday, Clara and Robert, dressed as if they ▶

had just come from church, were at her front door, inquiring about the apartment.

That was one of the last days in the park for them. Robert came to believe later that the tumor that would consume his wife's brain had been growing even on that rainy day. And it was there all those times he made love to her, and the thought that it was there, perhaps at first no bigger than a grain of salt, made him feel that he had somehow used her, taken from her even as she was moving toward death. He would not remember until much, much later the times she told him he gave her pleasure, when she whispered into his ear that she was glad she had found him, raised her head in that bed as she lay under him. And when he did remember, he would have to take out her photograph from the small box of valuables he kept in the dresser's top drawer, for he could not remember her face any other way.

Clara spent most of the first months of her pregnancy in bed, propped up, reading movie magazines and listening to the radio, waiting for Robert to come home from work. Her once pretty face slowly began to collapse in on itself like fruit too long in the sun, eaten away by the rot that despoiled from the inside out. The last month or so she spent in the bed on the third floor at Gallinger Hospital. One morning, toward four o'clock, they cut open her stomach and pulled out the child only moments after Clara died, mother and daughter passing each other as if along a corridor, one into death, the other into life.

The weeks after her death Robert and the infant were attended to by family and friends. They catered to him and to the baby to such an extent that sometimes in those weeks when he heard her cry, he would look about at the people in a room, momentarily confused about what was making the sound. But as all the people returned to their lives in other parts of Washington or in other cities, he was left with the ever-increasing vastness of the small apartment and with a being who hadn't the power to ask, yet seemed to demand everything.

"I don't think I can do this," he confessed to Miss Jenny one Friday evening when the baby was about a month old. "I know I can't do this." Robert's father had been the last to leave him, and Robert had just returned from taking the old man to Union Station a few blocks away. "If my daddy had just said the word, I'da been on that train with him." He and Miss Jenny were sitting at his kitchen table, and the child, sleeping, was in her cradle beside Miss Jenny. Miss Jenny watched him and said not a word.

"Woulda followed him all the way back home. . . . I never looked down the line and saw bein by myself like this."

"It's all right," Miss Jenny said finally. "I know how it is. You a young man. You got a whole life in front a you," and the stone on his heart grew lighter. "The city people can help out with this."

"The city?" He looked through the fluttering curtain onto the roof, at the oak tree, at the backs of houses on K Street.

"Yes, yes." She turned around in her chair to face him fully. "My niece works for the city, and she say they can take care of chirren like this who don't have parents. They have homes, good homes, for chirren like her. Bring em up real good. Feed em, clothe em, give em good schoolin. Give em everything they need." She stood, as if the matter were settled. "The city people care. Call my niece tomorra and find out what you need to do. A young man like you shouldn't have to worry yourself like this." She was at the door, and he stood up too, not wanting her to go. "Try to put all the worries out your mind." Before he could say anything, she closed the door quietly behind her.

She did not come back up, as he had hoped, and he spent his first night alone with the child. Each time he managed to get the baby back to sleep after he fed her or changed her diaper, he would place her in the crib in the front room and sit without light at the kitchen table listening to the trains coming and going just beyond his window. He was nineteen years old. There was a song about trains that kept rumbling in his head as the night wore on, a song his mother would sing when he was a boy.

The next morning, Saturday, he shaved and washed up while Betsy Ann was still sleeping, and after she woke and he had fed her again, he clothed her with a yellow outfit and its yellow bonnet that Wilma Ellis, the schoolteacher next door, had given Betsy Ann. He carried the carriage downstairs first, leaving the baby on a pallet of blankets. On the sidewalk he covered her with a light green blanket that Dr. Oscar Jackson and his family up the street had given the baby. The shades were down at Miss Jenny's windows, and he heard no sound, not even the dog's barking, as he came and went. At the child's kicking feet in the carriage he placed enough diapers and powdered formula to last an expedition to Baltimore. Beside her, he placed a blue rattle from the janitor Jake Horton across the street.

He was the only moving object within her sight and she watched him intently, which made him uncomfortable. She seemed the most helpless thing he had ever known. It occurred to him perversely, as he settled her in, that if he decided to walk away forever from her and the carriage and all her stuff, to walk but a few yards and make his way up or down ▶

13

The Girl Who Raised Pigeons (*continued*)

1st Street for no place in particular, there was not a damn thing in the world she could do about it. The carriage was facing 1st Street Northeast, and with some effort—because one of the wheels refused to turn with the others—he maneuvered it around, pointing toward North Capitol Street.

In those days, before the community was obliterated, a warm Myrtle Street Saturday morning filled both sidewalks and the narrow street itself with playing children oblivious to everything but their own merriment. A grownup's course was generally not an easy one, but that morning, as he made his way with the soundless wheels of the carriage, the children made way for Robert Morgan, for he was the man whose wife had passed away. At her wake, some of them had been held up by grownups so they could look down on Clara laid out in her pink casket in Miss Jenny's parlor. And though death and its rituals did not mean much beyond the wavering understanding that they would never see someone again, they knew from what their parents said and did that a clear path to the corner was perhaps the very least a widow man deserved.

Some of the children called to their parents still in their houses and apartments that Robert was passing with Clara's baby. The few grownups on porches came down to the sidewalk and made a fuss over Betsy Ann. More than midway down the block, Janet Gordon, who had been one of Clara's best friends, came out and picked up the baby. It was too nice a day to have that blanket over her, she told Robert. You expectin to go all the way to Baltimore with all them diapers? she said. It would be Janet who would teach him—practicing on string and a discarded blond-haired doll—how to part and plait a girl's hair.

He did not linger on Myrtle Street; he planned to make the visits there on his way back that evening. Janet's boys, Carlos and Carleton, walked on either side of him up Myrtle to North Capitol, then to the corner of K Street. There they knew to turn back. Carlos, seven years old, told him to take it easy. Carleton, younger by two years, did not want to repeat what his brother had said, so he repeated one of the things his grandfather, who was losing his mind, always told him: "Don't get lost in the city."

Robert nodded as if he understood and the boys turned back. He took off his tie and put it in his pocket and unbuttoned his suit coat and the top two buttons of his shirt. Then he adjusted his hat and placed the rattle nearer the baby, who paid it no mind. And when the light changed, he maneuvered the carriage down off the sidewalk and crossed North Capitol into Northwest.

. . .

Miles the barber gave Betsy Ann two pigeons, yearlings, a dull-white female with black spots and a sparkling red male. For several weeks, in the morning, soon after she had dutifully gone in to fill the feed dish and replace the water, and after they had fortified themselves, the pigeons took to the air and returned to Miles. The forlorn sound of their flapping wings echoed in her head as she stood watching them disappear into the colors of the morning, often still holding the old broom she used to sweep out their coop.

So in those first weeks, she went first to Miles's after school to retrieve the pigeons, usually bringing along Ralph Holley, her cousin. Miles would put the birds in the two pigeon baskets Robert would bring over each morning before he took to the street in his taxicab.

"They don't like me," Betsy Ann said to Miles one day in the second week. "They just gonna keep on flyin away. They hate me."

Miles laughed, the same way he laughed when she asked him the first day how he knew one was a girl pigeon and the other was a boy pigeon.

"I don't think that they even got to the place of likin or not likin you," Miles said. She handed her books to Ralph, and Miles gave her the two baskets.

"Well, they keep runnin away."

"Thas all they know to do," which was what he had told her the week before. "Right now, this is all the home they know for sure. It ain't got nothin to do with you, child. They just know to fly back here."

His explanations about everything, when he could manage an explanation, rarely satisfied her. He had been raising pigeons all his life, and whatever knowledge he had accumulated in those years was now such an inseparable part of his being that he could no more explain the birds than he could explain what went into the act of walking. He only knew that they did all that birds did and not something else, as he only knew that he walked and did not fall.

"You might try lockin em in for while," he said. "Maybe two, three days, however long it take em to get use to the new home. Let em know you the boss and you ain't gonna stand for none a this runnin away stuff."

She considered a moment, then shook her head. She watched her cousin peering into Miles's coop, his face hard against the wire. "I guess if I gotta lock em up there ain't no use havin em."

"Why you wanna mess with gotdamn pigeons anyway?" Ralph said as they walked to her home that day.

"Because," she said.

"Because what?" he said.

"Because, thas all," she said. "Just because." ▶

"You oughta get a puppy like I'm gonna get," Ralph said. "A puppy never run away."

"A puppy never fly either. So what?" she said. "You been talkin bout gettin a gotdamn puppy for a million years, but I never see you gettin one." Though Ralph was a year older and a head taller than his cousin, she often bullied him.

"You wait. You wait. You'll see," Ralph said.

"I ain't waitin. You the one waitin. When you get it, just let me know and I'll throw you a big party."

At her place, he handed over her books and went home. She considered following her cousin back to his house after she took the pigeons up to the coop, for the idea of being on the roof with birds who wanted to fly away to be with someone else pained her. At Ralph's L Street house, there were cookies almost as big as her face, and Aunt Thelma, Clara's oldest sister, who was, in fact, the very image of Clara. The girl had never had an overwhelming curiosity about her mother, but it fascinated her to see the face of the lady in all the pictures on a woman who moved and laughed and did mother things.

She put the pigeons back in the coop and put fresh water in the bath bowls. Then she stood back, outside the coop, its door open. At such moments they often seemed contented, hopping in and out of cubicles, inspecting the feed and water, all of which riled her. She would have preferred—and understood—agitation, some sign that they were unhappy and ready to fly to Miles again. But they merely pecked about, strutted, heads bobbing happily, oblivious of her. Pretending everything was all right.

"You shitheads!" she hissed, aware that Miss Jenny was downstairs within earshot. "You gotdamn stupid shitheads!"

That was the fall of 1957.

Myrtle Street was only one long block, running east to west. To the east, preventing the street from going any farther, was a high, medieval-like wall of stone across 1st Street, Northeast, and beyond the wall were the railroad tracks. To the west, across North Capitol, preventing Myrtle Street from going any farther in that direction, was the high school Gonzaga, where white boys were taught by white priests. When the colored people and their homes were gone, the wall and the tracks remained, and so did the high school, with the same boys being taught by the same priests.

It was late spring when Betsy Ann first noticed the nest, some two feet up from the coop's floor in one of the twelve cubicles that made up the entire structure. The nest was nothing special, a crude, ill-formed thing of straw and dead leaves and other, uncertain material she later figured only her hapless birds could manage to find. They had not flown back to Miles in a long time, but she had never stopped thinking that it was on their minds each time they took to the air. So the nest was the first solid indication that the pigeons would stay forever, would go but would always return.

About three weeks later, on an afternoon when she was about to begin the weekly job of thoroughly cleaning the entire coop, she saw the two eggs. She thought them a trick of the light at first—two small and perfect wonders alone in that wonderless nest without any hallelujahs from the world. She put off the cleaning and stood looking at the male bird, who had moved off the nest for only a few seconds, rearrange himself on the nest and look at her from time to time in that bored way he had. The female bird was atop the coop, dozing. Betsy Ann got a chair from the kitchen and continued watching the male bird and the nest through the wire. "Tell me bout this," she said to them.

As it happened, Robert discovered the newly hatched squabs when he went to look for dead birds before going to work. About six that morning he peered into the coop and shivered to find two hideous, bug-eyed balls of movement. They were a dirty orange and looked like baby vultures. He looked about as if there might be someone responsible for it all. This was, he knew now, a point of no return for his child. He went back in to have his first cup of coffee of the day.

He drank without enjoyment and listened to the chirping, unsettling, demanding. He would not wake his daughter just to let her know about the hatchlings. Two little monsters had changed the predictable world he was trying to create for his child and he was suddenly afraid for her. He turned on the radio and played it real low, but he soon shut it off, because the man on WOOK was telling him to go in and kill the hatchlings.

It turned out that the first pigeon to die was a stranger, and Robert never knew anything about it. The bird appeared out of nowhere and was dead less than a week later. By then, a year or so after Miles gave her the yearlings, she had eight birds of various ages, resulting from hatches in her coop and from trades with the barber ("for variety's sake," he told her) and with a family in Anacostia. One morning before going to school, she noticed the stranger perched in one of the lower cubicles, a few inches up from the floor, and though he seemed submissive enough, she sensed ▶

that he would peck with all he had if she tried to move him out. His entire body, what little there was left of it, was a witness to misery. One ragged cream-colored tail feather stuck straight up, as if with resignation. His bill was pitted as if it had been sprayed with minute pellets, and his left eye was covered with a patch of dried blood and dirt and decaying flesh.

She placed additional straw to either side of him in the cubicle and small bowls of water and feed in front of the cubicle. Then she began to worry that he had brought in some disease that would ultimately devastate her flock.

Days later, home for lunch with Ralph, she found the pigeon dead near the water tray, his wings spread out full as if he had been preparing for flight.

"Whatcha gonna do with him?" Ralph asked, kneeling down beside Betsy Ann and poking the dead bird with a pencil.

"Bury him. What else, stupid?" She snatched the pencil from him. "You don't think any a them gonna do it, do you?" and she pointed to the few stay-at-home pigeons who were not out flying about the city. The birds looked down uninterestedly at them from various places around the coop. She dumped the dead bird in a pillowcase and took it across 1st Street to the grassy spot of ground near the Esso filling station in front of the medieval wall. With a large tablespoon, she dug two feet or so into the earth and dropped the sack in.

"Beaver would say something over his grave," Ralph said.

"What?"

"Beaver. The boy on TV."

She gave him a cut-eye look and stood up. "You do it, preacher man," she said. "I gotta get back to school."

After school she said to Miss Jenny, "Don't tell Daddy bout that dead pigeon. You know how he is: He'll think it's the end of the world or somethin."

The two were in Miss Jenny's kitchen, and Miss Jenny was preparing supper while Betsy Ann did her homework.

"You know what he do in the mornin?" Betsy Ann said. "He go out and look at them pigeons."

"Oh?" Miss Jenny, who knew what Robert had been doing, did not turn around from the stove. "Wants to say good mornin to em, hunh?"

"I don't think so. I ain't figured out what he doin," the girl said. She was sitting at Miss Jenny's kitchen table. The dog, Bosco, was beside her and one of her shoes was off and her foot was rubbing the dog's back. "I was sleepin one time and this cold air hit me and I woke up. I couldn't get back to sleep cause I was cold, so I got up to see what window was open. Daddy wasn't in the bed and he wasn't in the kitchen or the bathroom. I thought he was downstairs warmin up the cab or somethin, but when I went to close the kitchen window, I could see him, peekin in the coop from the side with a flashlight. He scared me cause I didn't know who he was at first."

"You ask him what he was doin?"

"No. He wouldn't told me anyway, Miss Jenny. I just went back to my room and closed the door. If I'da asked him straight out, he would just make up something or say maybe I was dreamin. So now when I feel that cold air, I just look out to see if he in bed and then I shut my door."

Sometimes, when the weather allowed, the girl would sit on the roof plaiting her hair or reading the funny papers before school, or sit doing her homework in the late afternoon before going down to Miss Jenny's or out to play. She got pleasure just from the mere presence of the pigeons, a pleasure that was akin to what she felt when she followed her Aunt Thelma about her house, or when she jumped double dutch for so long she had to drop to the ground to catch her breath. In the morning, the new sun rising higher, she would place her chair at the roof's edge. She could look down at tail-wagging Bosco looking up at her, down through the thick rope fence around the roof that Robert had put up when she was a year old. She would hum or sing some nonsense song she'd made up, as the birds strutted and pecked and preened and flapped about in the bath water. And in the evening she watched the pigeons return home, first landing in the oak tree, then over to the coop's landing board. A few of them, generally the males, would settle on her book or on her head and shoulders. Stroking the breast of one, she would be rewarded with a cooing that was as pleasurable as music, and when the bird edged nearer so that it was less than an inch away, she smelled what seemed a mixture of dirt and rainy air and heard a heart that seemed to be hurling itself against the wall of the bird's breast.

She turned ten. She turned eleven.

In the early summer of 1960, there began a rumor among the children of Betsy Ann's age that the railroad people were planning to take all the land around Myrtle Street, perhaps up to L Street and down to H Street. This rumor—unlike the summer rumor among Washington's Negro children that Richard Nixon, if he were elected president, would make ▶

all the children go to school on Saturday from nine to twelve and cut their summer vacations in half—this rumor had a long life. And as the boys scraped their knuckles on the ground playing Poison, as the girls jumped rope until their bouncing plaits came loose, as the boys filled the neighborhood with the sounds of amateur hammering as they built skating trucks, as the girls made up talk for dolls with names they would one day bestow on their children, their conversations were flavored with light-hearted speculation about how far the railroad would go. When one child fell out with another, it became standard to try to hurt the other with the "true fact" that the railroad was going to take his or her home. "It's a true fact, they called my daddy at his work and told him we could stay, but yall gotta go. Yall gotta." And then the tormentor would stick out his or her tongue as far as it would go.

There were only two other girls on Myrtle Street who were comfortable around pigeons, and both of them moved away within a month of each other. One, LaDeidre Gordon, was a cousin of the brothers Carlos and Carleton. LaDeidre believed that the pigeons spoke a secret language among themselves, and that if she listened long enough and hard enough she could understand what they were saying and, ultimately, could communicate with them. For this, the world lovingly nicknamed her "Coo-Coo." After LaDeidre and the second girl moved, Betsy Ann would take the long way around to avoid passing where they had lived. And in those weeks she found a comfort of sorts at Thelma and Ralph's, for their house and everything else on the other side of North Capitol Street, the rumor went, would be spared by the railroad people.

Thelma Holley, her husband, and Ralph lived in a small house on L Street, Northwest, two doors from Mt. Airy Baptist Church, just across North Capitol Street. Thelma had suffered six miscarriages before God, as she put it, "took pity on my womb" and she had Ralph. But even then, she felt God had given with one hand and taken with the other, for the boy suffered with asthma. Thelma had waited until the seventh month of her pregnancy before she felt secure enough to begin loving him. And from then on, having given her heart, she thought nothing of giving him the world after he was born.

Ralph was the first colored child anyone knew to have his own television. In his house there had been three bedrooms, but Thelma persuaded her husband that an asthmatic child needed more space. Her husband knocked down the walls between the two back bedrooms and Ralph then had a bedroom that was nearly twice as large as that of his parents. And in that enormous room, she put as much of the world as she and her husband could afford.

Aside from watching Thelma, what Betsy Ann enjoyed most in that house was the electric train set, which dominated the center of Ralph's room. Over an area of more than four square feet, running on three levels, the trains moved through a marvelous and complete world Ralph's father had constructed. In that world, there were no simple plastic figures waving beside the tracks. Rather, it was populated with such people as a hand-carved woman of wood, in a floppy hat and gardener's outfit of real cloth, a woman who had nearly microscopic beads of sweat on her brow as she knelt down with concentration in her flower garden; several inches away, hand-carved schoolchildren romped about in the playground. One group of children was playing tag, and on one boy's face was absolute surprise as he was being tagged by a girl whose cheek was lightly smudged with dirt. A foot or so away, in a small field, two hand-carved farmers of wood were arguing, one with his finger in the other's face and the other with his fist heading toward the chest of the first. The world also included a goat-populated mountain with a tunnel large enough for the trains to go through, and a stream made of light blue glass. The stream covered several tiny fish of many colors which had almost invisible pins holding them suspended from the bottom up to give the impression that the fish were swimming.

What Thelma would not put in her son's enormous room, despite years of pleadings from him, was a dog, for she had learned in childhood that all animals had the power to suck the life out of asthmatics. "What you need with some ole puppy?" she would tease sometimes when he asked. "You'll be my little puppy dog forever and forever." And then she would grab and hug him until he wiggled out of her arms.

By the time he was six, the boy had learned that he could sometimes stay all day in the room and have Thelma minister to him by pretending he could barely breathe. He hoped that over time he could get out of her a promise for a dog. But his pretending to be at death's door only made her worry more, and by the middle of 1961, she had quit her part-time, GS-4 clerk-typist position at the Interior Department, because by then he was home two or three times a week.

Gradually, as more people moved out of Myrtle Street, the room became less attractive for Betsy Ann to visit, for Ralph grew difficult and would ▶

be mean and impatient with her and other visiting children. "You stupid, thas all! You just the stupidest person in the whole wide world," he would say to anyone who did not do what he wanted as fast as he wanted. Some children cried when he lit into them, and others wanted to fight him.

In time, the boy Betsy Ann once bullied disappeared altogether, and so when she took him assignments from school, she tried to stay only the amount of time necessary to show politeness. Then, too, the girl sensed that Thelma, with her increasing coldness, felt her son's problem was partly the result of visits from children who weren't altogether clean and from a niece who lived her life in what Thelma called "pigeon air" and "pigeon dust."

When he found out, the details of it did not matter to Robert Morgan: He only knew that his daughter had been somewhere doing bad while he was out doing the best he could. It didn't matter that it was Darlene Greenley who got Betsy Ann to go far away to 7th and Massachusetts and steal candy bars from Peoples Drug, candy she didn't even like, to go away the farthest she had ever been without her father or Miss Jenny or some other adult.

She knew Darlene, fast Darlene, from going to Ralph's ("You watch and see," Darlene would whisper to her, "I'm gonna make him my boyfriend"), but they had never gone off together before the Saturday that Thelma, for the last time, expelled all the children from her house. "Got any money?" Darlene said on the sidewalk after Thelma had thrown them out. She was stretching her bubble gum between her teeth and fingers and twirling the stuff the way she would a jump rope. When Betsy Ann shook her head, Darlene said she knew this Peoples that kinda like y'know gave children candy just for stopping by, and Betsy Ann believed her.

The assistant manager caught the girls before they were out of the candy and toy aisle and right away Darlene started to cry. "That didn't work the last time I told you to stay outa here," the woman said, taking the candy out of their dress pockets, "and it ain't gonna work now." Darlene handed her candy over, and Betsy Ann did the same. Darlene continued to cry. "Oh, just shut up, you little hussy, before I give you somethin to really cry about."

The assistant manager handed the candy to a clerk and was about to drag the girls into a back room when Etta O'Connell came up the aisle. "Yo daddy know you this far from home, Betsy Ann?" Miss Etta said, tapping Betsy Ann in the chest with her walking stick. She was, at ninety-two, the oldest person on Myrtle Street. It surprised Betsy Ann that she even knew her name, because the old woman, as far as Betsy Ann could remember, had never once spoken a word to her.

"You know these criminals?" the assistant manager said.

"Knowed this one since the day she born," Miss Etta said. The top of her stick had the head of an animal that no one had been able to identify, and the animal, perched a foot or so higher than Miss Etta's head, looked down at Betsy Ann with a better-you-than-me look. The old woman uncurled the fingers of the assistant manager's hand from around Betsy Ann's arm. "Child, whatcha done in this lady's sto?"

In the end, the assistant manager accepted Miss Etta's word that Betsy Ann would never again step foot in the store, that her father would know what she had done the minute he got home. Outside, standing at the corner, Miss Etta raised her stick and pointed to K Street. "You don't go straight home with no stoppin, I'll know," she said to Betsy Ann, and the girl sprinted off, never once looking back. Miss Etta and Darlene continued standing at the corner. "I think that old lady gave me the evil eye," Darlene told Betsy Ann the next time they met. "She done took all my good luck away. Yall got ghosties and shit on yo street." And thereafter, she avoided Betsy Ann.

Robert tanned her hide, as Miss Jenny called it, and then withheld her fifty-cents-a-week allowance for two months. For some three weeks he said very little to her, and when he did, it was almost always the same words: "You should be here, takin care a them damn birds! That's where you should be, not out there robbin somebody's grocery store!" She stopped correcting him about what kind of store it was after the first few times, because each time she did he would say, "Who the grownup here? You startin to sound like you runnin the show."

The candy episode killed something between them, and more and more he began checking up on her. He would show up at the house when she thought he was out working. She would come out of the coop with a bag of feed or the broom in her hand and a bird sitting on her head and she would find him standing at the kitchen window watching her. And several times a day he would call Miss Jenny. "Yo daddy wanna know if you up there," Miss Jenny would holler out her back window. Robert called the school so much that the principal herself wrote a letter telling him to stop.

He had been seeing Janet Gordon for two years, and about three or four times a month, they would take in a movie or a show at the Howard and then spend the night at a tourist home. But after the incident at ▶

Peoples, he saw Janet only once or twice a month. Then he began taking his daughter with him in the cab on most Saturdays. He tried to make it seem as if it were a good way to see the city.

Despite his reasons for taking her along, she enjoyed riding with him at first. She asked him for one of his old maps, and, with a blue crayon, she would chart the streets of Washington she had been on. Her father spent most of his time in Southeast and in Anacostia, but sometimes he went as far away as Virginia and Maryland, and she charted streets in those places as well. She also enjoyed watching him at work, seeing a part of him she had never known: The way he made deliberate notations in his log. Patted his thigh in time to music in his head until he noticed her looking at him. Raised his hat any time a woman entered or left the cab.

But the more she realized that being with him was just his way of keeping his eye on her, the more the travels began losing something for her. When she used the bathroom at some filling station during her travels, she found him waiting for her outside the bathroom door, his nail-bitten hands down at his sides, his hat sitting perfectly on his head, and a look on his face that said Nothin. Nothin's wrong. Before the autumn of 1961 had settled in, she only wanted to be left at home, and because the incident at Peoples was far behind them, he allowed it. But he went back to the old ways of checking up on her. "Tell him yes," she would say when Miss Jenny called out her back window. "Tell him a million times yes, I'm home."

Little by little that spring and summer of 1961 Myrtle Street emptied of people, of families who had known no other place in their lives. Robert dreaded coming home each evening and seeing the signs of still another abandoned house free to be picked clean by rogues coming in from other neighborhoods: old curtains flapping out of screenless windows, the street with every kind of litter, windows so naked he could see clean through to the backyard. For the first time since he had been knowing her, Miss Jenny did not plant her garden that year, and that small patch of ground, with alien growth tall as a man, reverted to the wild.

He vowed that until he could find a good place for himself and his child, he would try to make life as normal as possible for her. He had never stopped rising each morning before Betsy Ann and going out to the coop to see what pigeons might have died in the night. And that was what he did that last morning in midautumn. He touched down onto the roof and discovered it had snowed during the night. A light, nuisance powder, not thick enough to cover the world completely and make things beautiful the way he liked. Though there was enough sunlight, he did not at first notice the tiny tracks, with even tinier, intermittent spots of blood, leading from the coop, across his roof and over to the roof of the house next door, the schoolteacher's house that had been empty for more than four months. He did, however, hear the birds squawking before he reached the coop, but this meant nothing to him, because one pigeon sound was more or less like another to him.

The night before there had been sixteen pigeons of various ages, but when he reached the coop, five were already dead and three were in their last moments, dragging themselves crazily about the floor or from side to side in the lower cubicles. Six of them he would kill with his own hands. Though there were bodies with holes so deep he saw white flesh, essence, it was the sight of dozens of detached feathers that caused his body to shake, because the scattered feathers, more than the wrecked bodies, spoke to him of helplessness. He closed his eyes as tight as he could and began to pray, and when he opened them, the morning was even brighter.

He looked back at the window, for something had whispered that Betsy Ann was watching. But he was alone and he went into the coop. He took up one dead bird whose left wing and legs had been chewed off; he shook the bird gently, and gently he blew into its face. He prayed once more. The pigeons that were able had moved to the farthest corner of the coop and they watched him, quivering. He knew now that the squawking was the sound of pain and it drove him out of their house.

When he saw the tracks, he realized immediately that they had been made by rats. He bent down, and some logical piece of his mind was surprised that there was a kind of orderliness to the trail, even with its ragged bits of pigeon life, a fragment of feather here, a spot of blood there.

He did not knock at Walter and Miss Jenny's door and wait to go in, as he had done each morning for some thirteen years. He found them at the breakfast table, and because they had been used to thirteen years of knocking, they looked up at him, amazed. Most of his words were garbled, but they followed him back upstairs. Betsy Ann had heard the noise of her father coming through the kitchen window and bounded down the stairs. She stood barefoot in the doorway leading from the front room to the kitchen, blinking herself awake.

"Go back to bed!" Robert shouted at her.

When she asked what was the matter, the three only told her to go back to bed. From the kitchen closet, Robert took two burlap sacks. Walter followed him out onto the roof and Betsy Ann made her way around Miss Jenny to the window. ▶

Her father shouted at her to go to her room and Miss Jenny tried to grab her, but she managed to get onto the roof, where Walter held her. From inside, she had heard the squawking, a brand new sound for her. Even with Walter holding her, she got a few feet from the coop. And when Robert told her to go back inside, she gave him the only no of their lives. He looked but once at her and then began to wring the necks of the birds injured beyond all hope. Strangely, when he reached for them, the pigeons did not peck, did not resist. He placed all of the bodies in the sacks, and when he was all done and stood covered in blood and viscera and feathers, he began to cry.

Betsy Ann and her father noticed almost simultaneously that there were two birds completely unharmed, huddled in an upper corner of the coop. After he tied the mouths of the sacks, the two birds, as if of one mind, flew together to the landing board and from there to the oak tree in Miss Jenny's yard. Then they were gone. The girl buried her face in Walter's side, and when the old man saw that she was barefoot, he picked her up.

She missed them more than she ever thought she would. In school, her mind would wander and she would doodle so many pigeons on the backs of her hands and along her arms that teachers called her Nasty, nasty girl. In the bathtub at night, she would cry to have to wash them off. And as she slept, missing them would take shape and lean down over her bed and wake her just enough to get her to understand a whisper that told her all over again how much she missed them. And when she raged in her sleep, Robert would come in and hold her until she returned to peace. He would sit in a chair beside her bed for the rest of the night, for her rages usually came about four in the morning and with the night so near morning, he saw no use in going back to bed.

She roamed the city at will, and Robert said nothing. She came to know the city so well that had she been blindfolded and taken to practically any place in Washington, even as far away as Anacostia or Georgetown, she could have taken off the blindfold and walked home without a moment's trouble. Her favorite place became the library park at Mount Vernon Square, the same park where Miss Jenny had first seen Robert and Clara together, across the street from the Peoples where Betsy Ann had been caught stealing. And there on some warm days Robert would find her, sitting on a bench, or lying on the grass, eyes to the sky.

For many weeks, well into winter, one of the birds that had not been harmed would come to the ledge of a back window of an abandoned house that faced K Street. The bird, a typical gray, would stand on the ledge and appear to look across the backyards in the direction of Betsy Ann's roof, now an empty space because the coop had been dismantled for use as firewood in Miss Jenny's kitchen stove. When the girl first noticed him and realized who he was, she said nothing, but after a few days, she began to call to him, beseech him to come to her. She came to the very edge of the roof, for now the rope fence was gone and nothing held her back. When the bird would not come to her, she cursed him. After as much as an hour it would fly away and return the next morning.

On what turned out to be the last day, a very cold morning in February, she stepped out onto the roof to drink the last of her cocoa. At first she sipped, then she took one final swallow, and in the time it took her to raise the cup to her lips and lower it, the pigeon had taken a step and dropped from the ledge. He caught an upwind that took him nearly as high as the tops of the empty K Street houses. He flew farther into Northeast, into the colors and sounds of the city's morning. She did nothing, aside from following him, with her eyes, with her heart, as far as she could. ❧